AW YEAH COMICS!™

AND... ACTION!

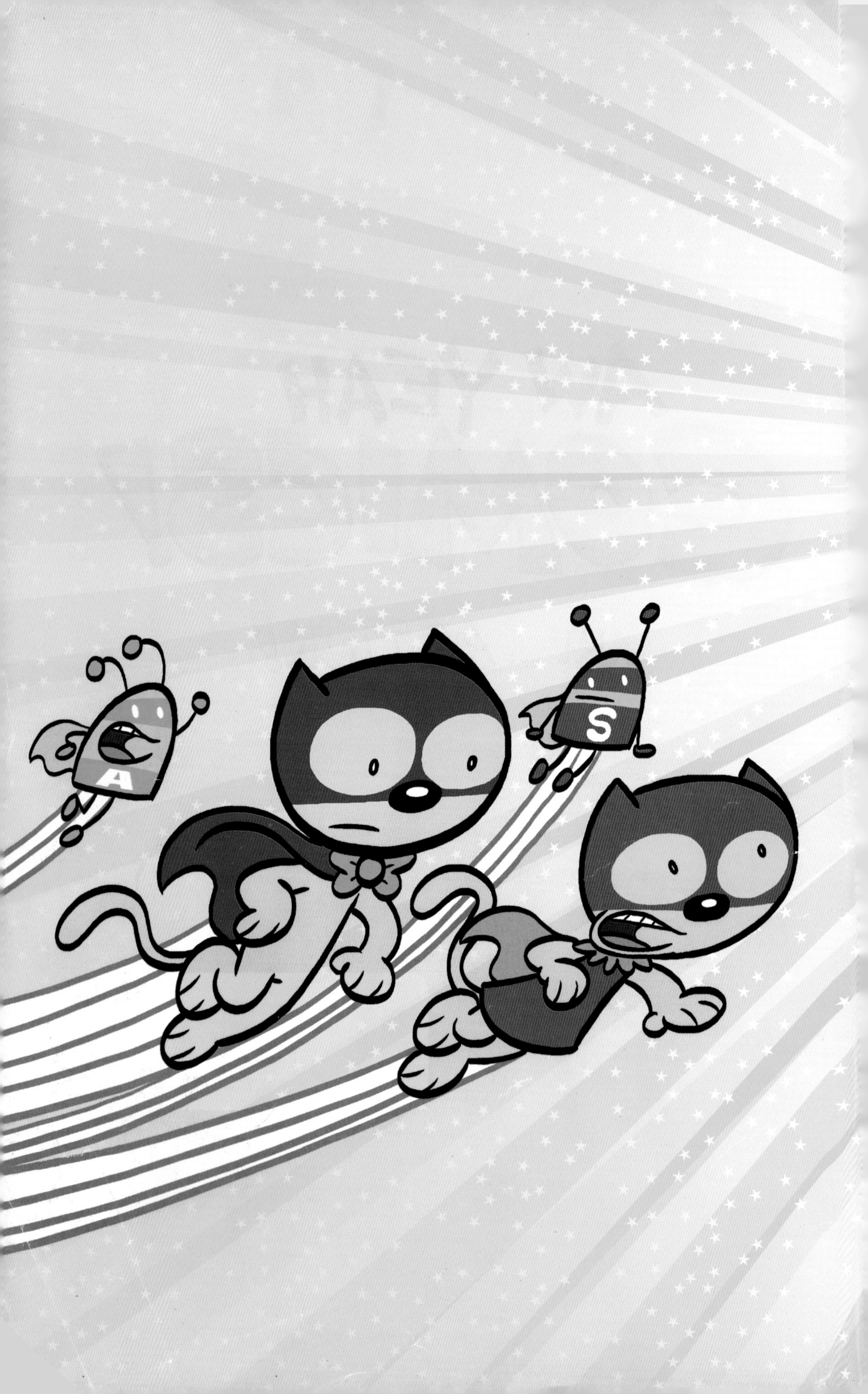
A
S

AW YEAH COMICS!

AND... ACTION!

STORY AND ARTWORK BY ART BALTAZAR AND FRANCO

FEATURING

Arthee, Jim Anderson, Nicolas Aureliani, Audrey Baltazar,
Denver Brubaker, Jamie Cosley, Jeff Couturier,
Chad Derdowski, Haas, Marc Hammond, Scoot McMahon,
Brad and Theo Meltzer, Aaron Pittman, Polito,
Alejandro Rosado, Chris Zod Smits, Kurt Wood, and Zac

Dark Horse Books

Designer KAT LARSON
Assistant Editor SHANTEL LAROCQUE
Editor SCOTT ALLIE
Publisher MIKE RICHARDSON

Published by
Dark Horse Books
A division of Dark Horse Comics, Inc.
10956 SE Main Street
Milwaukie, OR 97222

First edition: September 2014
ISBN 978-1-61655-558-0

1 3 5 7 9 10 8 6 4 2
Printed in China

This volume collects *Aw Yeah Comics!* #1–#4,
originally published by Aw Yeah Comics! Publishing.

AW YEAH COMICS! AND . . . ACTION!

President and Publisher MIKE RICHARDSON ★ Executive Vice President NEIL HANKERSON ★ Chief Financial Officer TOM WEDDLE ★ Vice President of Publishing RANDY STRADLEY ★ Vice President of Book Trade Sales MICHAEL MARTENS ★ Vice President of Business Affairs ANITA NELSON ★ Editor in Chief SCOTT ALLIE ★ Vice President of Marketing MATT PARKINSON ★ Vice President of Product Development DAVID SCROGGY ★ Vice President of Information Technology DALE LaFOUNTAIN ★ Senior Director of Print, Design, and Production DARLENE VOGEL ★ General Counsel KEN LIZZI ★ Editorial Director DAVEY ESTRADA ★ Senior Books Editor CHRIS WARNER ★ Executive Editor DIANA SCHUTZ ★ Director of Print and Development CARY GRAZZINI ★ Art Director LIA RIBACCHI ★ Director of Scheduling CARA NIECE ★ Director of International Licensing TIM WIESCH ★ Director of Digital Publishing MARK BERNARDI

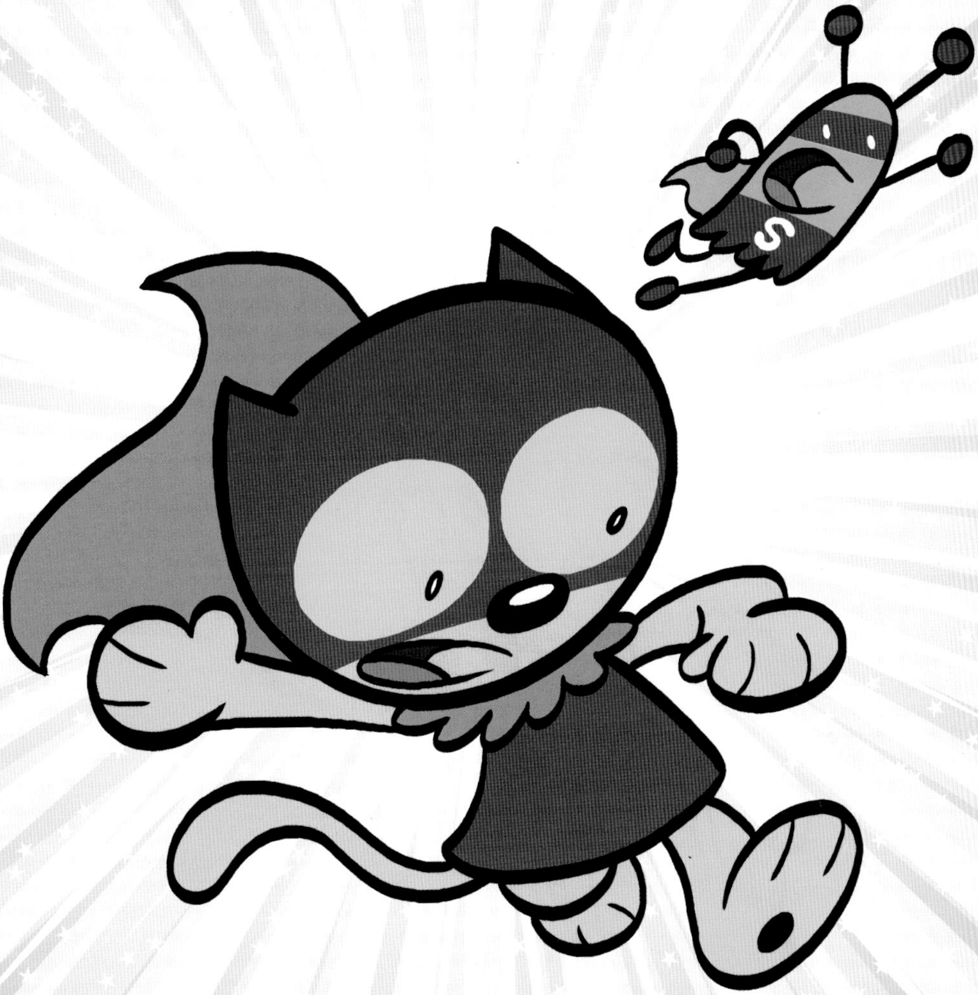
S

★ CHAPTER ONE ★

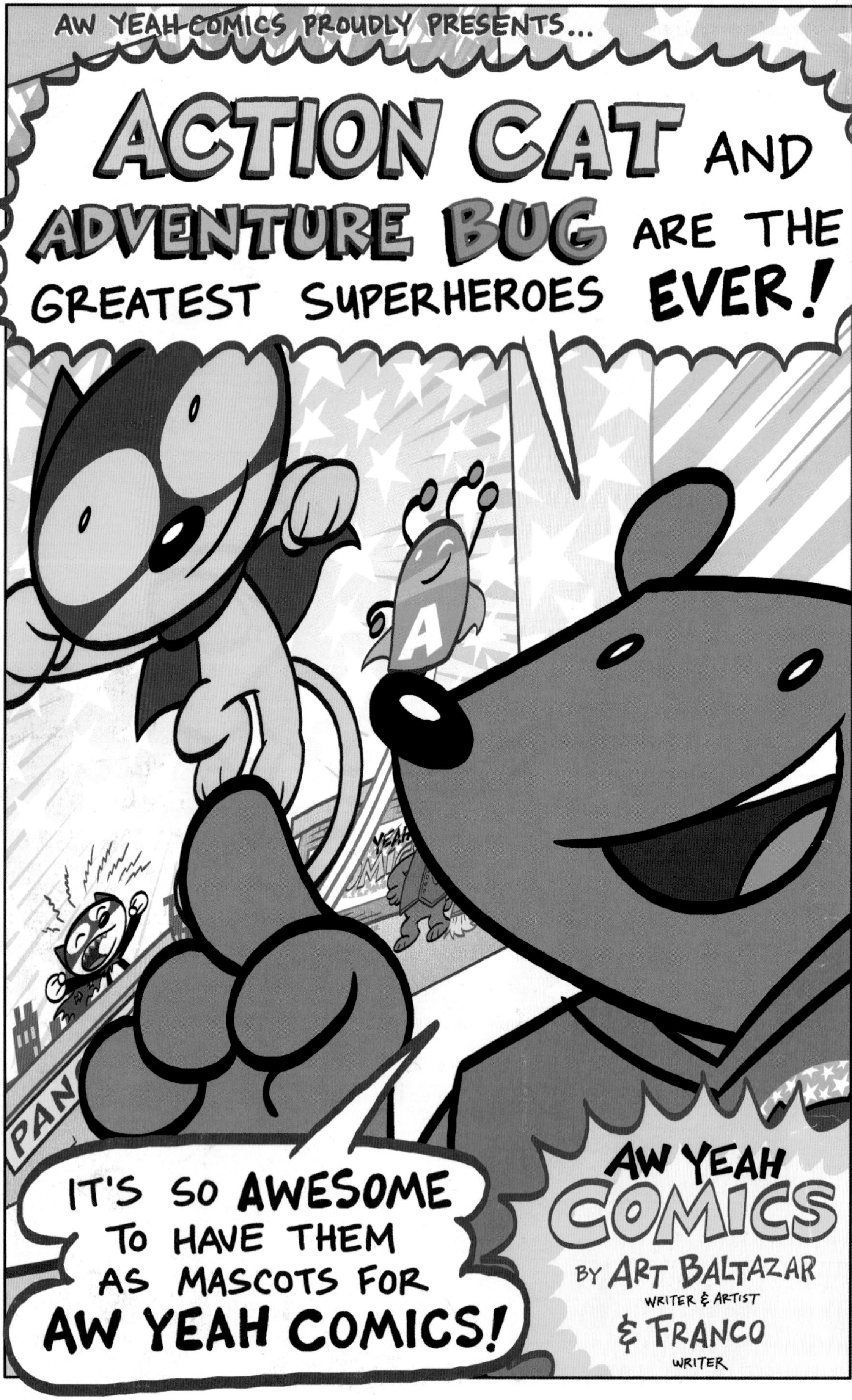
AW YEAH COMICS PROUDLY PRESENTS...
ACTION CAT AND ADVENTURE BUG ARE THE GREATEST SUPERHEROES EVER!
IT'S SO AWESOME TO HAVE THEM AS MASCOTS FOR AW YEAH COMICS!
AW YEAH COMICS
BY ART BALTAZAR
WRITER & ARTIST
& FRANCO
WRITER

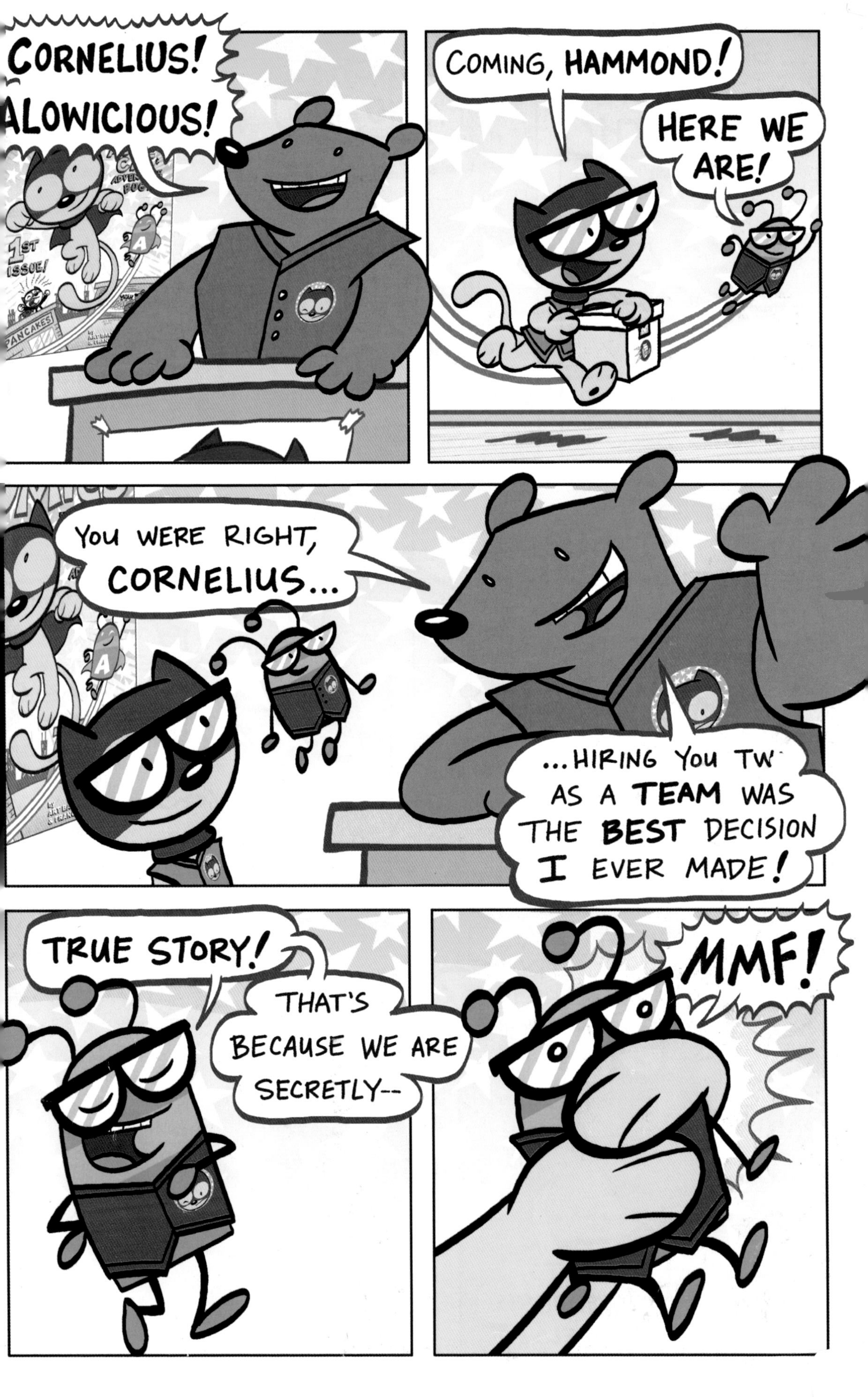
CORNELIUS!
ALOWICIOUS!
1ST ISSUE!
PANCAKES
COMING, HAMMOND!
HERE WE ARE!
YOU WERE RIGHT, CORNELIUS...
...HIRING YOU TW
AS A TEAM WAS THE BEST DECISION I EVER MADE!
TRUE STORY!
THAT'S BECAUSE WE ARE SECRETLY--
MMF!

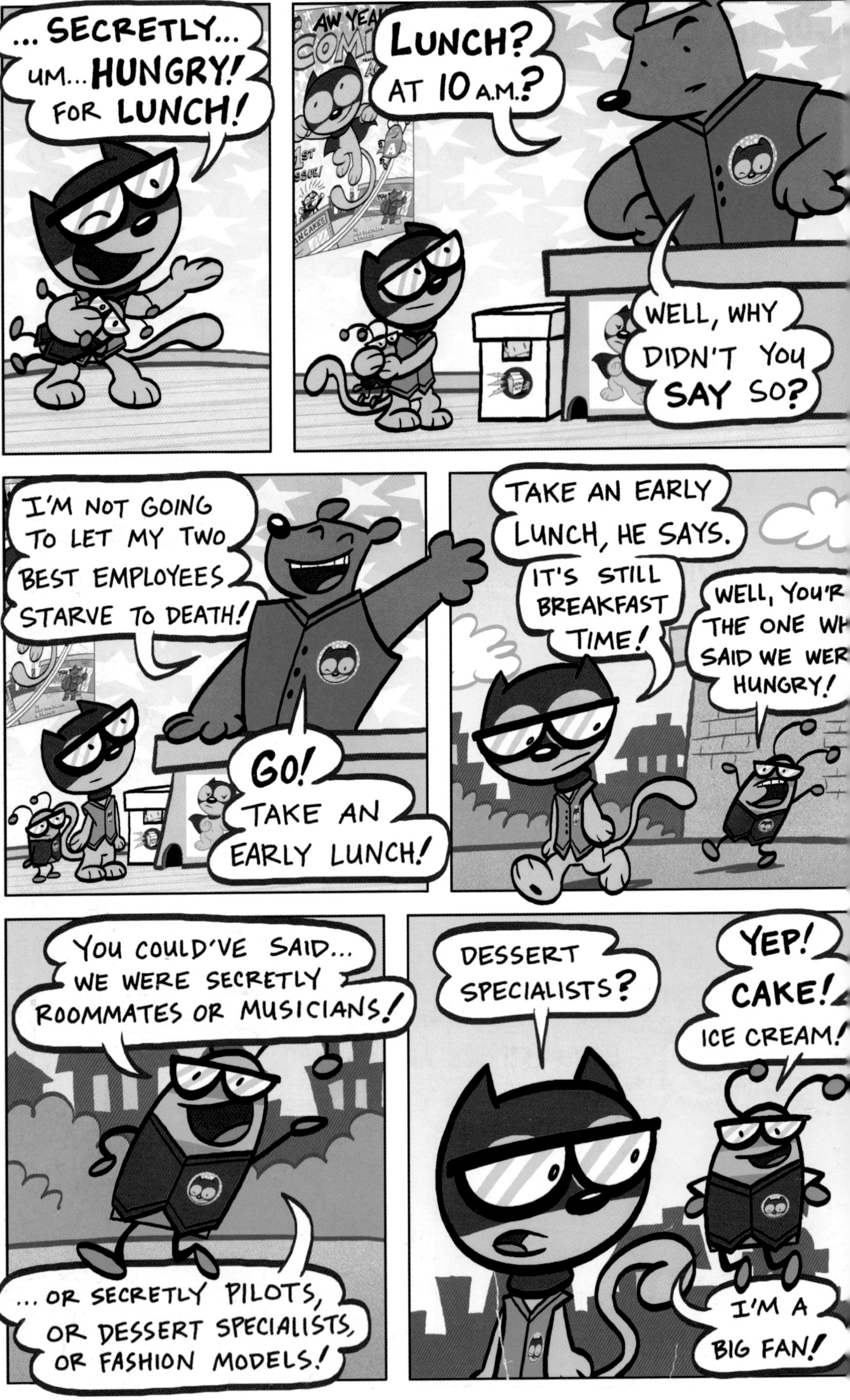
... SECRETLY... UM... HUNGRY! FOR LUNCH!
LUNCH? AT 10 A.M.?
WELL, WHY DIDN'T YOU SAY SO?
I'M NOT GOING TO LET MY TWO BEST EMPLOYEES STARVE TO DEATH!
GO! TAKE AN EARLY LUNCH!
TAKE AN EARLY LUNCH, HE SAYS.
IT'S STILL BREAKFAST TIME!
WELL, YOU'R THE ONE WH SAID WE WER HUNGRY!
YOU COULD'VE SAID... WE WERE SECRETLY ROOMMATES OR MUSICIANS!
... OR SECRETLY PILOTS, OR DESSERT SPECIALISTS, OR FASHION MODELS!
DESSERT SPECIALISTS?
YEP! CAKE! ICE CREAM!
I'M A BIG FAN!

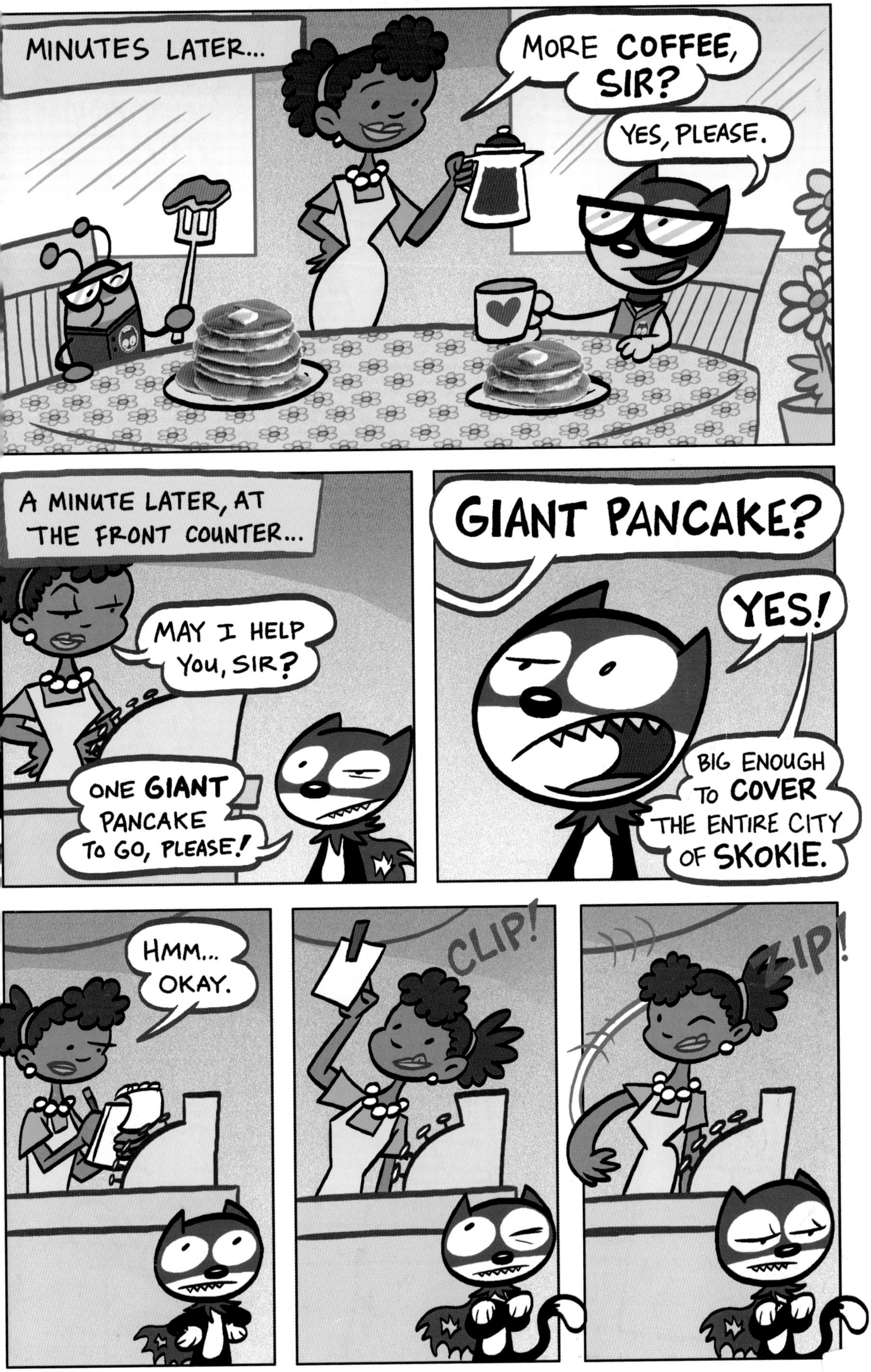
MINUTES LATER...
MORE COFFEE, SIR?
YES, PLEASE.
A MINUTE LATER, AT THE FRONT COUNTER...
MAY I HELP YOU, SIR?
ONE GIANT PANCAKE TO GO, PLEASE!
GIANT PANCAKE?
YES!
BIG ENOUGH TO COVER THE ENTIRE CITY OF SKOKIE.
HMM... OKAY.
CLIP!
ZIP!

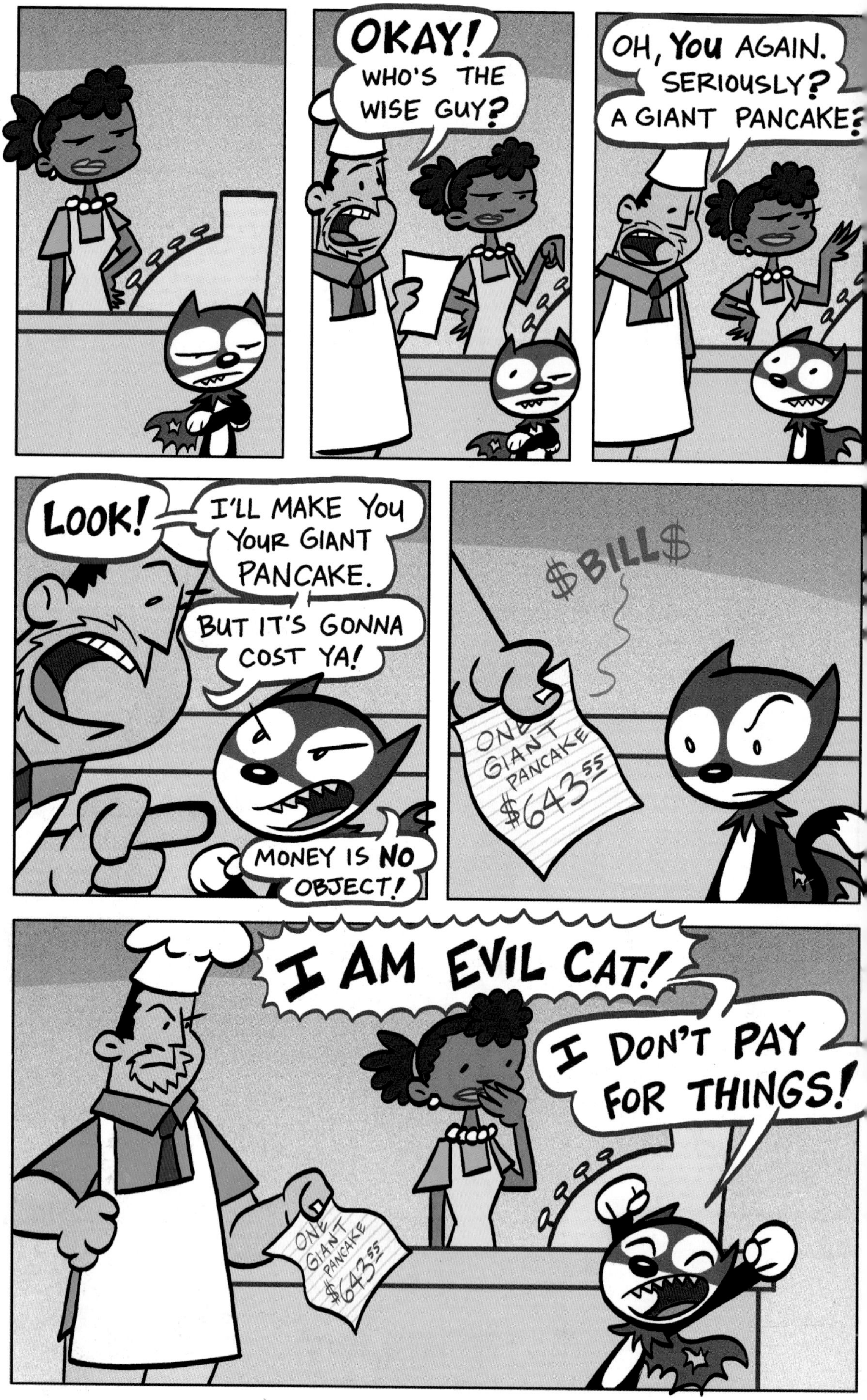
OKAY! WHO'S THE WISE GUY?
OH, YOU AGAIN. SERIOUSLY? A GIANT PANCAKE?
LOOK!
I'LL MAKE YOU YOUR GIANT PANCAKE.
BUT IT'S GONNA COST YA!
MONEY IS NO OBJECT!
$BILL$
ONE GIANT PANCAKE $643.55
I AM EVIL CAT!
I DON'T PAY FOR THINGS!
ONE GIANT PANCAKE $643.55

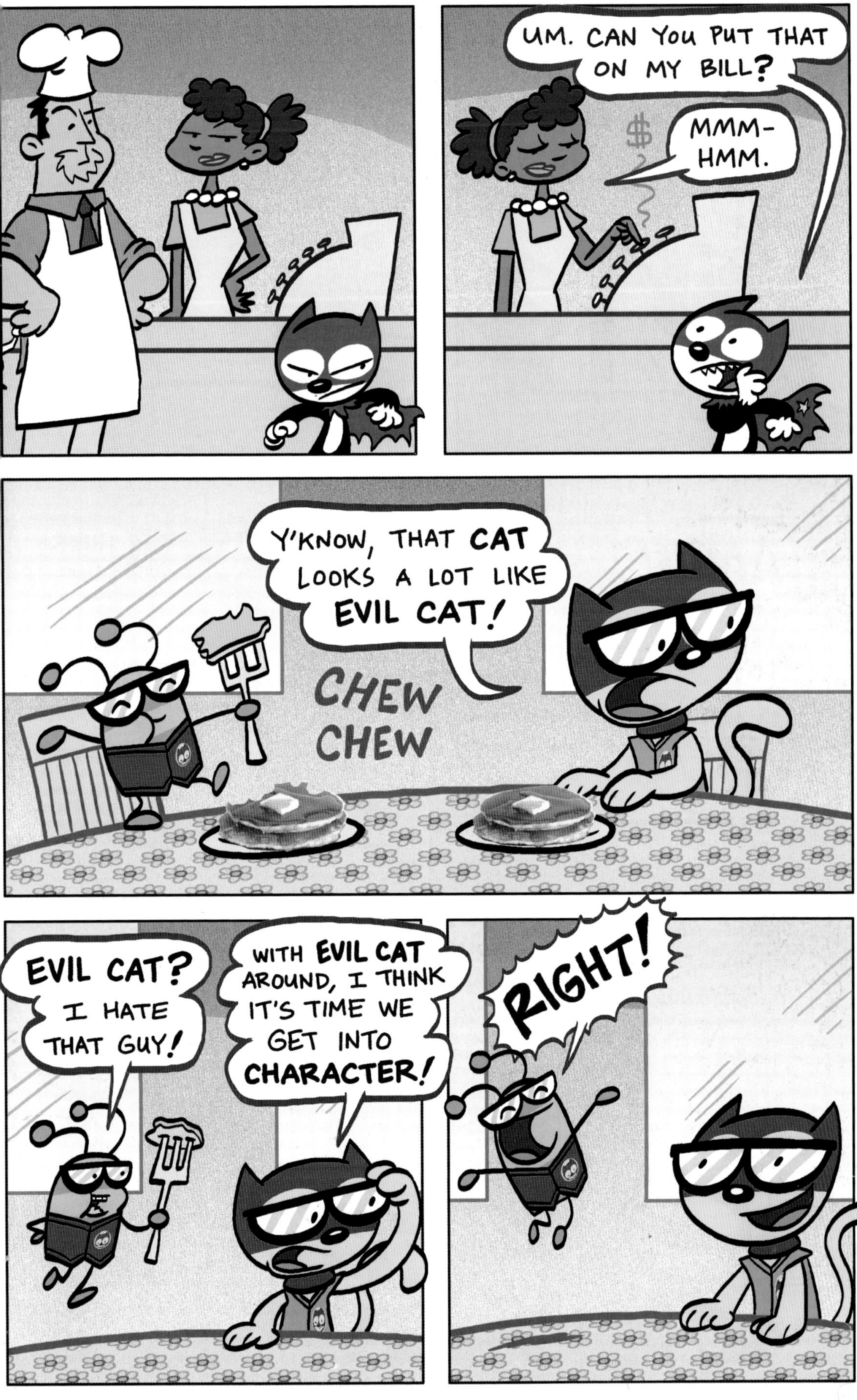
UM. CAN YOU PUT THAT ON MY BILL?
$
MMM-HMM.
Y'KNOW, THAT CAT LOOKS A LOT LIKE EVIL CAT!
CHEW CHEW
EVIL CAT? I HATE THAT GUY!
WITH EVIL CAT AROUND, I THINK IT'S TIME WE GET INTO CHARACTER!
RIGHT!

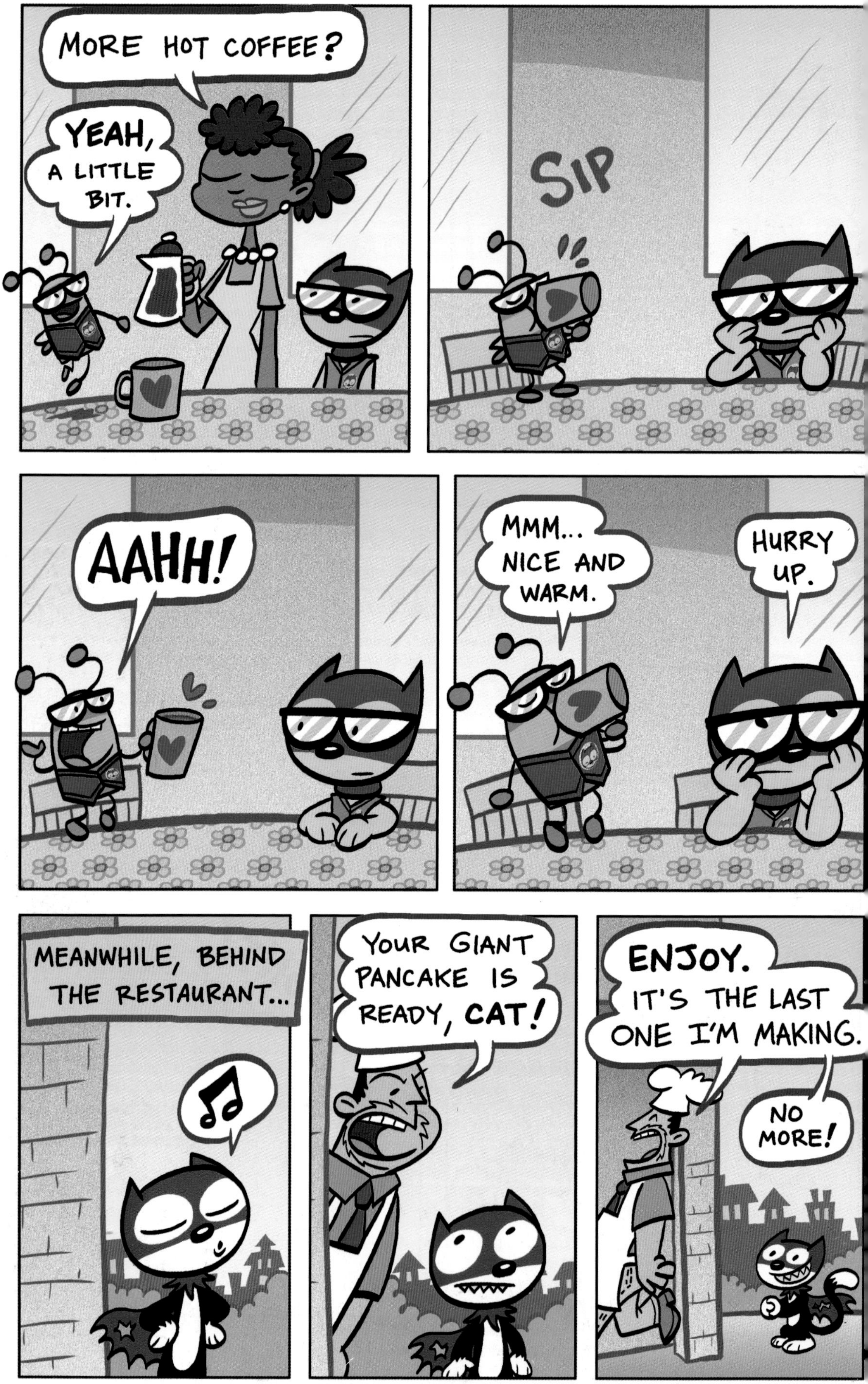
MORE HOT COFFEE?
YEAH, A LITTLE BIT.
SIP
AAHH!
MMM... NICE AND WARM.
HURRY UP.
MEANWHILE, BEHIND THE RESTAURANT...
YOUR GIANT PANCAKE IS READY, CAT!
ENJOY. IT'S THE LAST ONE I'M MAKING.
NO MORE!

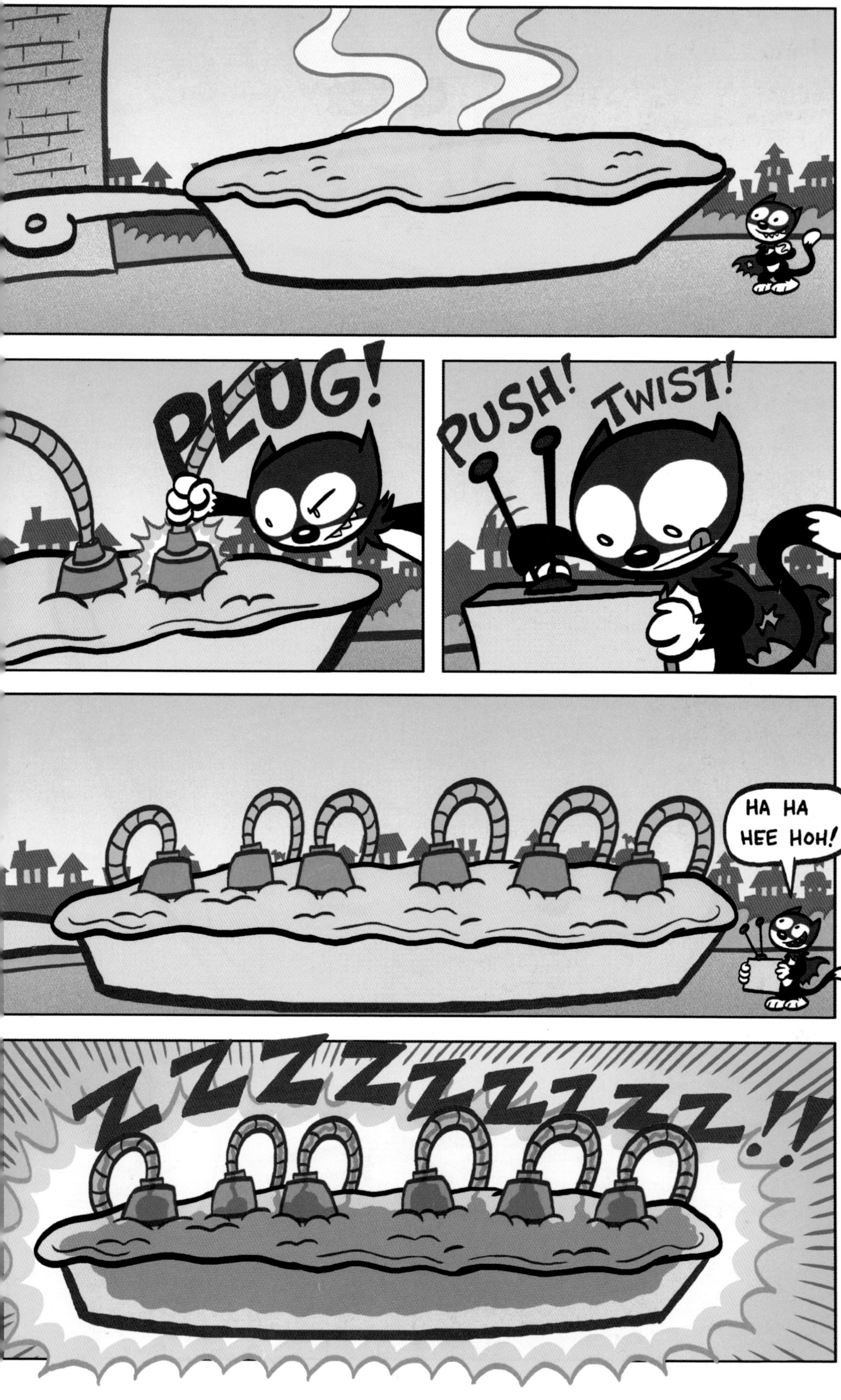
PLUG!
PUSH!
TWIST!
HA HA
HEE HOH!
ZZZZZZZZZZ!!

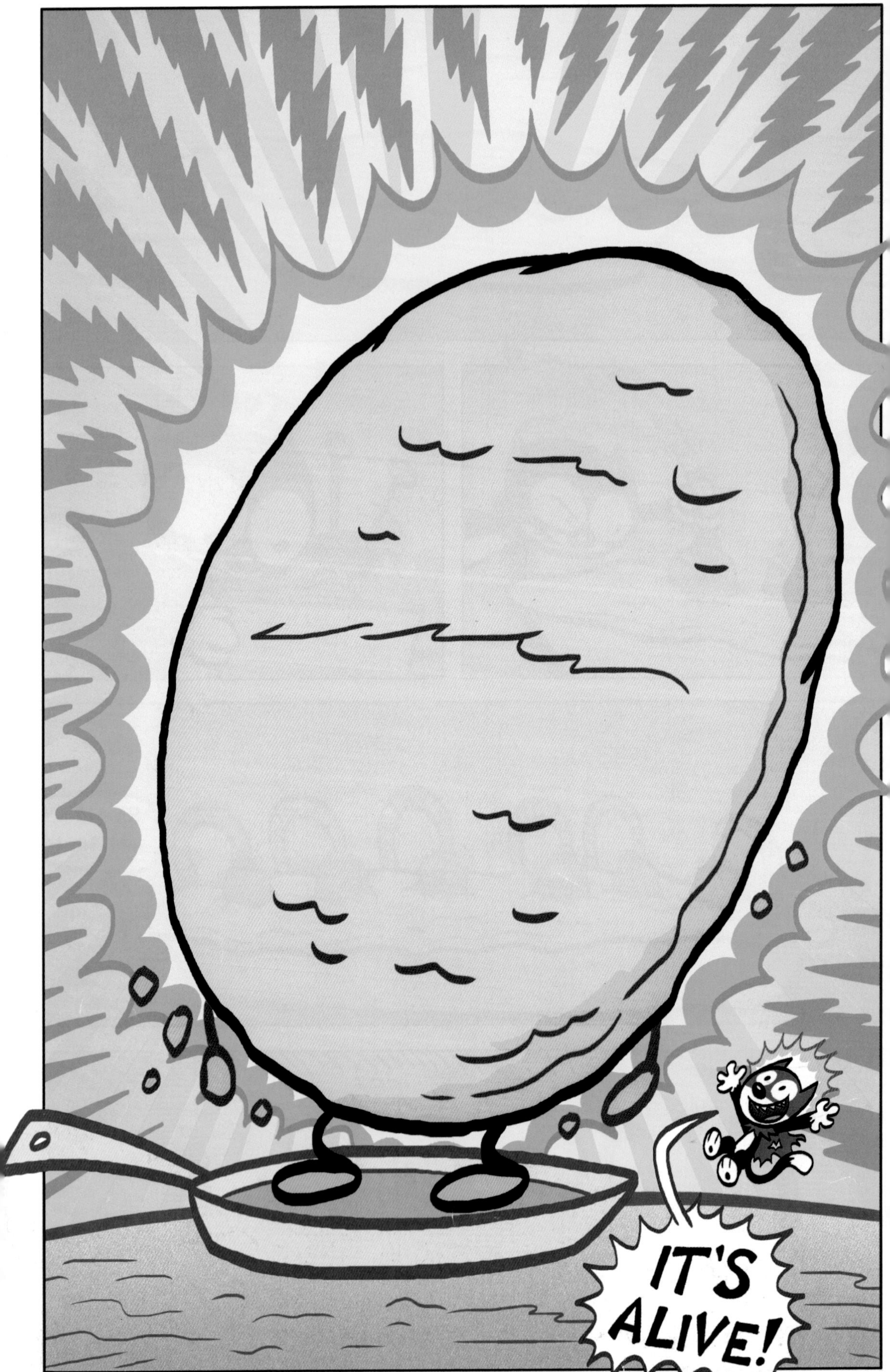
IT'S ALIVE!

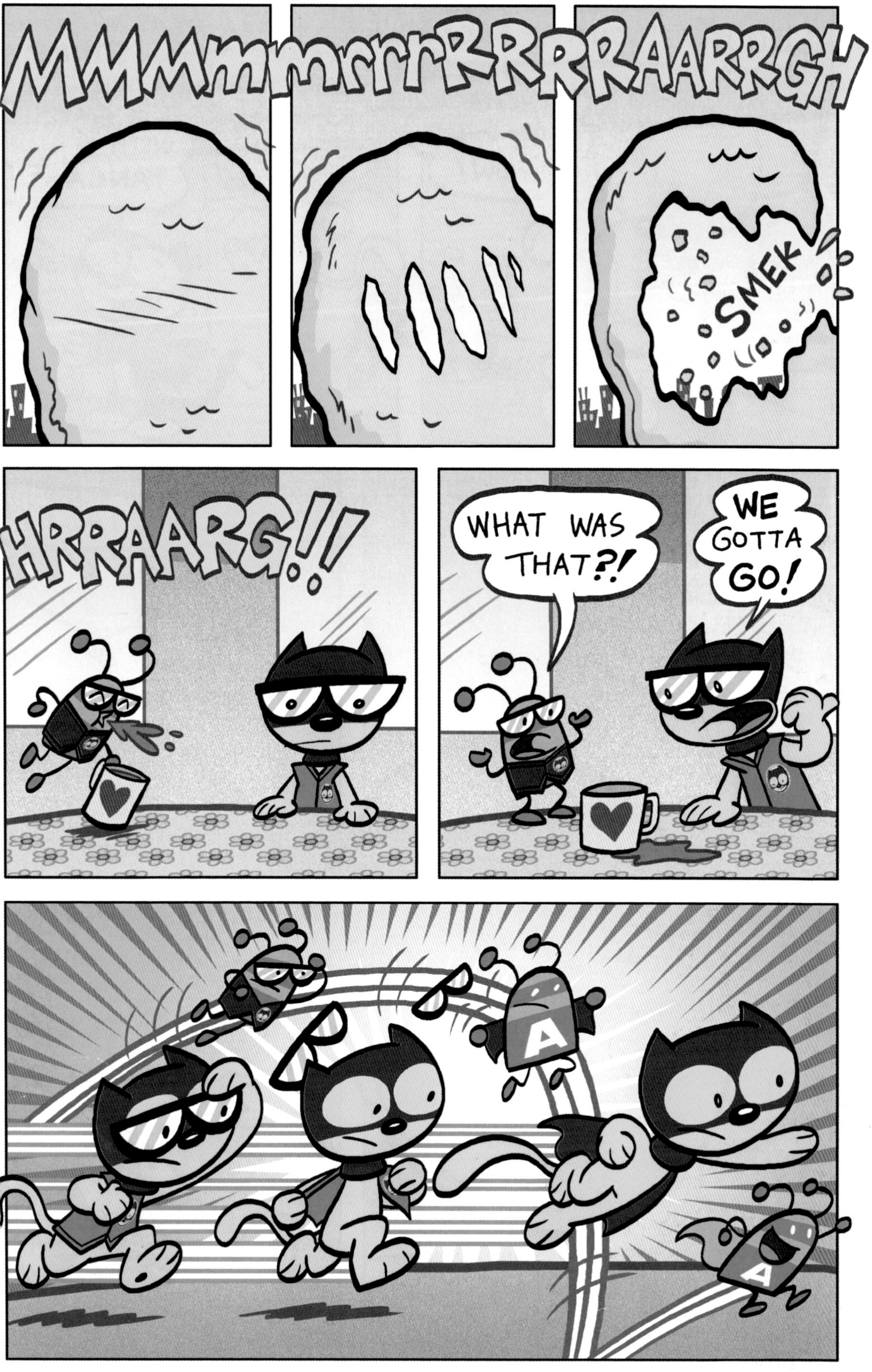
MMMmmrrrRRRRAARRGH
SMEK
HRRAARG!!!
WHAT WAS THAT?!
WE GOTTA GO!

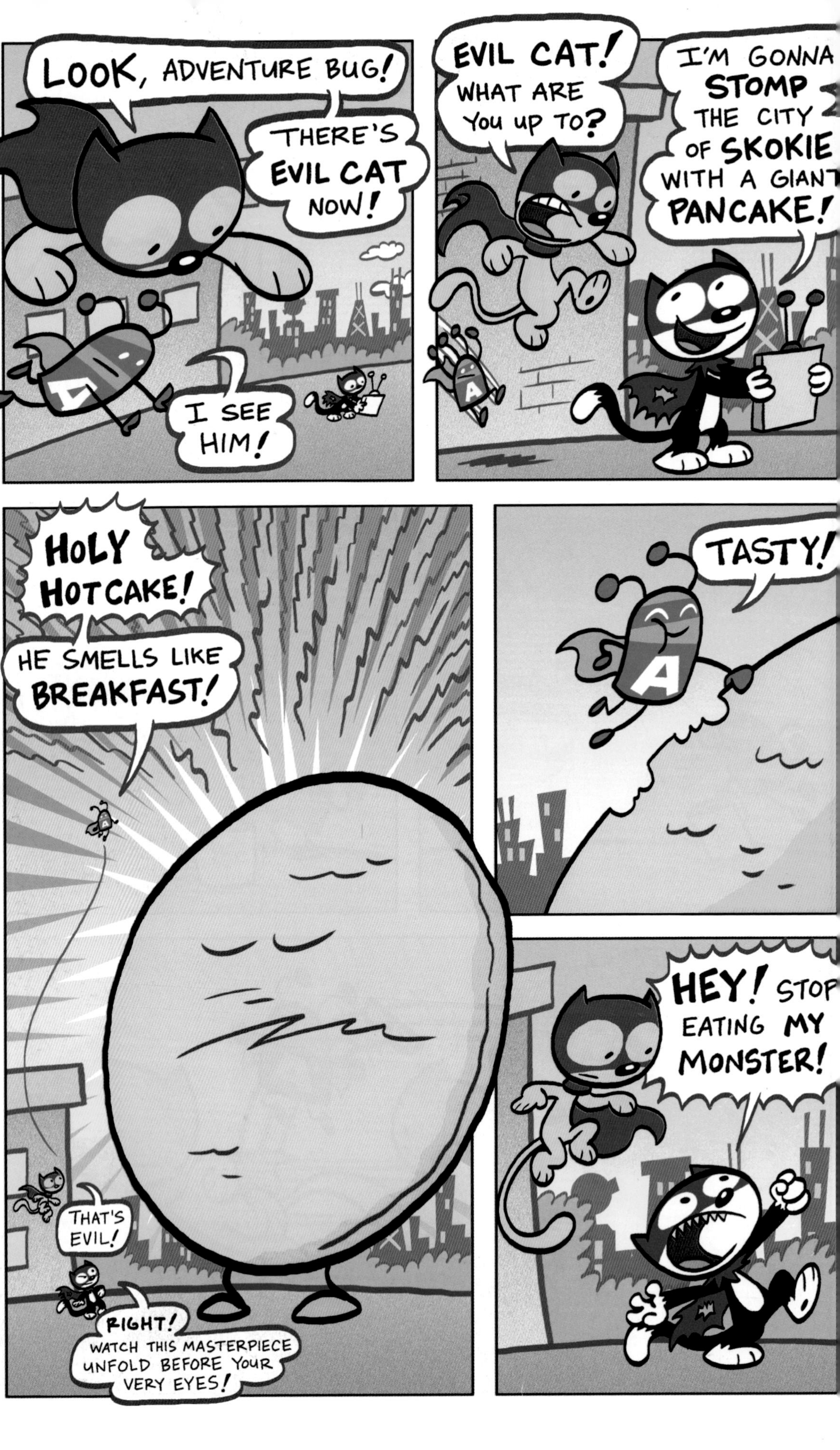
LOOK, ADVENTURE BUG!
THERE'S EVIL CAT NOW!
I SEE HIM!
EVIL CAT! WHAT ARE YOU UP TO?
I'M GONNA STOMP THE CITY OF SKOKIE WITH A GIANT PANCAKE!
HOLY HOTCAKE!
HE SMELLS LIKE BREAKFAST!
THAT'S EVIL!
RIGHT! WATCH THIS MASTERPIECE UNFOLD BEFORE YOUR VERY EYES!
TASTY!
HEY! STOP EATING MY MONSTER!

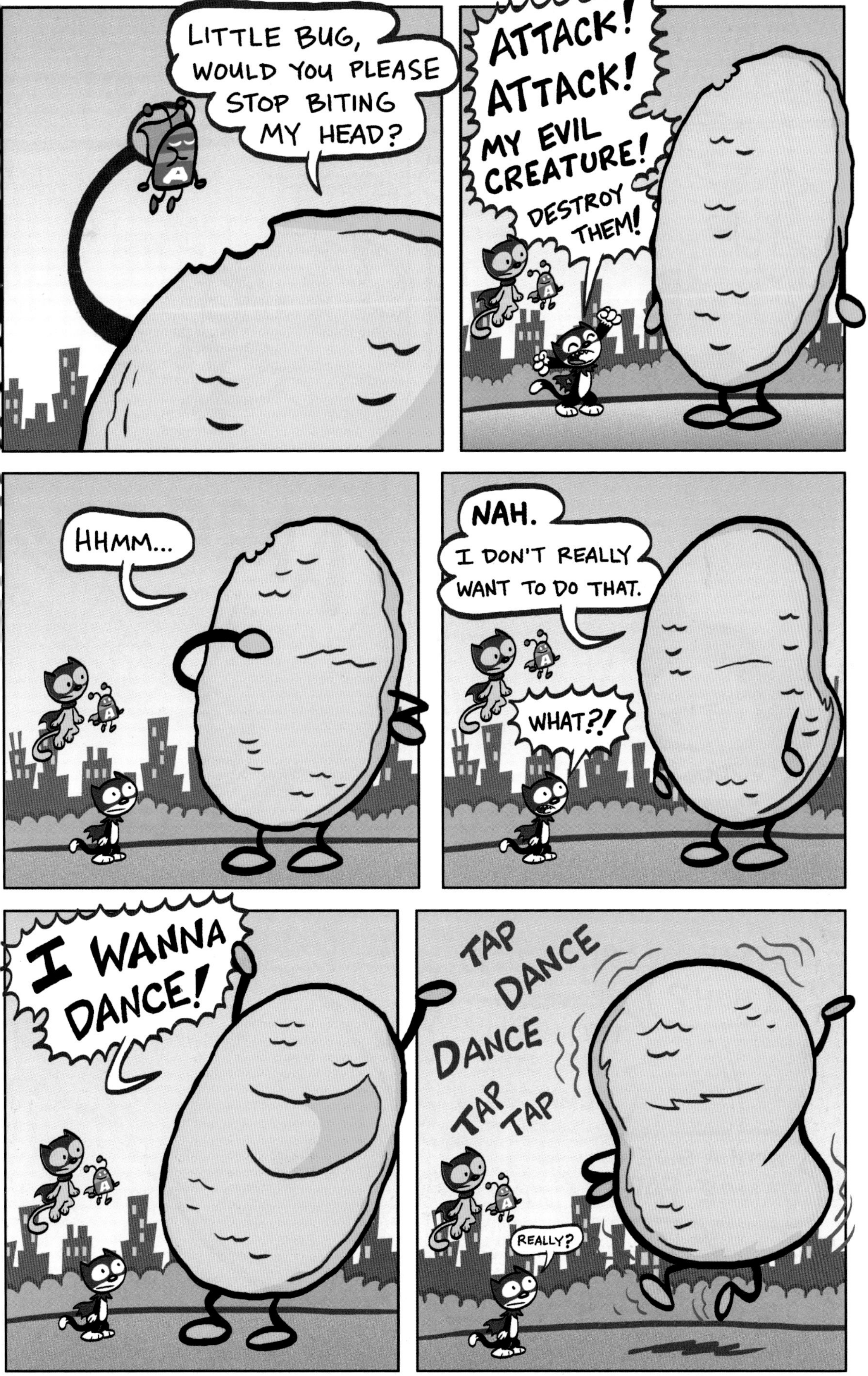
LITTLE BUG, WOULD YOU PLEASE STOP BITING MY HEAD?
ATTACK! ATTACK! MY EVIL CREATURE!
DESTROY THEM!
HHMM...
NAH.
I DON'T REALLY WANT TO DO THAT.
WHAT?!
I WANNA DANCE!
TAP DANCE DANCE TAP TAP
REALLY?

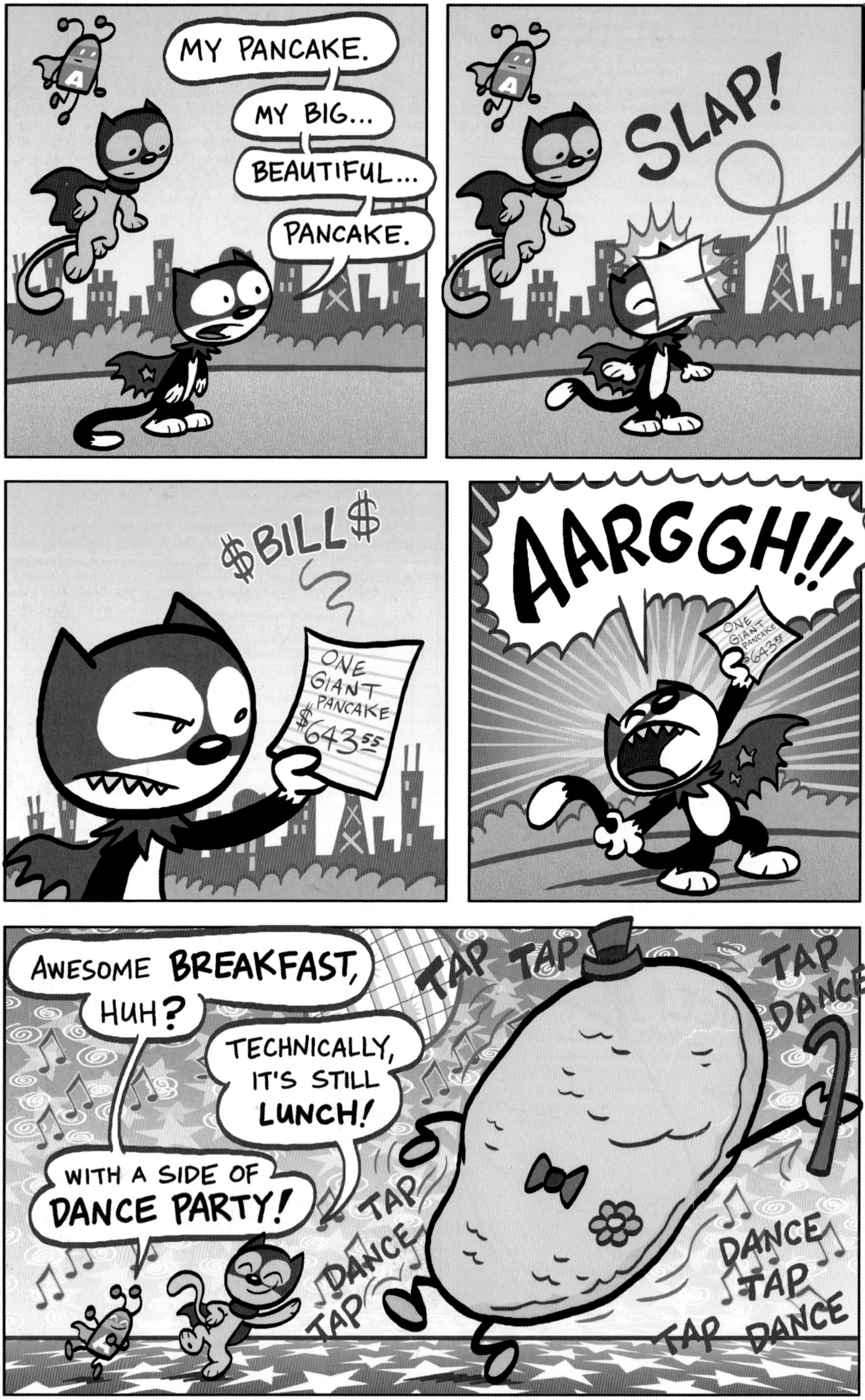
MY PANCAKE.
MY BIG...
BEAUTIFUL...
PANCAKE.
SLAP!
$BILL$
ONE GIANT PANCAKE $643.55
AARGGH!!
ONE GIANT PANCAKE $643.55
AWESOME BREAKFAST, HUH?
TECHNICALLY, IT'S STILL LUNCH!
WITH A SIDE OF DANCE PARTY!
TAP TAP
TAP DANCE
TAP DANCE TAP
DANCE TAP
TAP DANCE

—DINNER SHOULD BE INTERESTING.

ACTION CAT & ADVENTURE BUG IN: **THAT'S NOT FAIR!**

BY SCOOT MCMAHON

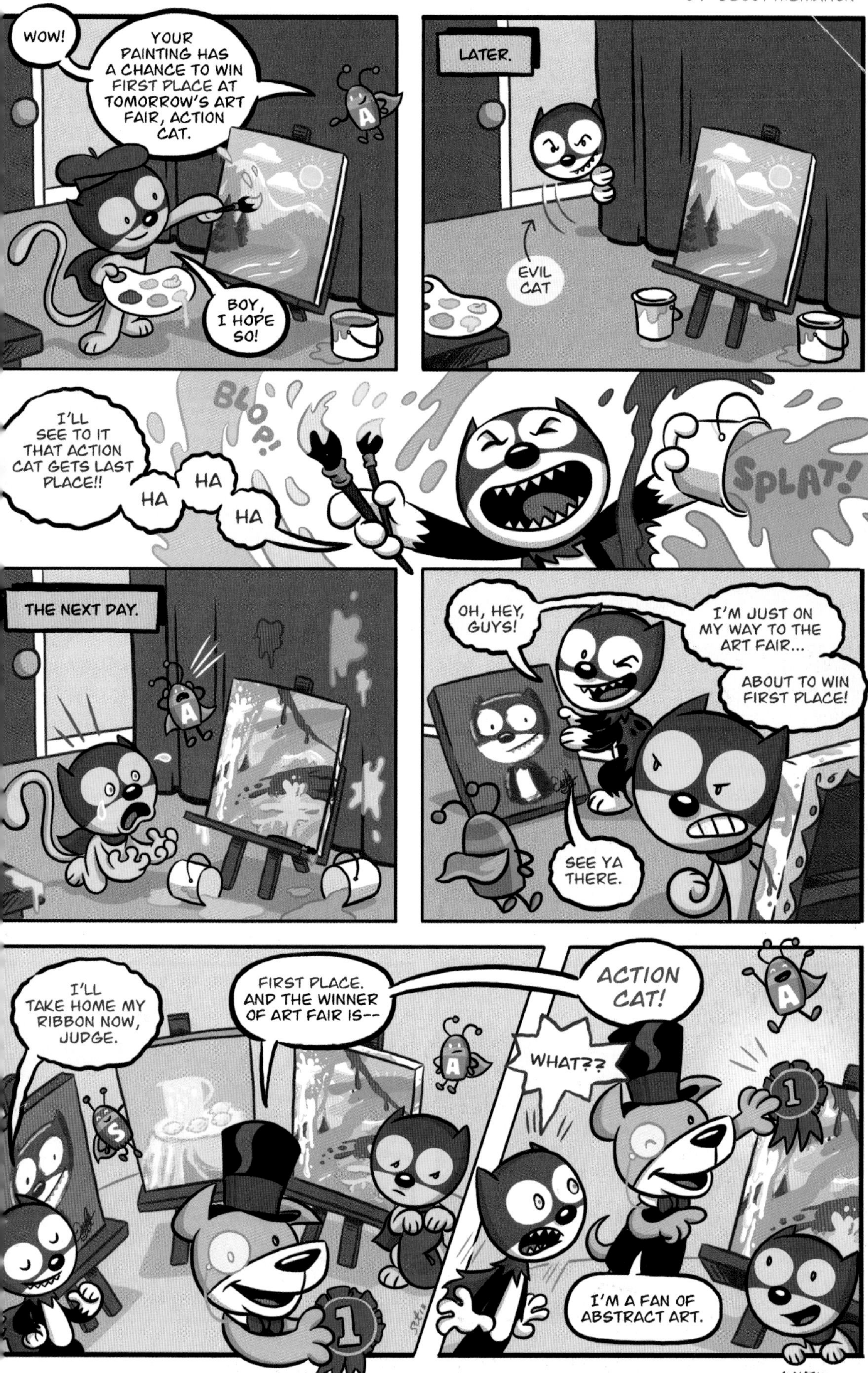
WOW!
YOUR PAINTING HAS A CHANCE TO WIN FIRST PLACE AT TOMORROW'S ART FAIR, ACTION CAT.
BOY, I HOPE SO!
LATER.
EVIL CAT
BLOP!
I'LL SEE TO IT THAT ACTION CAT GETS LAST PLACE!!
HA
HA
HA
SPLAT!
THE NEXT DAY.
OH, HEY, GUYS!
I'M JUST ON MY WAY TO THE ART FAIR...
ABOUT TO WIN FIRST PLACE!
SEE YA THERE.
I'LL TAKE HOME MY RIBBON NOW, JUDGE.
FIRST PLACE. AND THE WINNER OF ART FAIR IS--
ACTION CAT!
WHAT??
I'M A FAN OF ABSTRACT ART.

AW YEAH COMICS!

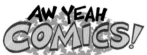

AW YEAH COMICS! PRESENTS... GHOST BUG! BY CHRIS ZOD SMITS & FRANCO

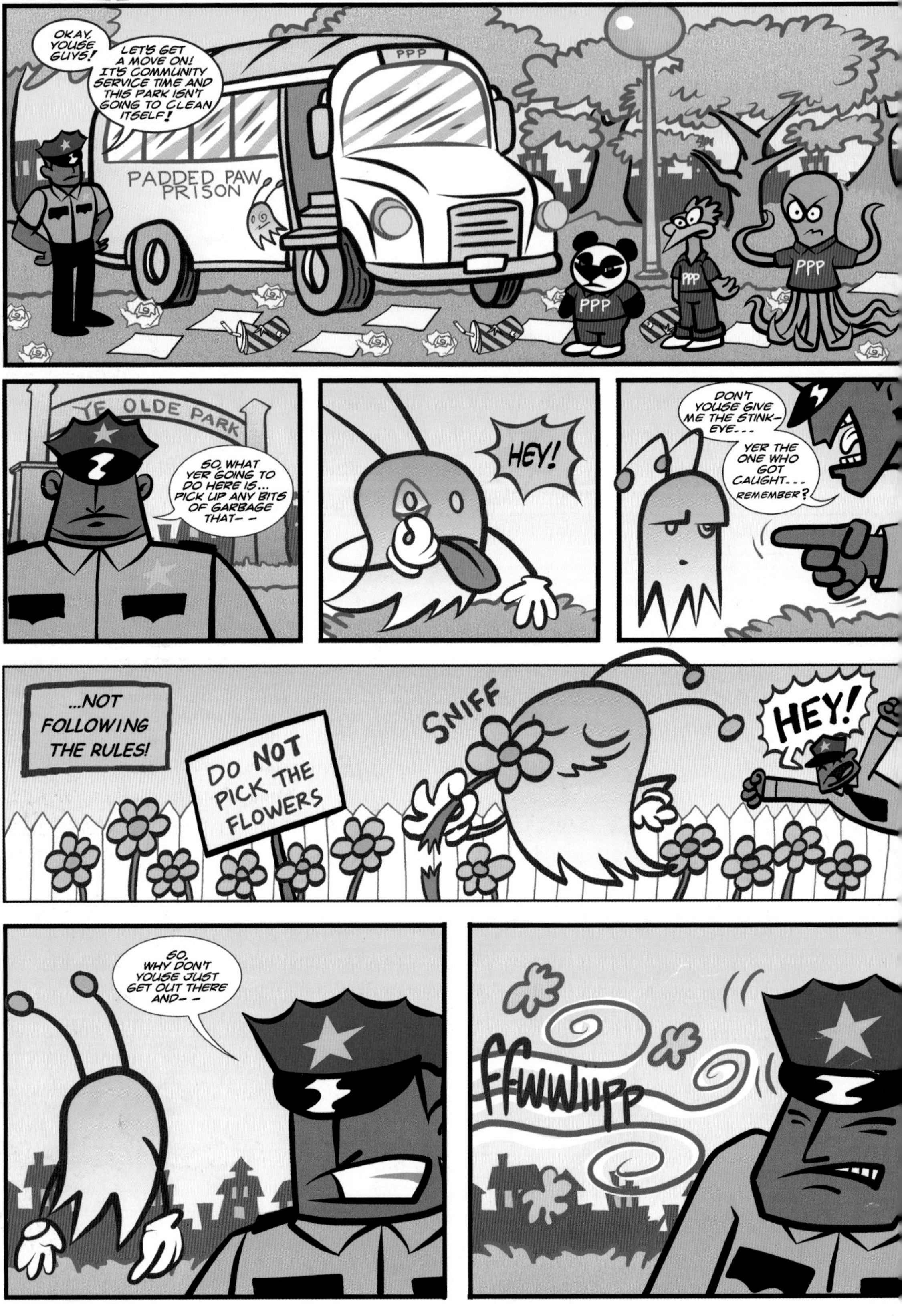
OKAY, YOUSE GUYS!
LET'S GET A MOVE ON! IT'S COMMUNITY SERVICE TIME AND THIS PARK ISN'T GOING TO CLEAN ITSELF!
PPP
PADDED PAW PRISON
PPP
PPP
PPP
YE OLDE PARK
SO, WHAT YER GOING TO DO HERE IS... PICK UP ANY BITS OF GARBAGE THAT--
HEY!
DON'T YOUSE GIVE ME THE STINK-EYE...
YER THE ONE WHO GOT CAUGHT... REMEMBER?
...NOT FOLLOWING THE RULES!
DO NOT PICK THE FLOWERS
SNIFF
HEY!
SO, WHY DON'T YOUSE JUST GET OUT THERE AND--
FFWWIIPP

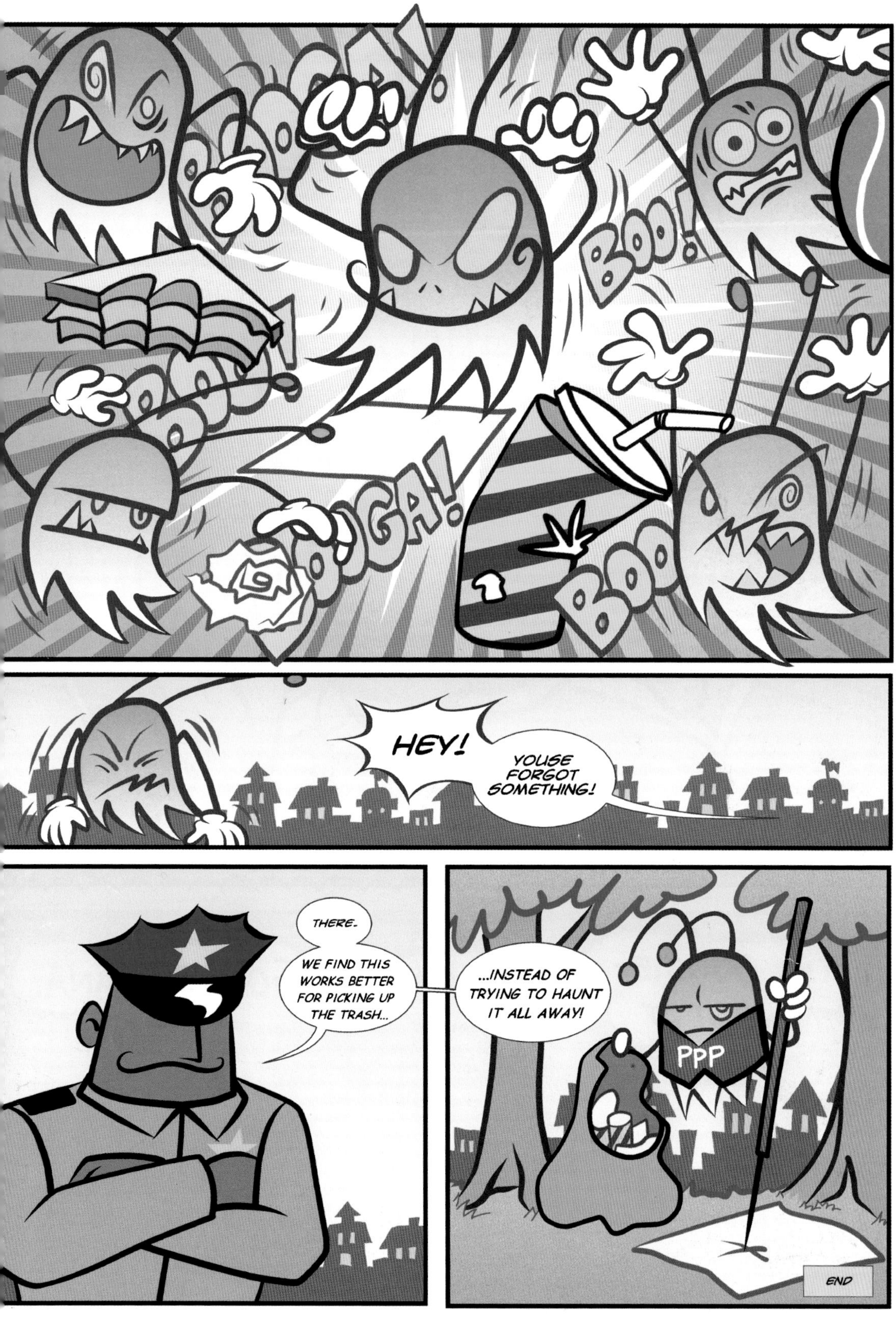
BOO!
HEY!
YOUSE FORGOT SOMETHING!
THERE.
WE FIND THIS WORKS BETTER FOR PICKING UP THE TRASH...
...INSTEAD OF TRYING TO HAUNT IT ALL AWAY!
PPP
END

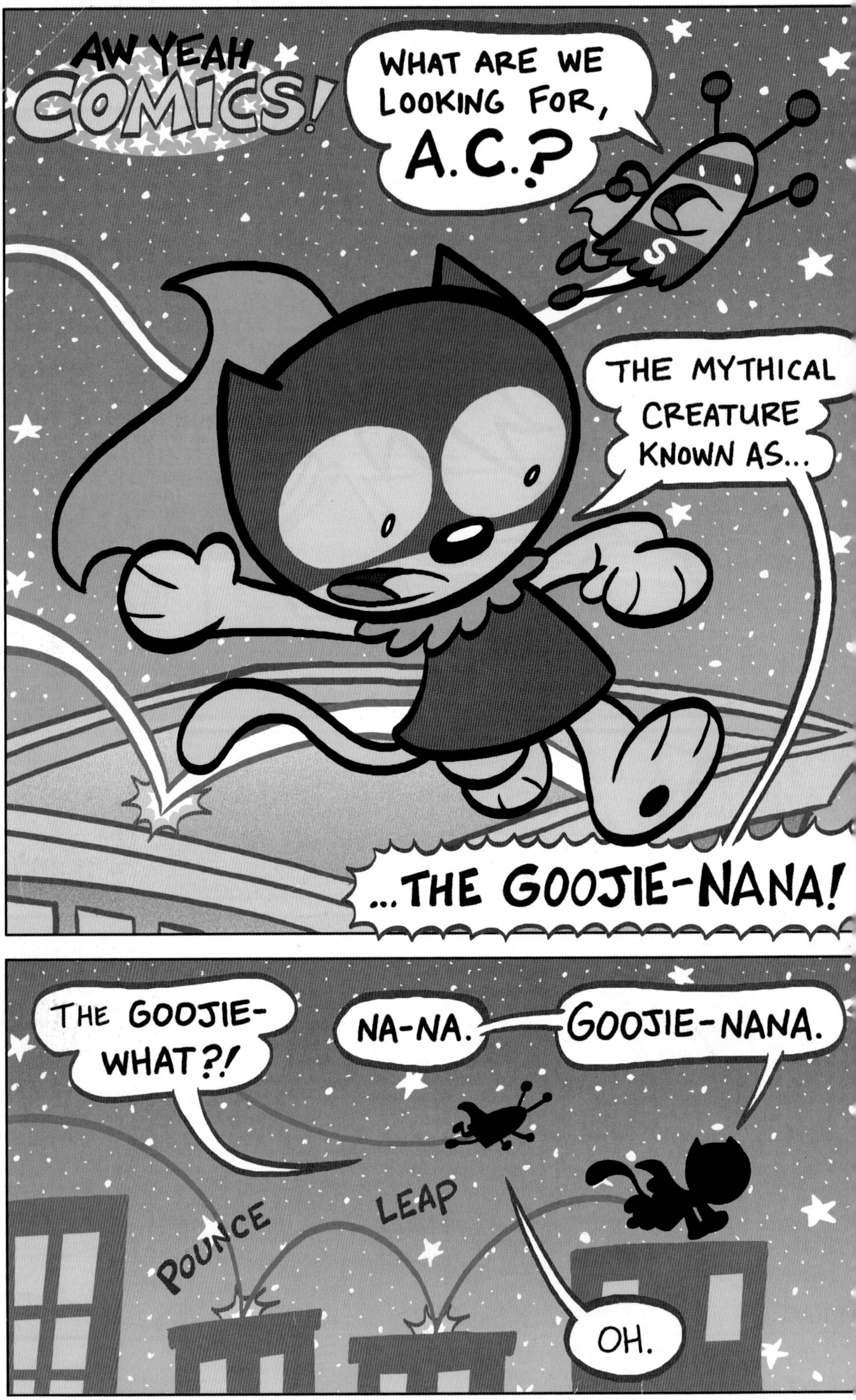
AW YEAH COMICS!
WHAT ARE WE LOOKING FOR, A.C.?
THE MYTHICAL CREATURE KNOWN AS...
...THE GOOJIE-NANA!
THE GOOJIE-WHAT?!
NA-NA.
GOOJIE-NANA.
POUNCE
LEAP
OH.

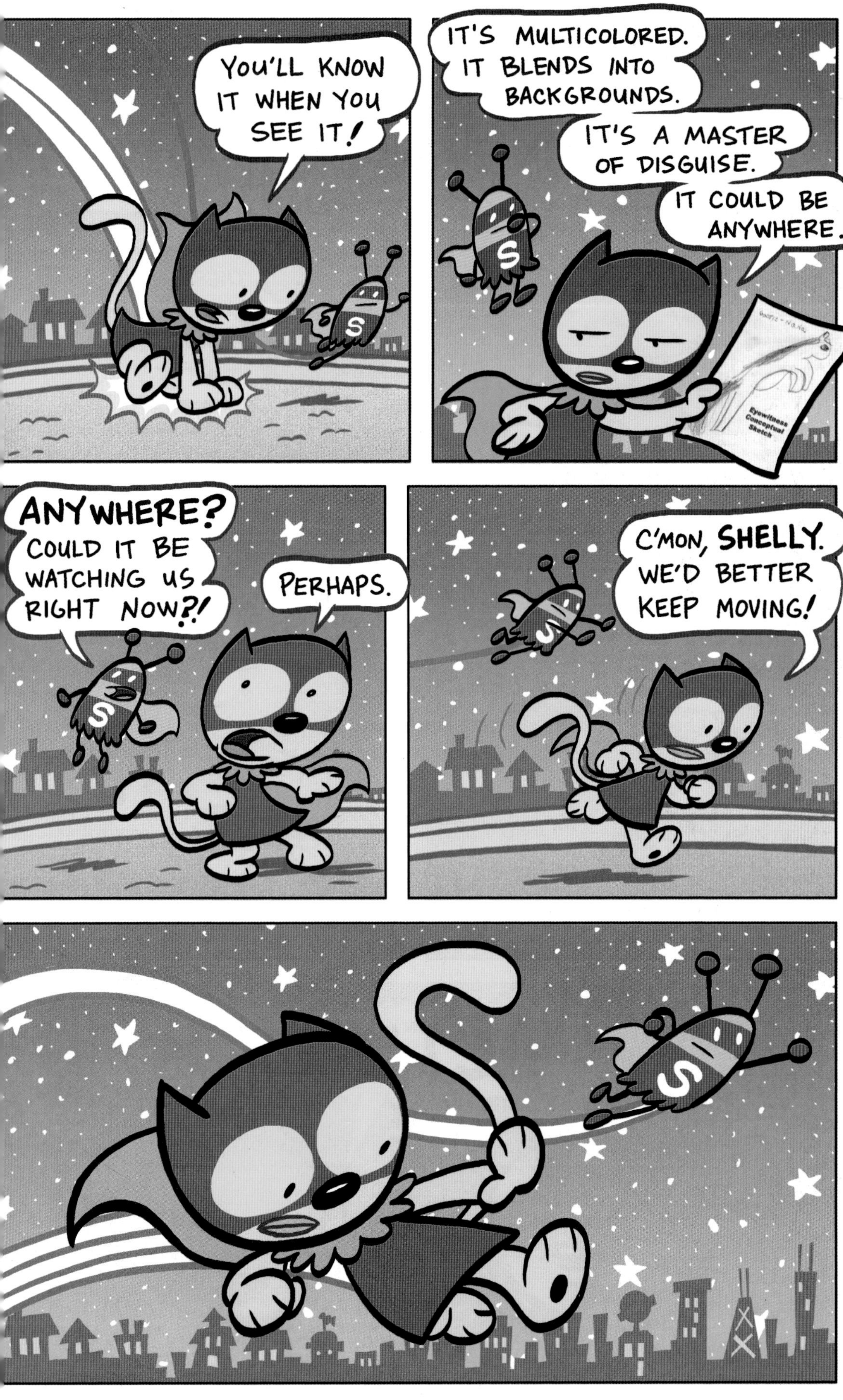
YOU'LL KNOW IT WHEN YOU SEE IT!
IT'S MULTICOLORED. IT BLENDS INTO BACKGROUNDS.
IT'S A MASTER OF DISGUISE.
IT COULD BE ANYWHERE.
Eyewitness Conceptual Sketch
ANYWHERE? COULD IT BE WATCHING US RIGHT NOW?!
PERHAPS.
C'MON, SHELLY. WE'D BETTER KEEP MOVING!

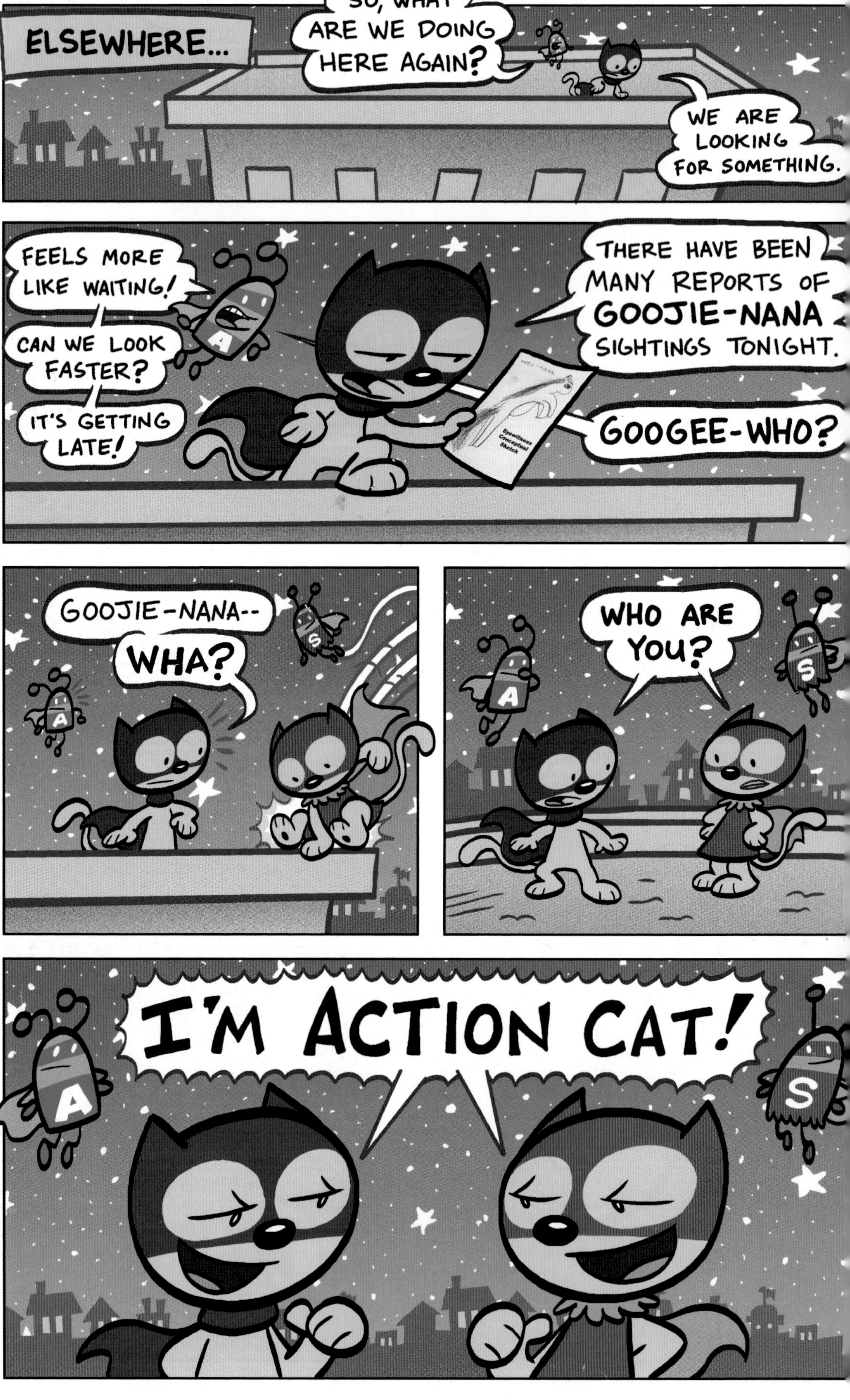
ELSEWHERE...
SO, WHAT ARE WE DOING HERE AGAIN?
WE ARE LOOKING FOR SOMETHING.
FEELS MORE LIKE WAITING!
CAN WE LOOK FASTER?
IT'S GETTING LATE!
THERE HAVE BEEN MANY REPORTS OF GOOJIE-NANA SIGHTINGS TONIGHT.
Eyewitness Conceptual Sketch
GOOGEE-WHO?
GOOJIE-NANA--
WHA?
WHO ARE YOU?
I'M ACTION CAT!

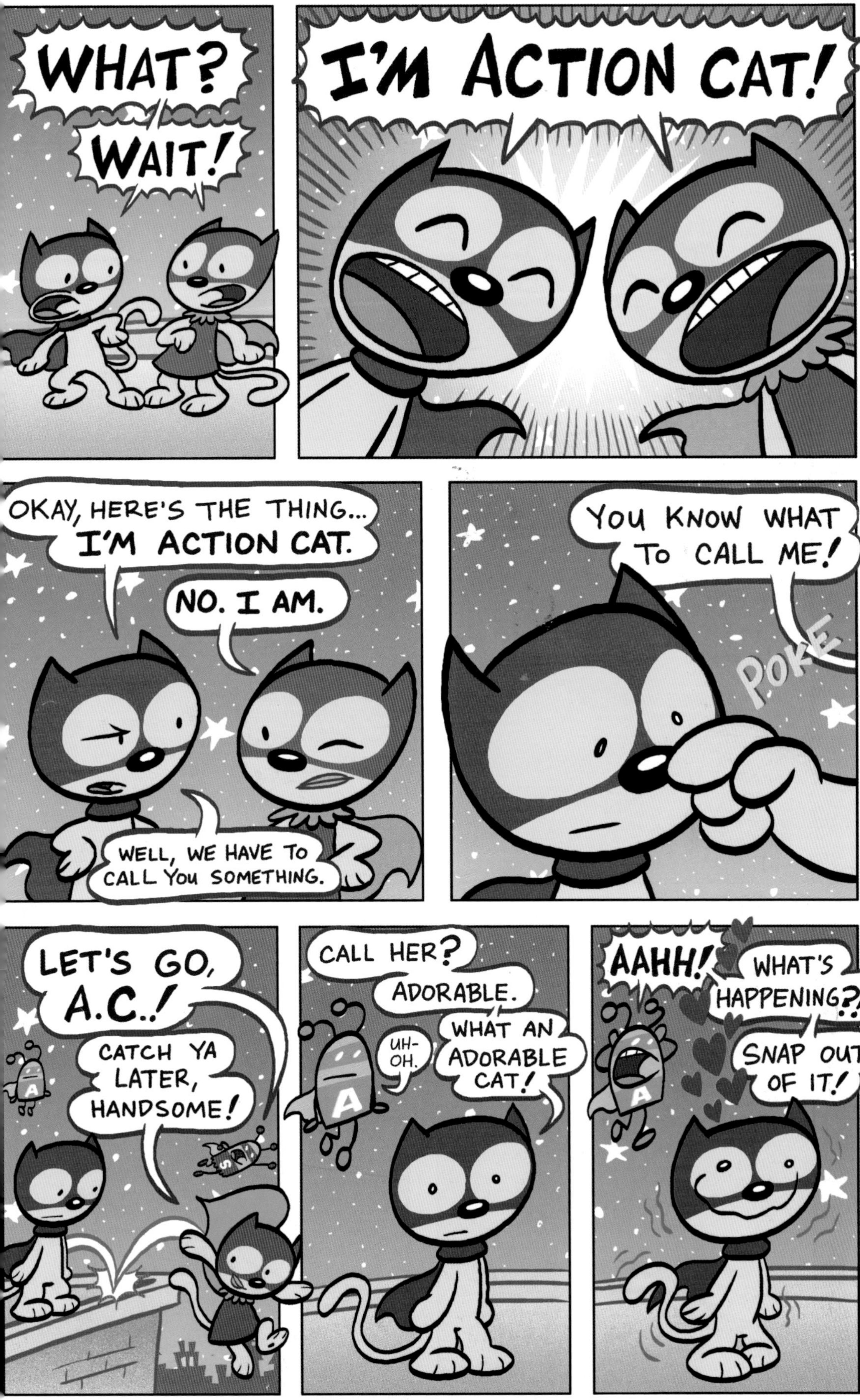
WHAT?
WAIT!
I'M ACTION CAT!
OKAY, HERE'S THE THING... I'M ACTION CAT.
NO. I AM.
WELL, WE HAVE TO CALL YOU SOMETHING.
YOU KNOW WHAT TO CALL ME!
POKE
LET'S GO, A.C.!
CATCH YA LATER, HANDSOME!
CALL HER?
ADORABLE.
UH-OH.
WHAT AN ADORABLE CAT!
AAHH!
WHAT'S HAPPENING?!
SNAP OUT OF IT!

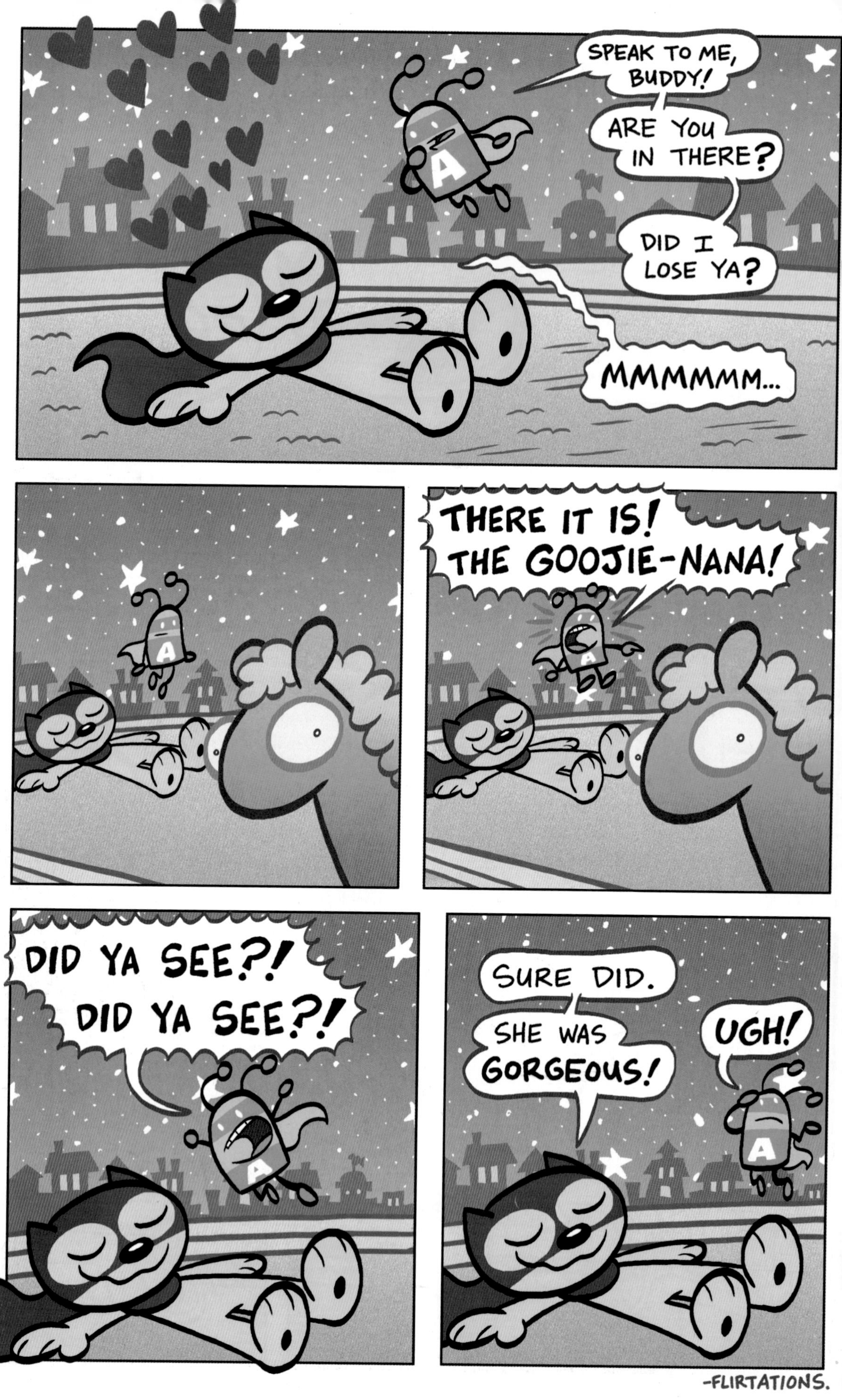
SPEAK TO ME, BUDDY!
ARE YOU IN THERE?
DID I LOSE YA?
MMMMMM...
THERE IT IS! THE GOOJIE-NANA!
DID YA SEE?! DID YA SEE?!
SURE DID.
SHE WAS GORGEOUS!
UGH!

-FLIRTATIONS.

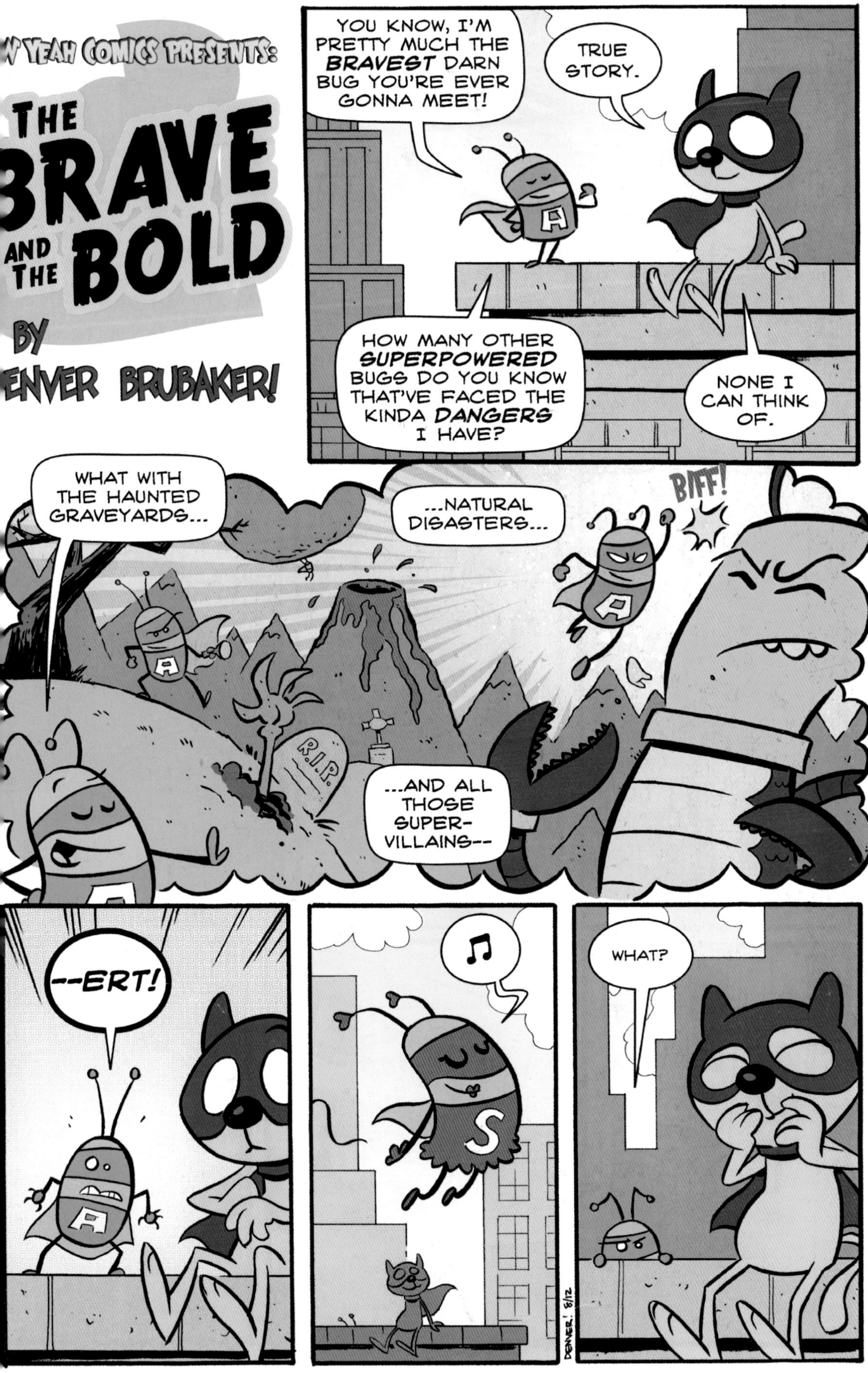
W YEAH COMICS PRESENTS:
THE BRAVE AND THE BOLD
BY
ENVER BRUBAKER!
YOU KNOW, I'M PRETTY MUCH THE BRAVEST DARN BUG YOU'RE EVER GONNA MEET!
TRUE STORY.
HOW MANY OTHER SUPERPOWERED BUGS DO YOU KNOW THAT'VE FACED THE KINDA DANGERS I HAVE?
NONE I CAN THINK OF.
WHAT WITH THE HAUNTED GRAVEYARDS...
...NATURAL DISASTERS...
BIFF!
R.I.P.
...AND ALL THOSE SUPER-VILLAINS--
--ERT!
♫
WHAT?
DENVER! 8/12

AW YEAH COMICS! PRESENTS...

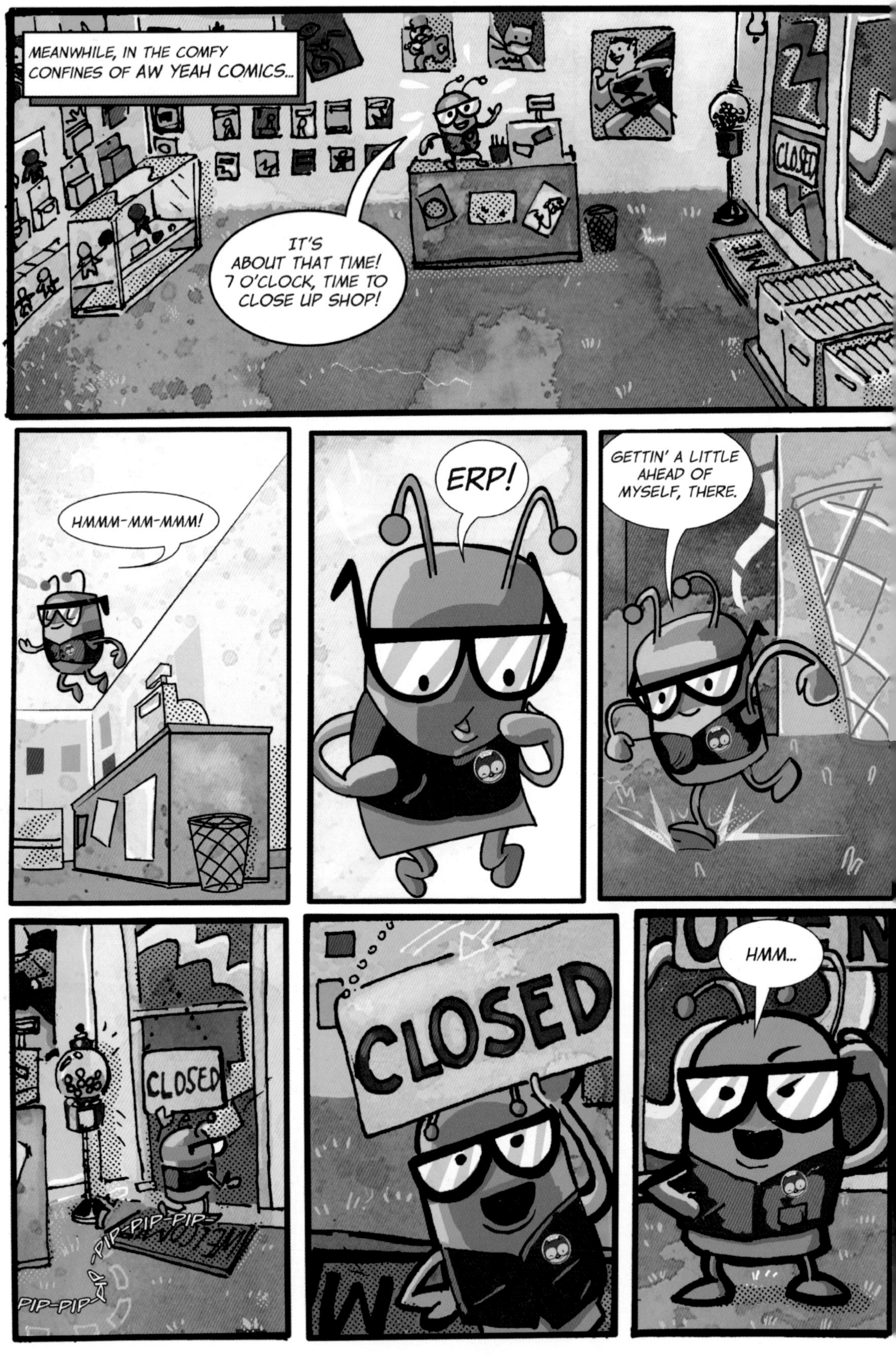
MEANWHILE, IN THE COMFY CONFINES OF AW YEAH COMICS...
IT'S ABOUT THAT TIME! 7 O'CLOCK, TIME TO CLOSE UP SHOP!
CLOSED
HMMM-MM-MMM!
ERP!
GETTIN' A LITTLE AHEAD OF MYSELF, THERE.
CLOSED
PIP-PIP-PIP-PIP-PIP-PIP-
CLOSED
HMM...

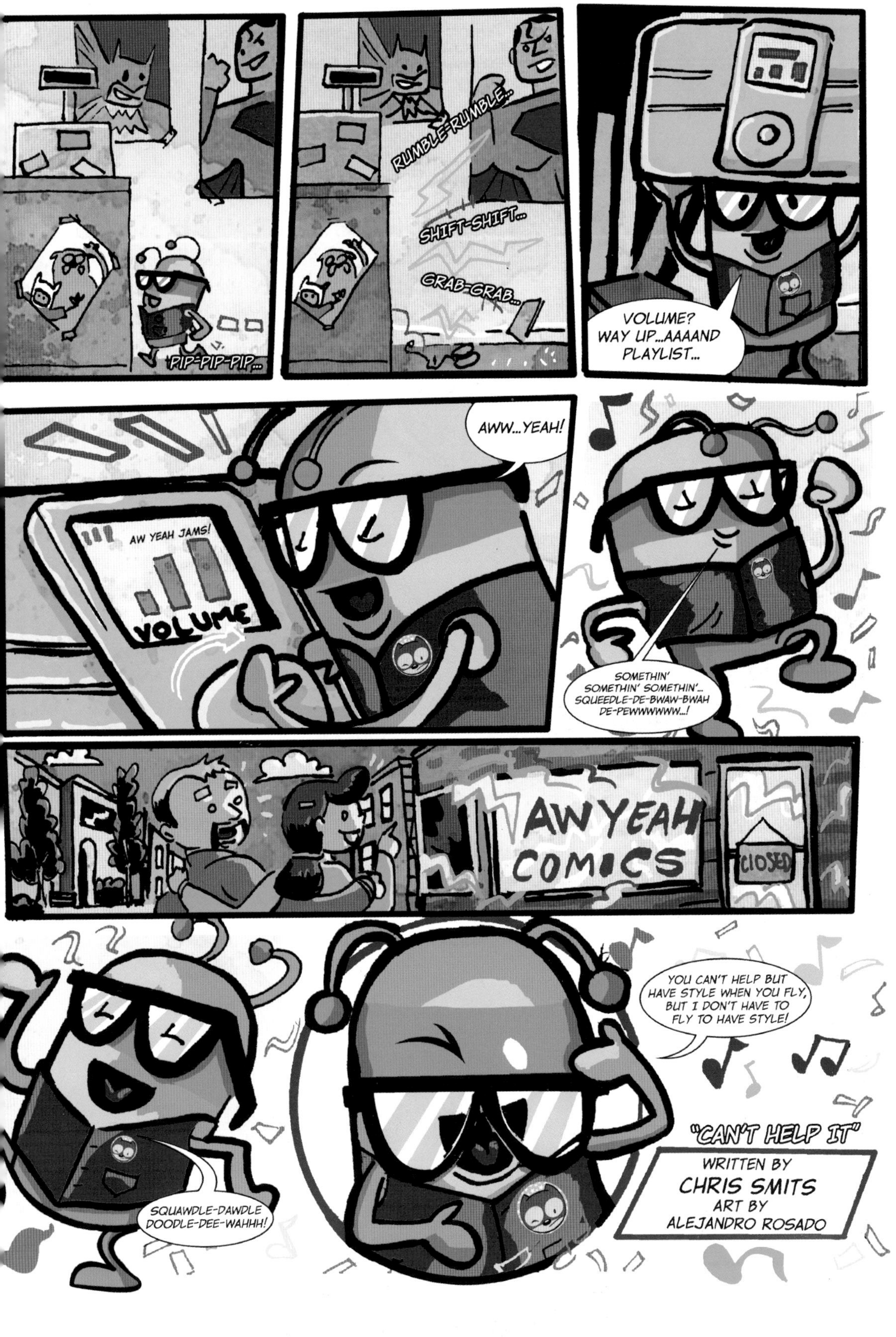
PIP-PIP-PIP...
RUMBLE-RUMBLE...
SHIFT-SHIFT...
GRAB-GRAB...
VOLUME? WAY UP...AAAAND PLAYLIST...
AW YEAH JAMS!
VOLUME
AWW...YEAH!
SOMETHIN' SOMETHIN' SOMETHIN'... SQUEEDLE-DE-BWAW-BWAH DE-PEWWWWWW...!
AWYEAH COMICS
CLOSED
SQUAWDLE-DAWDLE DOODLE-DEE-WAHHH!
YOU CAN'T HELP BUT HAVE STYLE WHEN YOU FLY, BUT I DON'T HAVE TO FLY TO HAVE STYLE!
"CAN'T HELP IT"
WRITTEN BY
CHRIS SMITS
ART BY
ALEJANDRO ROSADO

AND NOW...

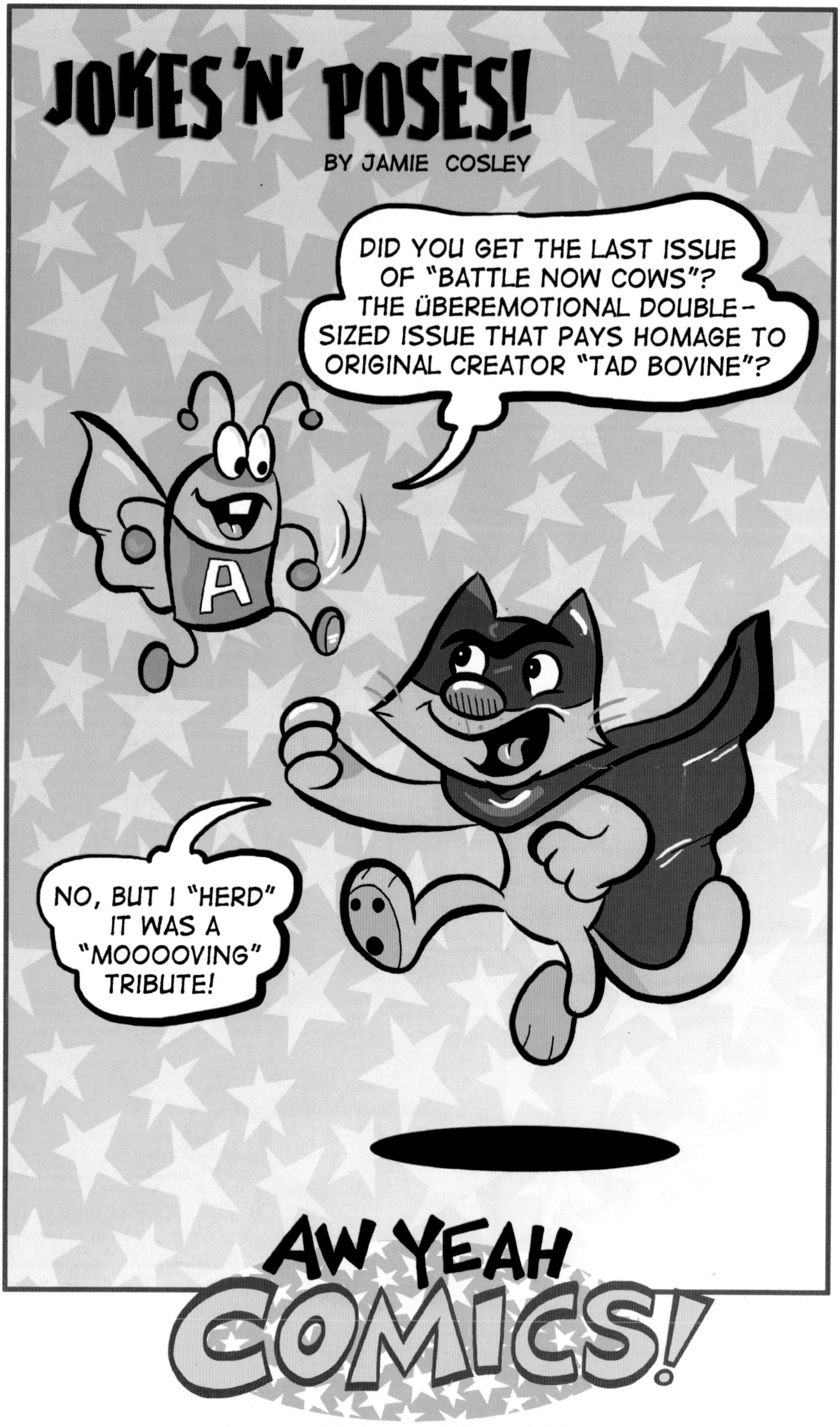
JOKES 'N' POSES!
BY JAMIE COSLEY
DID YOU GET THE LAST ISSUE OF "BATTLE NOW COWS"? THE ÜBEREMOTIONAL DOUBLE-SIZED ISSUE THAT PAYS HOMAGE TO ORIGINAL CREATOR "TAD BOVINE"?
NO, BUT I "HERD" IT WAS A "MOOOOVING" TRIBUTE!
AW YEAH COMICS!

★ CHAPTER TWO ★

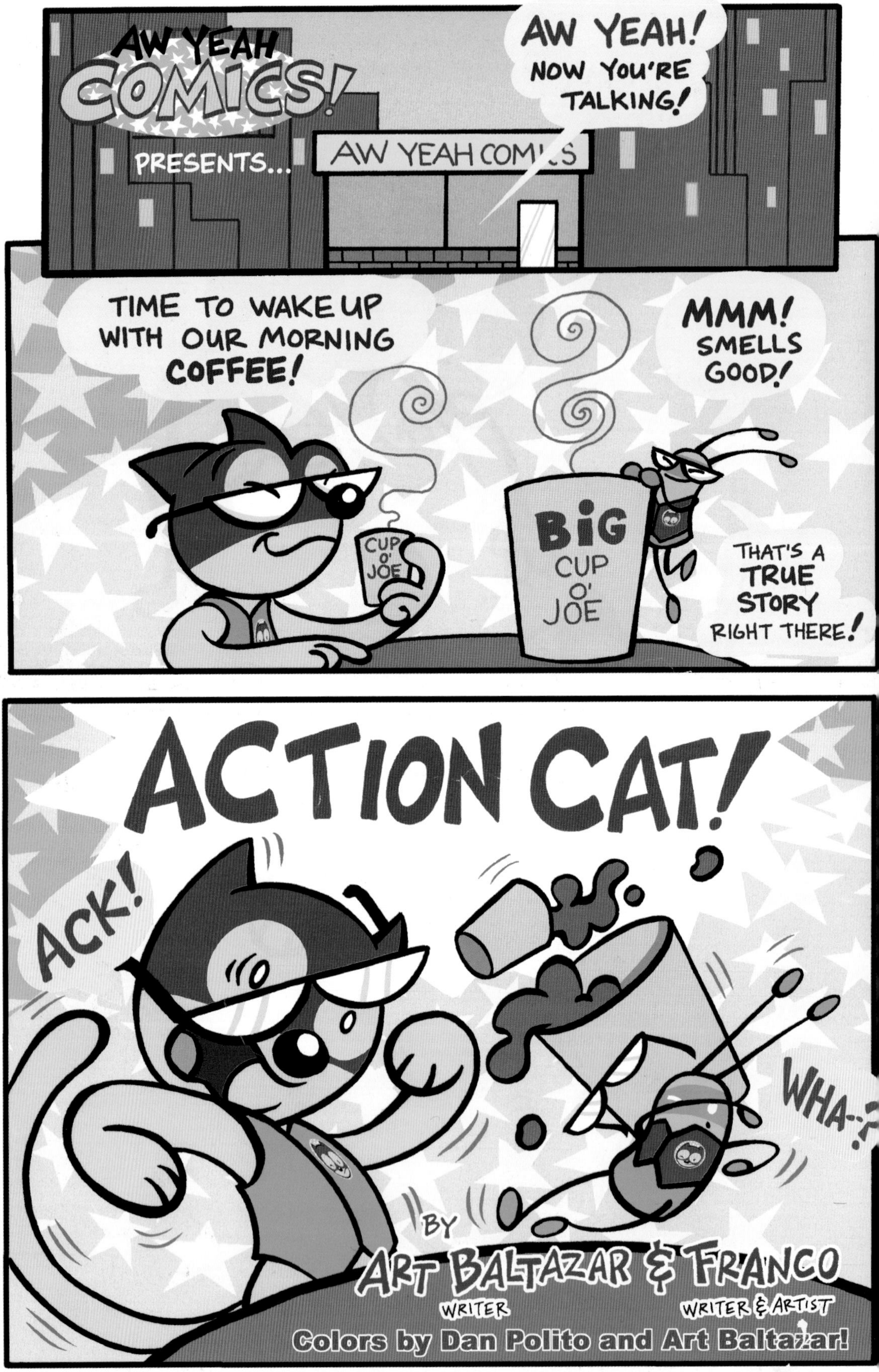
AW YEAH COMICS!
PRESENTS...
AW YEAH COMICS
AW YEAH! NOW YOU'RE TALKING!
TIME TO WAKE UP WITH OUR MORNING COFFEE!
MMM! SMELLS GOOD!
CUP O' JOE
BIG CUP O' JOE
THAT'S A TRUE STORY RIGHT THERE!
ACTION CAT!
ACK!
WHA--?
BY
ART BALTAZAR & FRANCO
WRITER
WRITER & ARTIST
Colors by Dan Polito and Art Baltazar!

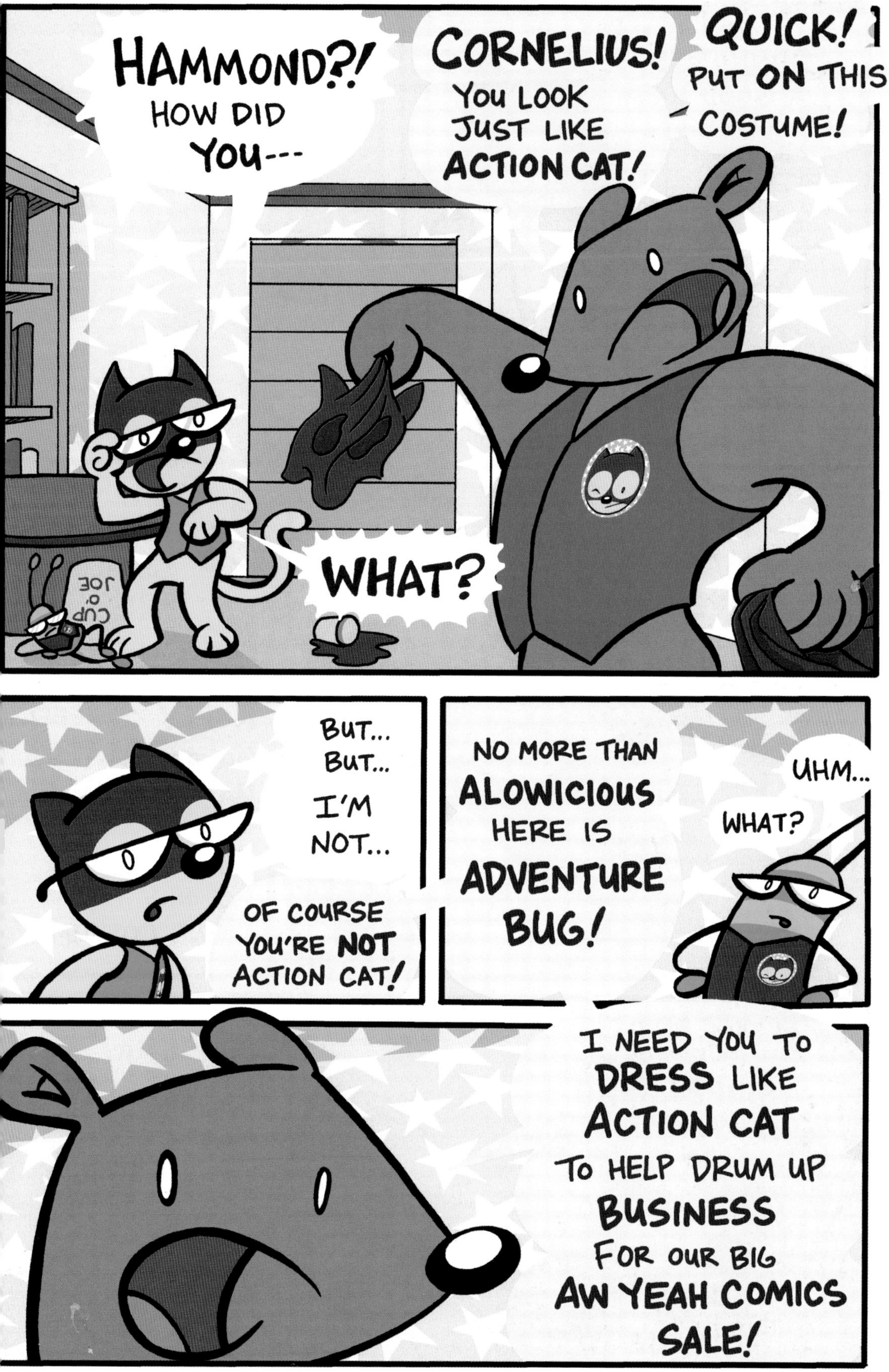
HAMMOND?! HOW DID YOU---
CORNELIUS! YOU LOOK JUST LIKE ACTION CAT!
QUICK! PUT ON THIS COSTUME!
WHAT?
CUP O' JOE
BUT... BUT... I'M NOT...
OF COURSE YOU'RE NOT ACTION CAT!
NO MORE THAN ALOWICIOUS HERE IS ADVENTURE BUG!
UHM... WHAT?
I NEED YOU TO DRESS LIKE ACTION CAT TO HELP DRUM UP BUSINESS FOR OUR BIG AW YEAH COMICS SALE!

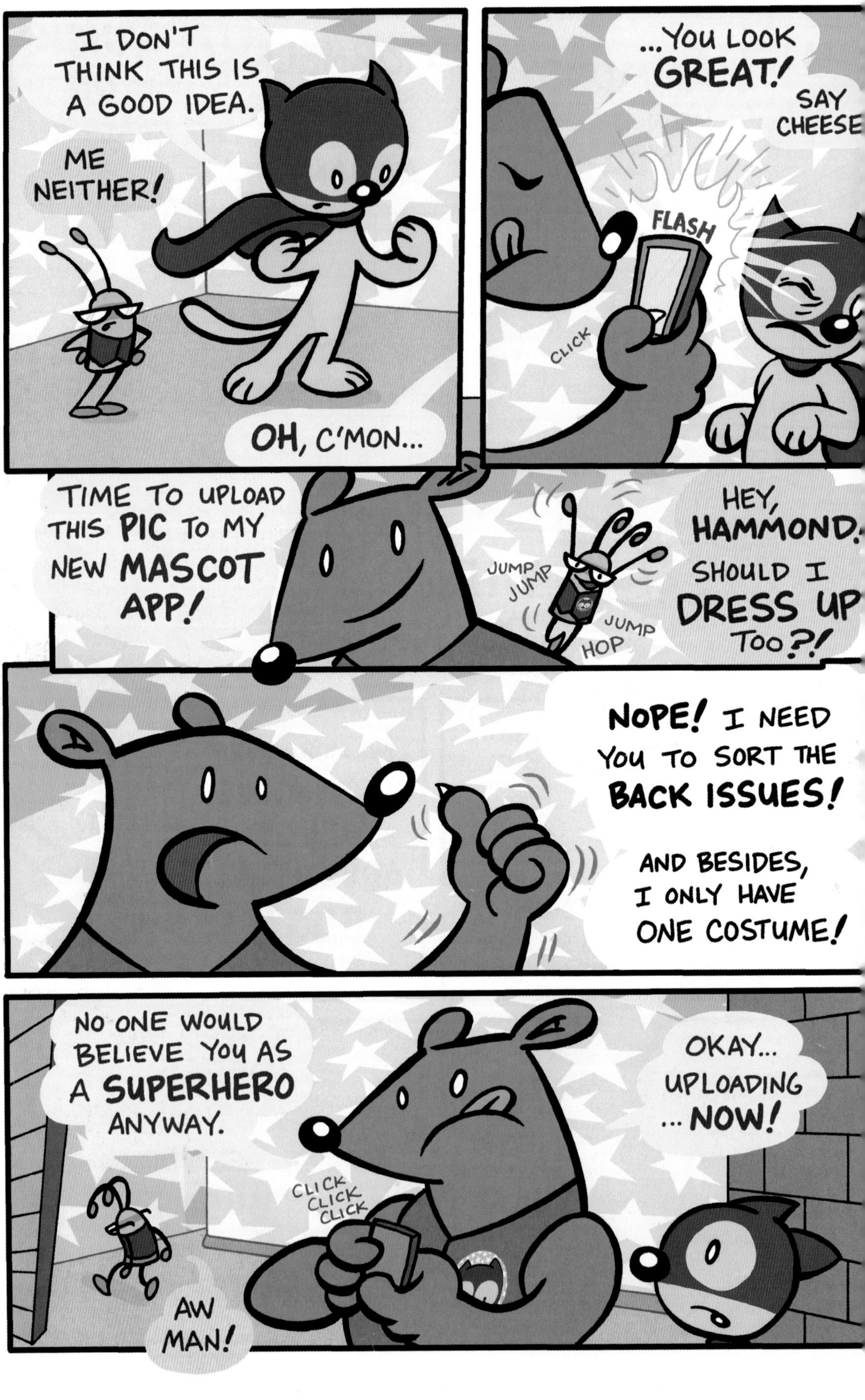
I DON'T THINK THIS IS A GOOD IDEA.
ME NEITHER!
OH, C'MON...
...YOU LOOK GREAT!
SAY CHEESE
FLASH
CLICK
TIME TO UPLOAD THIS PIC TO MY NEW MASCOT APP!
JUMP
JUMP
JUMP
HOP
HEY, HAMMOND. SHOULD I DRESS UP TOO?!
NOPE! I NEED YOU TO SORT THE BACK ISSUES!
AND BESIDES, I ONLY HAVE ONE COSTUME!
NO ONE WOULD BELIEVE YOU AS A SUPERHERO ANYWAY.
OKAY... UPLOADING ...NOW!
CLICK CLICK CLICK
AW MAN!

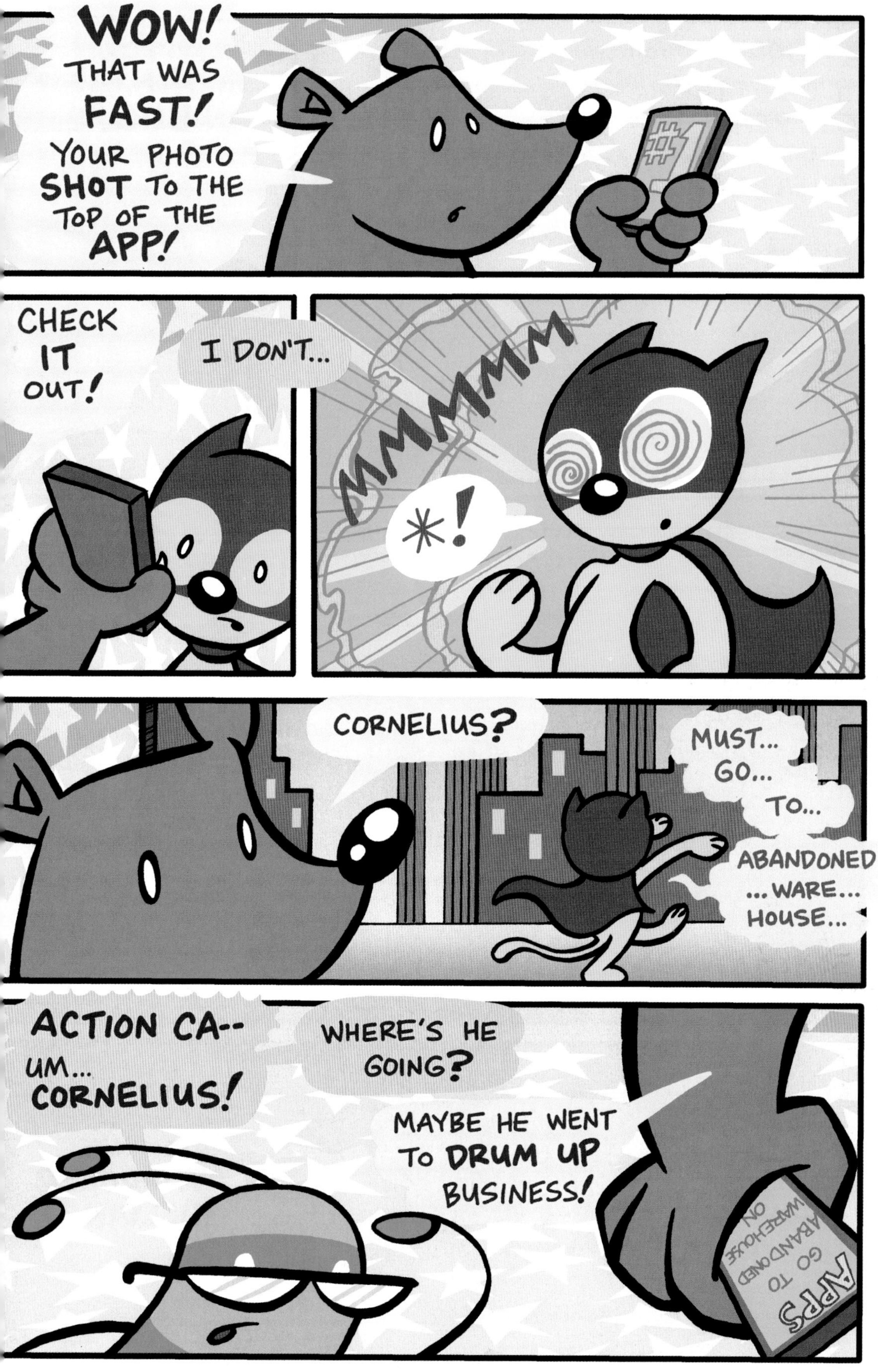

WOW! THAT WAS FAST! YOUR PHOTO SHOT TO THE TOP OF THE APP!
#1
CHECK IT OUT!
I DON'T...
MMMMMM
*!
CORNELIUS?
MUST... GO... TO... ABANDONED ... WARE... HOUSE...
ACTION CA-- UM... CORNELIUS!
WHERE'S HE GOING?
MAYBE HE WENT TO DRUM UP BUSINESS!
APPS
GO TO
ABANDONED
WAREHOUSE
ON

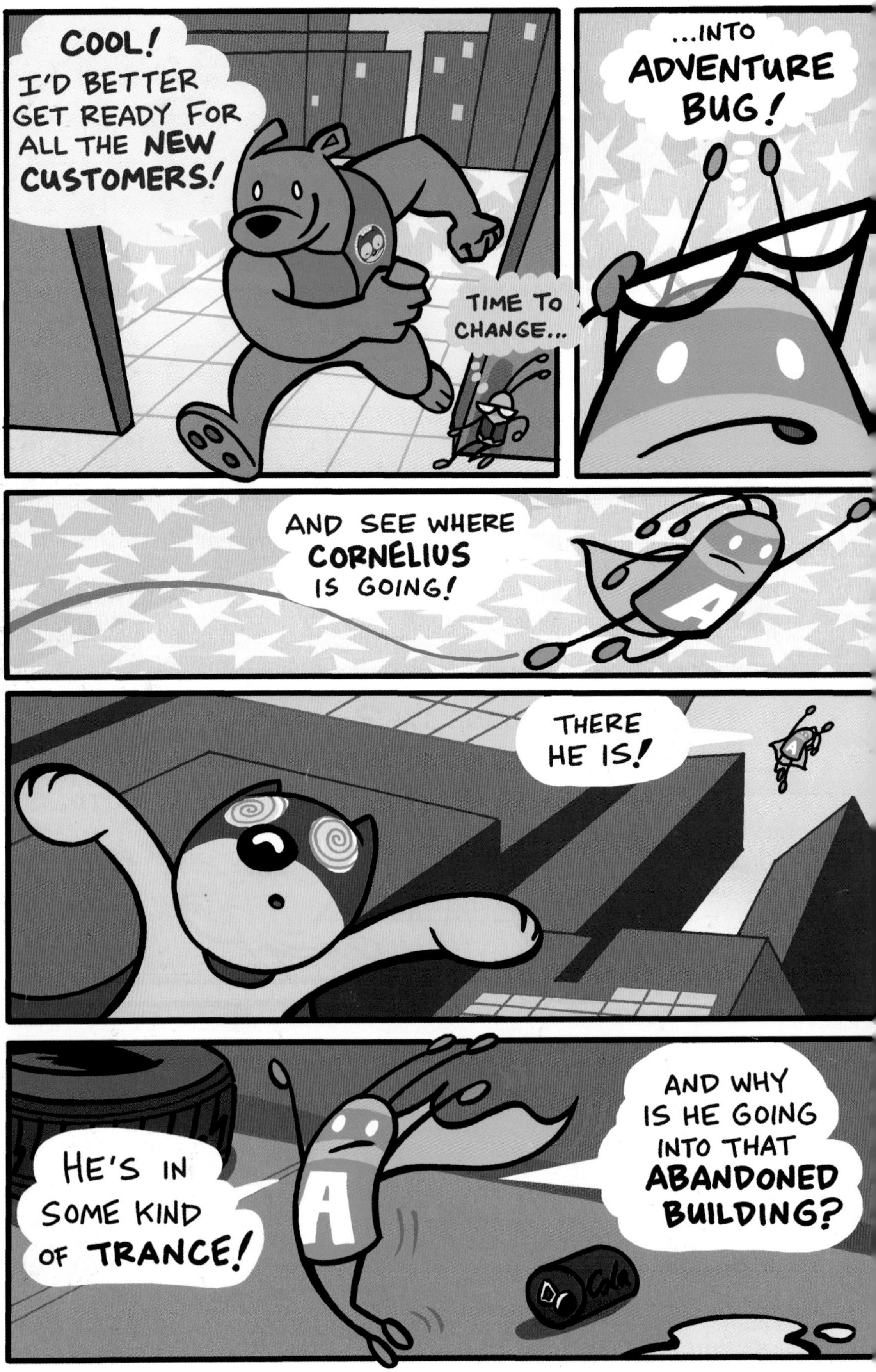
COOL! I'D BETTER GET READY FOR ALL THE NEW CUSTOMERS!
TIME TO CHANGE...
...INTO ADVENTURE BUG!
AND SEE WHERE CORNELIUS IS GOING!
THERE HE IS!
HE'S IN SOME KIND OF TRANCE!
AND WHY IS HE GOING INTO THAT ABANDONED BUILDING?

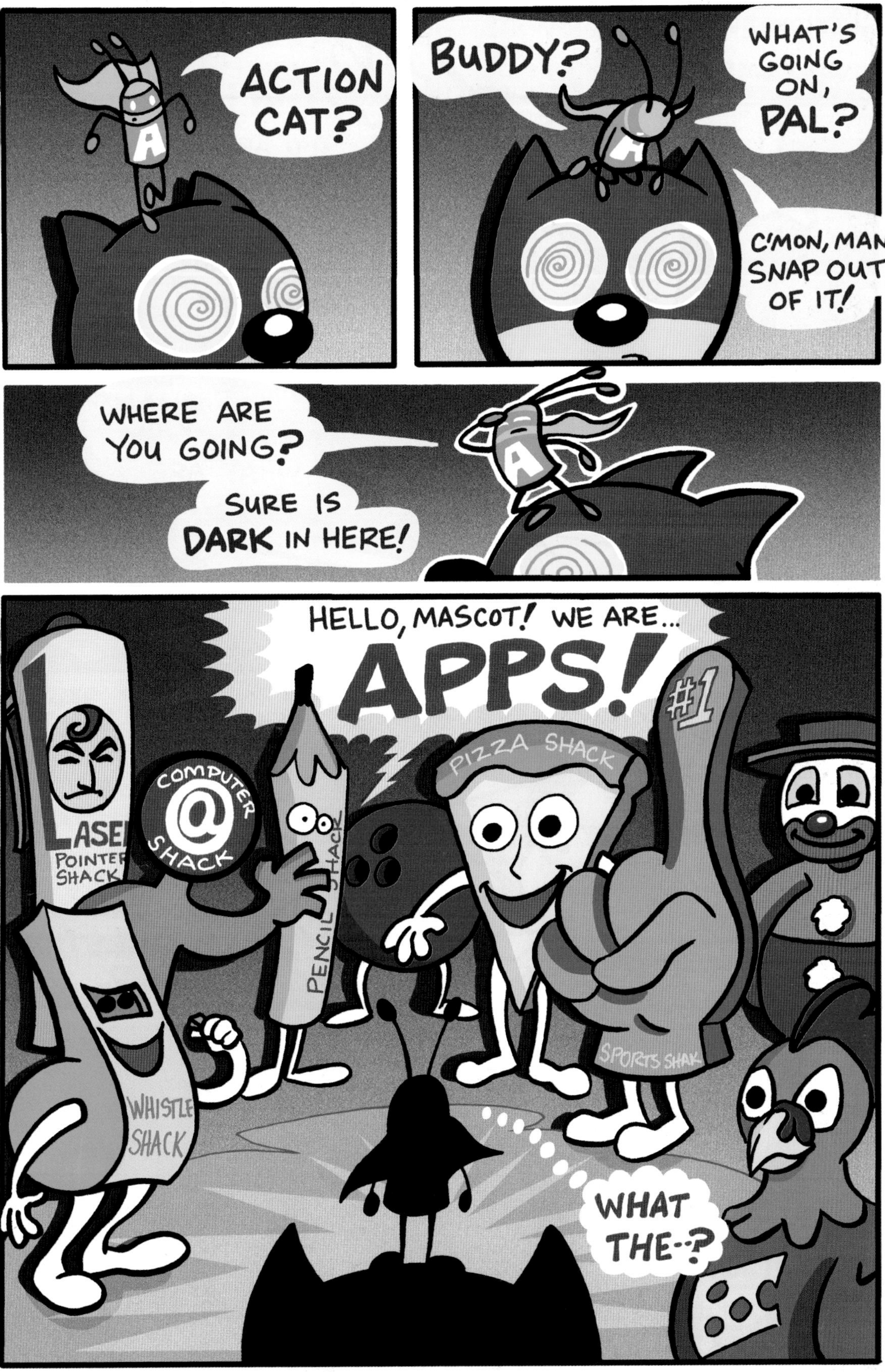
ACTION CAT?
BUDDY?
WHAT'S GOING ON, PAL?
C'MON, MAN, SNAP OUT OF IT!
WHERE ARE YOU GOING?
SURE IS DARK IN HERE!
HELLO, MASCOT! WE ARE... APPS!
POINTER SHACK
COMPUTER SHACK
PIZZA SHACK
#1
SPORTS SHAK
WHISTLE SHACK
WHAT THE--?

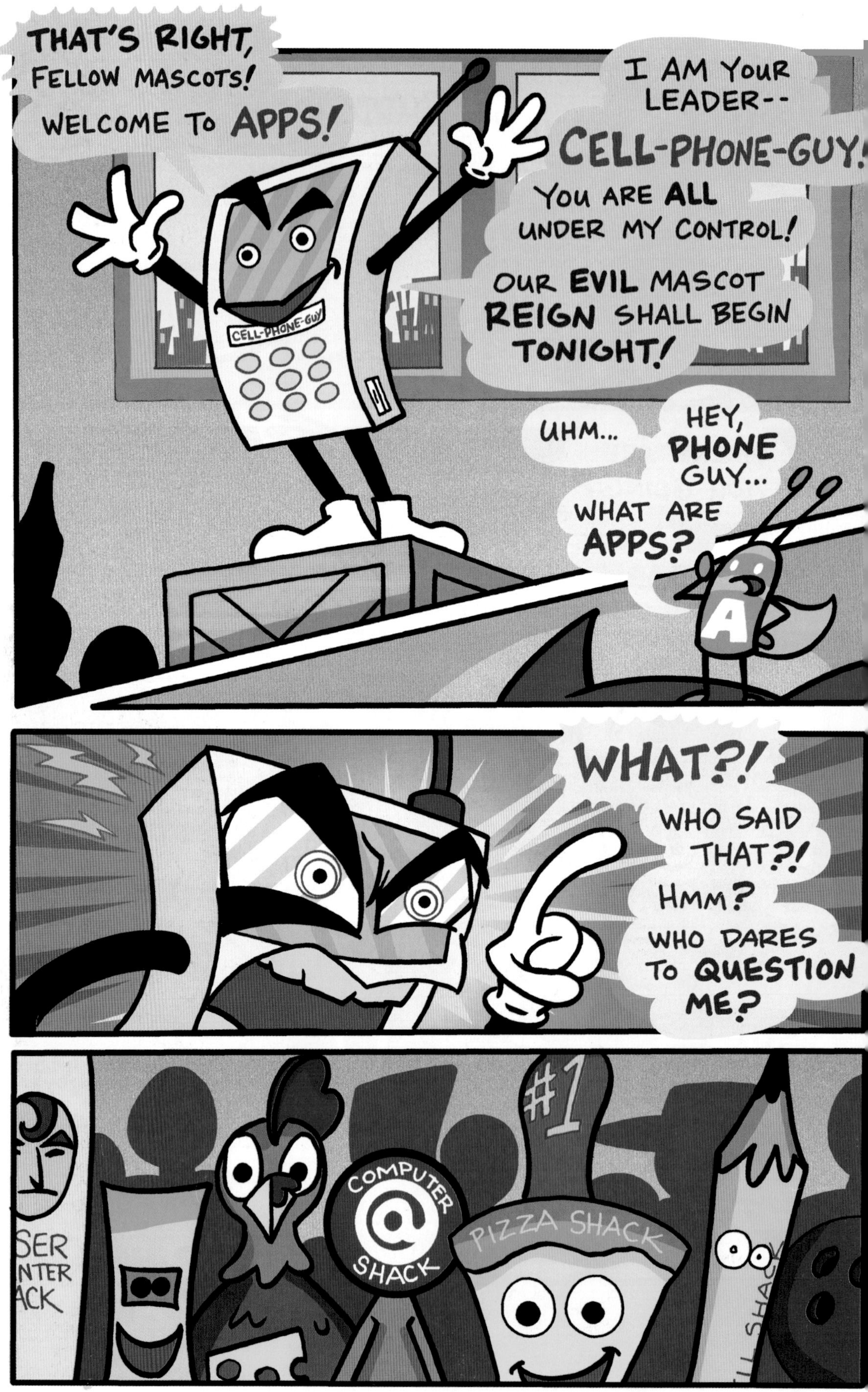
THAT'S RIGHT, FELLOW MASCOTS! WELCOME TO APPS!
I AM YOUR LEADER-- CELL-PHONE-GUY!
YOU ARE ALL UNDER MY CONTROL!
OUR EVIL MASCOT REIGN SHALL BEGIN TONIGHT!
CELL-PHONE-GUY
UHM...
HEY, PHONE GUY... WHAT ARE APPS?
A
WHAT?!
WHO SAID THAT?!
HMM? WHO DARES TO QUESTION ME?
#1
COMPUTER SHACK
PIZZA SHACK
SER
NTER
ACK

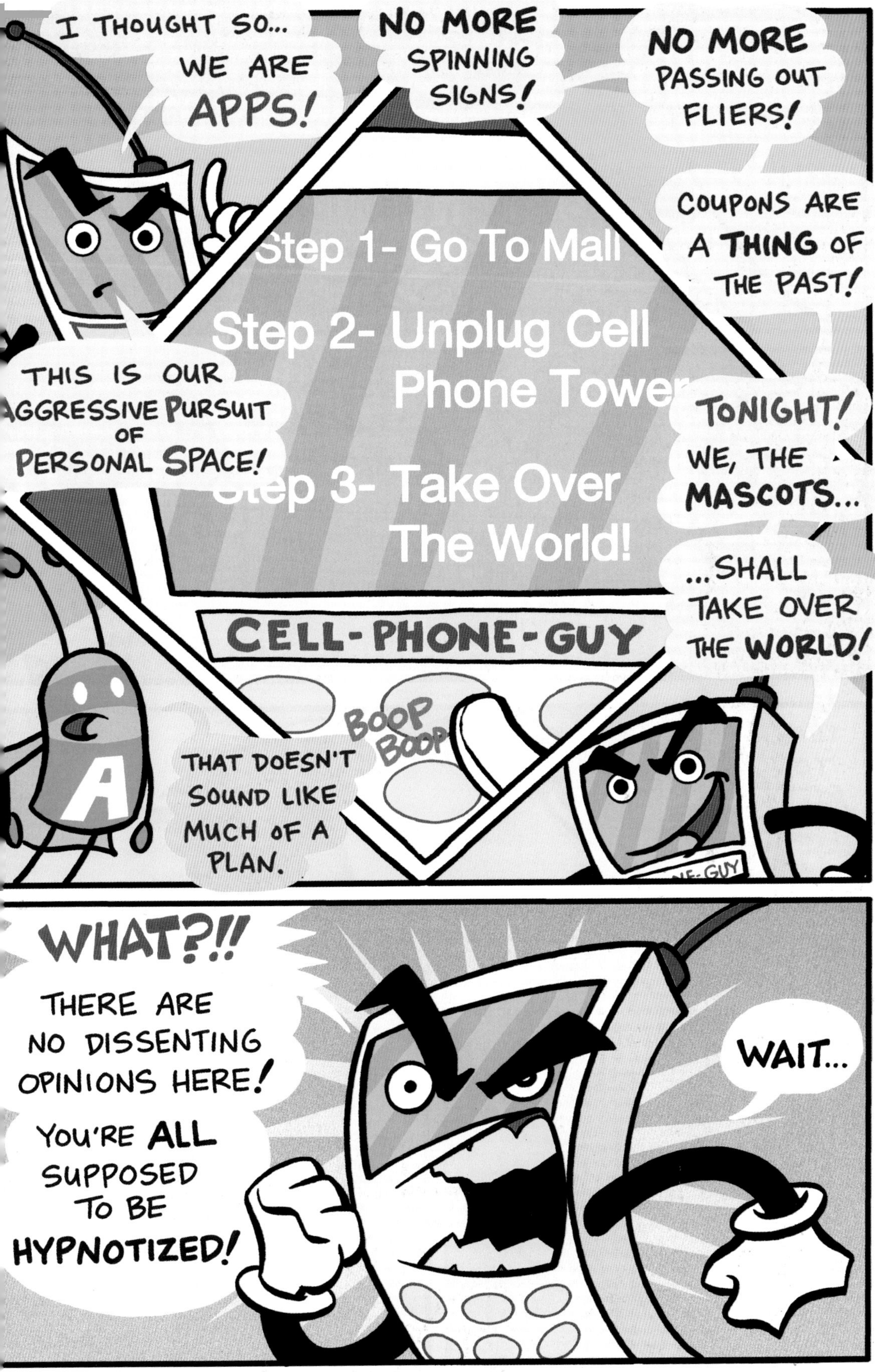
I THOUGHT SO... WE ARE APPS!
NO MORE SPINNING SIGNS!
NO MORE PASSING OUT FLIERS!
COUPONS ARE A THING OF THE PAST!
Step 1- Go To Mall
Step 2- Unplug Cell Phone Tower
Step 3- Take Over The World!
THIS IS OUR AGGRESSIVE PURSUIT OF PERSONAL SPACE!
CELL-PHONE-GUY
TONIGHT! WE, THE MASCOTS...
...SHALL TAKE OVER THE WORLD!
BOOP BOOP
THAT DOESN'T SOUND LIKE MUCH OF A PLAN.
WHAT?!!
THERE ARE NO DISSENTING OPINIONS HERE!
YOU'RE ALL SUPPOSED TO BE HYPNOTIZED!
WAIT...

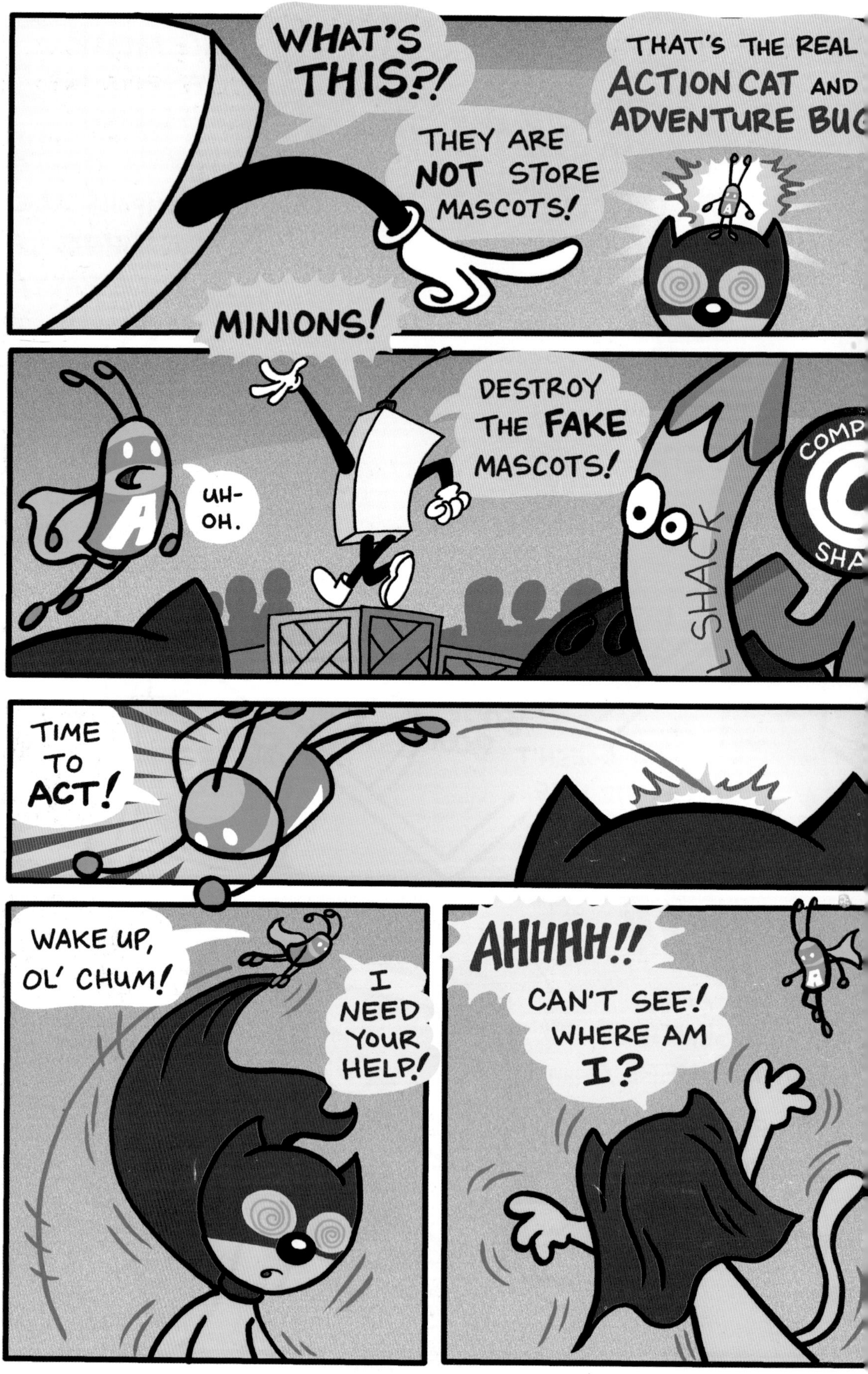
WHAT'S THIS?!
THAT'S THE REAL ACTION CAT AND ADVENTURE BUG
THEY ARE NOT STORE MASCOTS!
MINIONS!
DESTROY THE FAKE MASCOTS!
UH-OH.
SHACK
TIME TO ACT!
WAKE UP, OL' CHUM!
I NEED YOUR HELP!
AHHHH!!
CAN'T SEE! WHERE AM I?

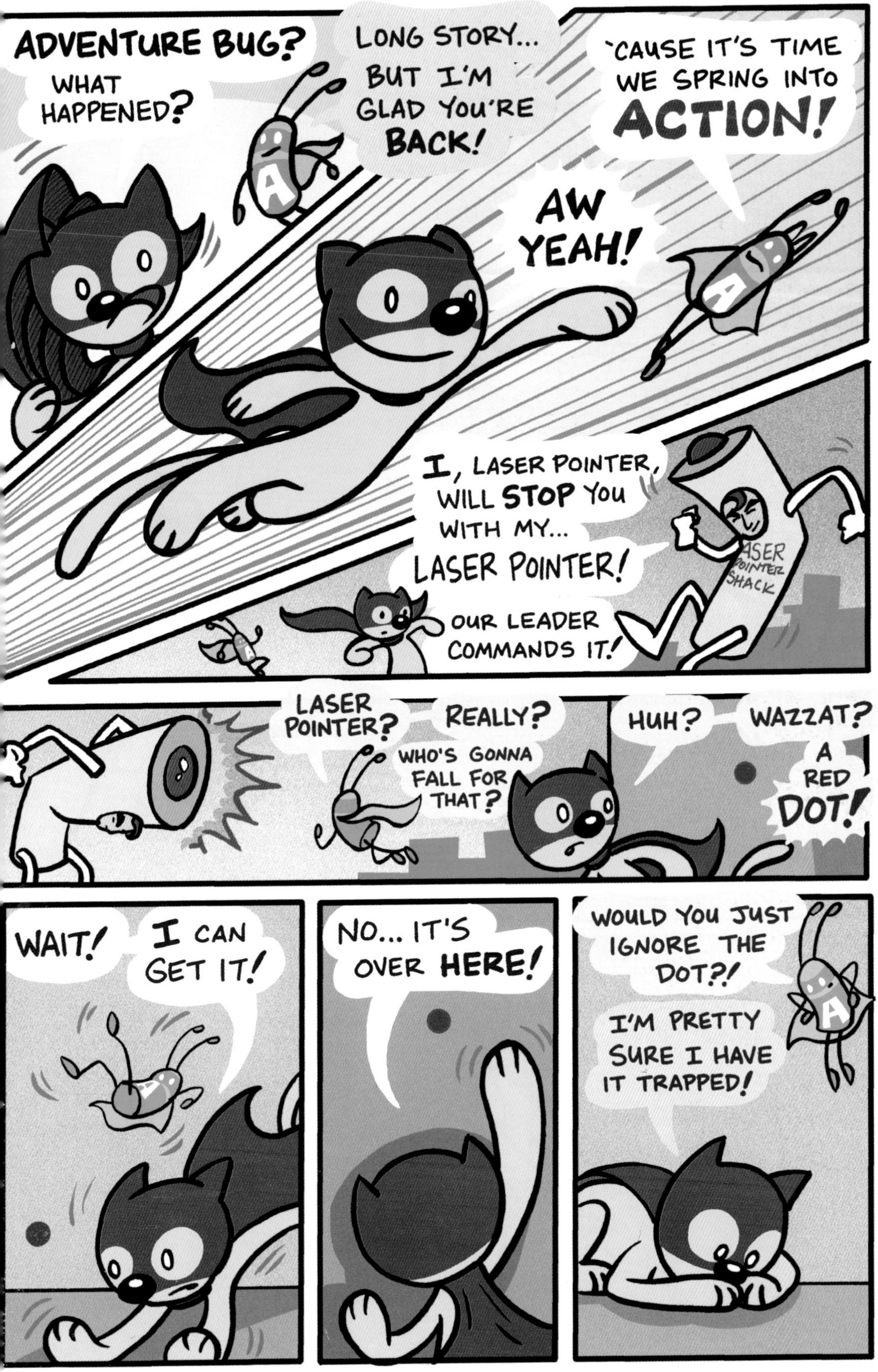
ADVENTURE BUG? WHAT HAPPENED?
LONG STORY...
BUT I'M GLAD YOU'RE BACK!
'CAUSE IT'S TIME WE SPRING INTO ACTION!
AW YEAH!
I, LASER POINTER, WILL STOP YOU WITH MY...
LASER POINTER!
OUR LEADER COMMANDS IT!
LASER POINTER SHACK
LASER POINTER?
REALLY?
WHO'S GONNA FALL FOR THAT?
HUH?
WAZZAT?
A RED DOT!
WAIT!
I CAN GET IT!
NO... IT'S OVER HERE!
WOULD YOU JUST IGNORE THE DOT?!
I'M PRETTY SURE I HAVE IT TRAPPED!

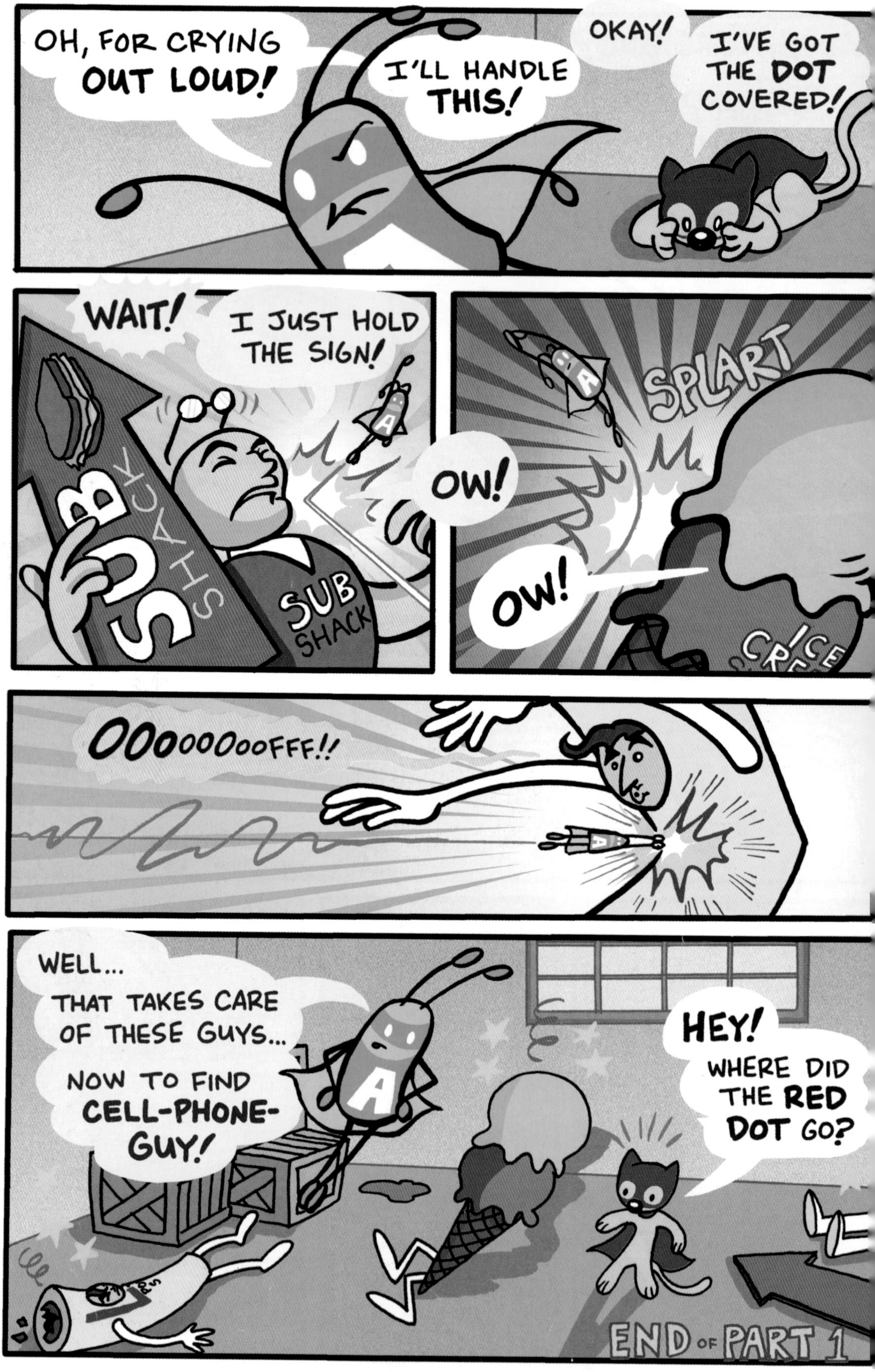

OH, FOR CRYING OUT LOUD!
I'LL HANDLE THIS!
OKAY!
I'VE GOT THE DOT COVERED!
WAIT!
I JUST HOLD THE SIGN!
SUB SHACK
SUB SHACK
OW!
SPLART
OW!
OOOOOOOOFFF!!
WELL... THAT TAKES CARE OF THESE GUYS...
NOW TO FIND CELL-PHONE-GUY!
HEY! WHERE DID THE RED DOT GO?
END OF PART 1

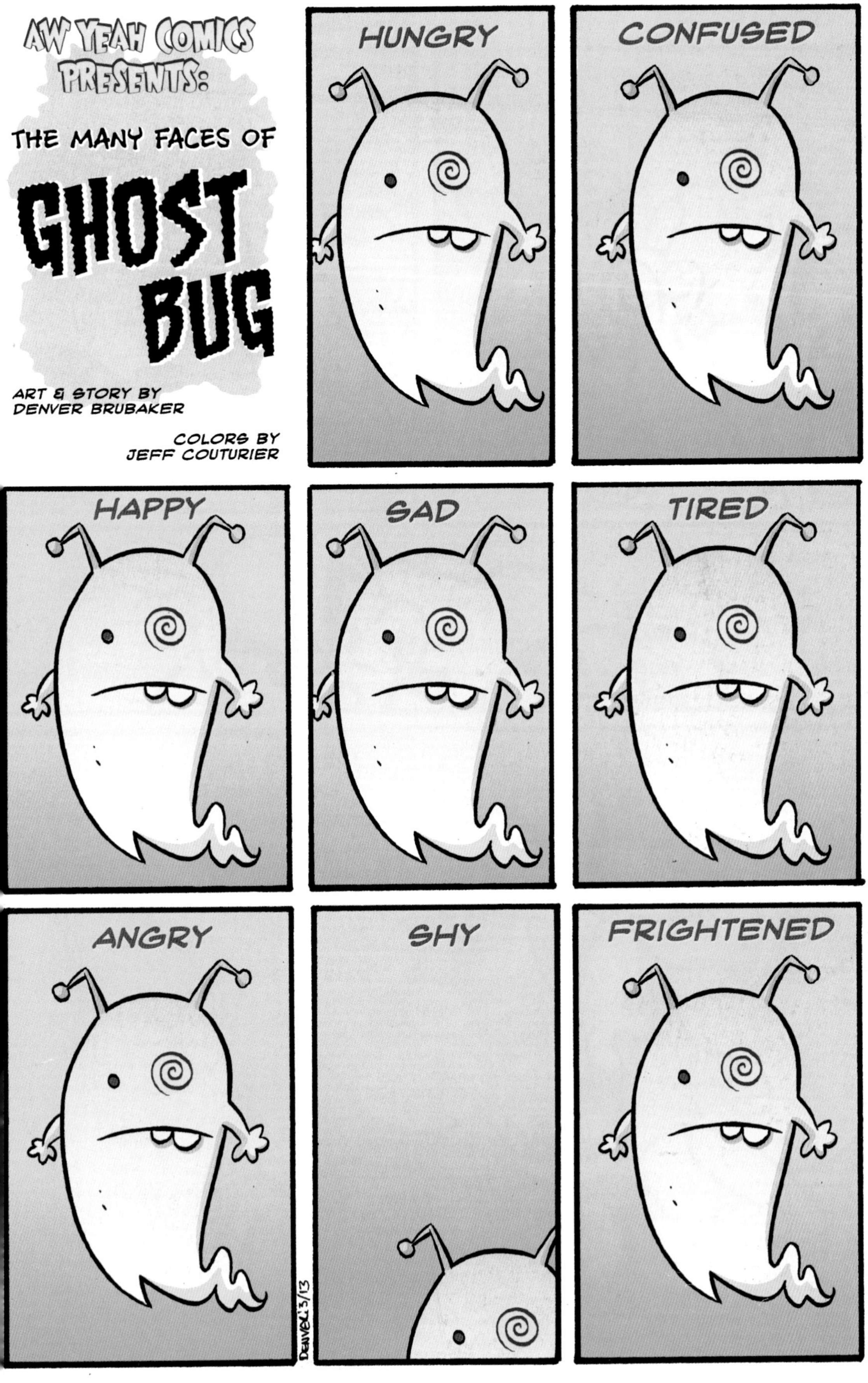
AW YEAH COMICS PRESENTS:
THE MANY FACES OF
GHOST BUG
ART & STORY BY DENVER BRUBAKER
COLORS BY JEFF COUTURIER
HUNGRY
CONFUSED
HAPPY
SAD
TIRED
ANGRY
SHY
FRIGHTENED

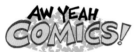

AW YEAH COMICS! PRESENTS... "THE BEST FIGHT EVER!"

written by Brad & Theo Meltzer with artwork by Franco

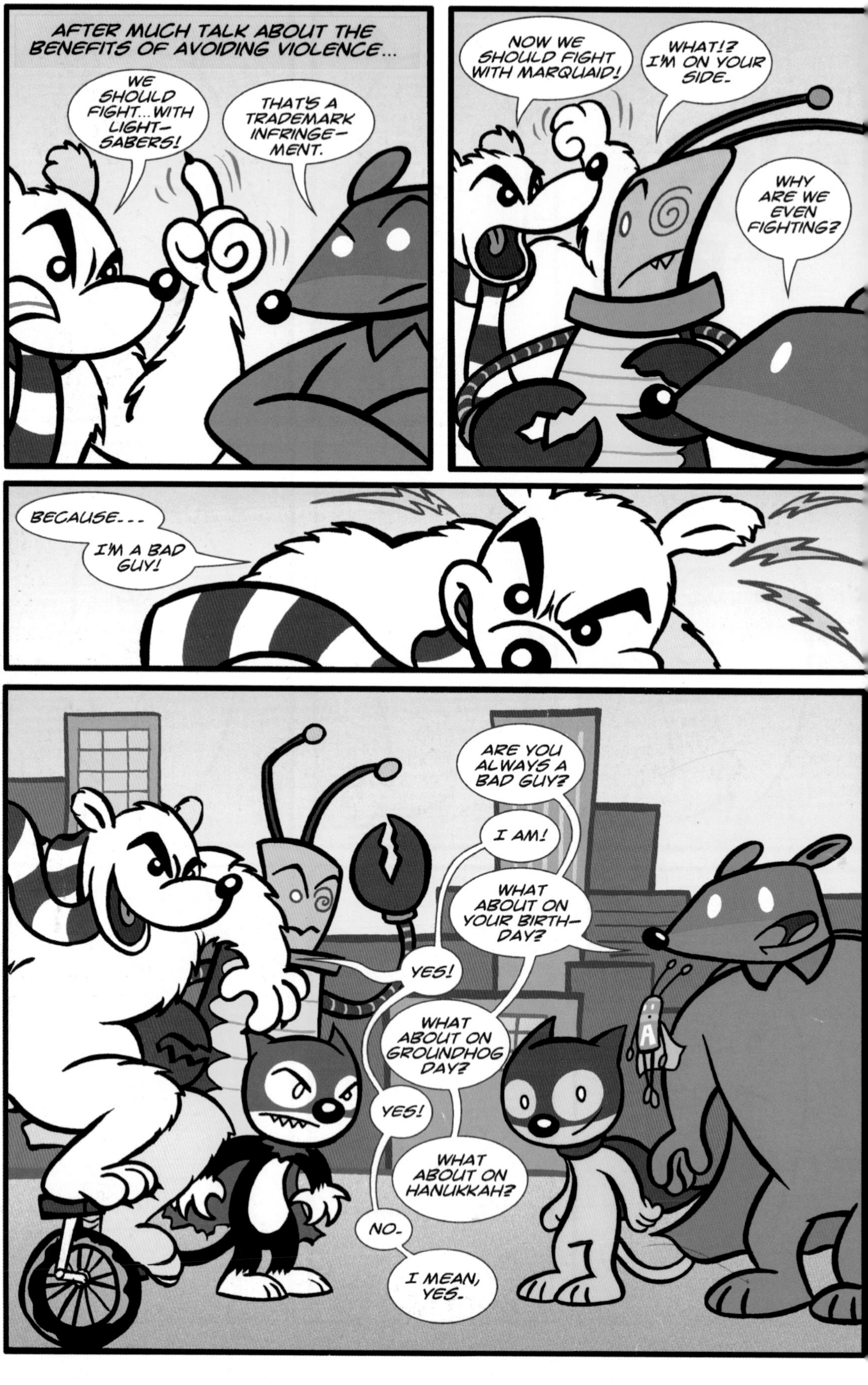

AFTER MUCH TALK ABOUT THE BENEFITS OF AVOIDING VIOLENCE...
WE SHOULD FIGHT...WITH LIGHT-SABERS!
THAT'S A TRADEMARK INFRINGE-MENT.
NOW WE SHOULD FIGHT WITH MARQUAID!
WHAT!? I'M ON YOUR SIDE.
WHY ARE WE EVEN FIGHTING?
BECAUSE...
I'M A BAD GUY!
ARE YOU ALWAYS A BAD GUY?
I AM!
WHAT ABOUT ON YOUR BIRTH-DAY?
YES!
WHAT ABOUT ON GROUNDHOG DAY?
YES!
WHAT ABOUT ON HANUKKAH?
NO.
I MEAN, YES.

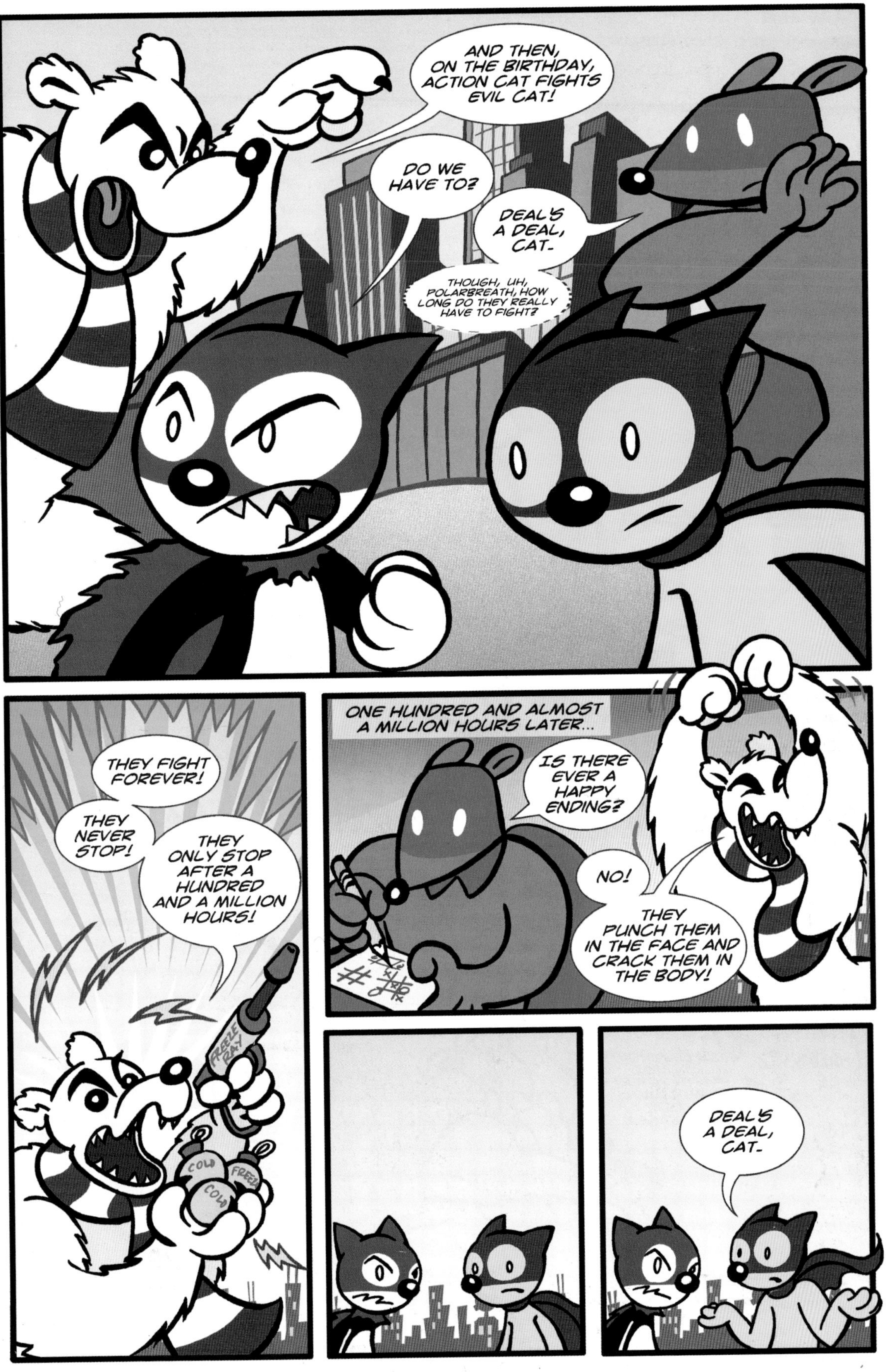
AND THEN, ON THE BIRTHDAY, ACTION CAT FIGHTS EVIL CAT!
DO WE HAVE TO?
DEAL'S A DEAL, CAT.
THOUGH, UH, POLARBREATH, HOW LONG DO THEY REALLY HAVE TO FIGHT?
THEY FIGHT FOREVER!
THEY NEVER STOP!
THEY ONLY STOP AFTER A HUNDRED AND A MILLION HOURS!
FREEZE RAY
COLD
FREEZE
COLD
ONE HUNDRED AND ALMOST A MILLION HOURS LATER...
IS THERE EVER A HAPPY ENDING?
NO!
THEY PUNCH THEM IN THE FACE AND CRACK THEM IN THE BODY!
DEAL'S A DEAL, CAT.

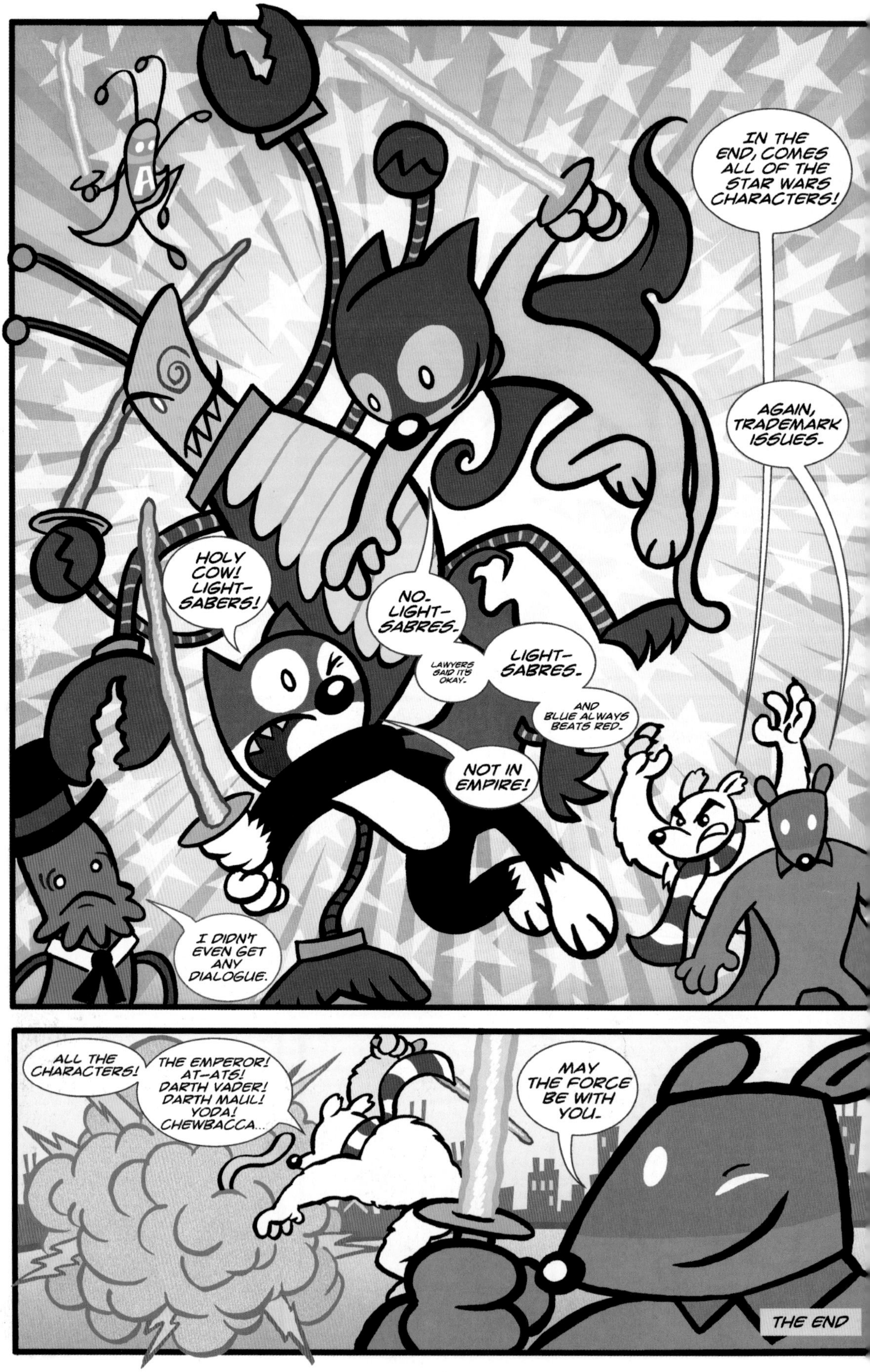
IN THE END, COMES ALL OF THE STAR WARS CHARACTERS!
AGAIN, TRADEMARK ISSUES.
HOLY COW! LIGHT-SABERS!
NO. LIGHT-SABRES.
LAWYERS SAID IT'S OKAY.
LIGHT-SABRES.
AND BLUE ALWAYS BEATS RED.
NOT IN EMPIRE!
I DIDN'T EVEN GET ANY DIALOGUE.
ALL THE CHARACTERS!
THE EMPEROR! AT-ATS! DARTH VADER! DARTH MAUL! YODA! CHEWBACCA...
MAY THE FORCE BE WITH YOU.
THE END

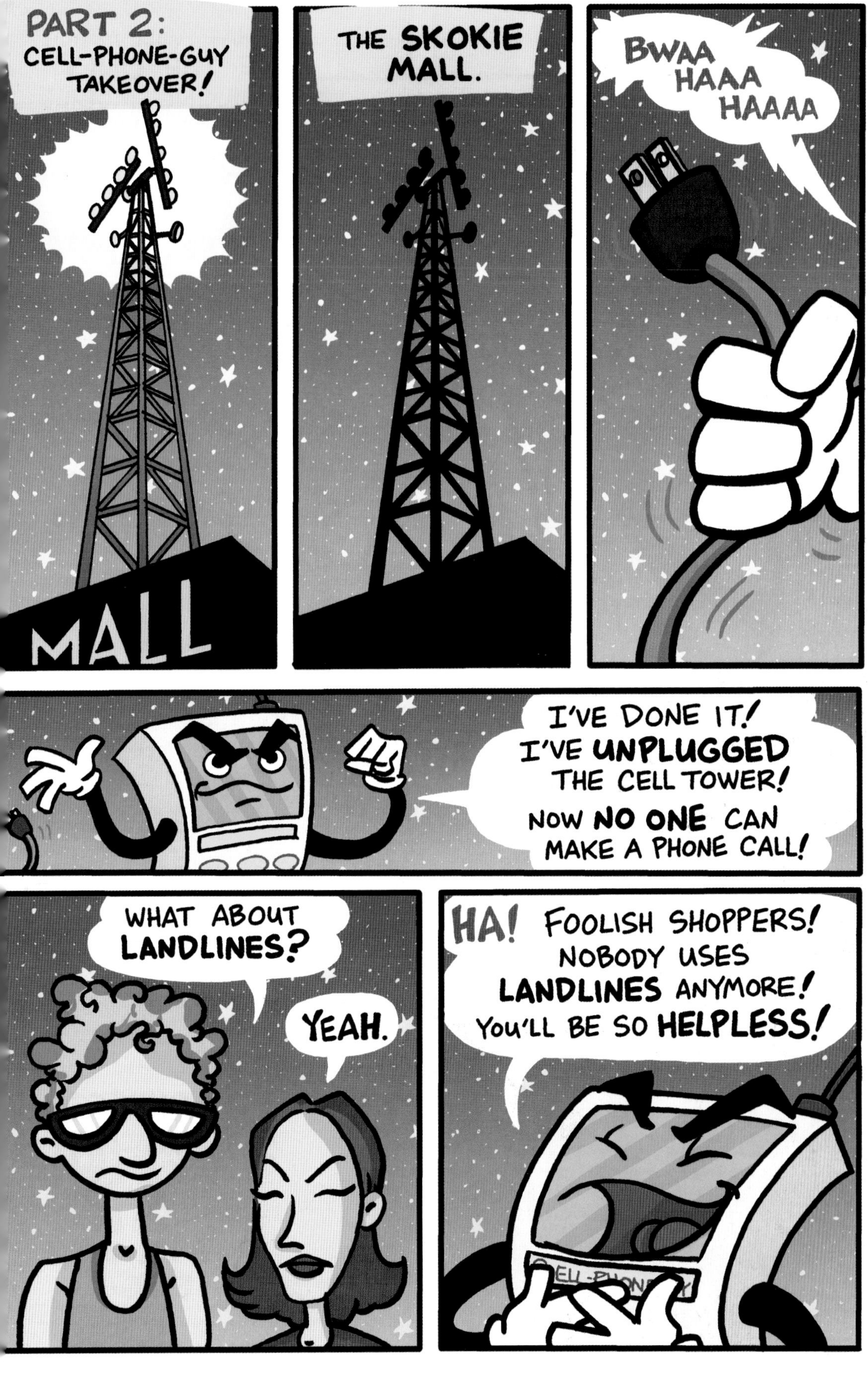
PART 2:
CELL-PHONE-GUY TAKEOVER!
MALL
THE SKOKIE MALL.
BWAA HAAA HAAAA
I'VE DONE IT!
I'VE UNPLUGGED THE CELL TOWER!
NOW NO ONE CAN MAKE A PHONE CALL!
WHAT ABOUT LANDLINES?
YEAH.
HA! FOOLISH SHOPPERS! NOBODY USES LANDLINES ANYMORE! YOU'LL BE SO HELPLESS!

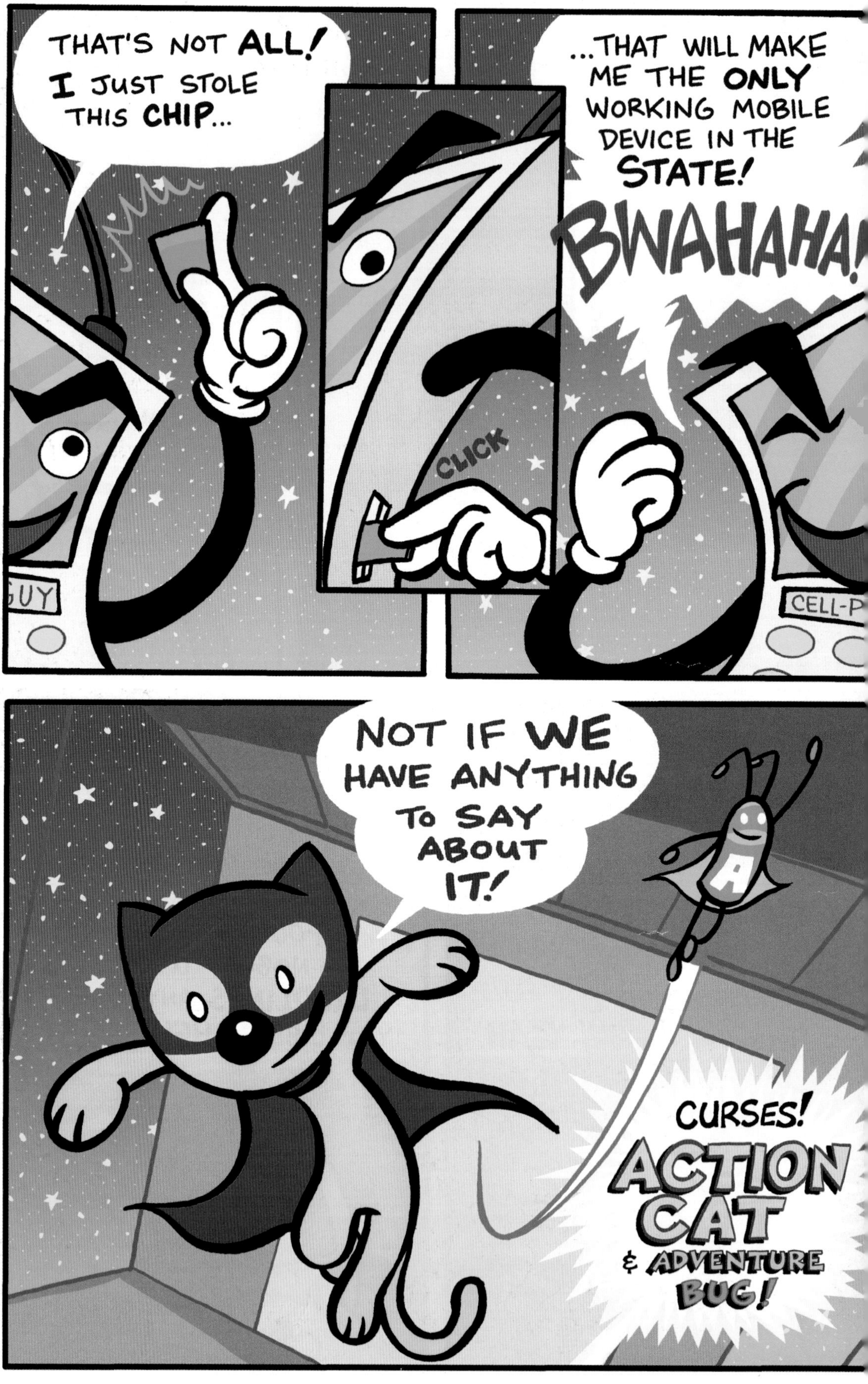
THAT'S NOT ALL! I JUST STOLE THIS CHIP...
CLICK
...THAT WILL MAKE ME THE ONLY WORKING MOBILE DEVICE IN THE STATE!
BWAHAHA!
NOT IF WE HAVE ANYTHING TO SAY ABOUT IT!
CURSES! ACTION CAT & ADVENTURE BUG!

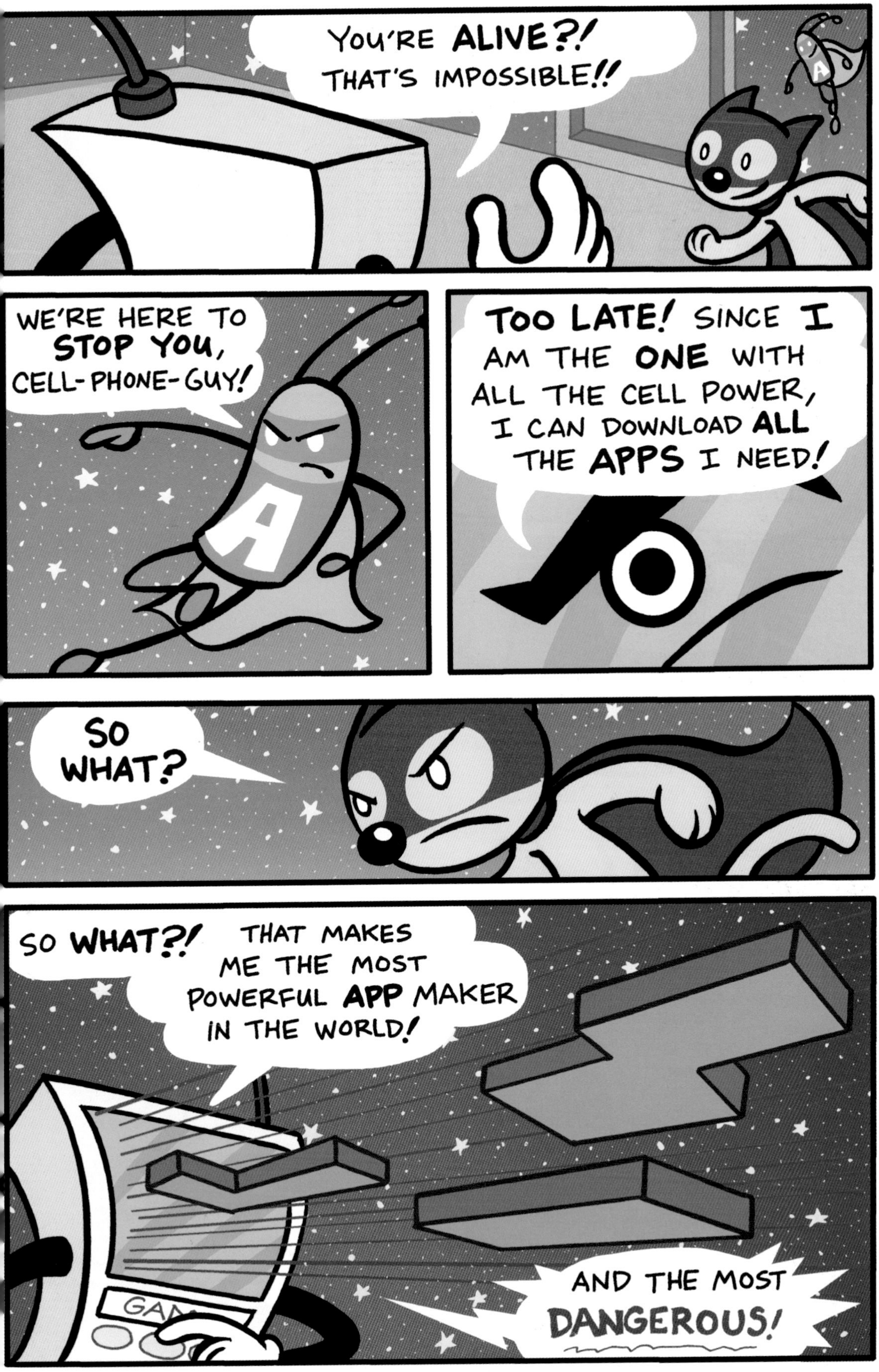
YOU'RE ALIVE?! THAT'S IMPOSSIBLE!!
WE'RE HERE TO STOP YOU, CELL-PHONE-GUY!
TOO LATE! SINCE I AM THE ONE WITH ALL THE CELL POWER, I CAN DOWNLOAD ALL THE APPS I NEED!
SO WHAT?
SO WHAT?! THAT MAKES ME THE MOST POWERFUL APP MAKER IN THE WORLD!
AND THE MOST DANGEROUS!

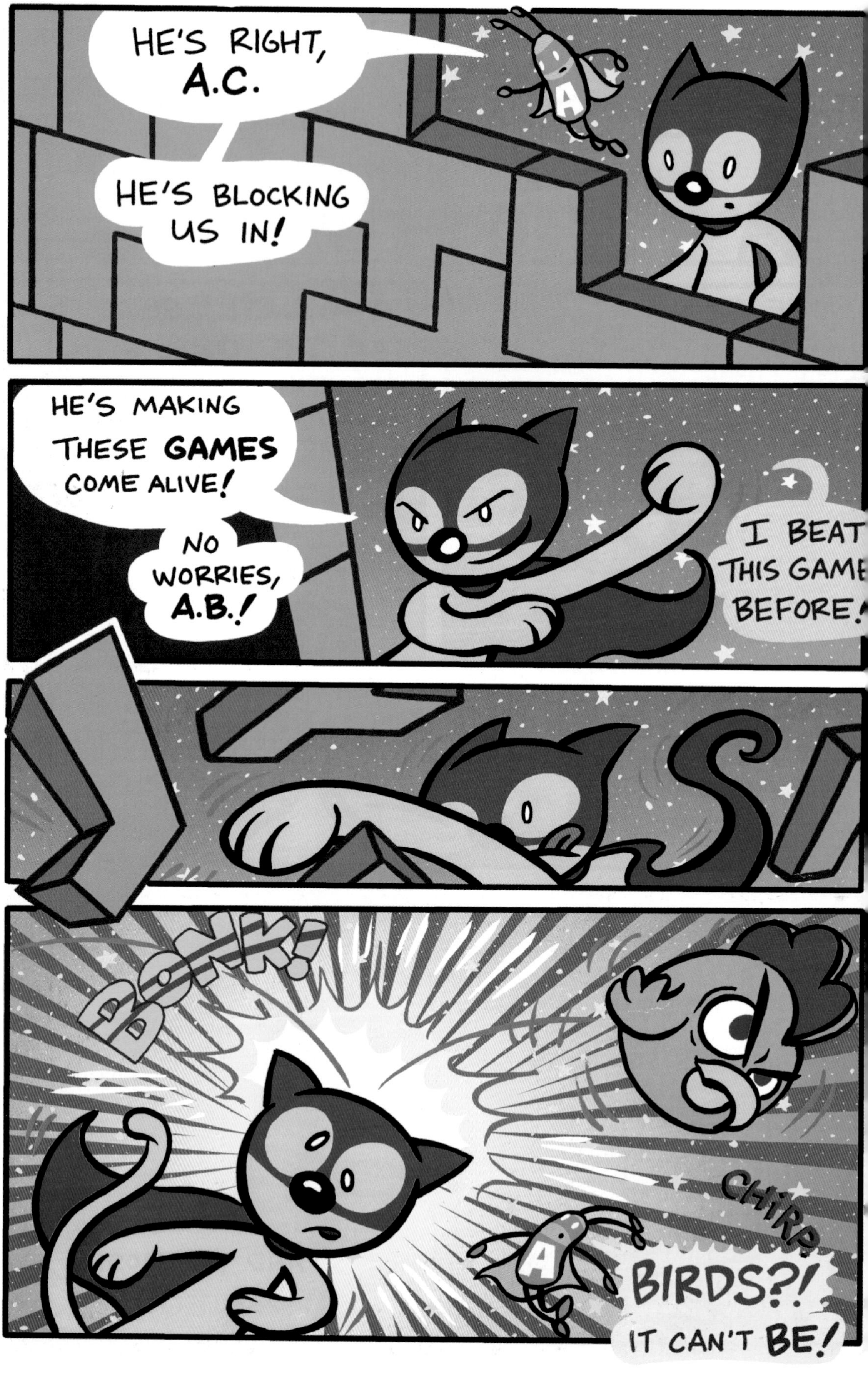
HE'S RIGHT, A.C.
HE'S BLOCKING US IN!
HE'S MAKING THESE GAMES COME ALIVE!
NO WORRIES, A.B.!
I BEAT THIS GAME BEFORE!
BONK!
CHIRP
BIRDS?!
IT CAN'T BE!

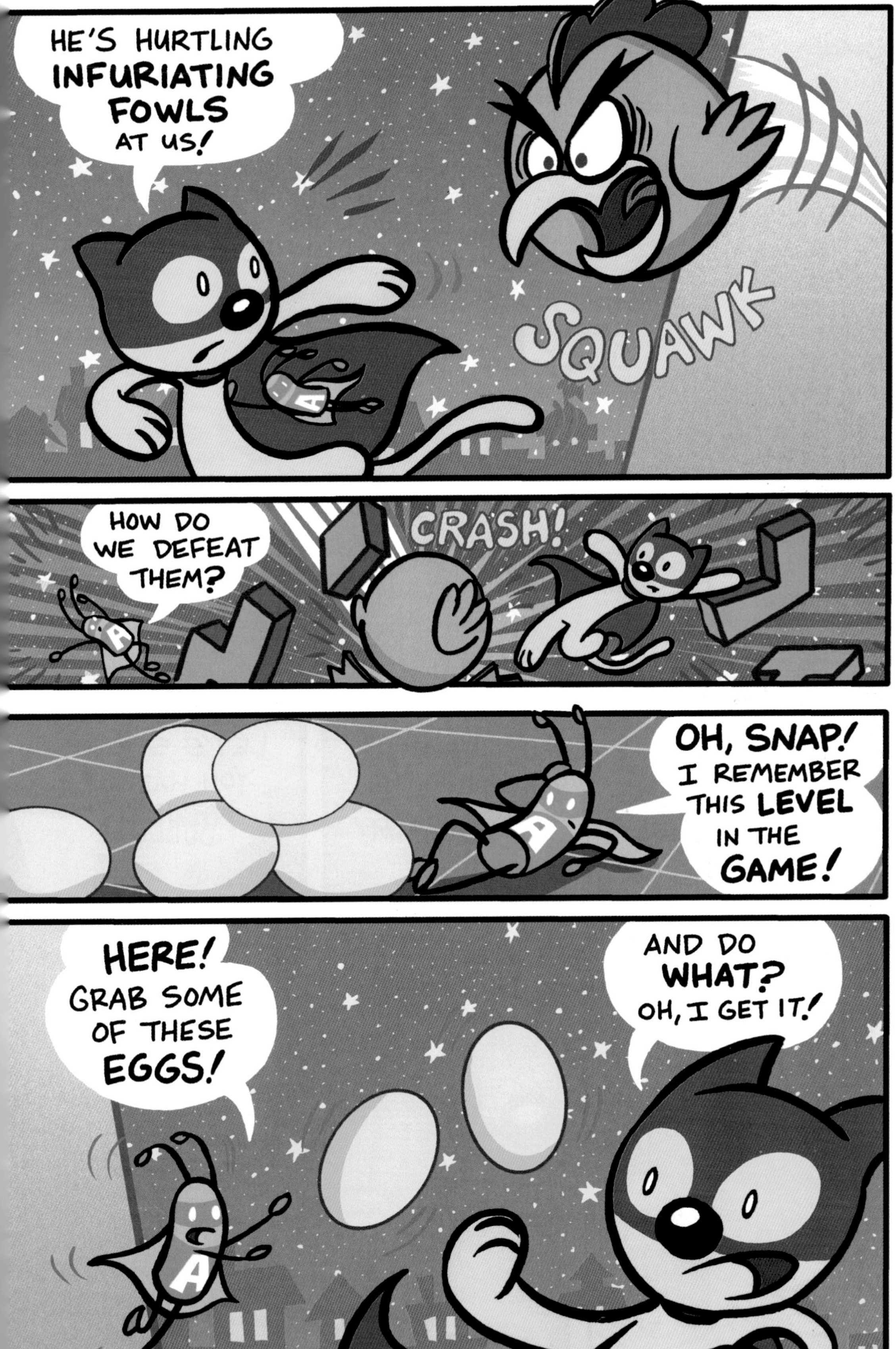
HE'S HURTLING INFURIATING FOWLS AT US!
SQUAWK
HOW DO WE DEFEAT THEM?
CRASH!
OH, SNAP! I REMEMBER THIS LEVEL IN THE GAME!
HERE! GRAB SOME OF THESE EGGS!
AND DO WHAT? OH, I GET IT!

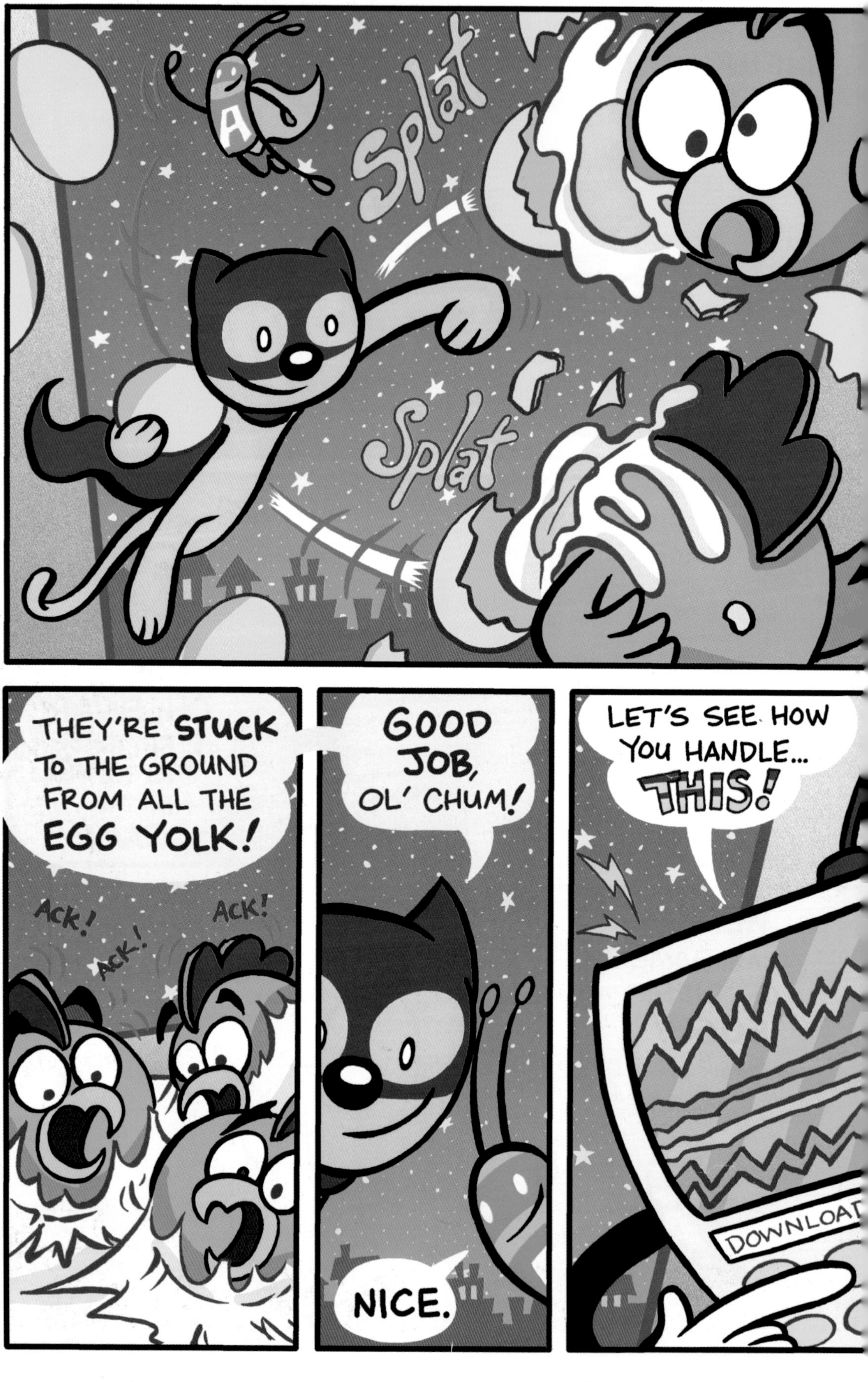
Splat
Splat
THEY'RE STUCK TO THE GROUND FROM ALL THE EGG YOLK!
ACK!
ACK!
ACK!
GOOD JOB, OL' CHUM!
NICE.
LET'S SEE HOW YOU HANDLE... THIS!
DOWNLOAD

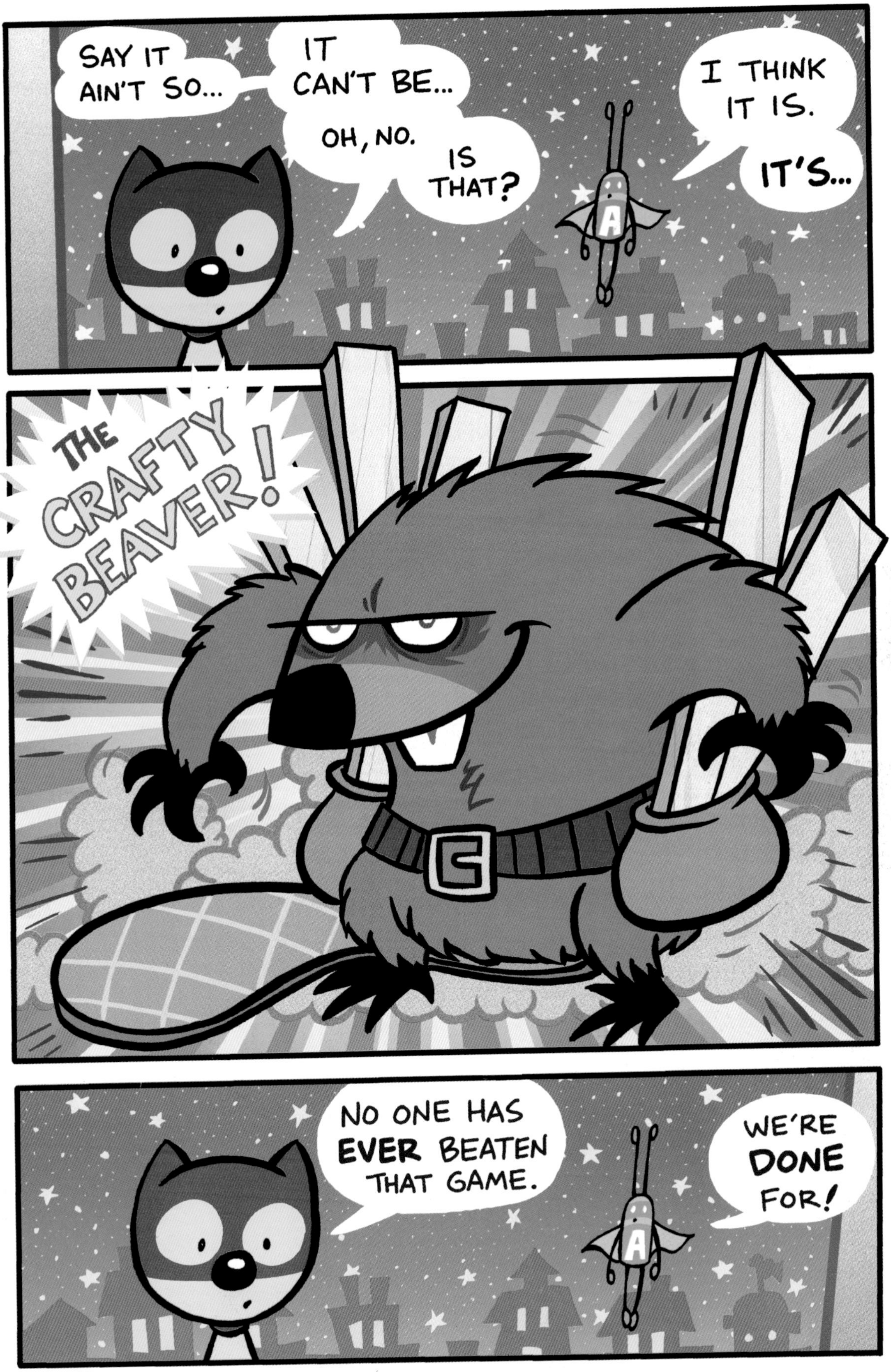
SAY IT AIN'T SO...
IT CAN'T BE...
OH, NO.
IS THAT?
I THINK IT IS.
IT'S...
THE CRAFTY BEAVER!
NO ONE HAS EVER BEATEN THAT GAME.
WE'RE DONE FOR!

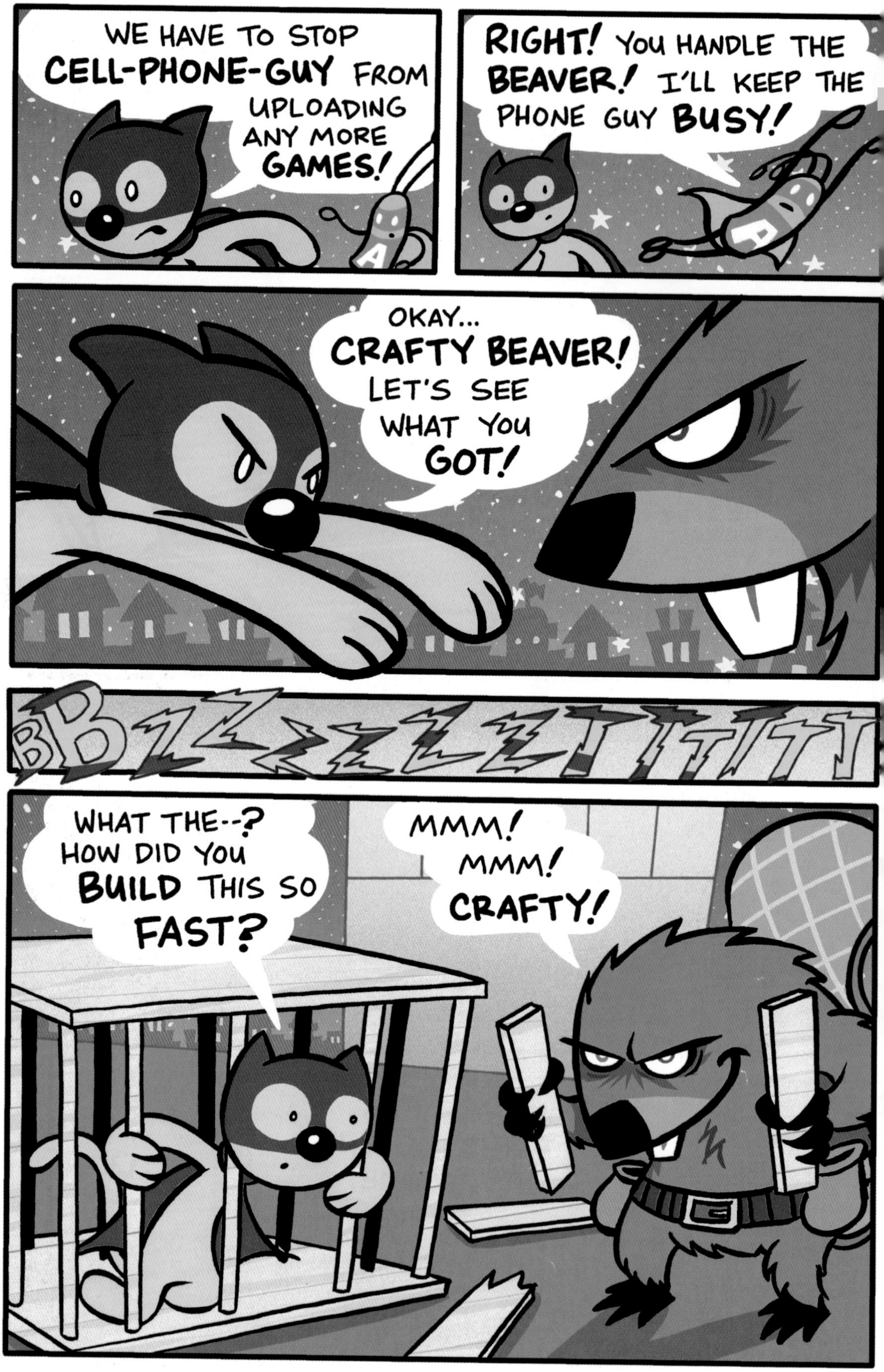
WE HAVE TO STOP CELL-PHONE-GUY FROM UPLOADING ANY MORE GAMES!
RIGHT! YOU HANDLE THE BEAVER! I'LL KEEP THE PHONE GUY BUSY!
OKAY... CRAFTY BEAVER! LET'S SEE WHAT YOU GOT!
BBZZZZZZTTTT
WHAT THE--? HOW DID YOU BUILD THIS SO FAST?
MMM! MMM! CRAFTY!

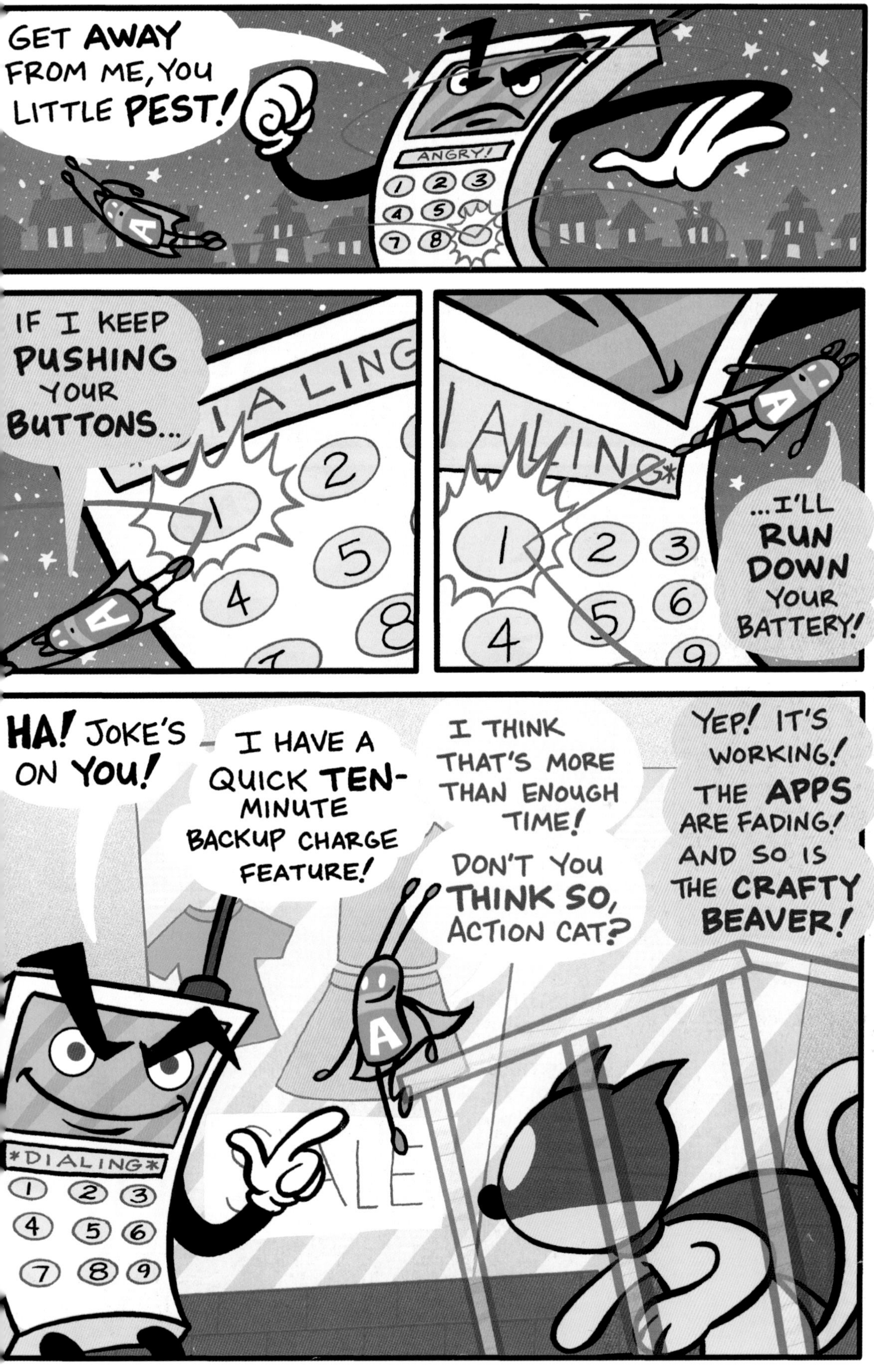
GET AWAY FROM ME, YOU LITTLE PEST!
ANGRY!
IF I KEEP PUSHING YOUR BUTTONS...
DIALING
...I'LL RUN DOWN YOUR BATTERY!
HA! JOKE'S ON YOU!
I HAVE A QUICK TEN-MINUTE BACKUP CHARGE FEATURE!
I THINK THAT'S MORE THAN ENOUGH TIME!
DON'T YOU THINK SO, ACTION CAT?
YEP! IT'S WORKING! THE APPS ARE FADING! AND SO IS THE CRAFTY BEAVER!
DIALING

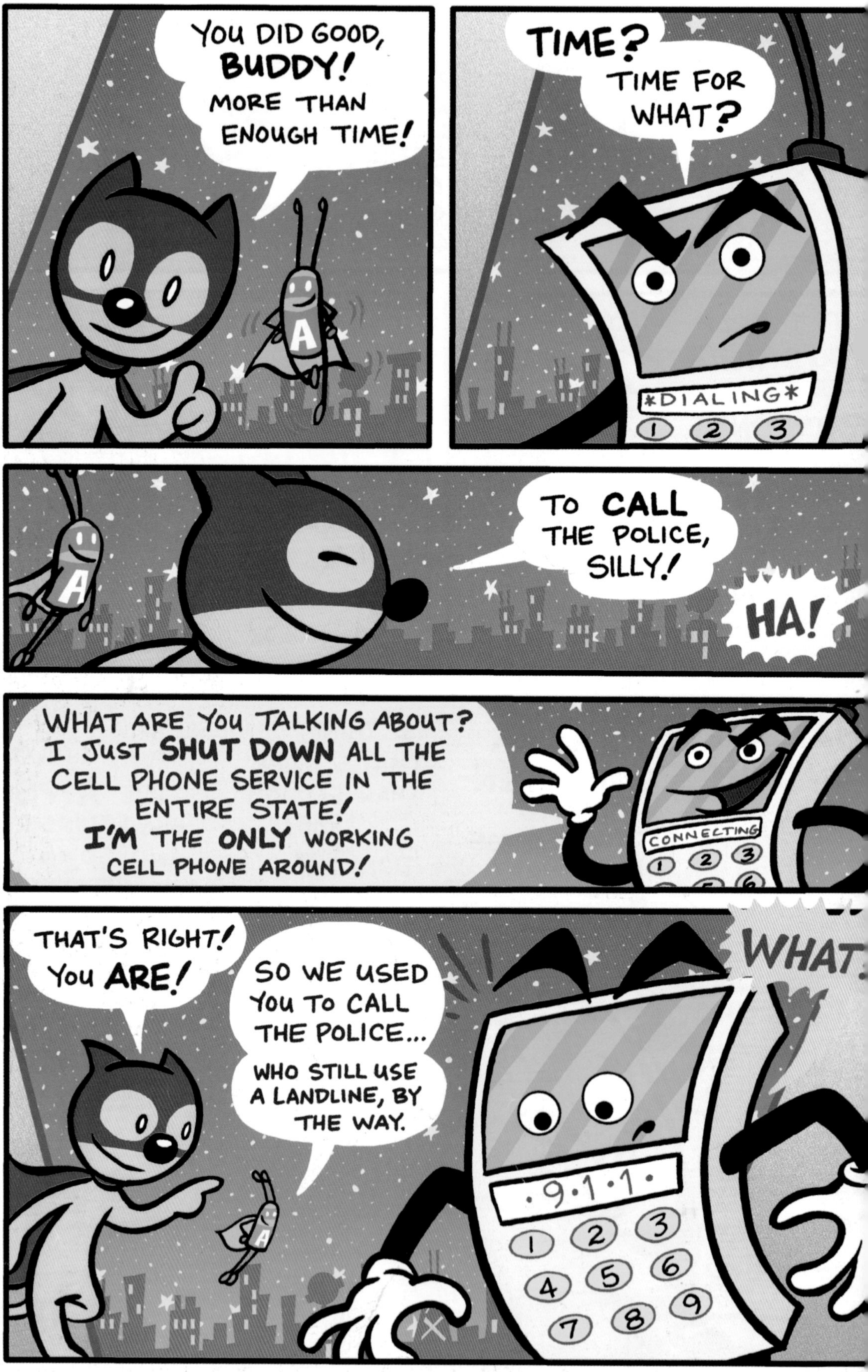
YOU DID GOOD, BUDDY! MORE THAN ENOUGH TIME!
TIME? TIME FOR WHAT?
DIALING
TO CALL THE POLICE, SILLY!
HA!
WHAT ARE YOU TALKING ABOUT? I JUST SHUT DOWN ALL THE CELL PHONE SERVICE IN THE ENTIRE STATE! I'M THE ONLY WORKING CELL PHONE AROUND!
CONNECTING
THAT'S RIGHT! YOU ARE!
SO WE USED YOU TO CALL THE POLICE...
WHO STILL USE A LANDLINE, BY THE WAY.
WHAT
·9·1·1·

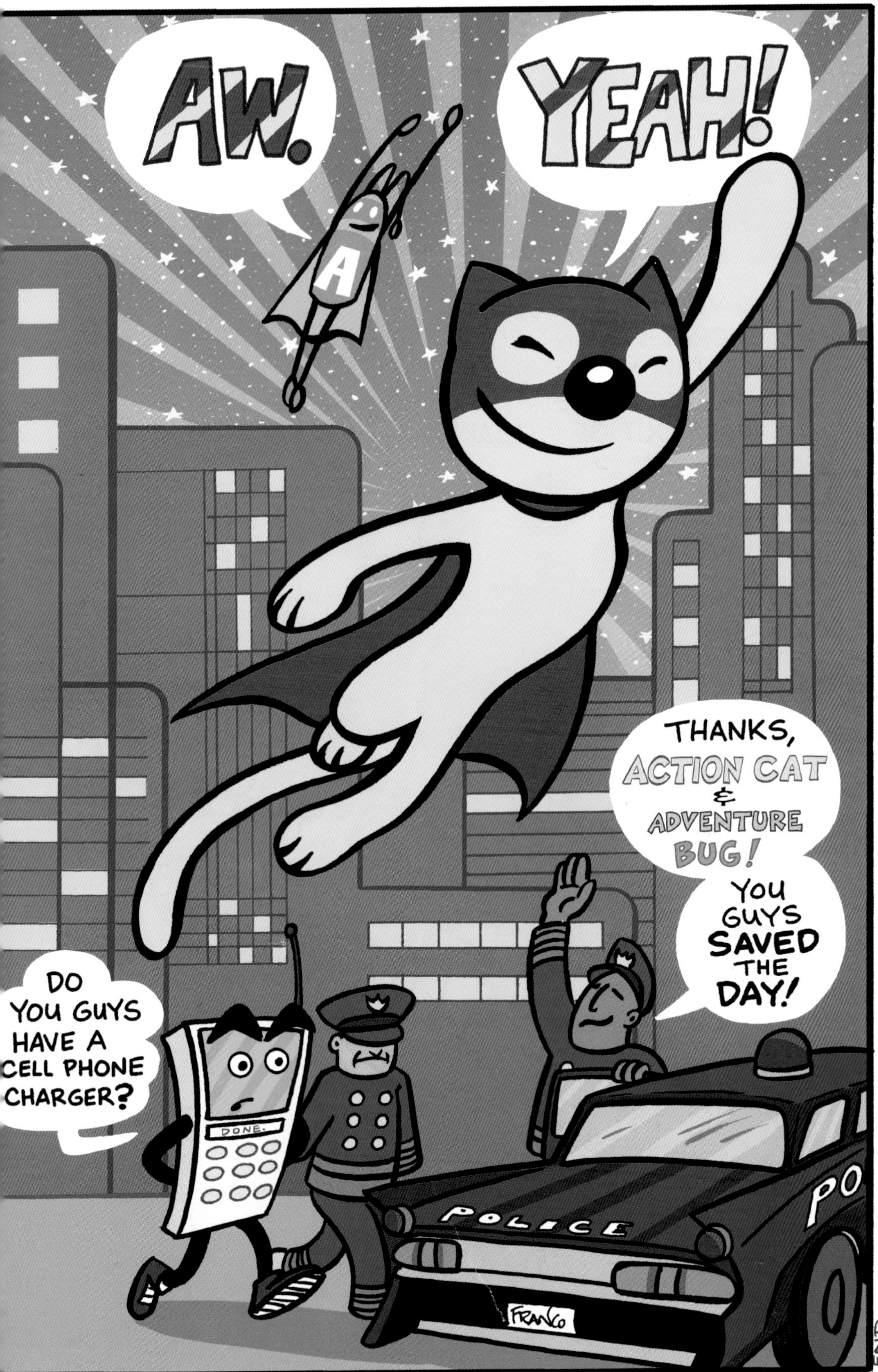
AW.
YEAH!
THANKS, ACTION CAT & ADVENTURE BUG!
YOU GUYS SAVED THE DAY!
DO YOU GUYS HAVE A CELL PHONE CHARGER?
DONE.
POLICE
PO
FRANCO
END

AW YEAH

AND NOW...

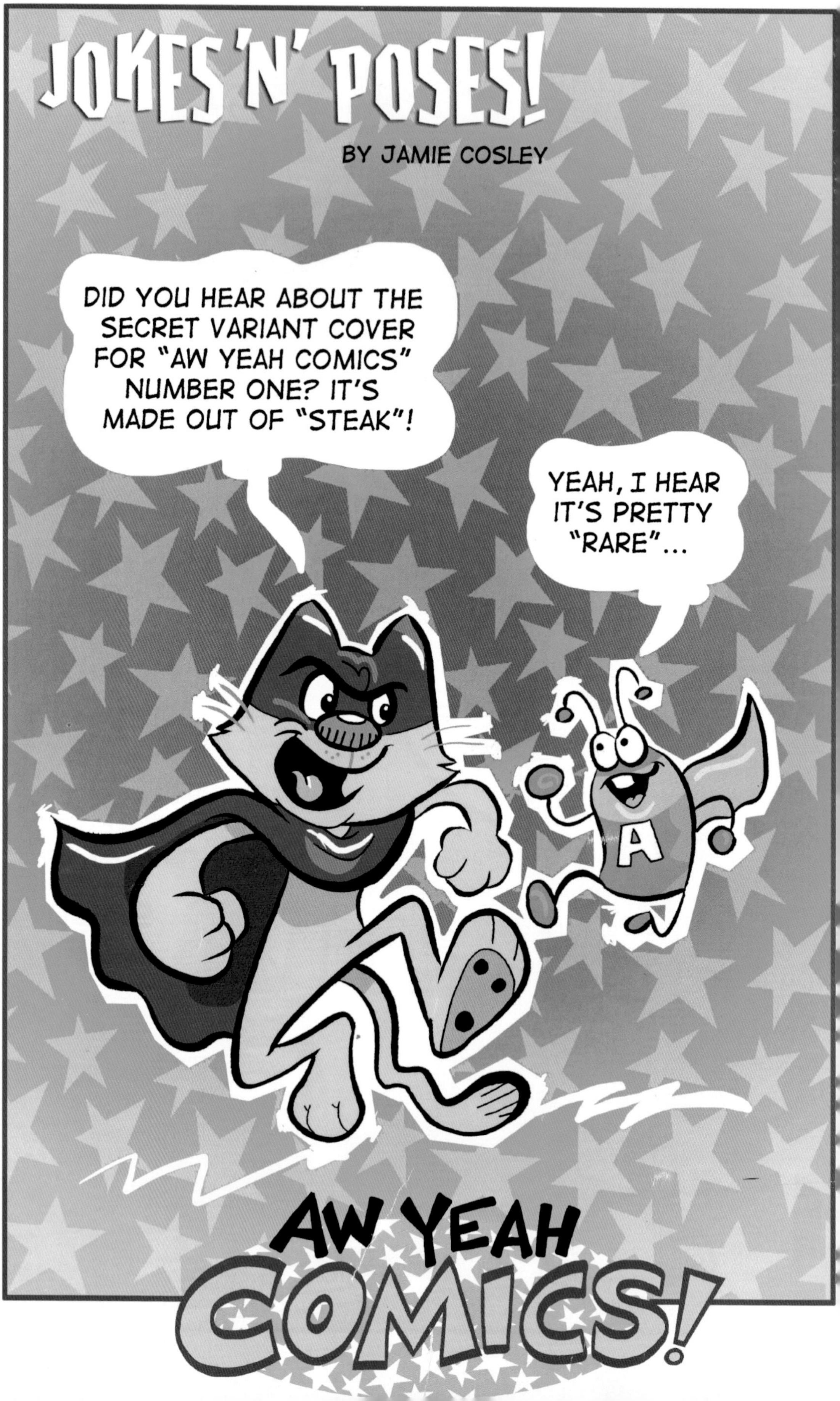

JOKES 'N' POSES!
BY JAMIE COSLEY
DID YOU HEAR ABOUT THE SECRET VARIANT COVER FOR "AW YEAH COMICS" NUMBER ONE? IT'S MADE OUT OF "STEAK"!
YEAH, I HEAR IT'S PRETTY "RARE"...
A
AW YEAH COMICS!

★ CHAPTER THREE ★

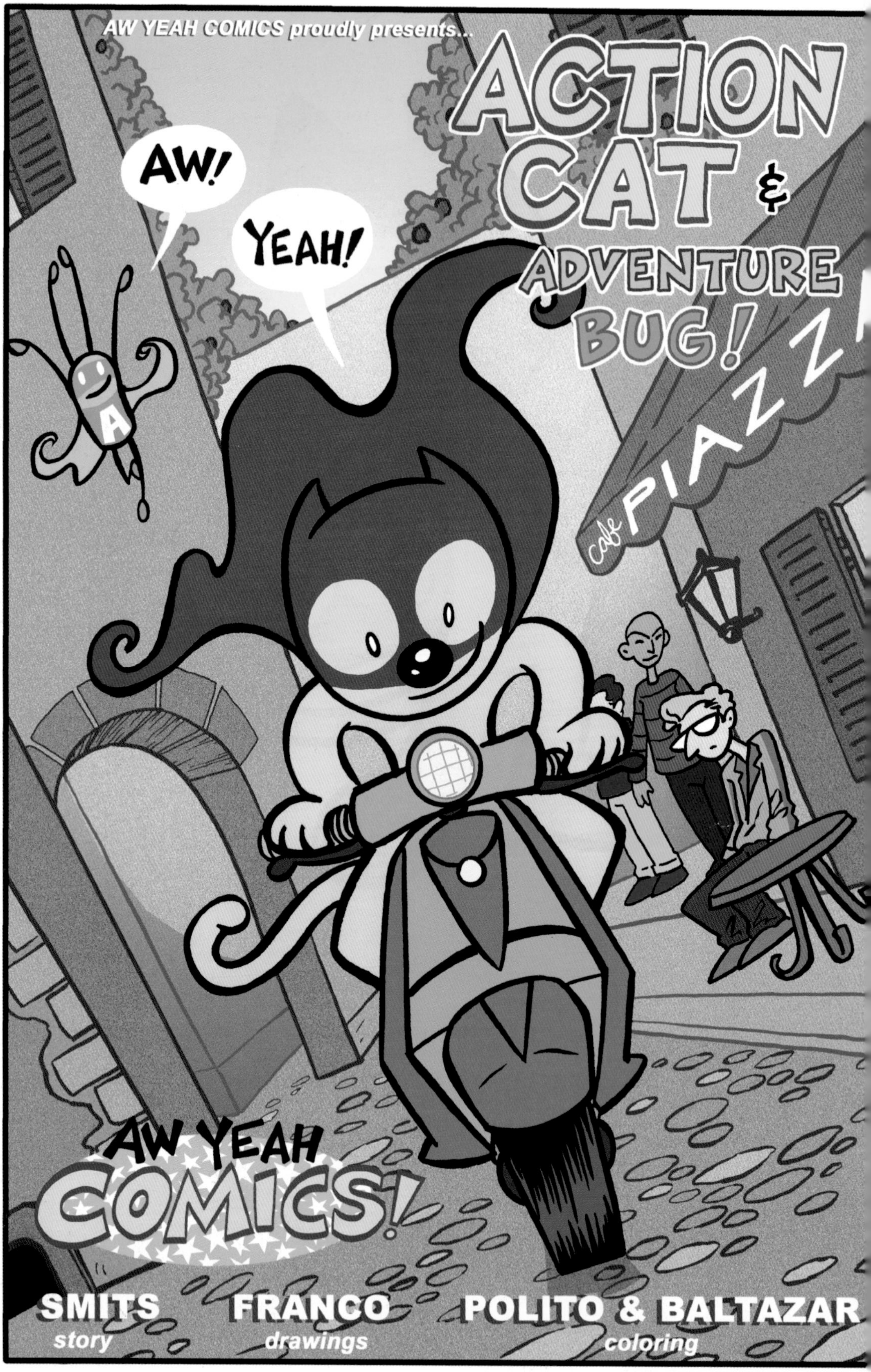
AW YEAH COMICS proudly presents...
ACTION CAT & ADVENTURE BUG!
AW!
YEAH!
cafe PIAZZ
AW YEAH COMICS!
SMITS story
FRANCO drawings
POLITO & BALTAZAR coloring

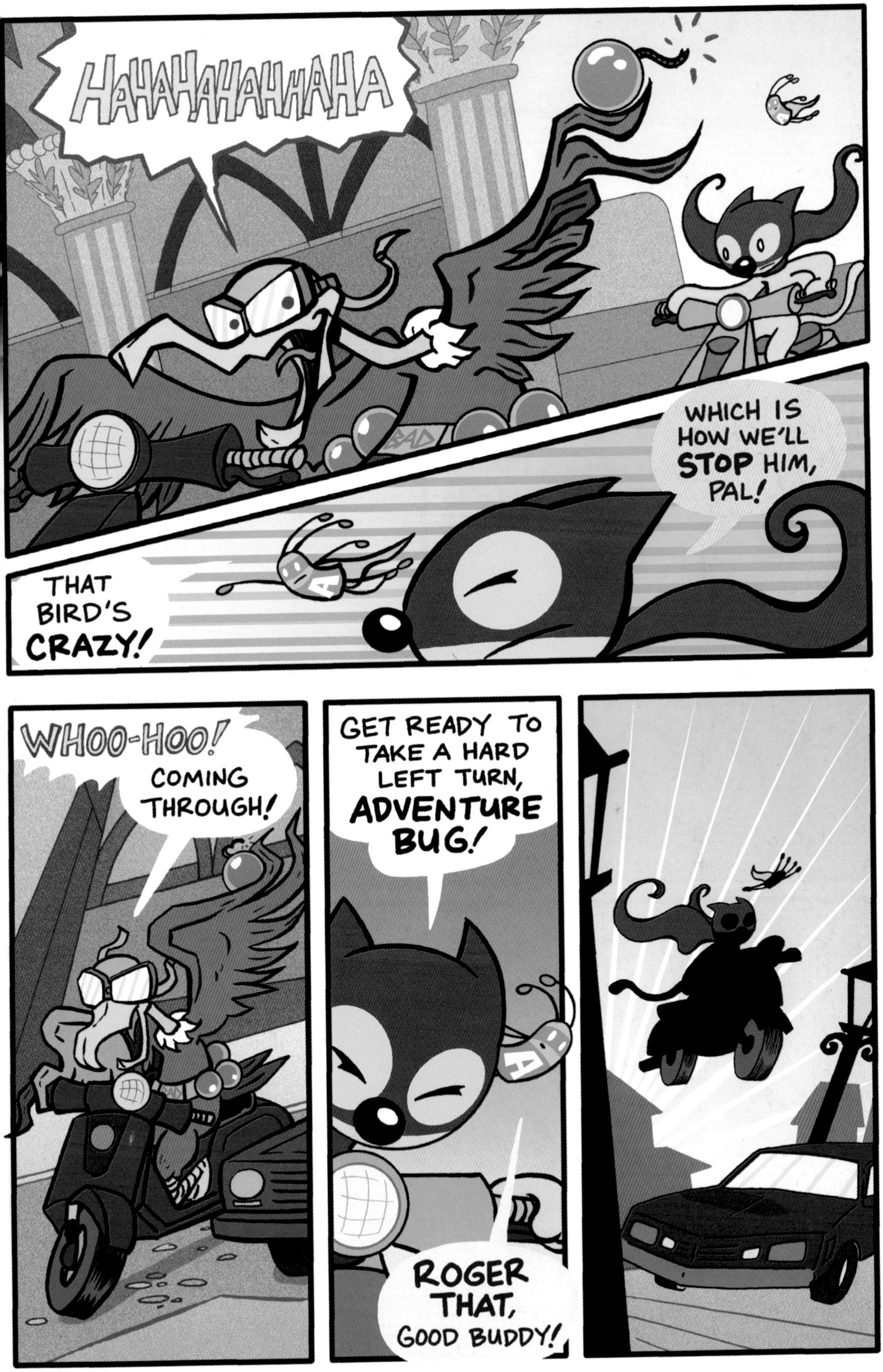
HAHAHAHAHHAHA
WHICH IS HOW WE'LL STOP HIM, PAL!
THAT BIRD'S CRAZY!
WHOO-HOO! COMING THROUGH!
GET READY TO TAKE A HARD LEFT TURN, ADVENTURE BUG!
ROGER THAT, GOOD BUDDY!

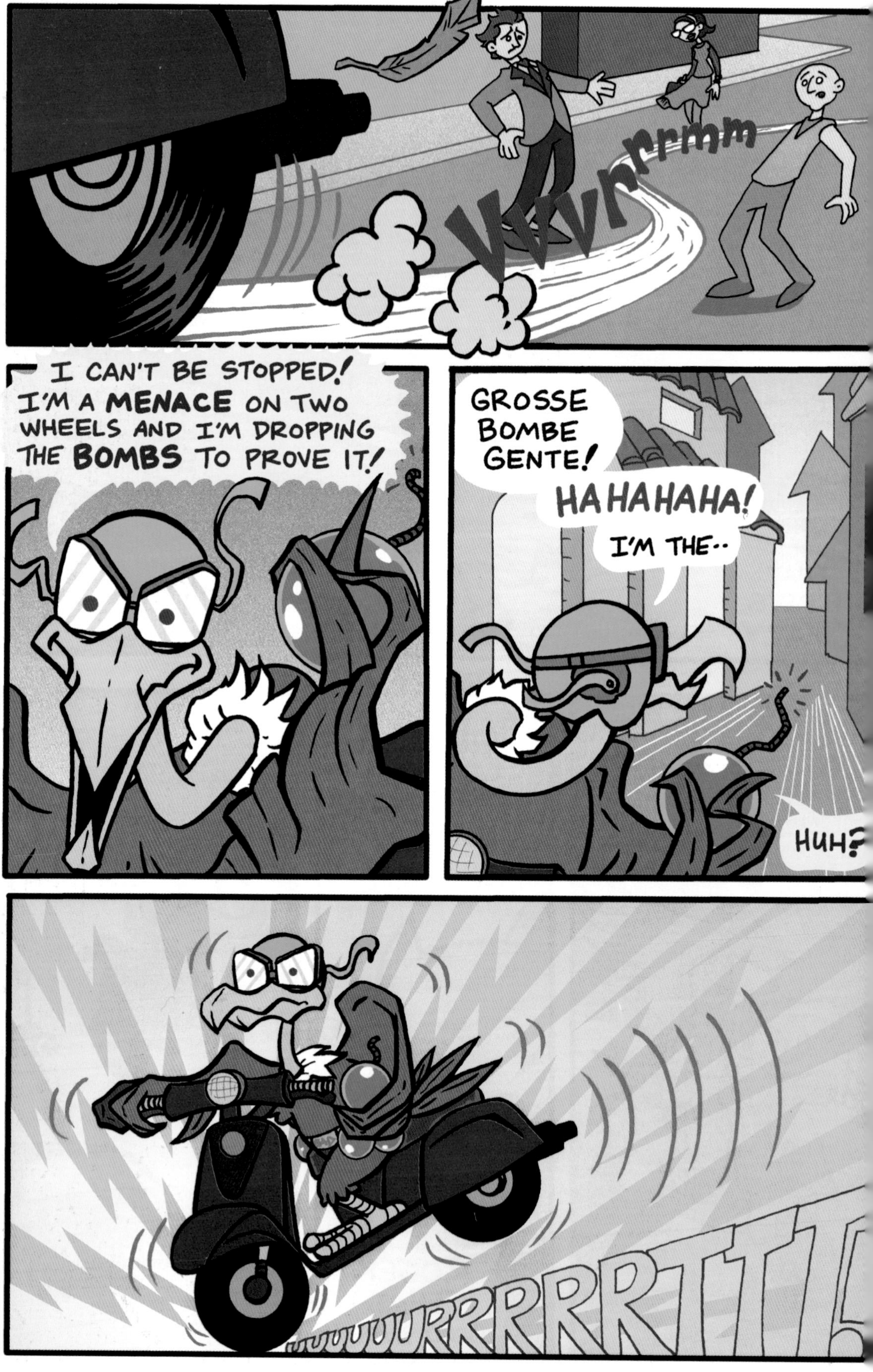
VVVVrrrmm
I CAN'T BE STOPPED! I'M A MENACE ON TWO WHEELS AND I'M DROPPING THE BOMBS TO PROVE IT!
GROSSE BOMBE GENTE!
HAHAHAHA!
I'M THE..
HUH?
UUUUUURRRRRRTTT!

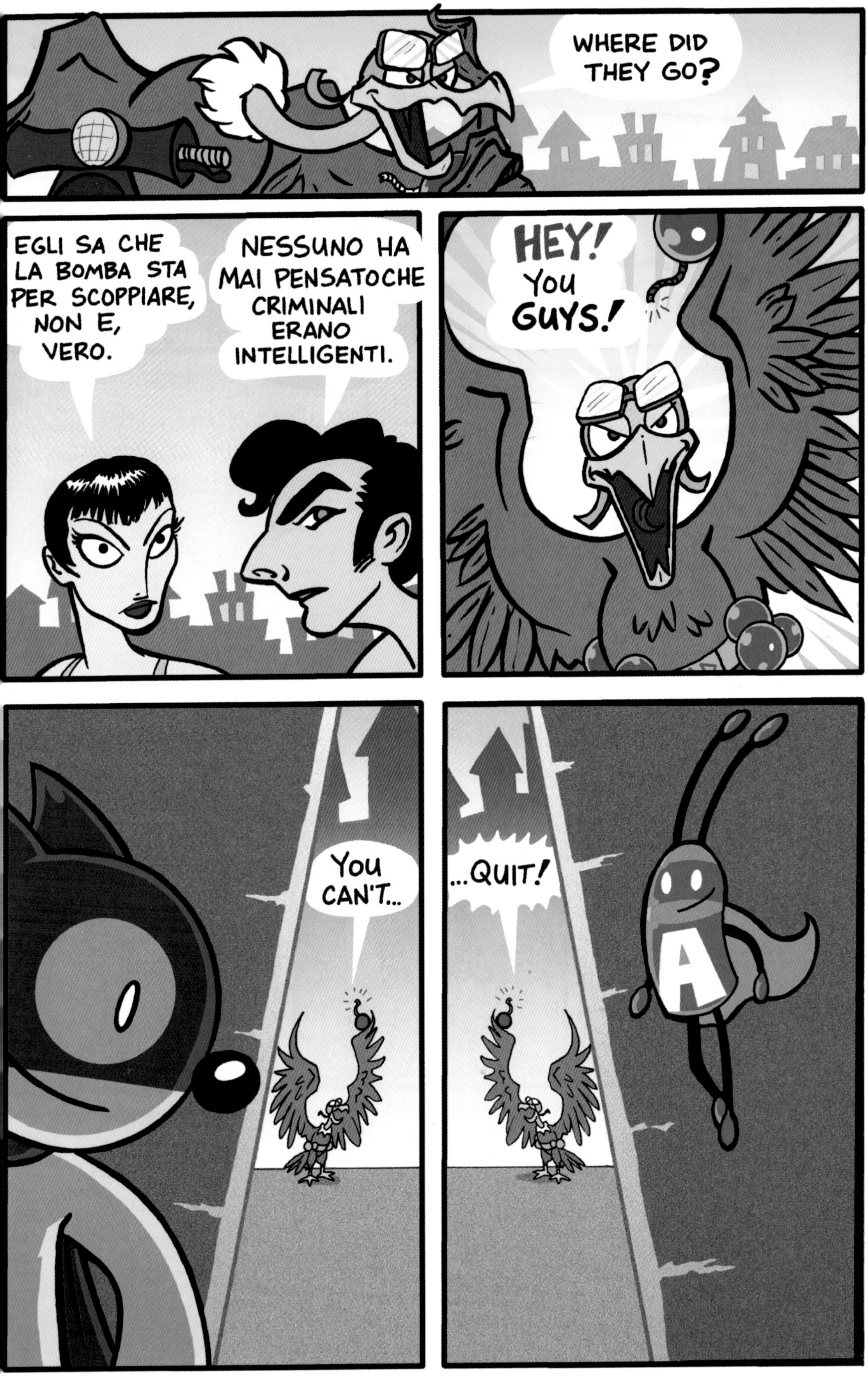

WHERE DID THEY GO?
EGLI SA CHE LA BOMBA STA PER SCOPPIARE, NON E, VERO.
NESSUNO HA MAI PENSATOCHE CRIMINALI ERANO INTELLIGENTI.
HEY! You GUYS!
You CAN'T...
...QUIT!

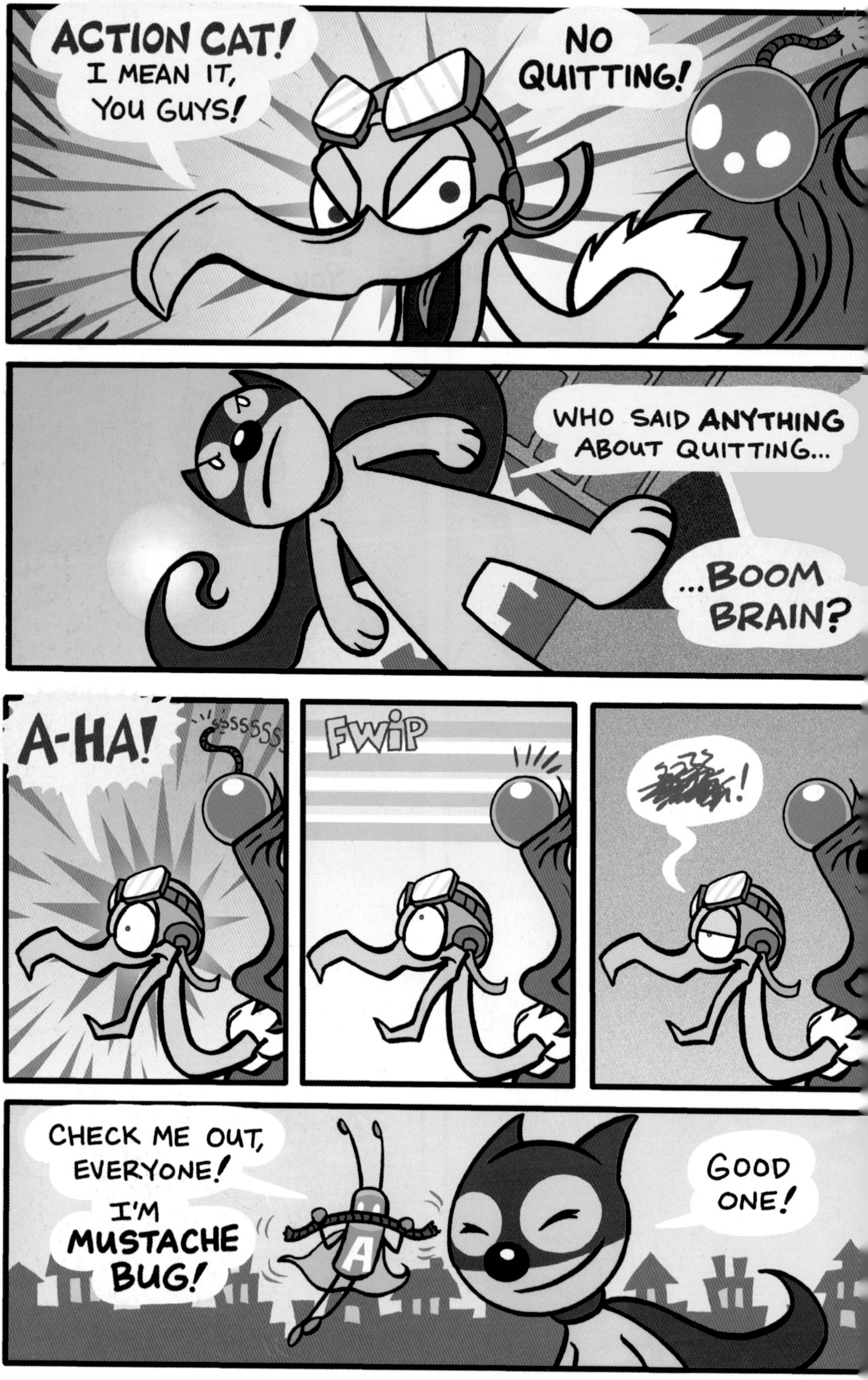
ACTION CAT! I MEAN IT, YOU GUYS!
NO QUITTING!
WHO SAID ANYTHING ABOUT QUITTING...
...BOOM BRAIN?
A-HA!
SSSSSSS
FWIP
CHECK ME OUT, EVERYONE!
I'M MUSTACHE BUG!
GOOD ONE!

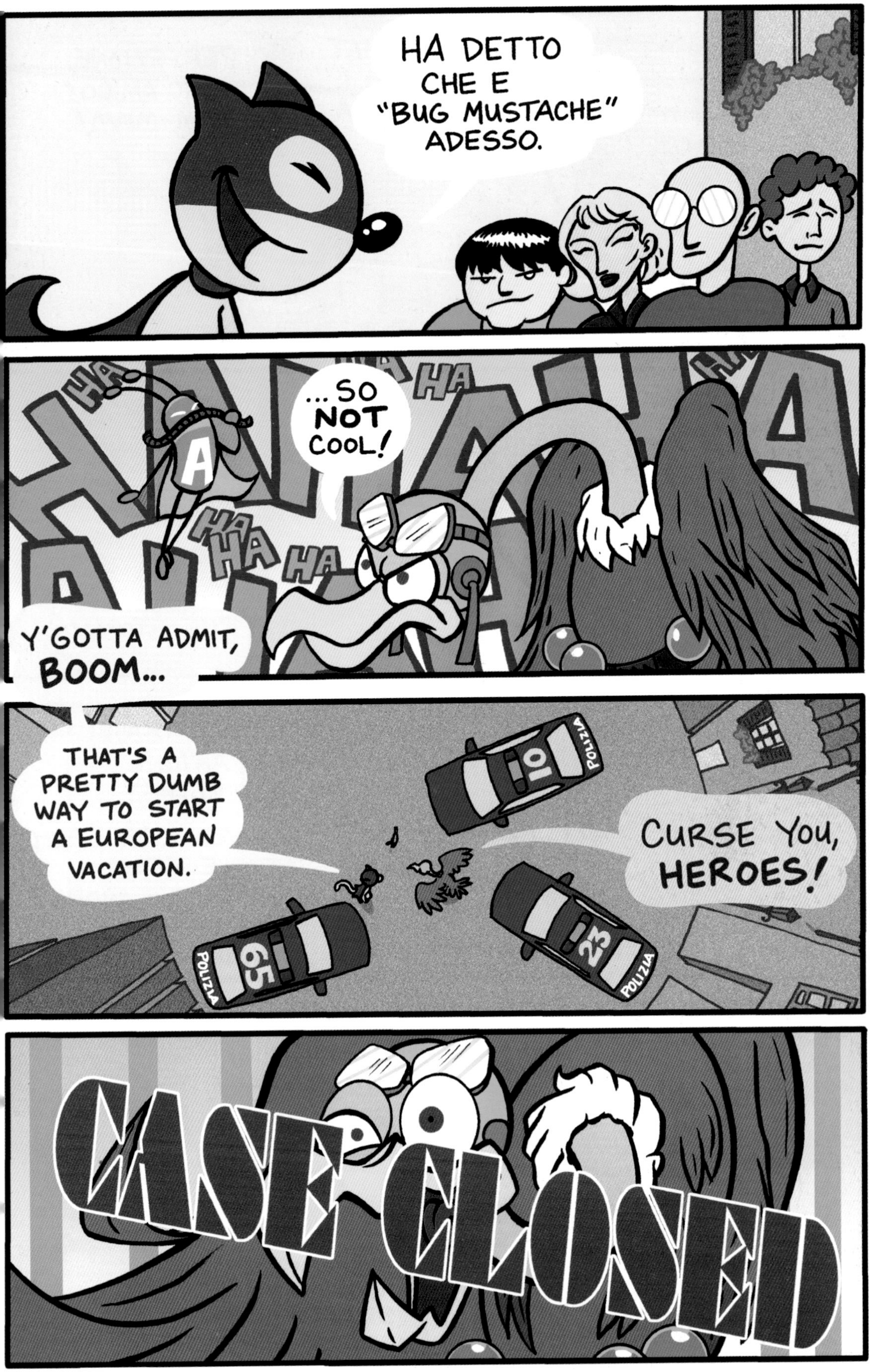
HA DETTO CHE E "BUG MUSTACHE" ADESSO.
HA
HA
HA
HA
HA
HA
...SO NOT COOL!
Y'GOTTA ADMIT, BOOM...
THAT'S A PRETTY DUMB WAY TO START A EUROPEAN VACATION.
CURSE YOU, HEROES!
POLIZIA
10
POLIZIA
65
POLIZIA
23
CASE CLOSED

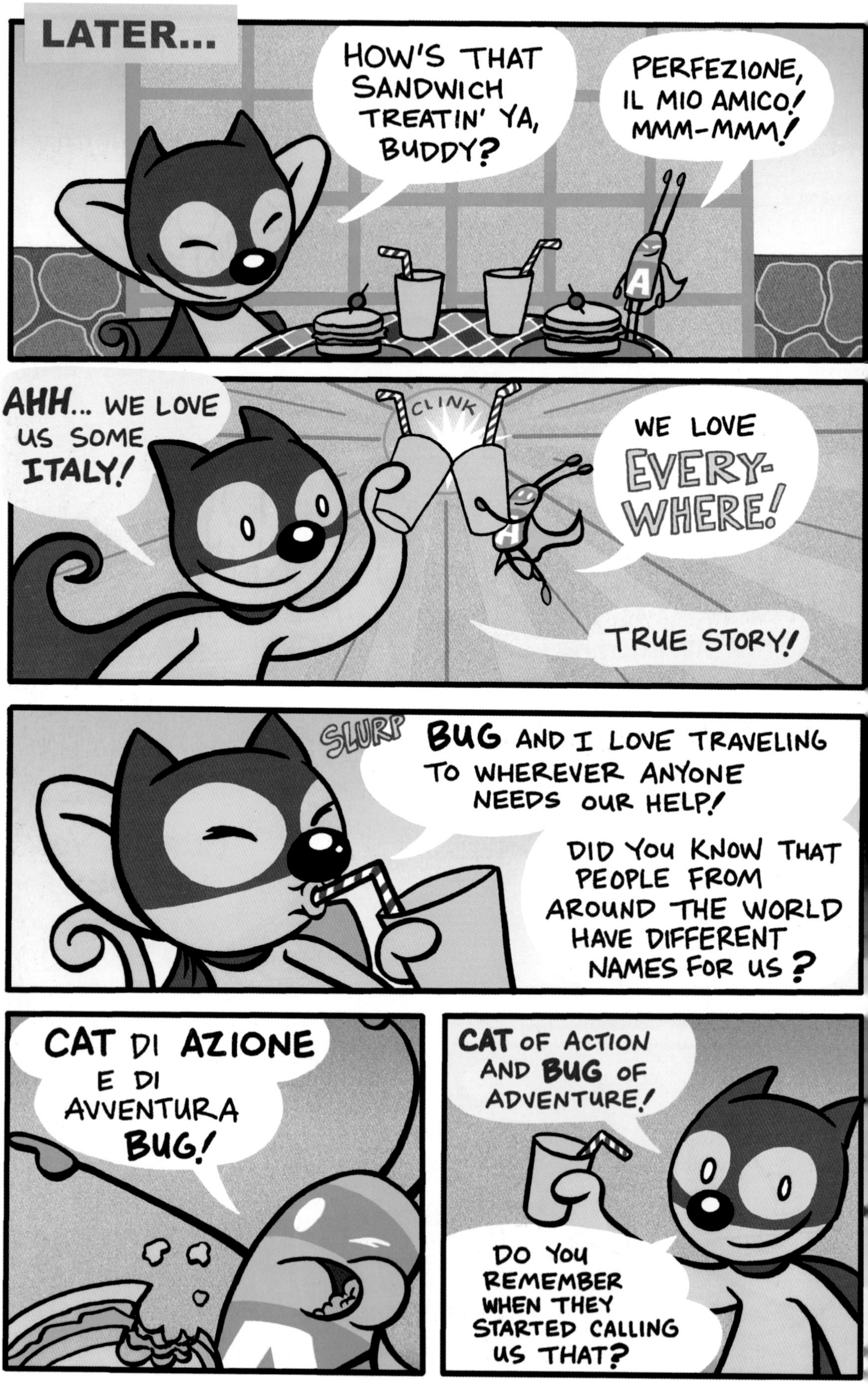
LATER...
HOW'S THAT SANDWICH TREATIN' YA, BUDDY?
PERFEZIONE, IL MIO AMICO! MMM-MMM!
AHH... WE LOVE US SOME ITALY!
CLINK
WE LOVE EVERY-WHERE!
TRUE STORY!
SLURP
BUG AND I LOVE TRAVELING TO WHEREVER ANYONE NEEDS OUR HELP!
DID YOU KNOW THAT PEOPLE FROM AROUND THE WORLD HAVE DIFFERENT NAMES FOR US?
CAT DI AZIONE E DI AVVENTURA BUG!
CAT OF ACTION AND BUG OF ADVENTURE!
DO YOU REMEMBER WHEN THEY STARTED CALLING US THAT?

"YEP!"

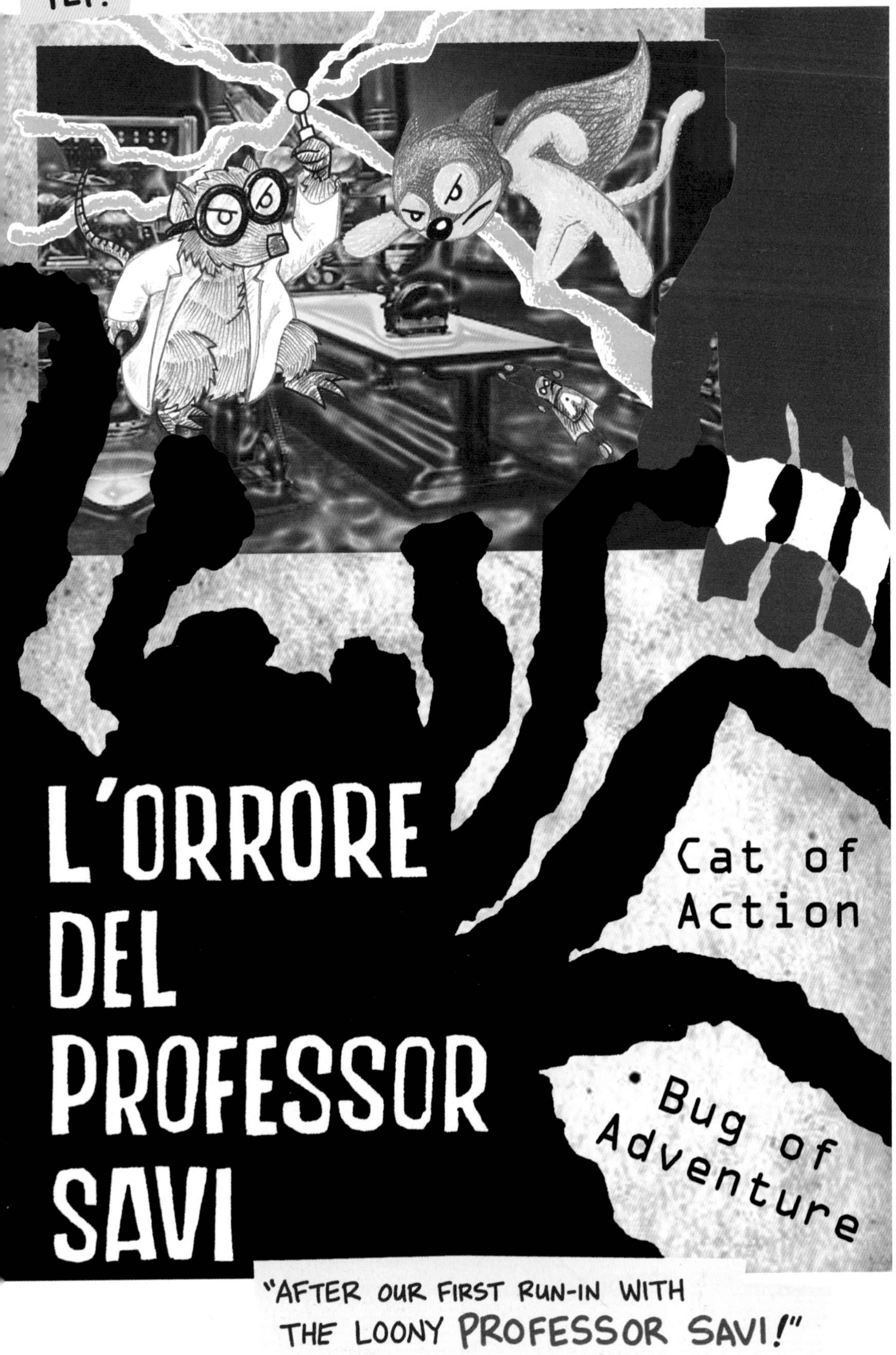
L'ORRORE DEL PROFESSOR SAVI
Cat of Action
Bug of Adventure

"AFTER OUR FIRST RUN-IN WITH THE LOONY PROFESSOR SAVI!"

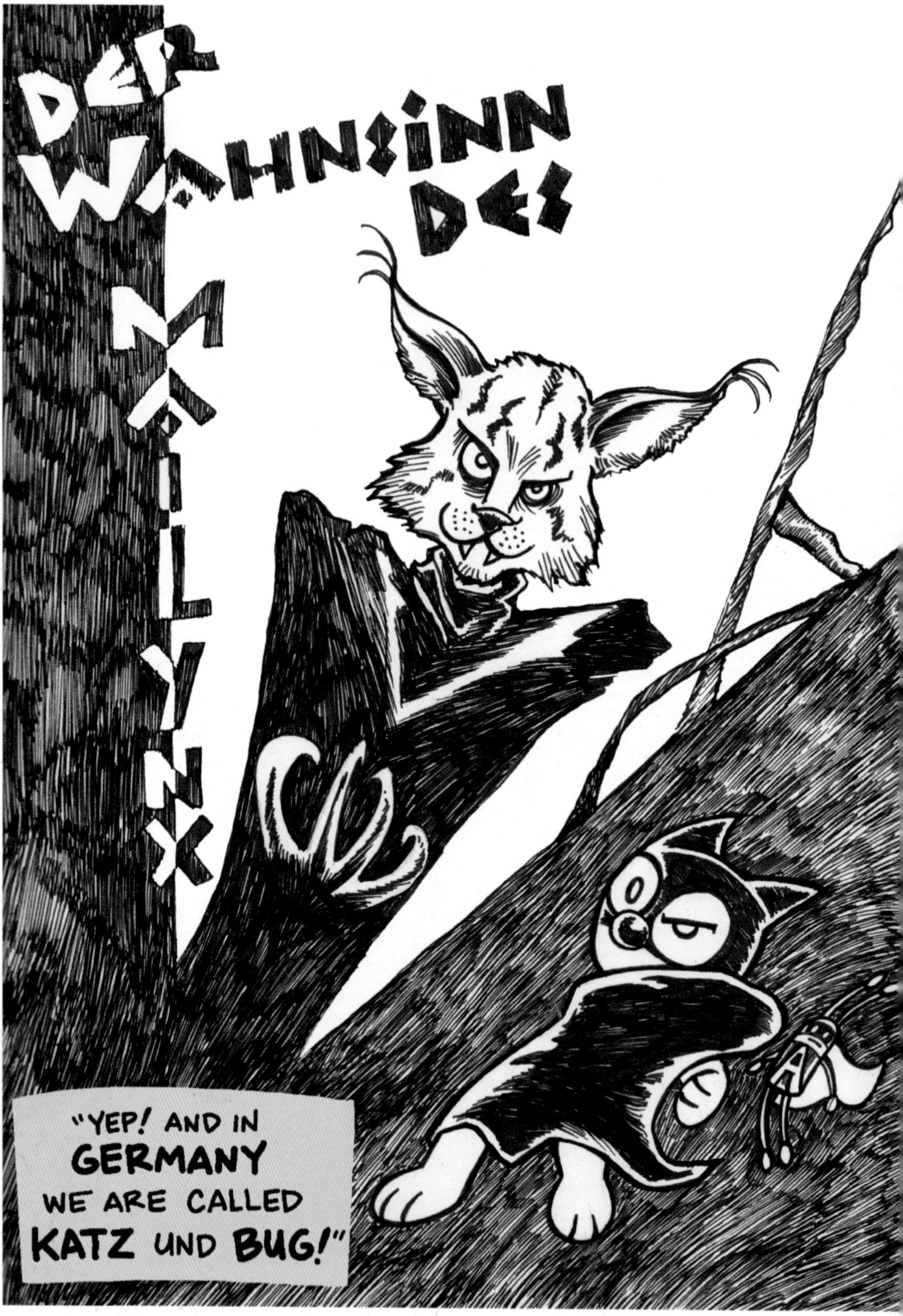
DER WAHNSINN DES MEL LYNX
"YEP! AND IN GERMANY WE ARE CALLED KATZ UND BUG!"

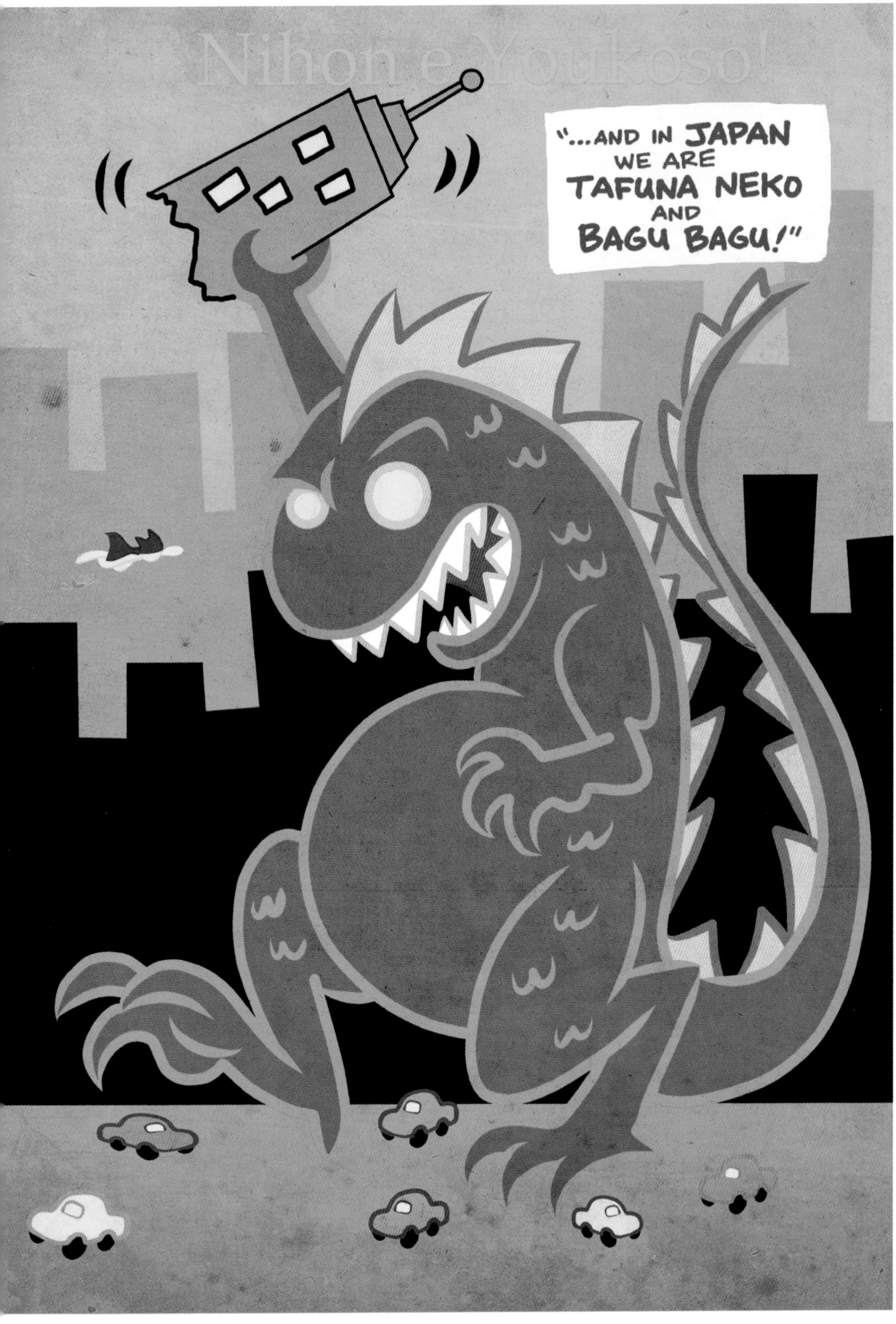
Nihon e Youkoso!
"...AND IN JAPAN WE ARE TAFUNA NEKO AND BAGU BAGU!"

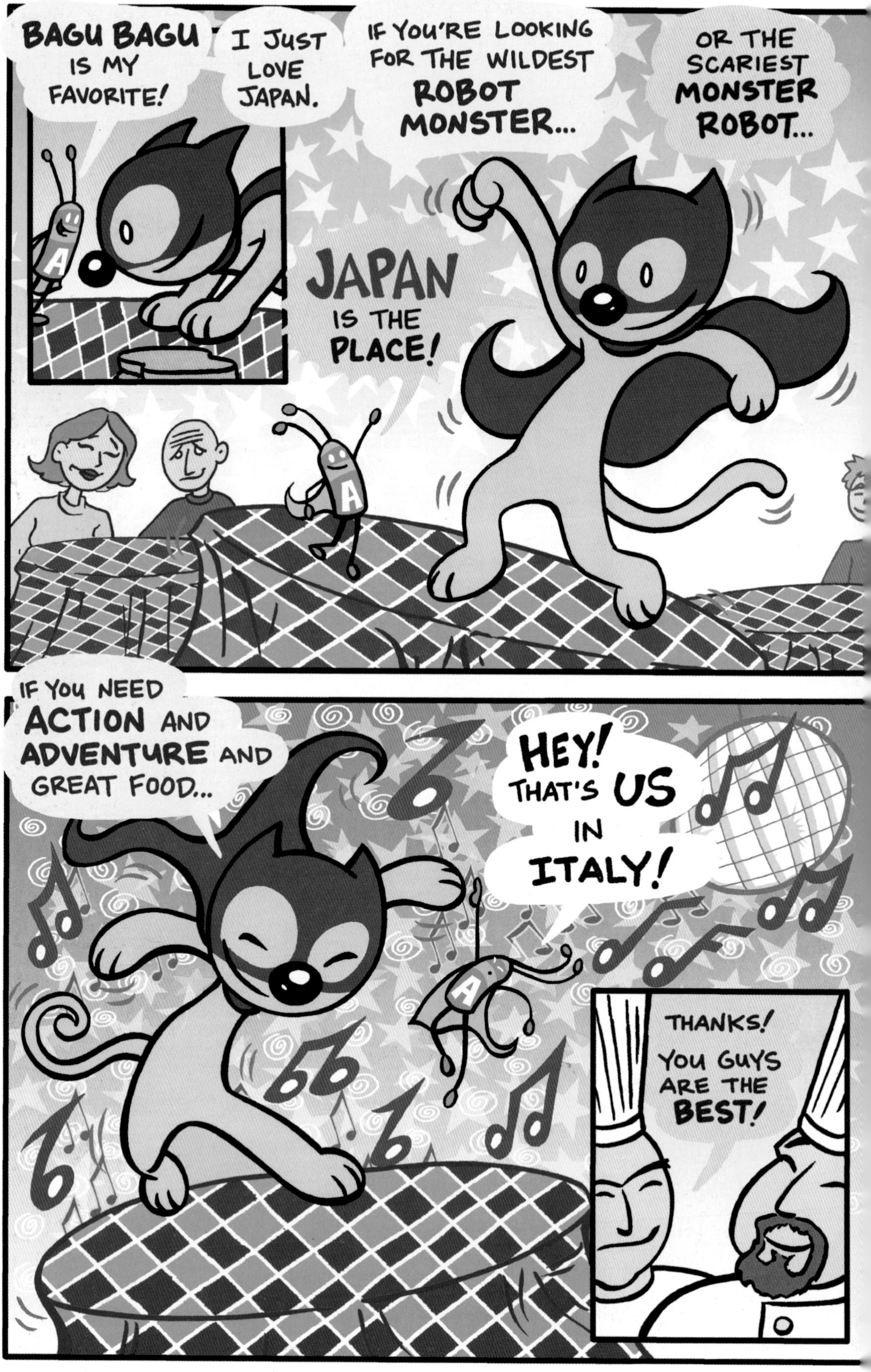
BAGU BAGU IS MY FAVORITE!
I JUST LOVE JAPAN.
IF YOU'RE LOOKING FOR THE WILDEST ROBOT MONSTER...
OR THE SCARIEST MONSTER ROBOT...
JAPAN IS THE PLACE!
IF YOU NEED ACTION AND ADVENTURE AND GREAT FOOD...
HEY! THAT'S US IN ITALY!
THANKS! YOU GUYS ARE THE BEST!

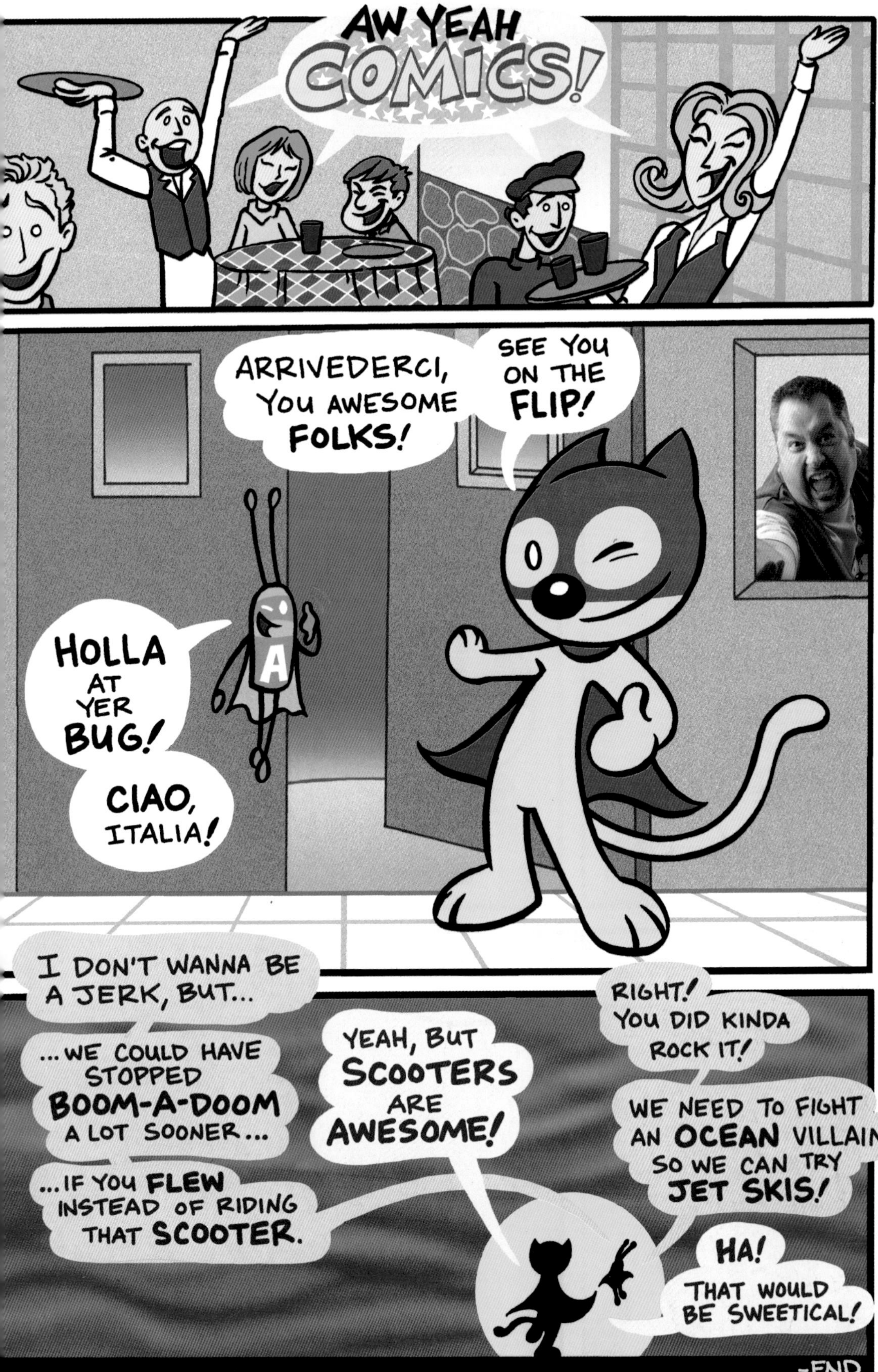
AW YEAH COMICS!
ARRIVEDERCI, YOU AWESOME FOLKS!
SEE YOU ON THE FLIP!
HOLLA AT YER BUG!
CIAO, ITALIA!
I DON'T WANNA BE A JERK, BUT...
...WE COULD HAVE STOPPED BOOM-A-DOOM A LOT SOONER...
...IF YOU FLEW INSTEAD OF RIDING THAT SCOOTER.
YEAH, BUT SCOOTERS ARE AWESOME!
RIGHT! YOU DID KINDA ROCK IT!
WE NEED TO FIGHT AN OCEAN VILLAIN SO WE CAN TRY JET SKIS!
HA! THAT WOULD BE SWEETICAL!
-END

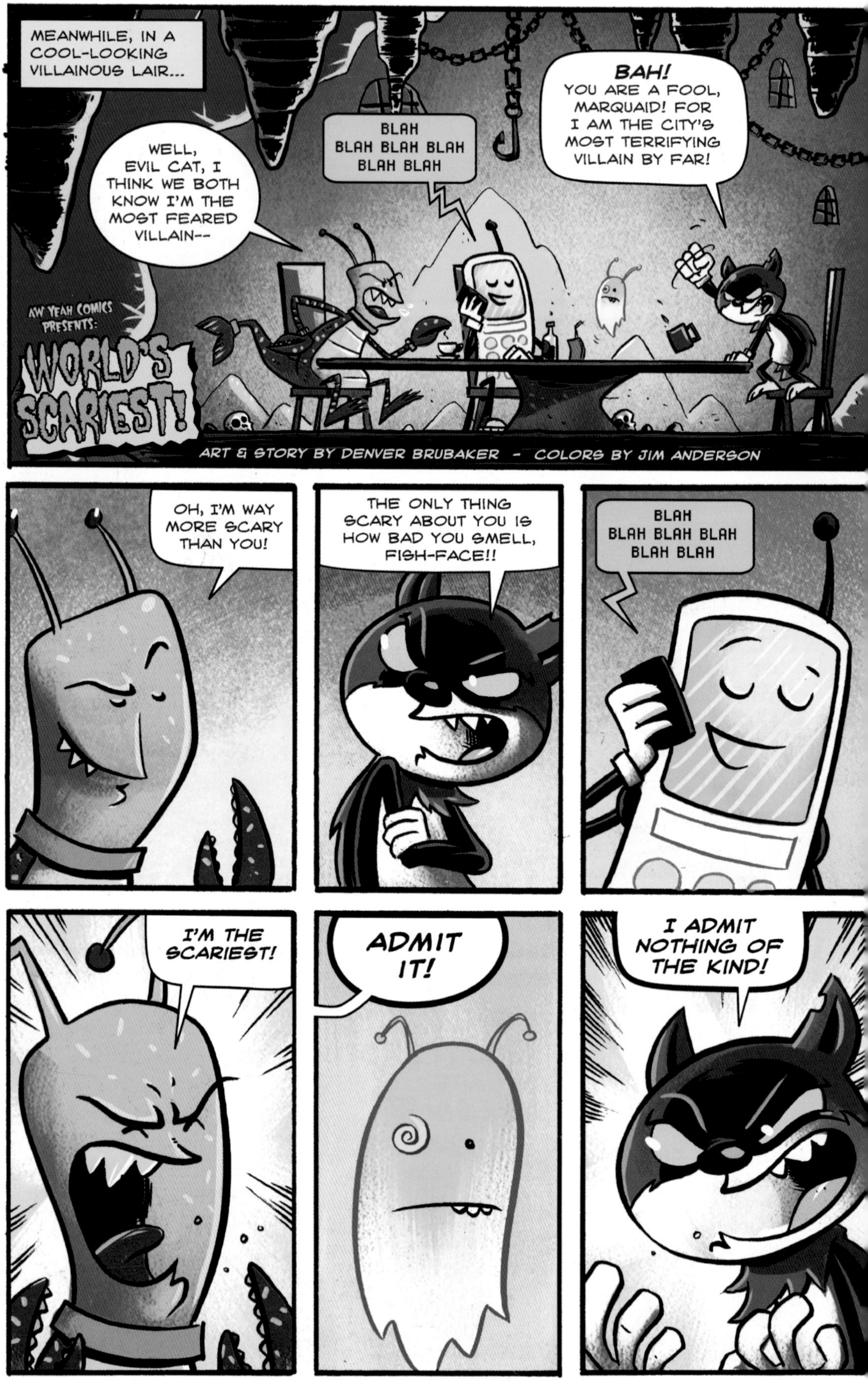
MEANWHILE, IN A COOL-LOOKING VILLAINOUS LAIR...
WELL, EVIL CAT, I THINK WE BOTH KNOW I'M THE MOST FEARED VILLAIN--
BLAH BLAH BLAH BLAH BLAH BLAH
BAH! YOU ARE A FOOL, MARQUAID! FOR I AM THE CITY'S MOST TERRIFYING VILLAIN BY FAR!
AW YEAH COMICS PRESENTS:
WORLD'S SCARIEST!
ART & STORY BY DENVER BRUBAKER - COLORS BY JIM ANDERSON
OH, I'M WAY MORE SCARY THAN YOU!
THE ONLY THING SCARY ABOUT YOU IS HOW BAD YOU SMELL, FISH-FACE!!
BLAH BLAH BLAH BLAH BLAH BLAH
I'M THE SCARIEST!
ADMIT IT!
I ADMIT NOTHING OF THE KIND!

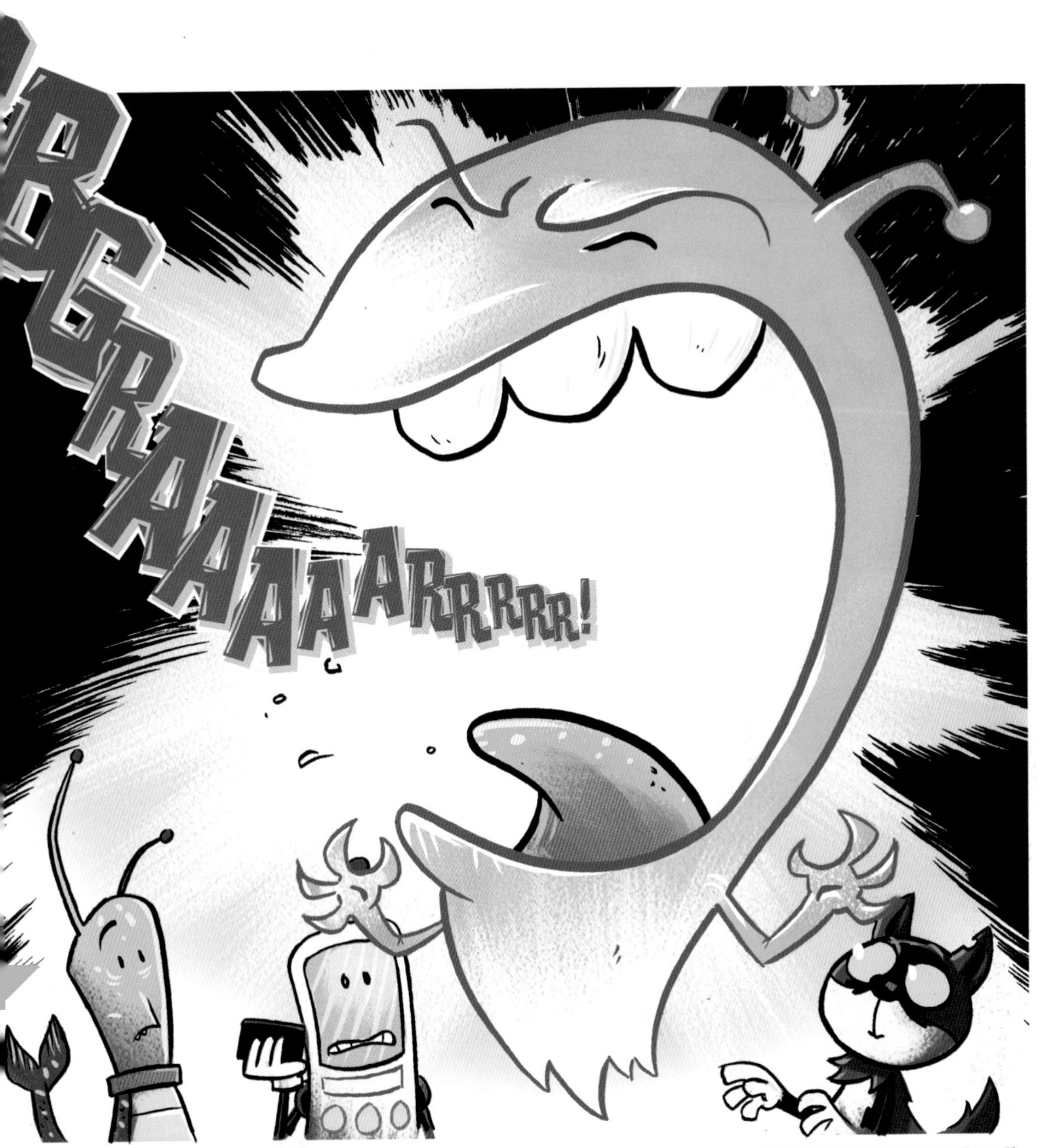
BGRAAAAAARRRRRR!

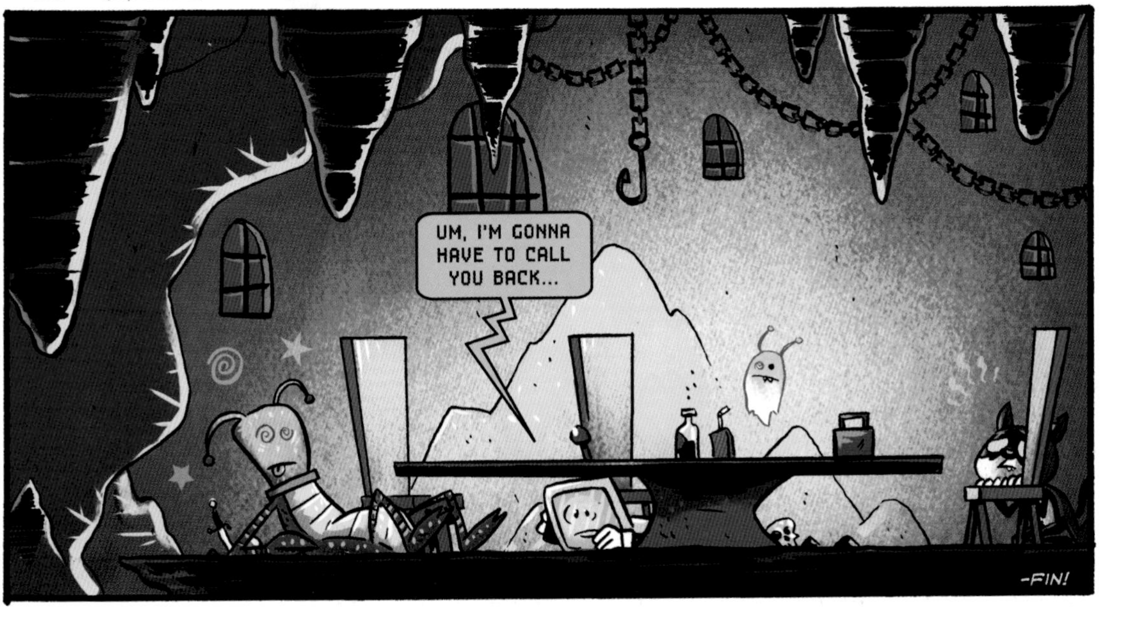
UM, I'M GONNA HAVE TO CALL YOU BACK...
-FIN!

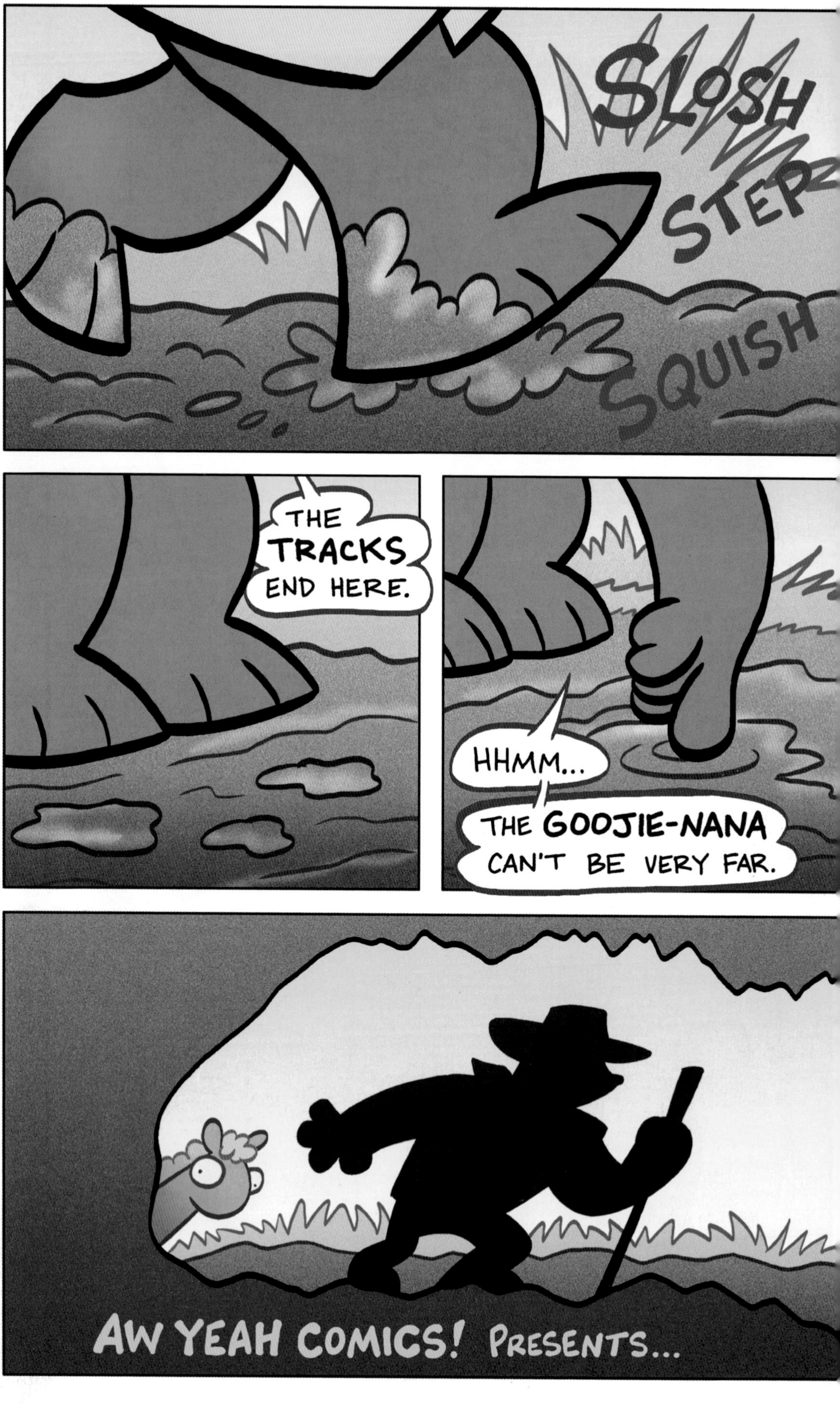
SLOSH
STEP
SQUISH
THE TRACKS END HERE.
HHMM...
THE GOOJIE-NANA CAN'T BE VERY FAR.
AW YEAH COMICS! PRESENTS...

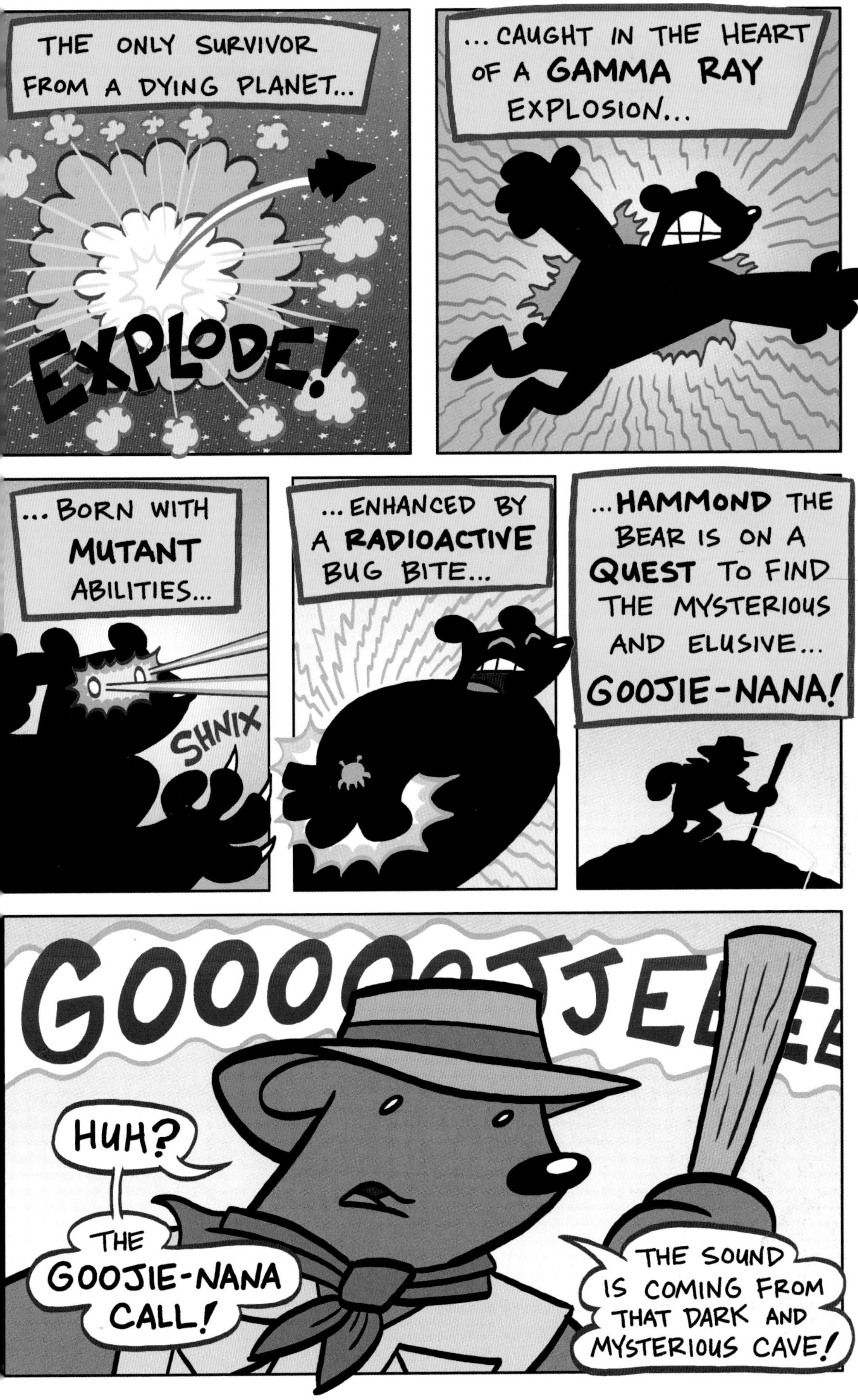
THE ONLY SURVIVOR FROM A DYING PLANET...
EXPLODE!
... CAUGHT IN THE HEART OF A GAMMA RAY EXPLOSION...
... BORN WITH MUTANT ABILITIES...
SHNIX
... ENHANCED BY A RADIOACTIVE BUG BITE...
... HAMMOND THE BEAR IS ON A QUEST TO FIND THE MYSTERIOUS AND ELUSIVE... GOOJIE-NANA!
HUH?
THE GOOJIE-NANA CALL!
THE SOUND IS COMING FROM THAT DARK AND MYSTERIOUS CAVE!

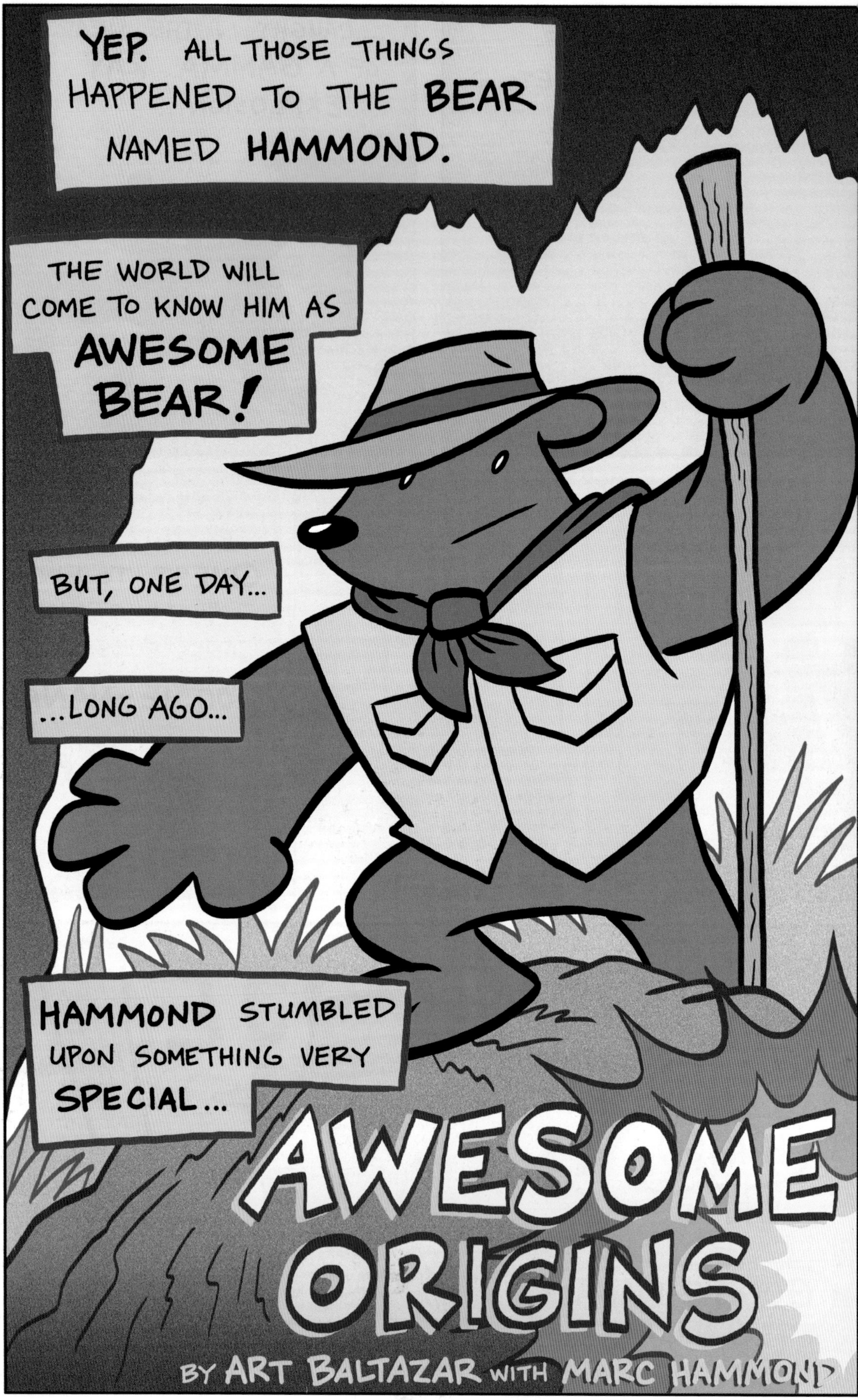
YEP. ALL THOSE THINGS HAPPENED TO THE BEAR NAMED HAMMOND.
THE WORLD WILL COME TO KNOW HIM AS AWESOME BEAR!
BUT, ONE DAY...
...LONG AGO...
HAMMOND STUMBLED UPON SOMETHING VERY SPECIAL...
AWESOME ORIGINS
BY ART BALTAZAR WITH MARC HAMMOND

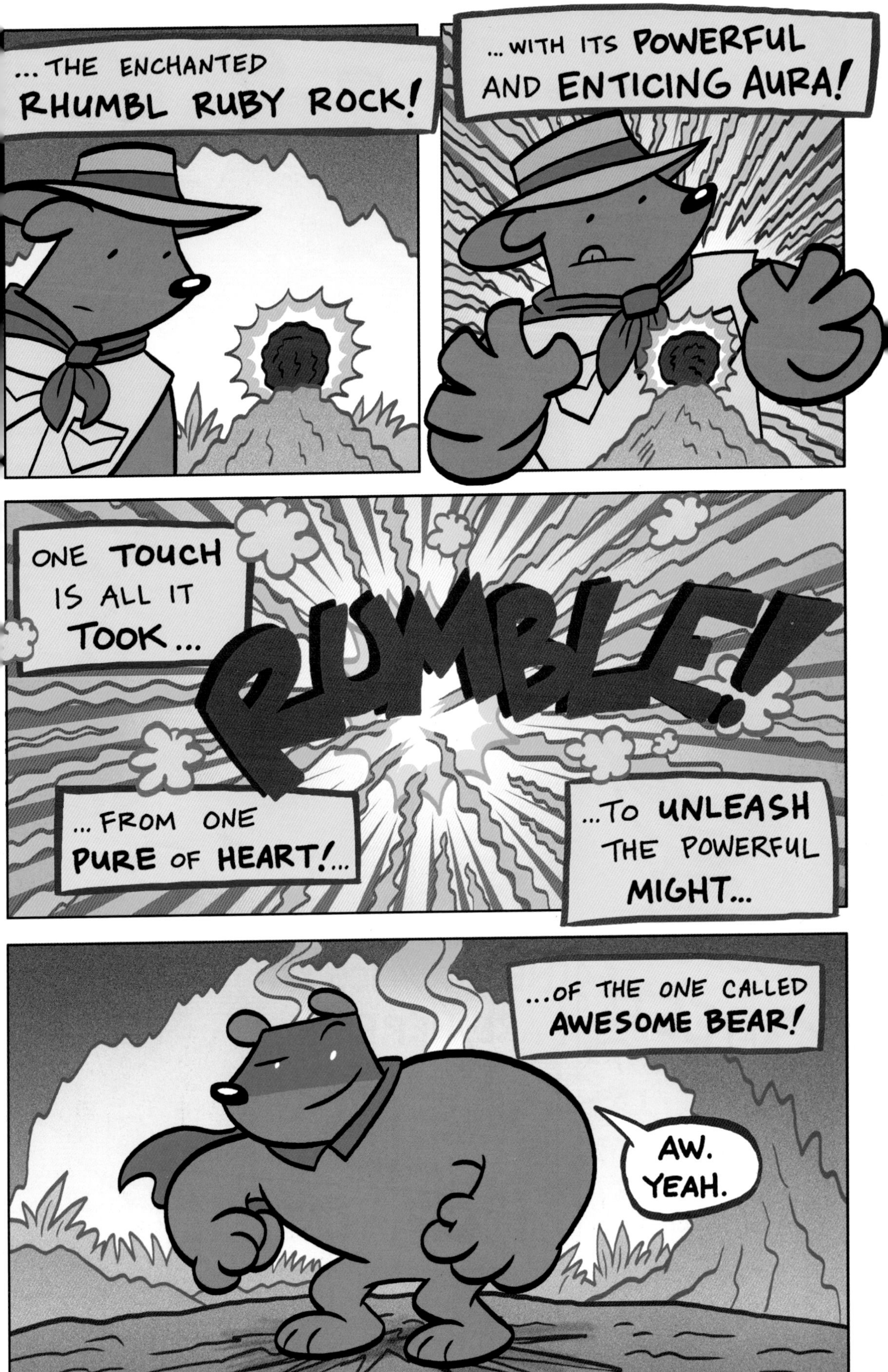
...THE ENCHANTED RHUMBL RUBY ROCK!
...WITH ITS POWERFUL AND ENTICING AURA!
ONE TOUCH IS ALL IT TOOK...
RUMBLE!!
...FROM ONE PURE OF HEART!...
...TO UNLEASH THE POWERFUL MIGHT...
...OF THE ONE CALLED AWESOME BEAR!
AW. YEAH.

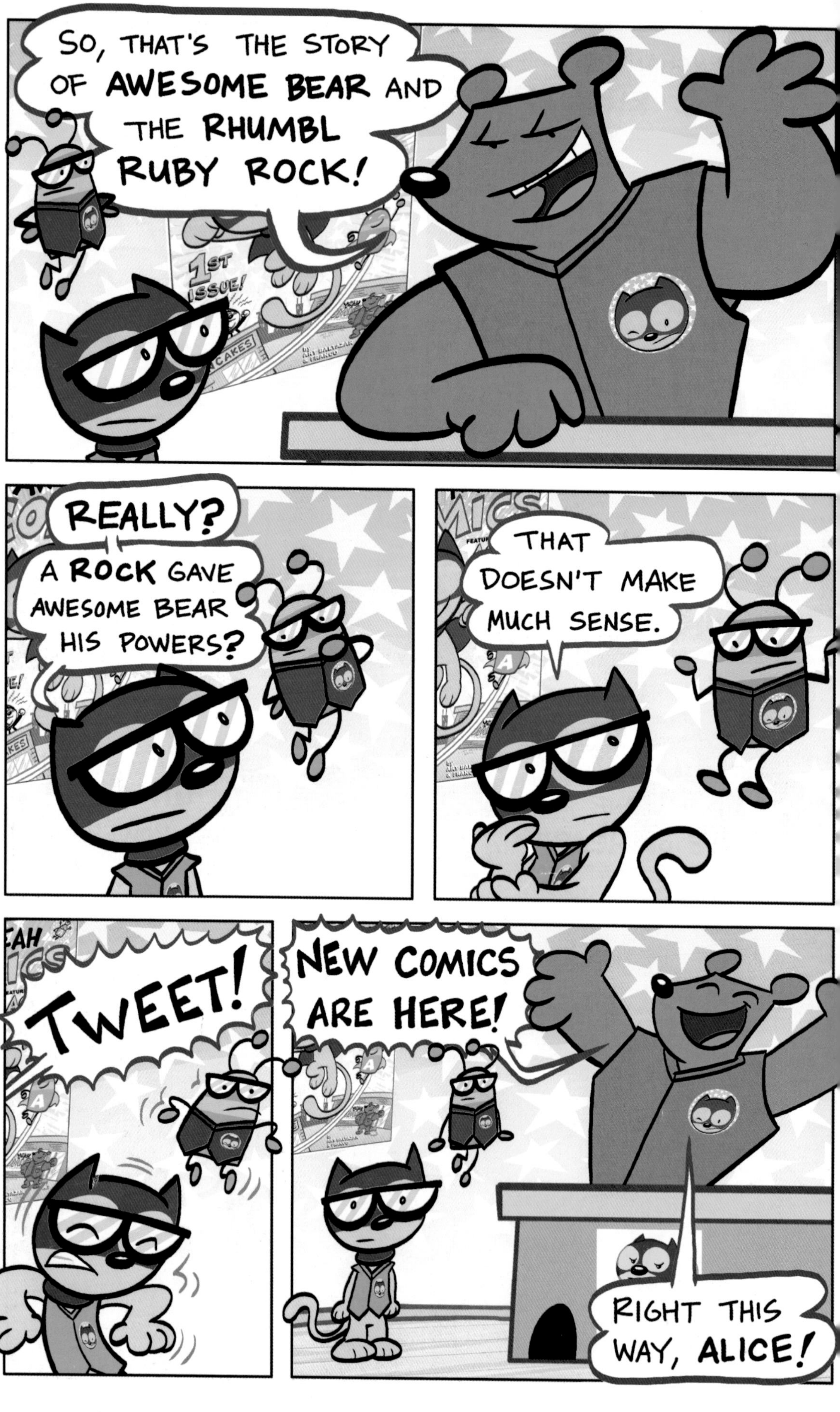
SO, THAT'S THE STORY OF AWESOME BEAR AND THE RHUMBL RUBY ROCK!
1ST ISSUE!
REALLY?
A ROCK GAVE AWESOME BEAR HIS POWERS?
THAT DOESN'T MAKE MUCH SENSE.
TWEET!
NEW COMICS ARE HERE!
RIGHT THIS WAY, ALICE!

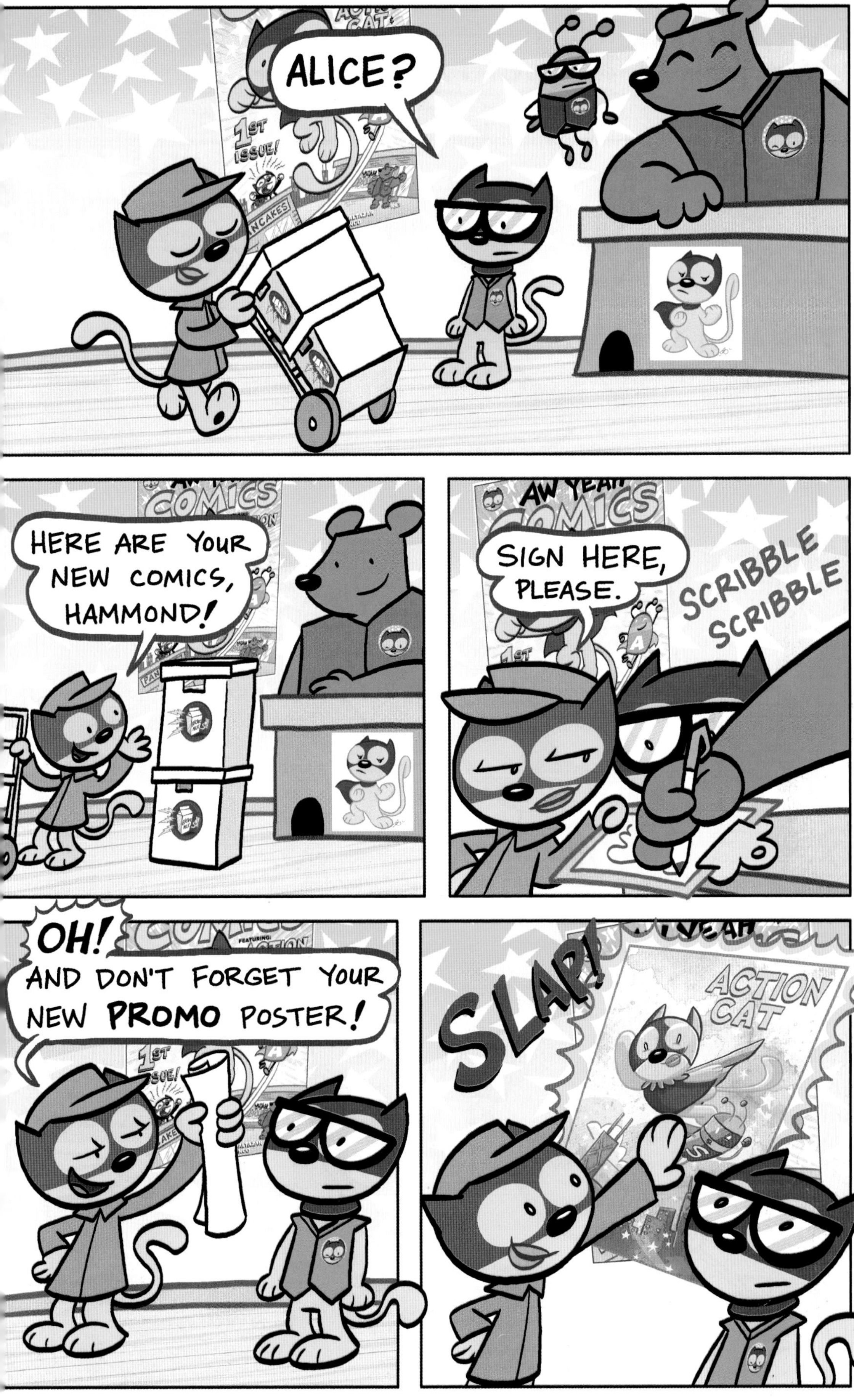
ALICE?
HERE ARE YOUR NEW COMICS, HAMMOND!
SIGN HERE, PLEASE.
SCRIBBLE SCRIBBLE
OH!
AND DON'T FORGET YOUR NEW **PROMO** POSTER!
SLAP!
ACTION CAT

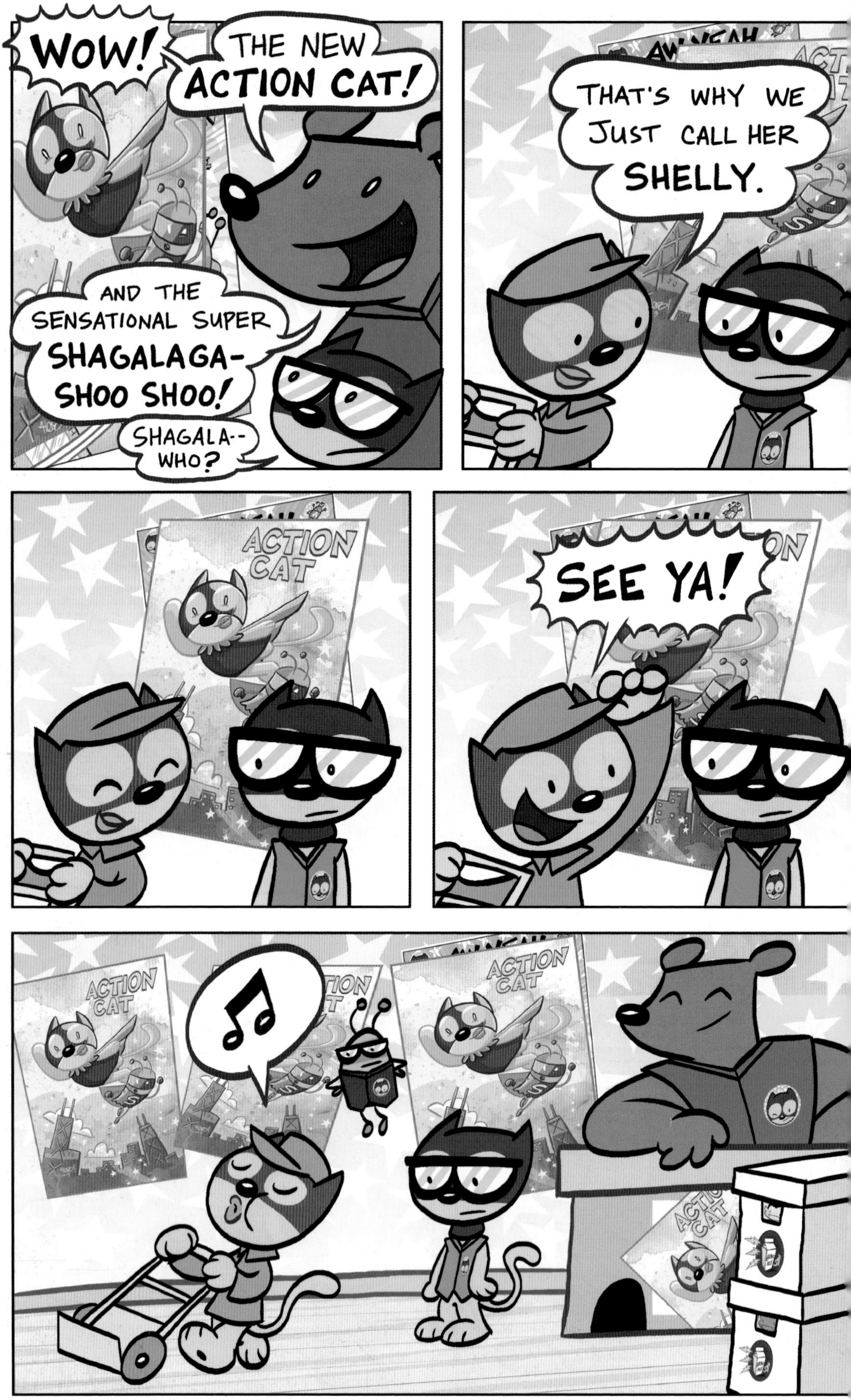
WOW!
THE NEW ACTION CAT!
AND THE SENSATIONAL SUPER SHAGALAGA-SHOO SHOO!
SHAGALA--WHO?
THAT'S WHY WE JUST CALL HER SHELLY.
ACTION CAT
SEE YA!
ACTION CAT
ACTION CAT
ACTION CAT

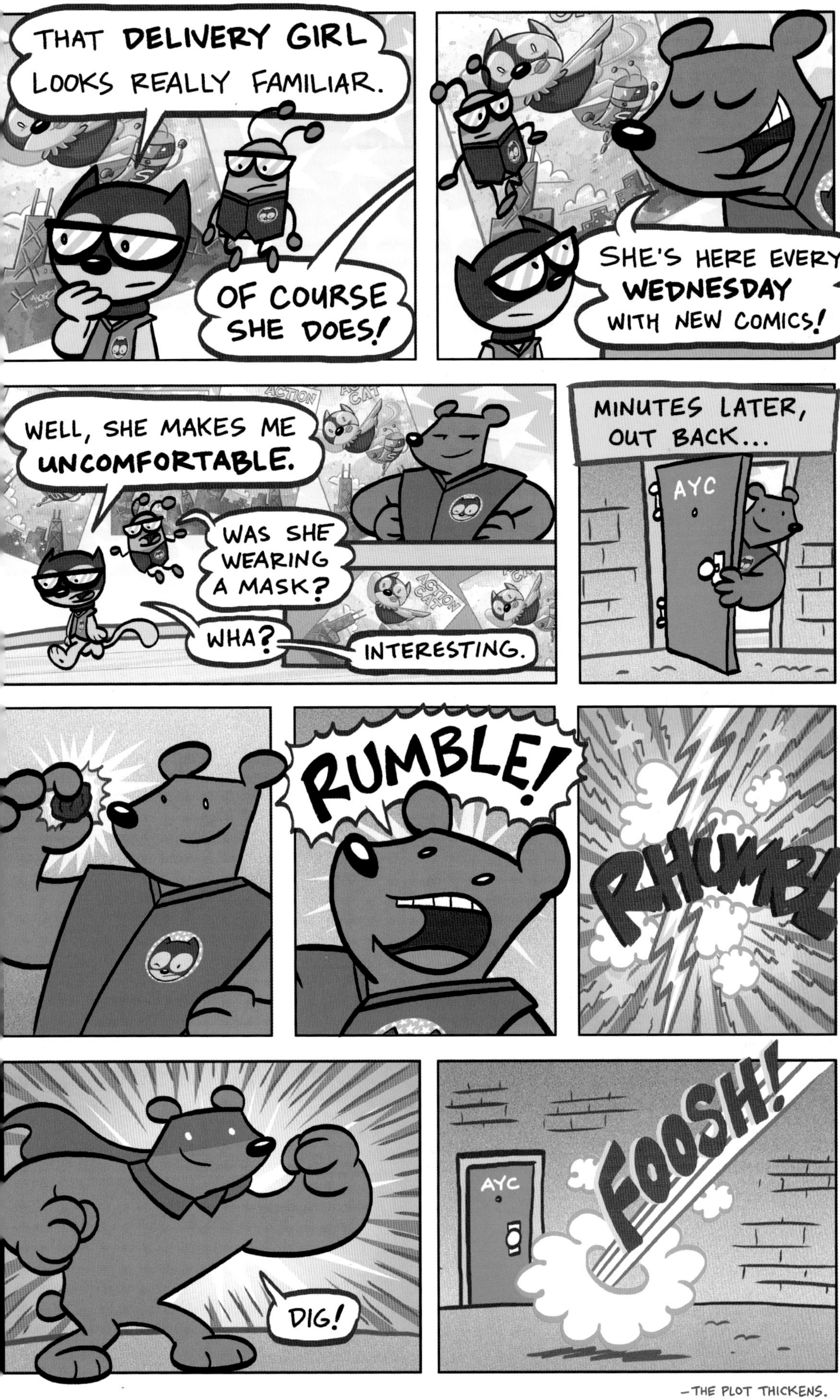
THAT DELIVERY GIRL LOOKS REALLY FAMILIAR.
OF COURSE SHE DOES!
SHE'S HERE EVERY WEDNESDAY WITH NEW COMICS!
WELL, SHE MAKES ME UNCOMFORTABLE.
WAS SHE WEARING A MASK?
WHA?
INTERESTING.
MINUTES LATER, OUT BACK...
AYC
RUMBLE!
RHUMB!
DIG!
AYC
FOOSH!

–THE PLOT THICKENS.

AWESOME BEAR in: LOOK BEFORE YOU LEAP!

by: SCOOT

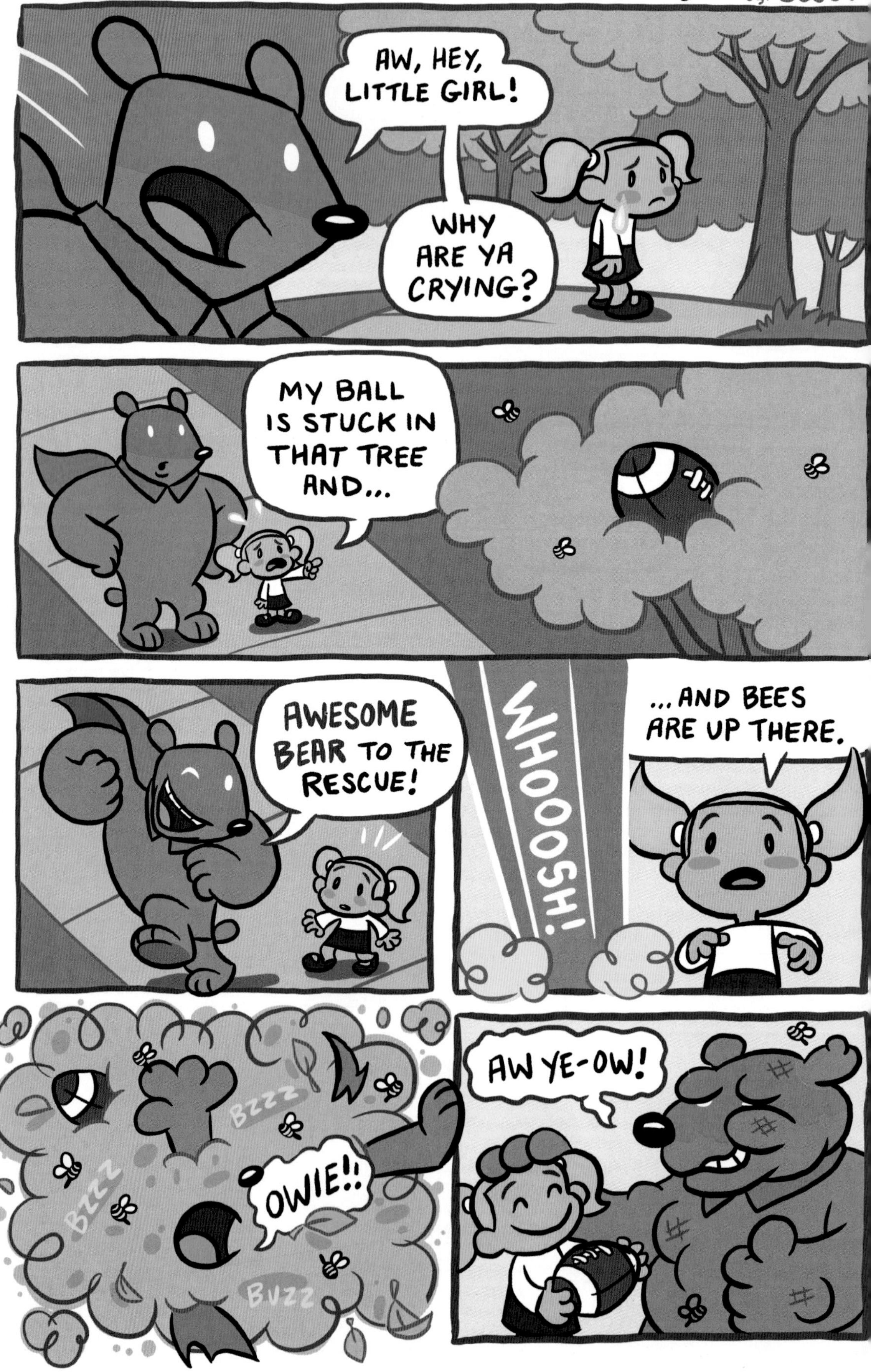
AW, HEY, LITTLE GIRL!
WHY ARE YA CRYING?
MY BALL IS STUCK IN THAT TREE AND...
AWESOME BEAR TO THE RESCUE!
WHOOOSH!
...AND BEES ARE UP THERE.
BZZZ
BZZZ
OWIE!!
BUZZ
AW YE-OW!

★ CHAPTER FOUR ★

AW YEAH COMICS! presents...

ZOMBIE Cat

by FRANCO & NICOLAS AURELIANI

THE TRAVELER

SKELETON

PRISONE

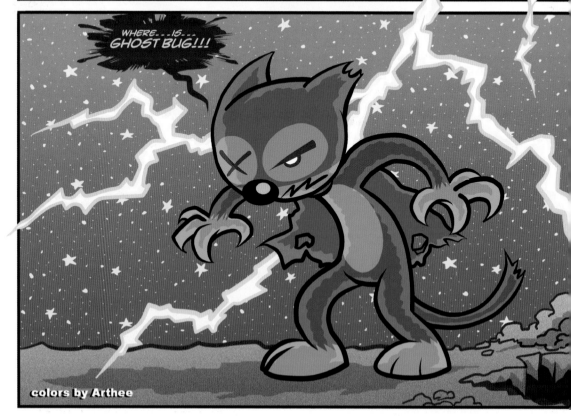

WHERE...IS... GHOST BUG!!!

colors by Arthee

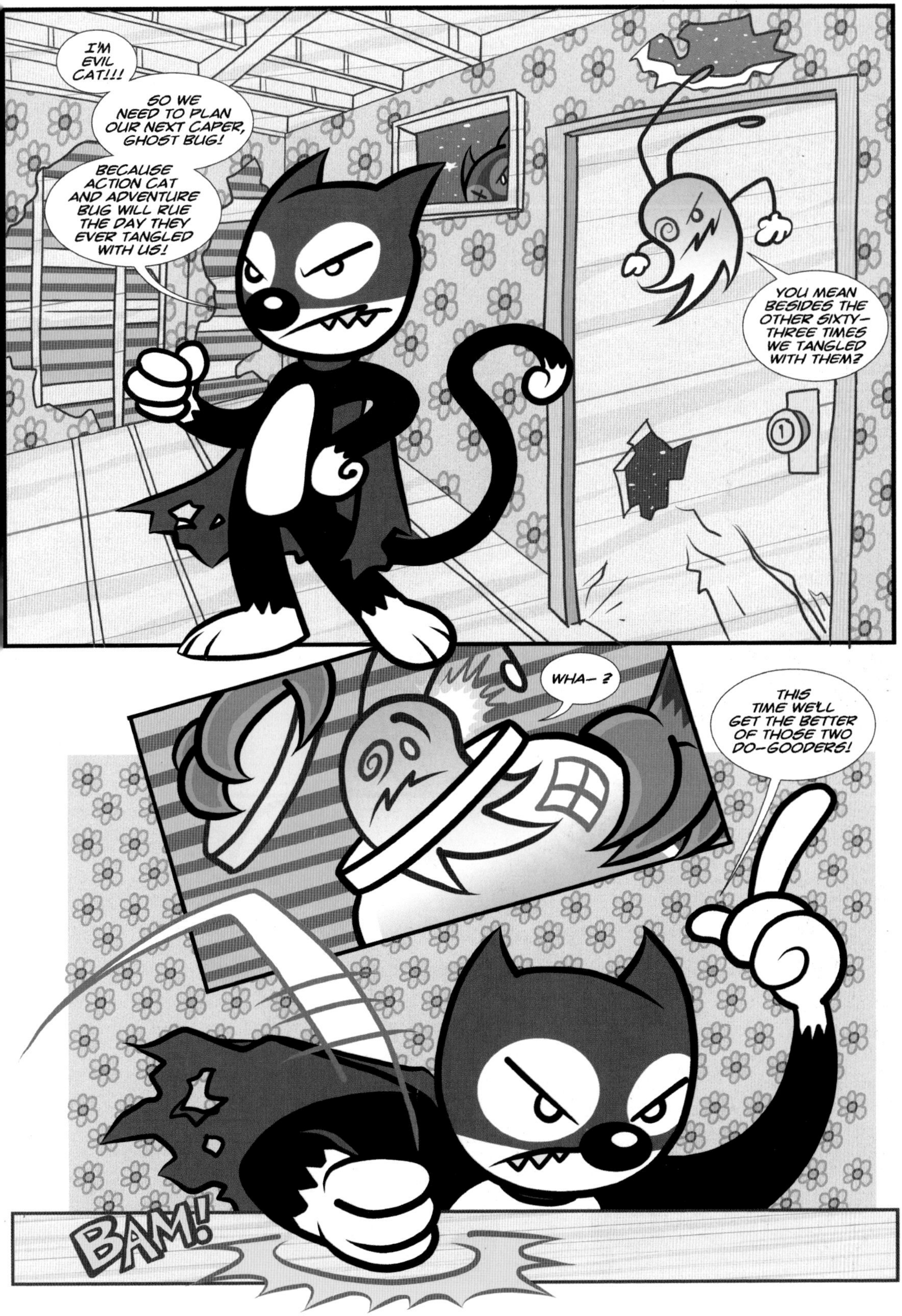
I'M EVIL CAT!!!
SO WE NEED TO PLAN OUR NEXT CAPER, GHOST BUG!
BECAUSE ACTION CAT AND ADVENTURE BUG WILL RUE THE DAY THEY EVER TANGLED WITH US!
YOU MEAN BESIDES THE OTHER SIXTY-THREE TIMES WE TANGLED WITH THEM?
WHA- ?
THIS TIME WE'LL GET THE BETTER OF THOSE TWO DO-GOODERS!
BAM!

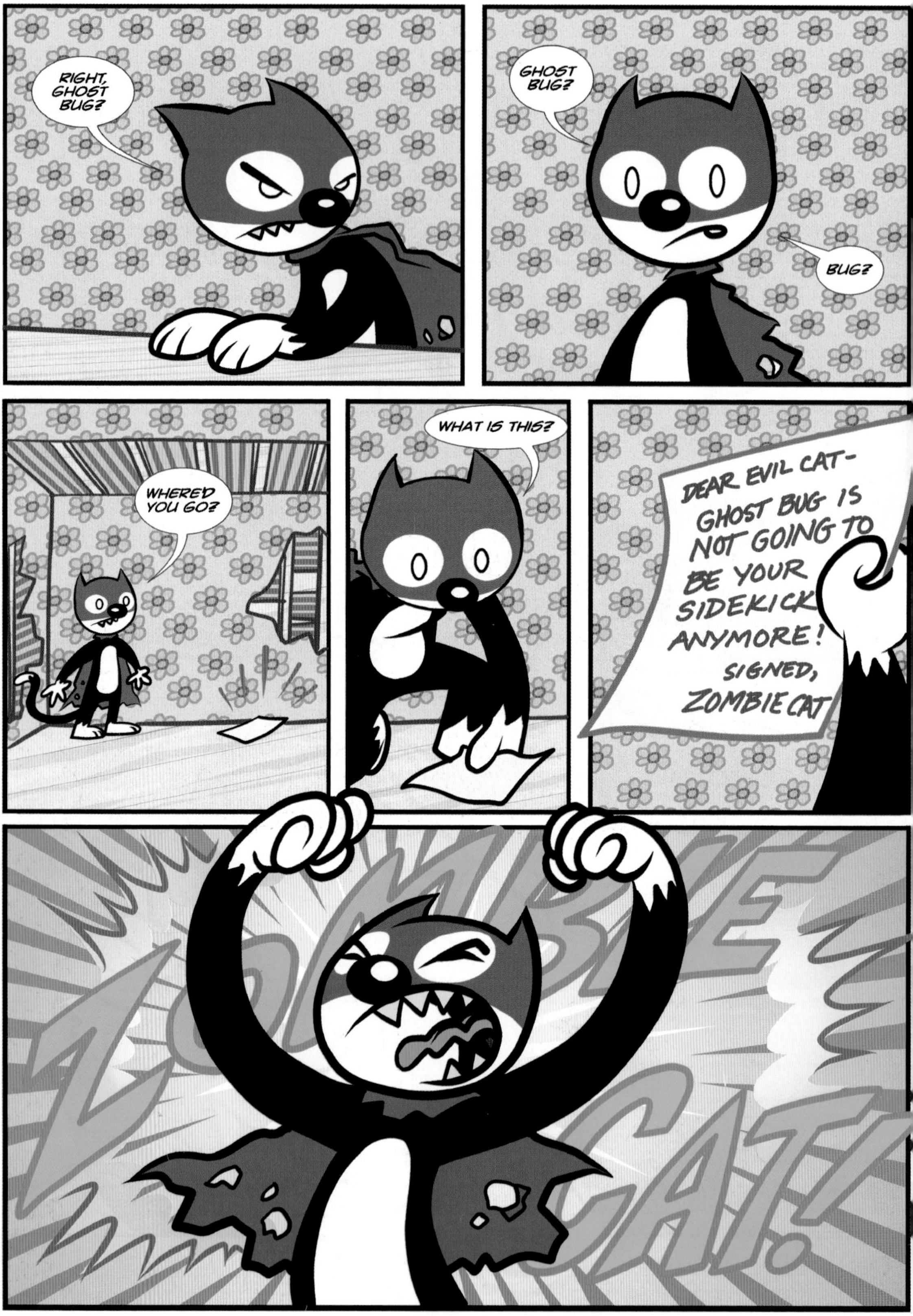
RIGHT, GHOST BUG?
GHOST BUG?
BUG?
WHERE'D YOU GO?
WHAT IS THIS?
DEAR EVIL CAT-
GHOST BUG IS NOT GOING TO BE YOUR SIDEKICK ANYMORE!
SIGNED, ZOMBIE CAT
ZOMBIE CAT!

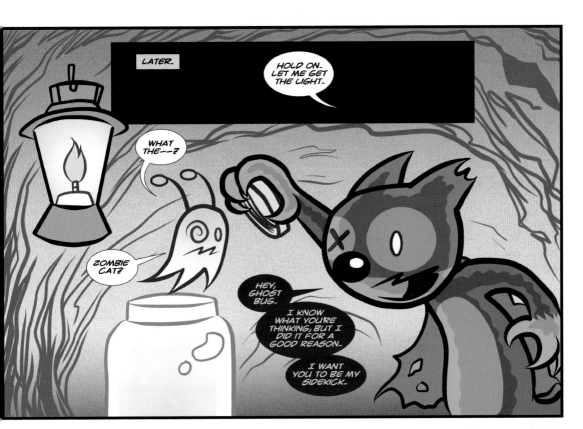

LATER.

HOLD ON. LET ME GET THE LIGHT.

WHAT THE--?

ZOMBIE CAT?

HEY, GHOST BUG.

I KNOW WHAT YOU'RE THINKING, BUT I DID IT FOR A GOOD REASON.

I WANT YOU TO BE MY SIDEKICK.

REALLY?

ZOMBIE CAT AND GHOST BUG?

IT DOES HAVE A NICE RING TO IT.

I KNOW HE'S NOT VERY NICE TO YOU...

...AND EVIL CAT IS, LIKE--EVIL. NOT A ZOMBIE LIKE ME.

YOU ARE A ZOMBIE... AND I'M A GHOST. WE ARE MORE ALIKE THAN EVIL CAT AND I ARE.

HIS EVIL PLANS NEVER REALLY WORK EITHER.

AND HE'S ALWAYS GETTING STOPPED OR CAPTURED BY ACTION CAT.

LET ME ASK YOU THIS:

WHAT WOULD HAPPEN IF I WERE TO DO THIS--

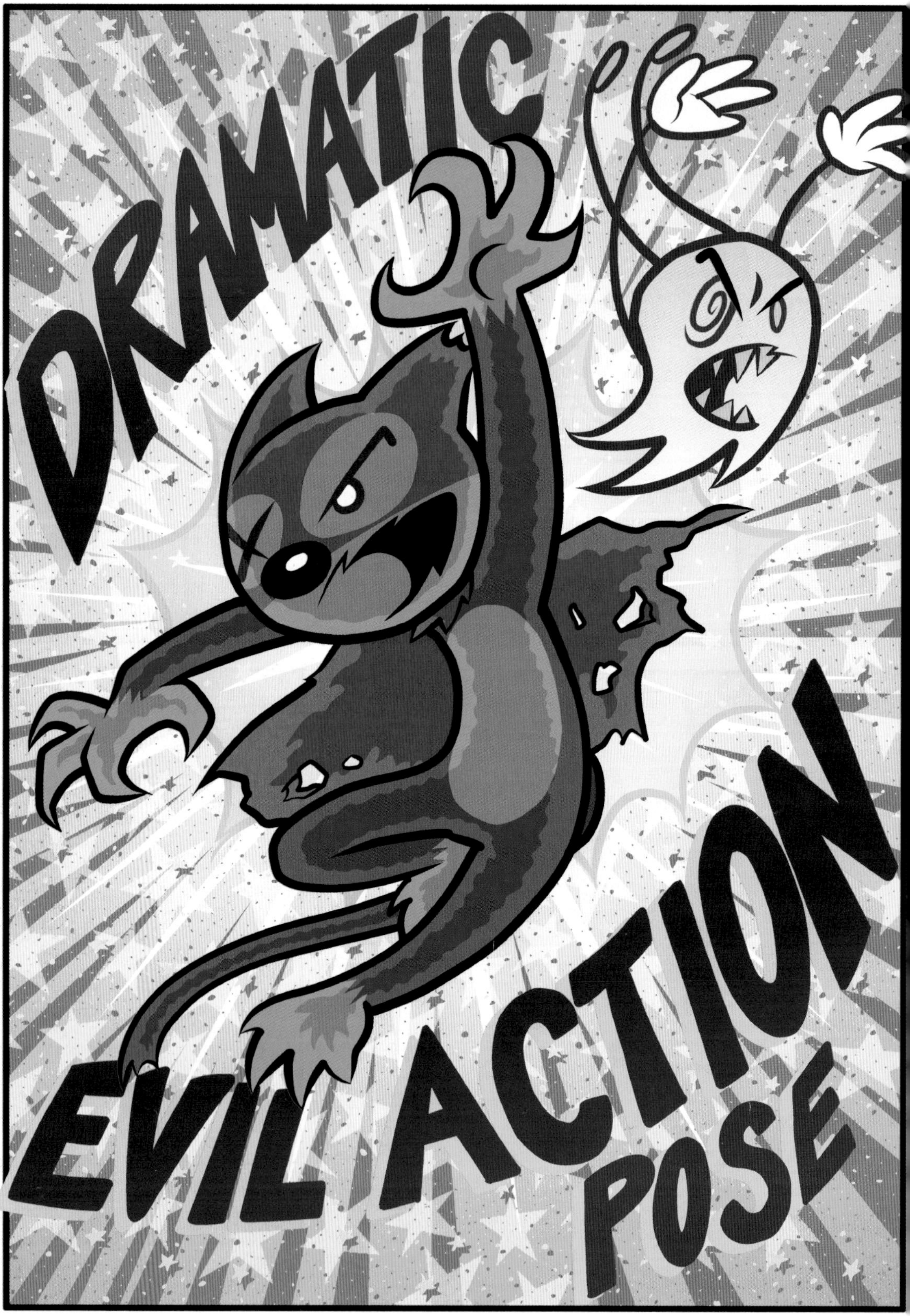
DRAMATIC
EVIL ACTION
POSE

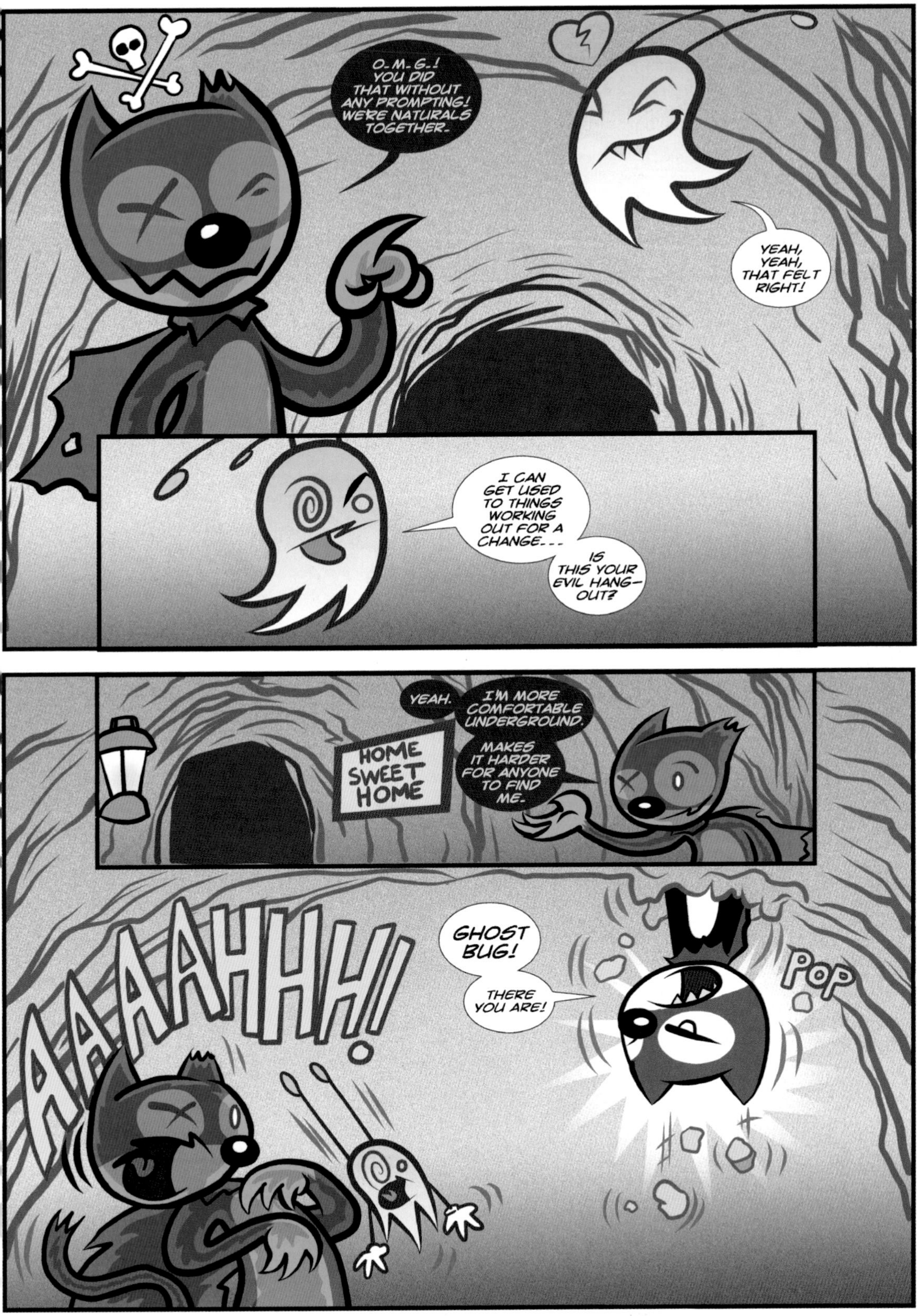
O.M.G.! YOU DID THAT WITHOUT ANY PROMPTING! WE'RE NATURALS TOGETHER.
YEAH, YEAH, THAT FELT RIGHT!
I CAN GET USED TO THINGS WORKING OUT FOR A CHANGE...
IS THIS YOUR EVIL HANG-OUT?
YEAH.
I'M MORE COMFORTABLE UNDERGROUND.
MAKES IT HARDER FOR ANYONE TO FIND ME.
HOME SWEET HOME
AAAAHHH!
GHOST BUG!
THERE YOU ARE!
POP

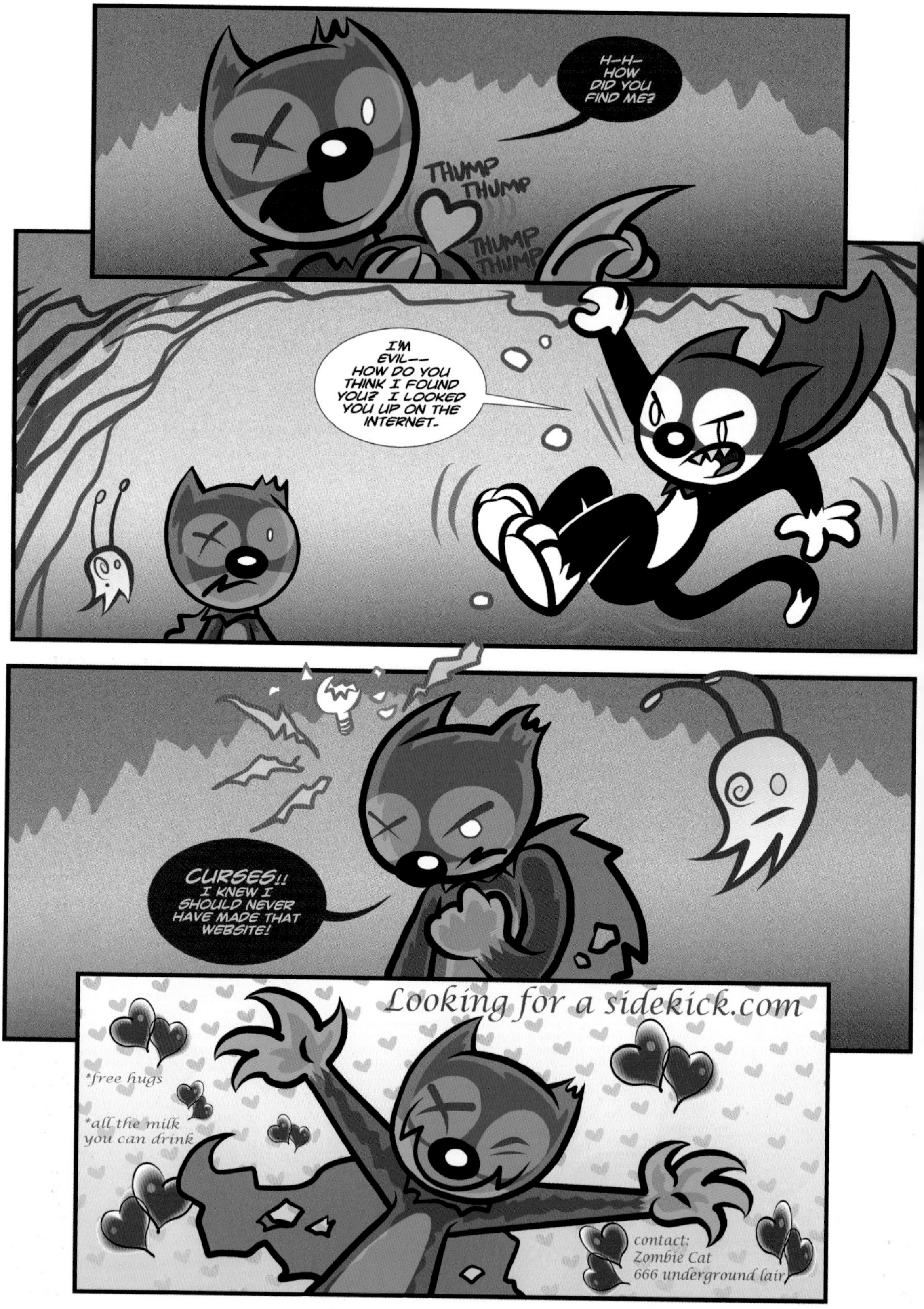
H-H-HOW DID YOU FIND ME?
THUMP THUMP
THUMP THUMP
I'M EVIL-- HOW DO YOU THINK I FOUND YOU? I LOOKED YOU UP ON THE INTERNET.
CURSES!! I KNEW I SHOULD NEVER HAVE MADE THAT WEBSITE!
Looking for a sidekick.com
*free hugs
*all the milk you can drink
contact:
Zombie Cat
666 underground lair

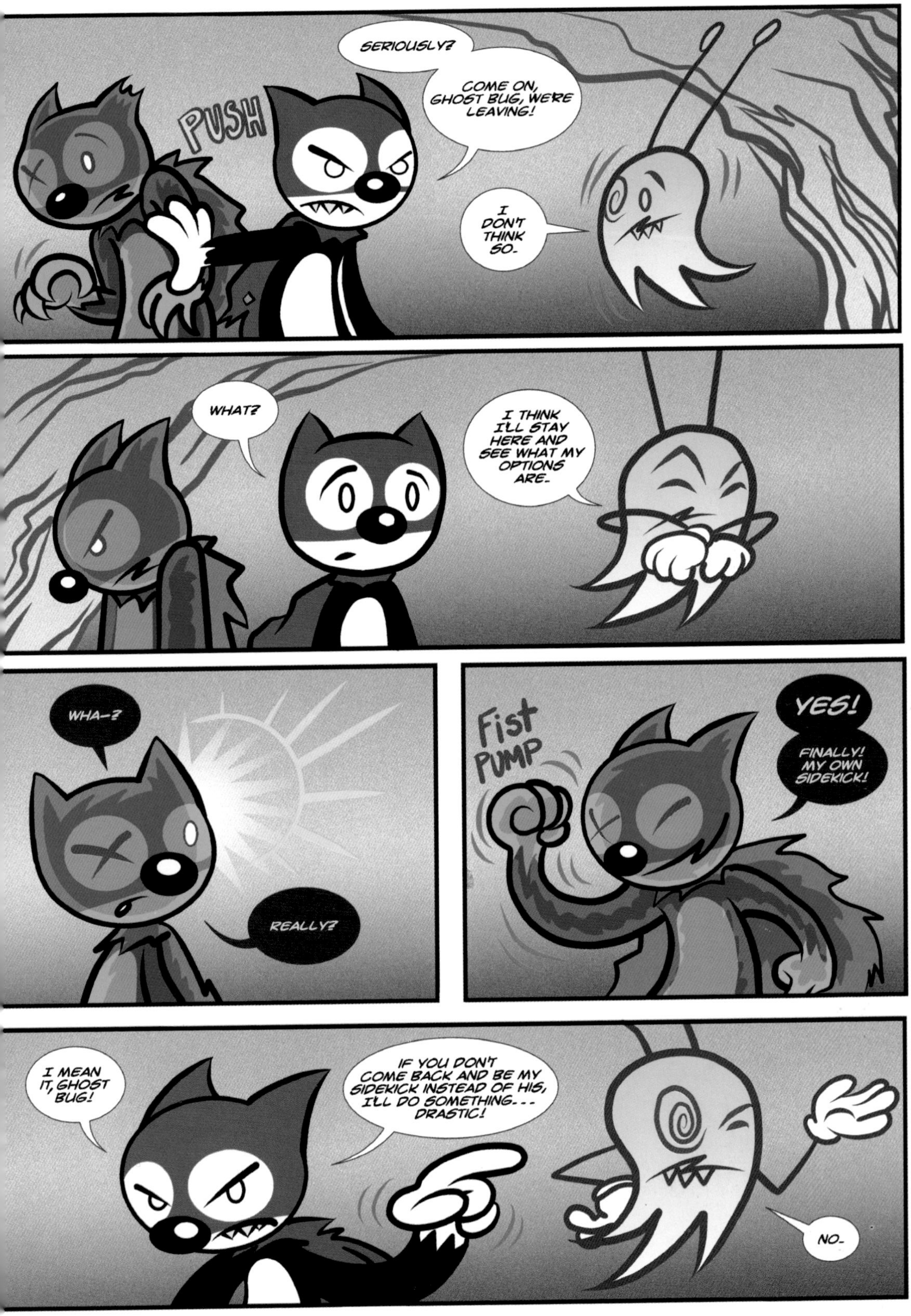
SERIOUSLY?
COME ON, GHOST BUG, WE'RE LEAVING!
PUSH
I DON'T THINK SO.
WHAT?
I THINK I'LL STAY HERE AND SEE WHAT MY OPTIONS ARE.
WHA--?
REALLY?
Fist PUMP
YES!
FINALLY! MY OWN SIDEKICK!
I MEAN IT, GHOST BUG!
IF YOU DON'T COME BACK AND BE MY SIDEKICK INSTEAD OF HIS, I'LL DO SOMETHING... DRASTIC!
NO.

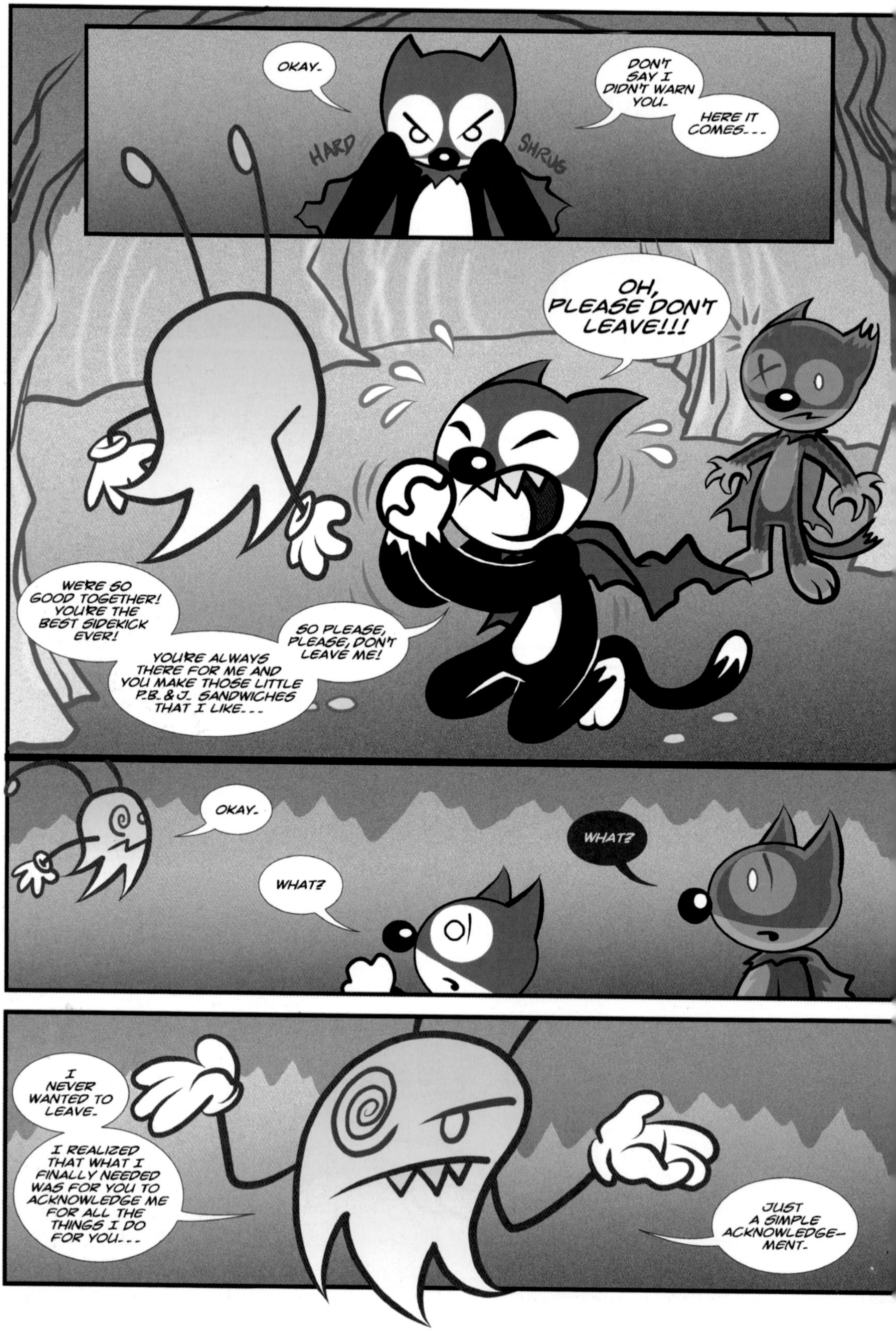
OKAY.
HARD
SHRUG
DON'T SAY I DIDN'T WARN YOU.
HERE IT COMES...
OH, PLEASE DON'T LEAVE!!!
WE'RE SO GOOD TOGETHER! YOU'RE THE BEST SIDEKICK EVER!
YOU'RE ALWAYS THERE FOR ME AND YOU MAKE THOSE LITTLE P.B. & J. SANDWICHES THAT I LIKE...
SO PLEASE, PLEASE, DON'T LEAVE ME!
OKAY.
WHAT?
WHAT?
I NEVER WANTED TO LEAVE.
I REALIZED THAT WHAT I FINALLY NEEDED WAS FOR YOU TO ACKNOWLEDGE ME FOR ALL THE THINGS I DO FOR YOU...
JUST A SIMPLE ACKNOWLEDGE-MENT.

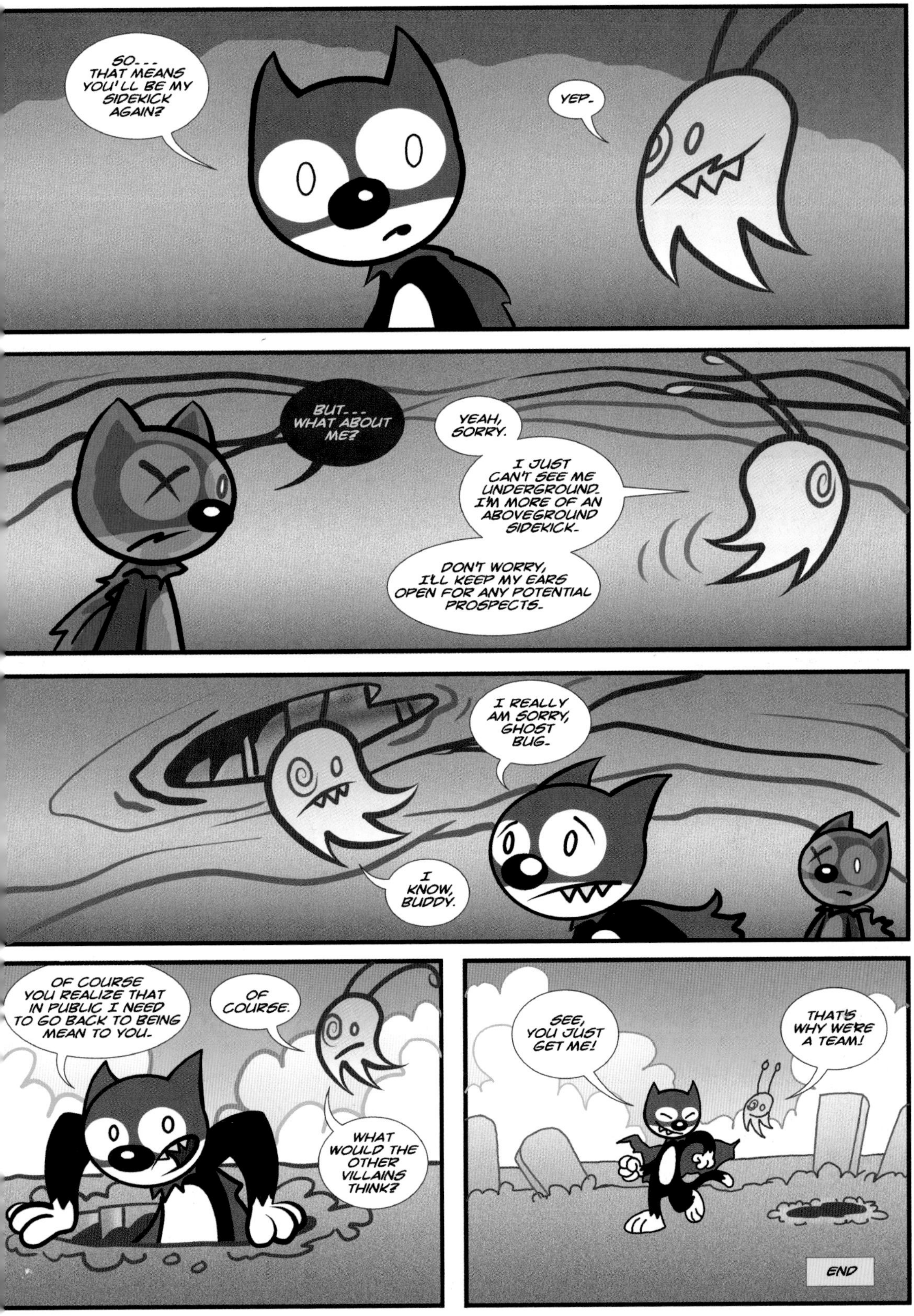
SO... THAT MEANS YOU'LL BE MY SIDEKICK AGAIN?
YEP.
BUT... WHAT ABOUT ME?
YEAH, SORRY.
I JUST CAN'T SEE ME UNDERGROUND. I'M MORE OF AN ABOVEGROUND SIDEKICK.
DON'T WORRY, I'LL KEEP MY EARS OPEN FOR ANY POTENTIAL PROSPECTS.
I REALLY AM SORRY, GHOST BUG.
I KNOW, BUDDY.
OF COURSE YOU REALIZE THAT IN PUBLIC I NEED TO GO BACK TO BEING MEAN TO YOU.
OF COURSE.
WHAT WOULD THE OTHER VILLAINS THINK?
SEE, YOU JUST GET ME!
THAT'S WHY WE'RE A TEAM!
END

ACTION CAT in: HEY TROUBLE! by: SCOOT

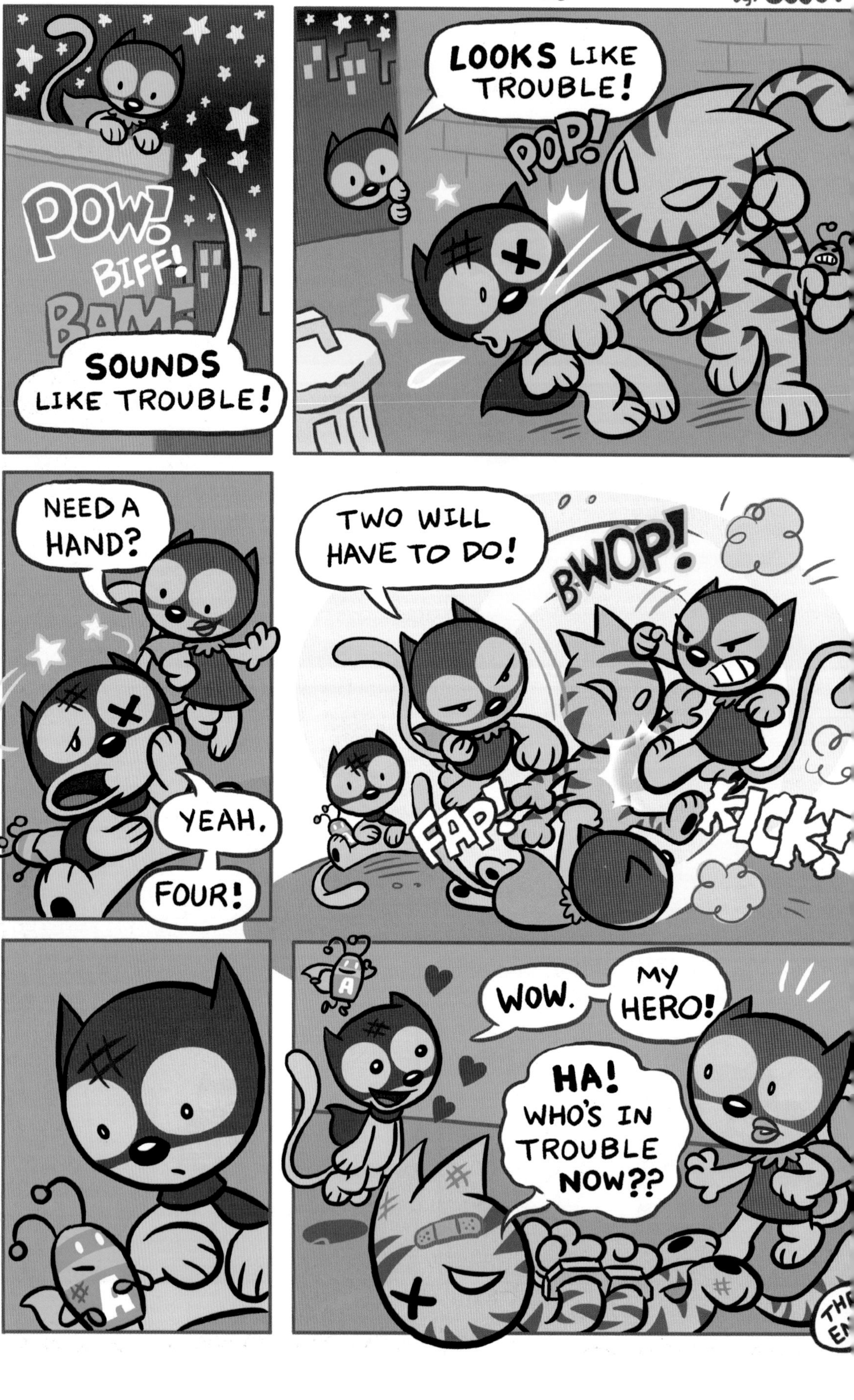
POW!
BIFF!
BAM!
SOUNDS LIKE TROUBLE!
LOOKS LIKE TROUBLE!
POP!
NEED A HAND?
YEAH.
FOUR!
TWO WILL HAVE TO DO!
BWOP!
FAP!
KICK!
WOW.
MY HERO!
HA! WHO'S IN TROUBLE NOW??

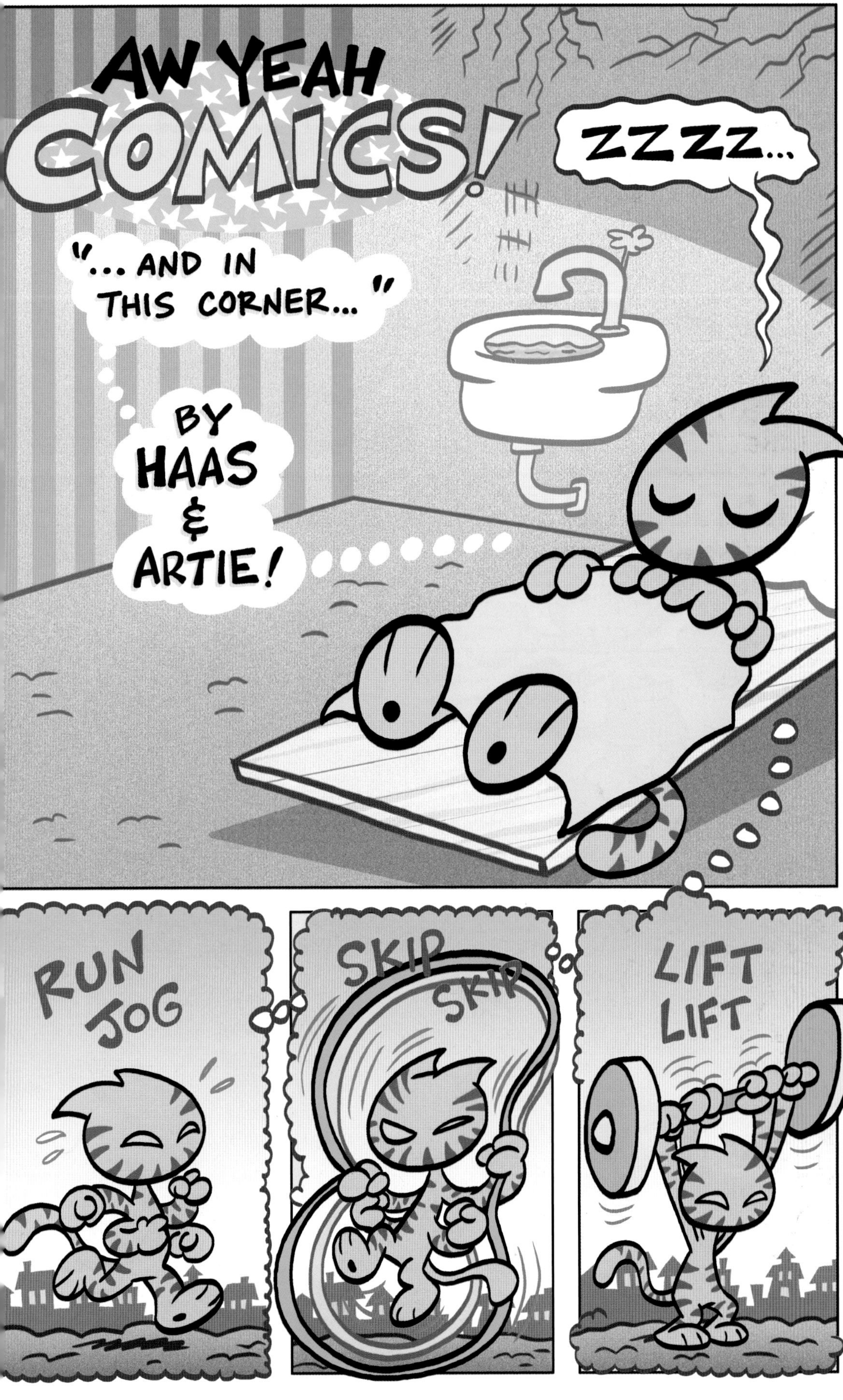
AW YEAH COMICS!
ZZZZ...
"... AND IN THIS CORNER..."
BY HAAS & ARTIE!
RUN
JOG
SKIP
SKIP
LIFT
LIFT

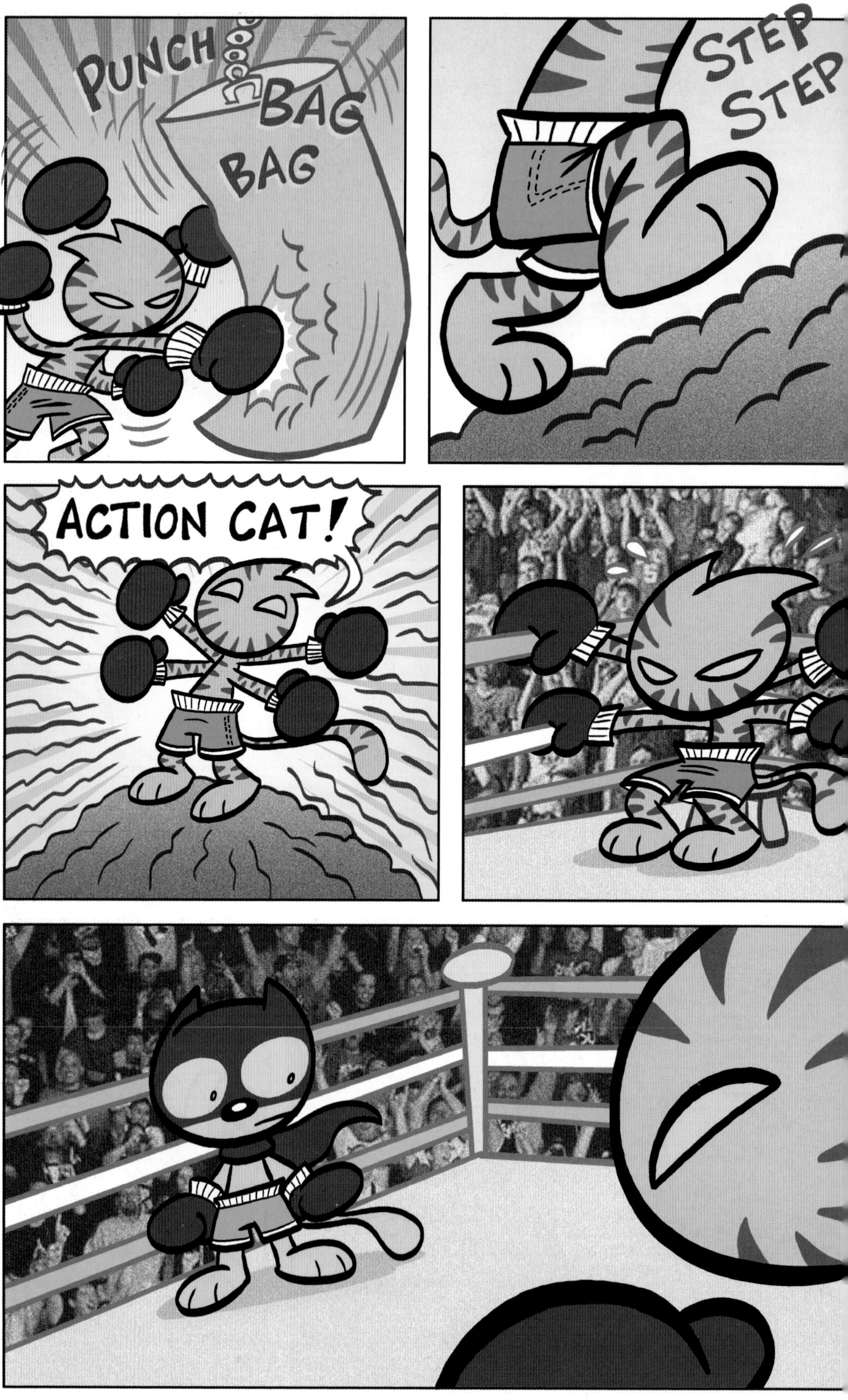
PUNCH
BAG
BAG
STEP
STEP
ACTION CAT!

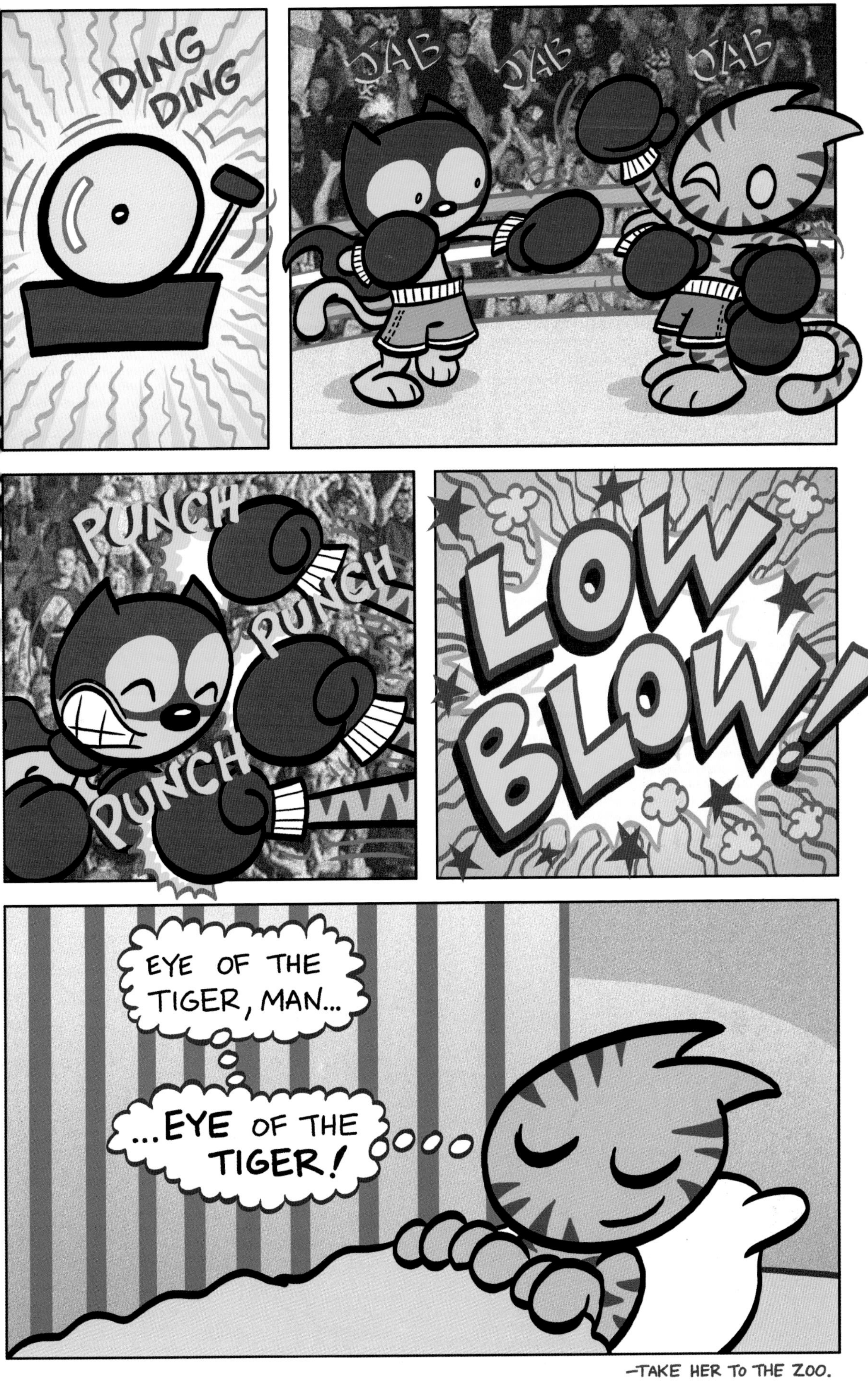
DING
DING
JAB
JAB
JAB
PUNCH
PUNCH
PUNCH
LOW BLOW!
EYE OF THE TIGER, MAN...
...EYE OF THE TIGER!

—TAKE HER TO THE ZOO.

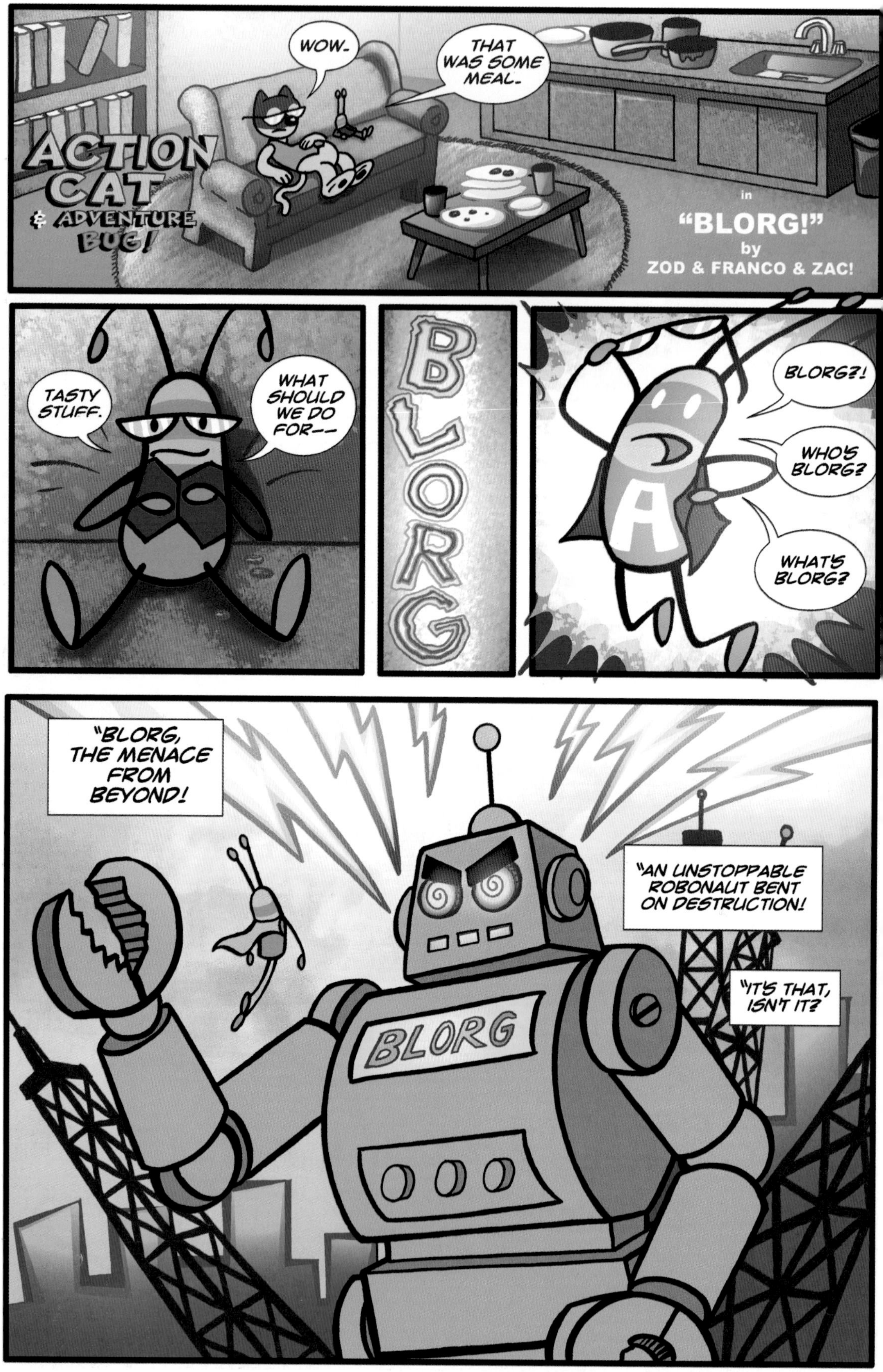
ACTION CAT & ADVENTURE BUG!
WOW.
THAT WAS SOME MEAL.
in
"BLORG!"
by
ZOD & FRANCO & ZAC!
TASTY STUFF.
WHAT SHOULD WE DO FOR--
BLORG
BLORG?!
WHO'S BLORG?
WHAT'S BLORG?
"BLORG, THE MENACE FROM BEYOND!
"AN UNSTOPPABLE ROBONAUT BENT ON DESTRUCTION!
"IT'S THAT, ISN'T IT?
BLORG

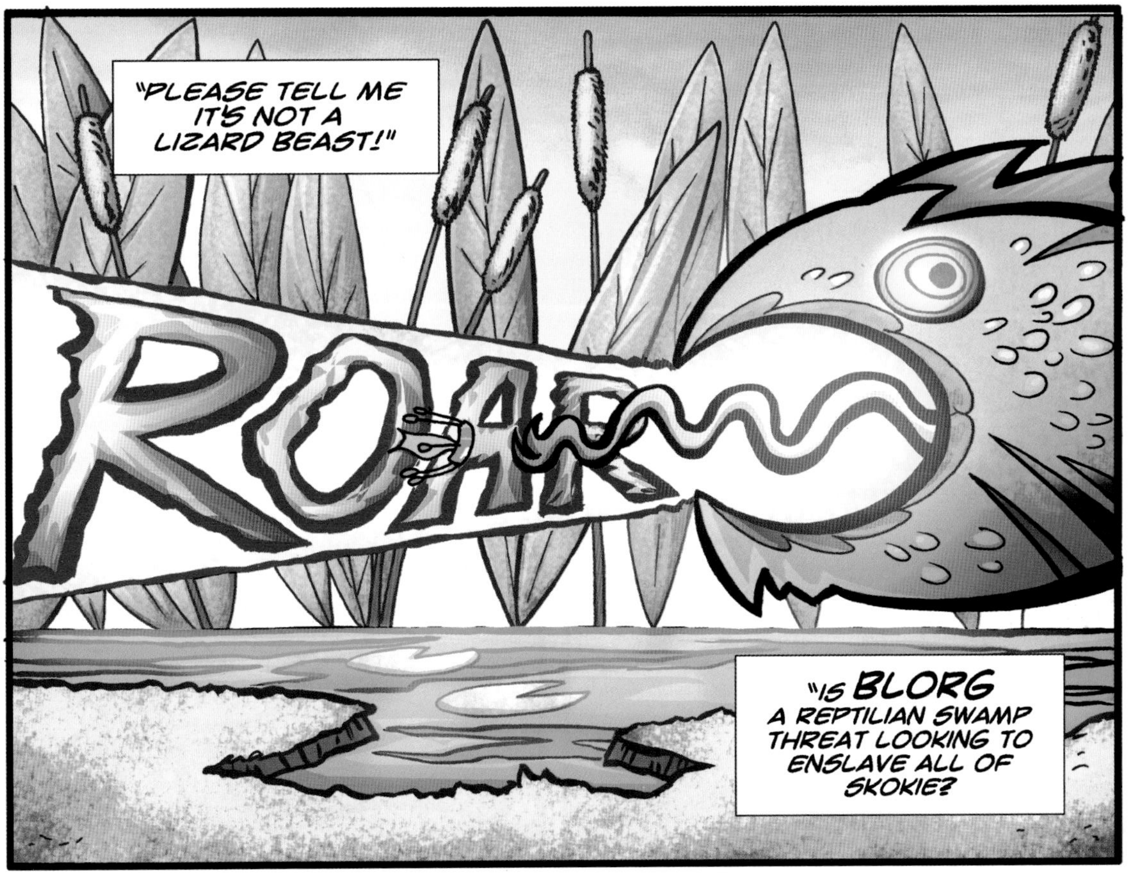
"PLEASE TELL ME IT'S NOT A LIZARD BEAST!"
ROAR
"IS BLORG A REPTILIAN SWAMP THREAT LOOKING TO ENSLAVE ALL OF SKOKIE?

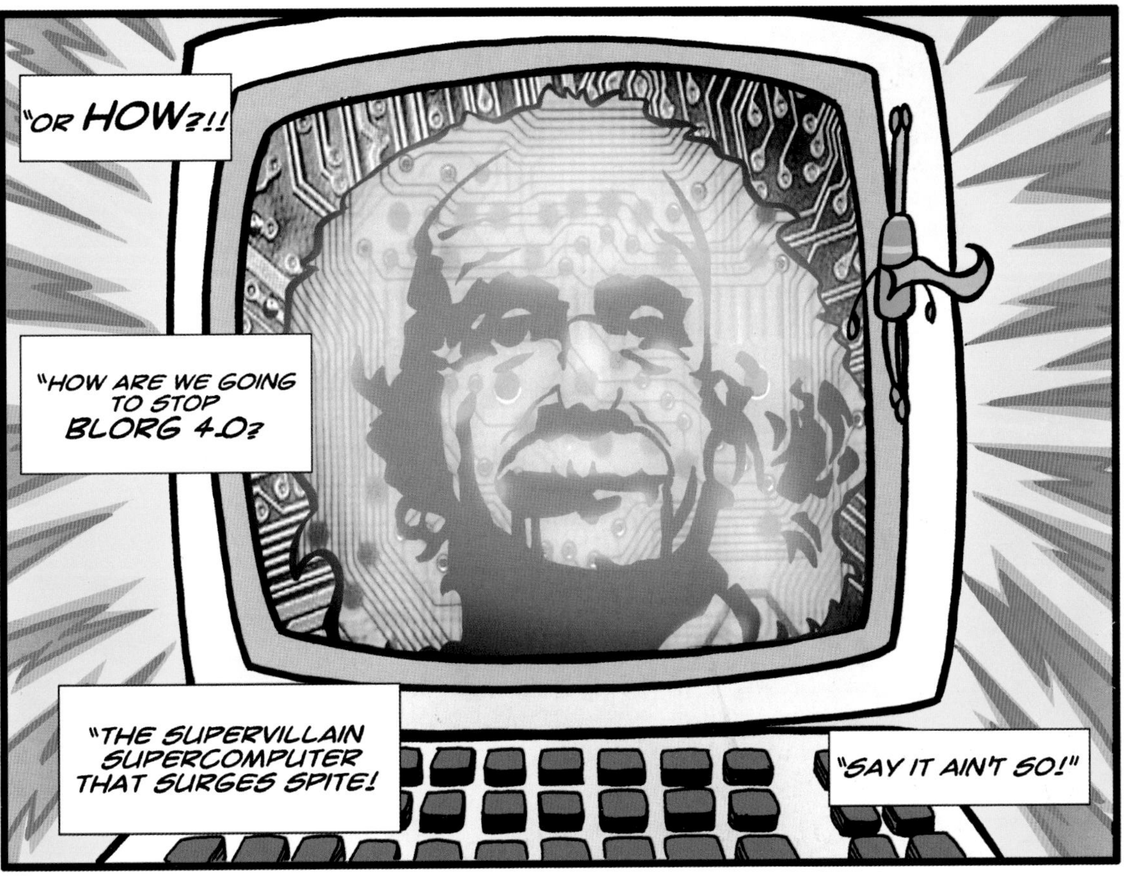
"OR HOW?!!
"HOW ARE WE GOING TO STOP BLORG 4.0?
"THE SUPERVILLAIN SUPERCOMPUTER THAT SURGES SPITE!
"SAY IT AIN'T SO!"

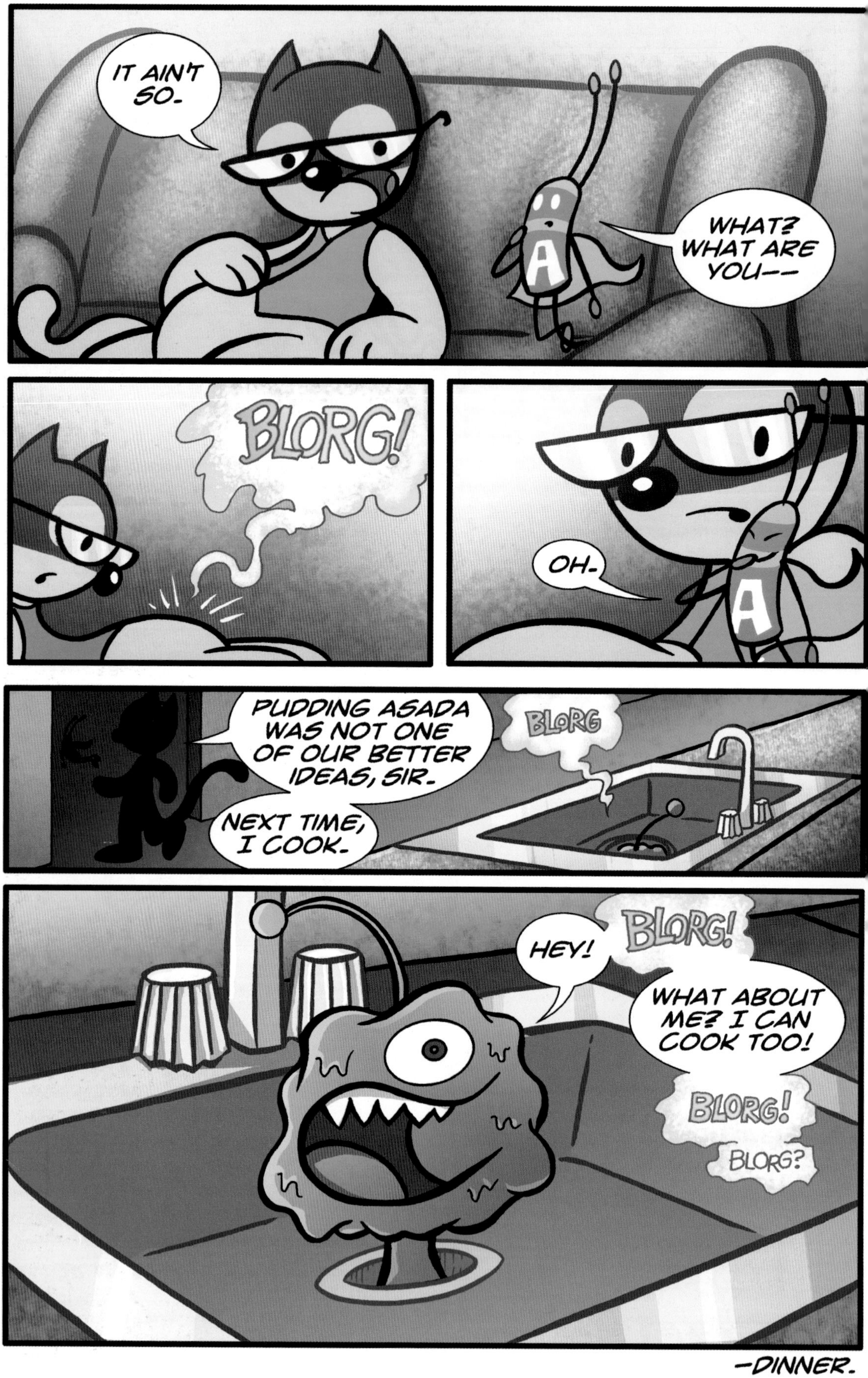
IT AIN'T SO.
WHAT? WHAT ARE YOU--
BLORG!
OH.
PUDDING ASADA WAS NOT ONE OF OUR BETTER IDEAS, SIR.
NEXT TIME, I COOK.
BLORG
HEY!
BLORG!
WHAT ABOUT ME? I CAN COOK TOO!
BLORG!
BLORG?

-DINNER.

AW YEAH FUNNIES

BY DENVER BRUBAKER

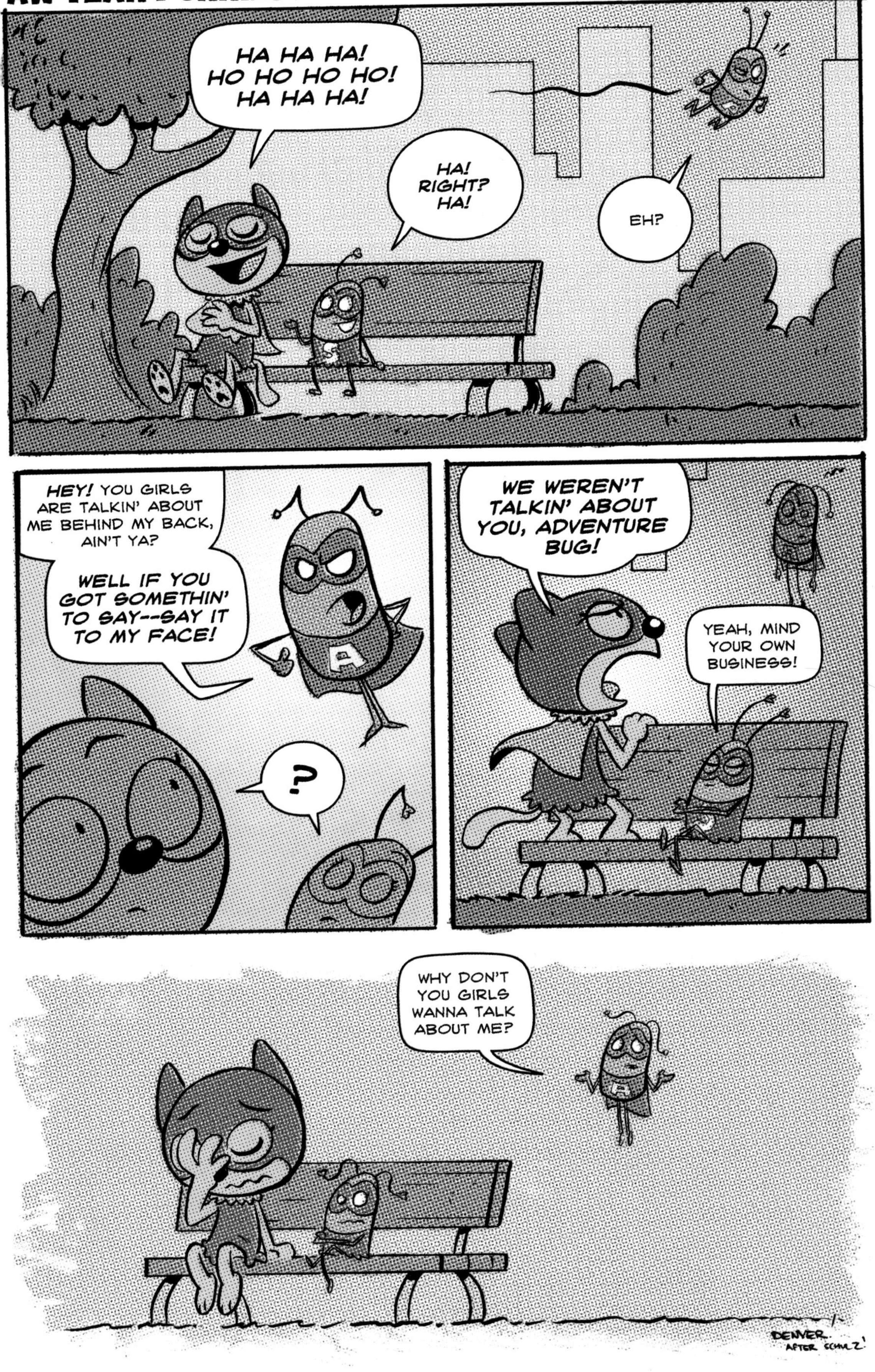

HA HA HA! HO HO HO HO! HA HA HA!
HA! RIGHT? HA!
EH?
HEY! YOU GIRLS ARE TALKIN' ABOUT ME BEHIND MY BACK, AIN'T YA?
WELL IF YOU GOT SOMETHIN' TO SAY--SAY IT TO MY FACE!
?
WE WEREN'T TALKIN' ABOUT YOU, ADVENTURE BUG!
YEAH, MIND YOUR OWN BUSINESS!
WHY DON'T YOU GIRLS WANNA TALK ABOUT ME?
DENVER.

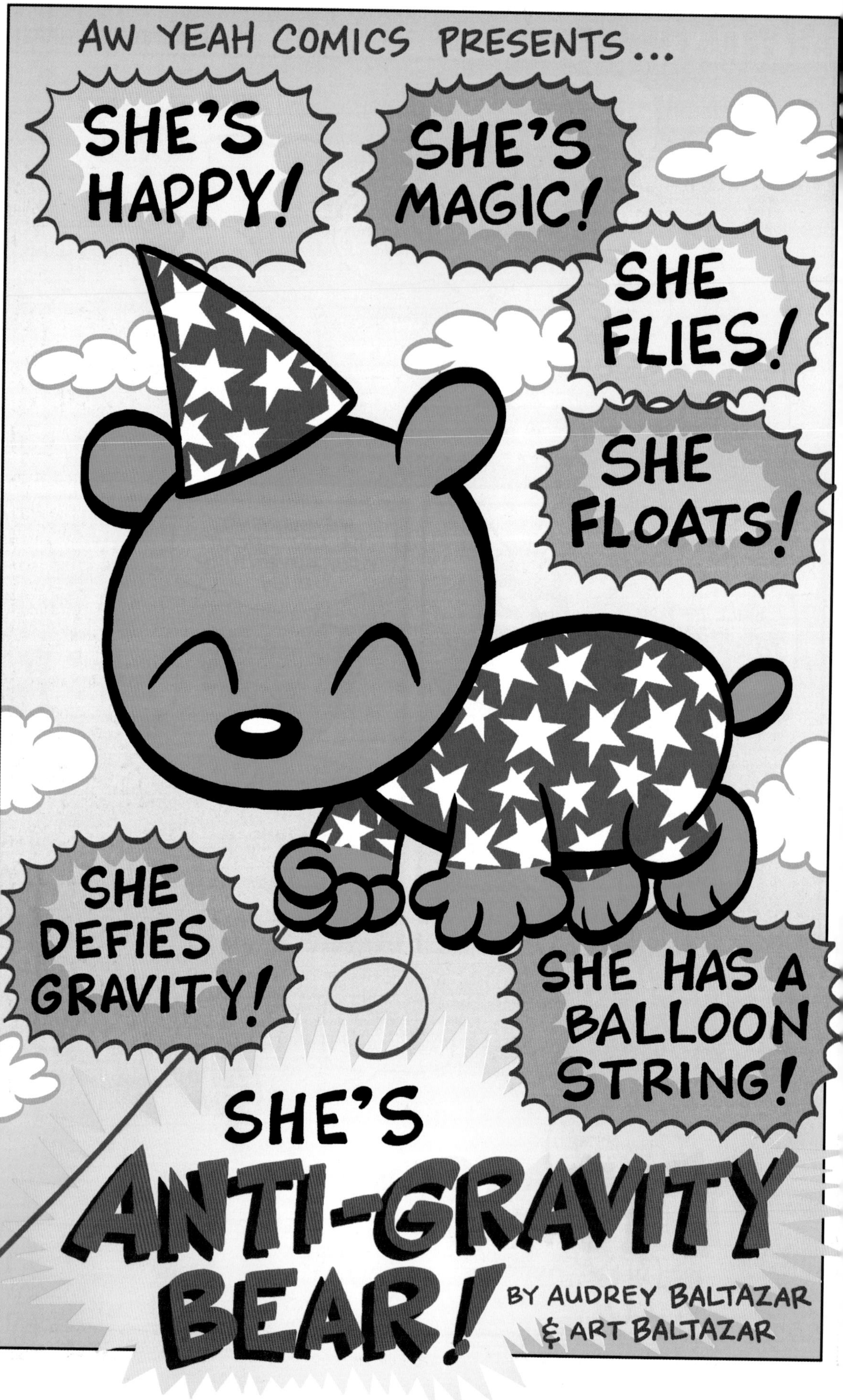
AW YEAH COMICS PRESENTS...
SHE'S HAPPY!
SHE'S MAGIC!
SHE FLIES!
SHE FLOATS!
SHE DEFIES GRAVITY!
SHE HAS A BALLOON STRING!
SHE'S
ANTI-GRAVITY BEAR!
BY AUDREY BALTAZAR & ART BALTAZAR

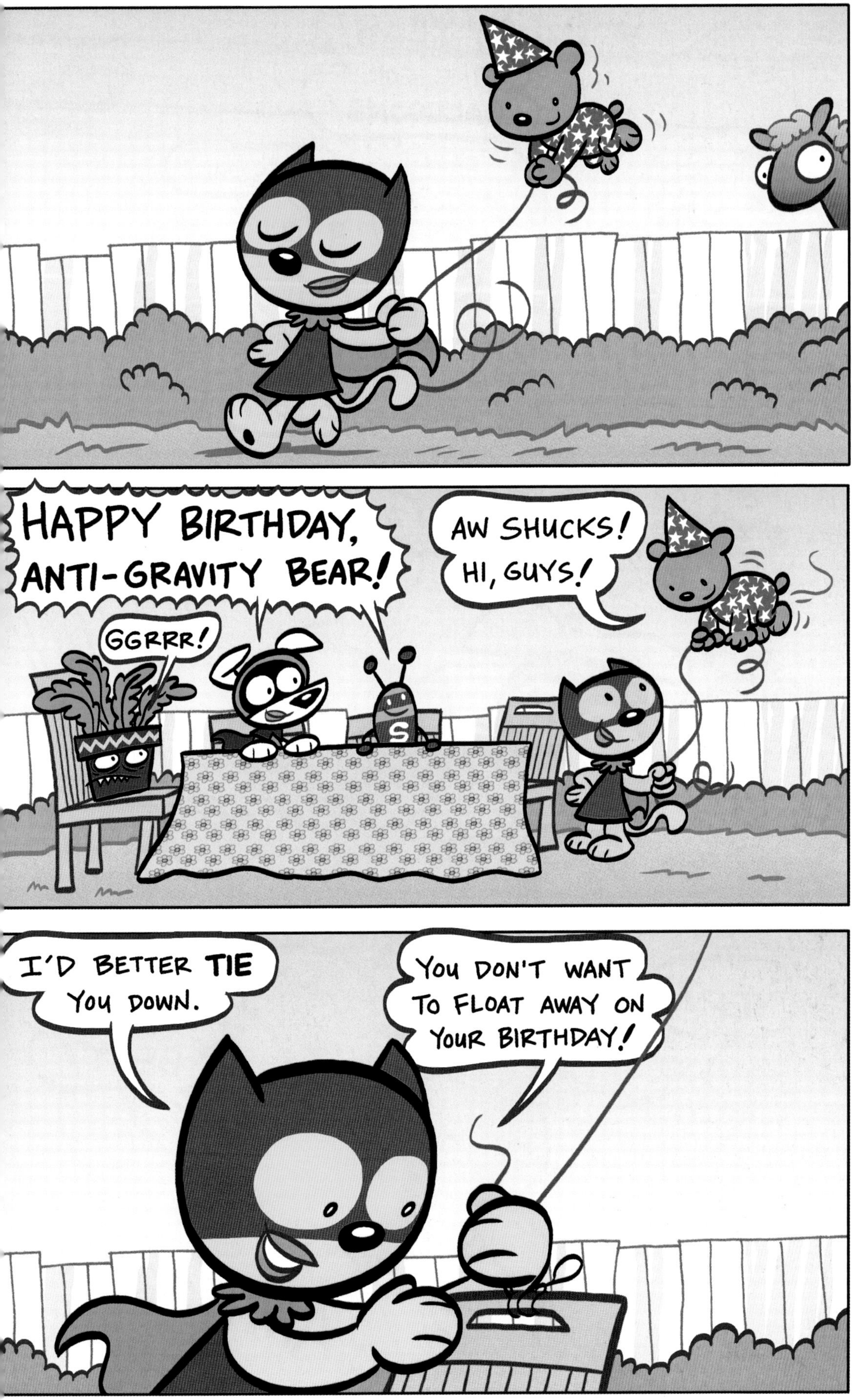
HAPPY BIRTHDAY, ANTI-GRAVITY BEAR!
AW SHUCKS! HI, GUYS!
GGRRR!
S
I'D BETTER TIE YOU DOWN.
YOU DON'T WANT TO FLOAT AWAY ON YOUR BIRTHDAY!

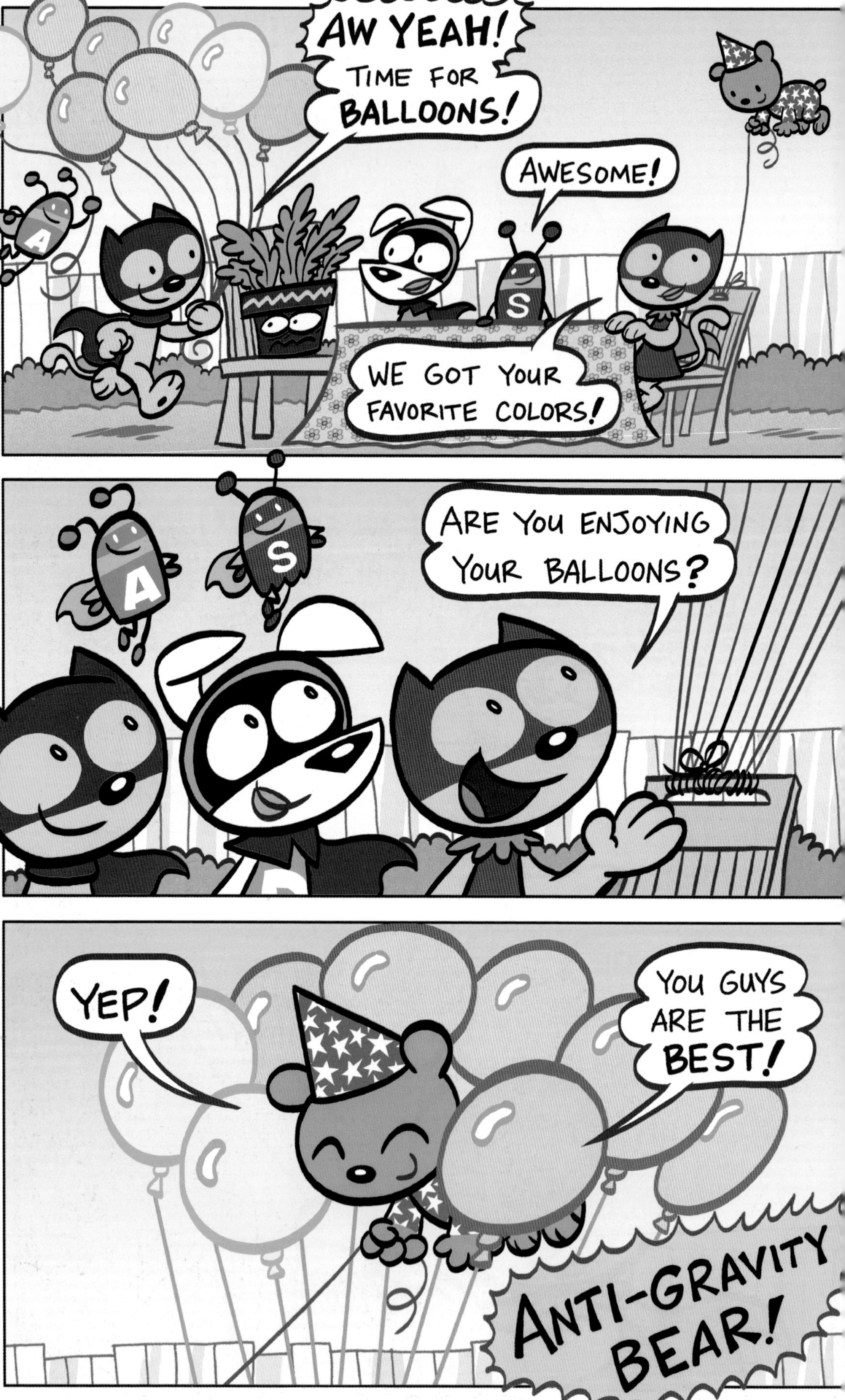
AW YEAH! TIME FOR BALLOONS!
AWESOME!
WE GOT YOUR FAVORITE COLORS!
ARE YOU ENJOYING YOUR BALLOONS?
YEP!
YOU GUYS ARE THE BEST!
ANTI-GRAVITY BEAR!

ZOMBIE CAT

STORY BY KURT WOOD

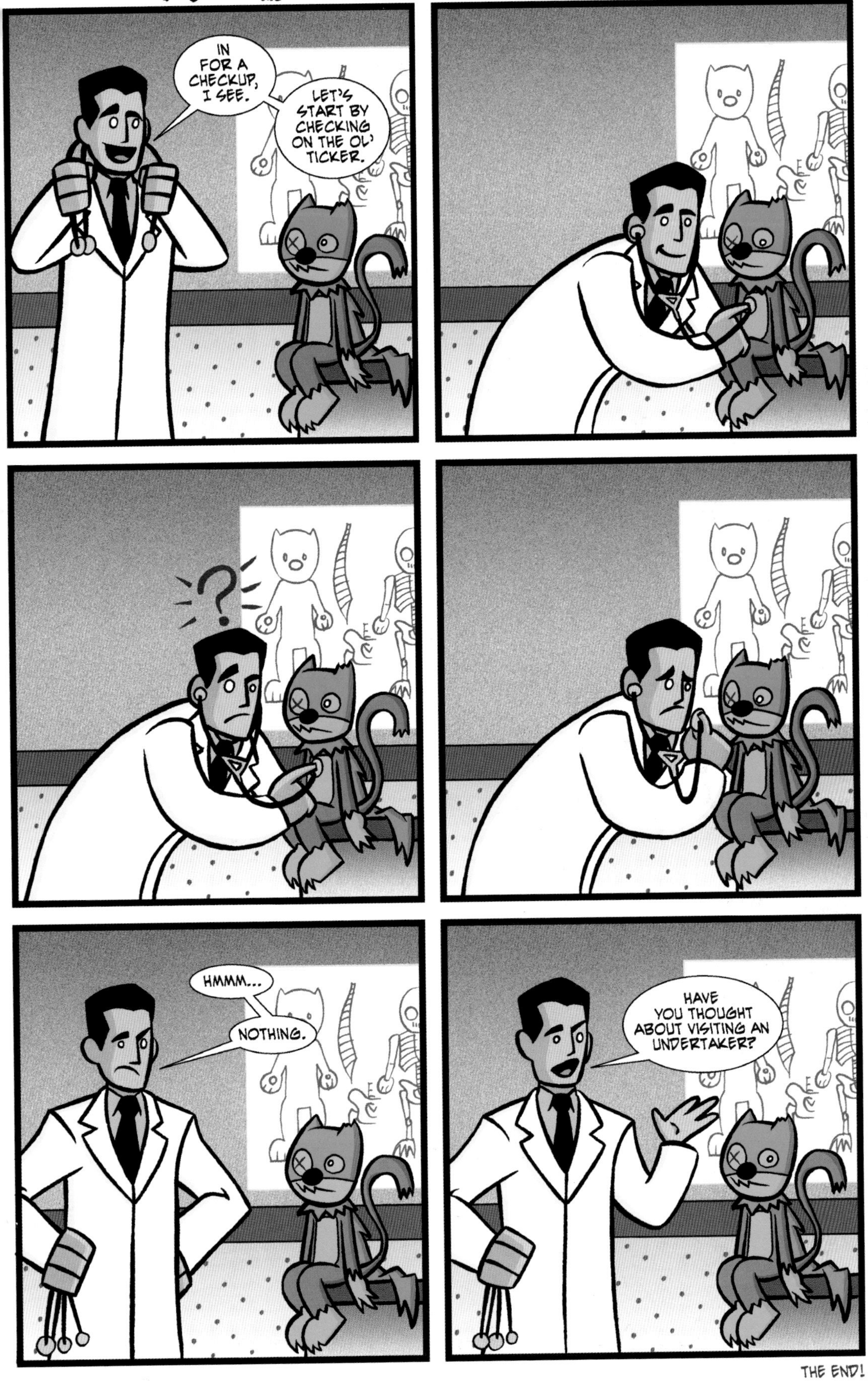
IN FOR A CHECKUP, I SEE.
LET'S START BY CHECKING ON THE OL' TICKER.
?
HMMM...
NOTHING.
HAVE YOU THOUGHT ABOUT VISITING AN UNDERTAKER?

THE END!

MAGMA BUSINESS

Story: Chad Derdowski Art: Scoot McMahon

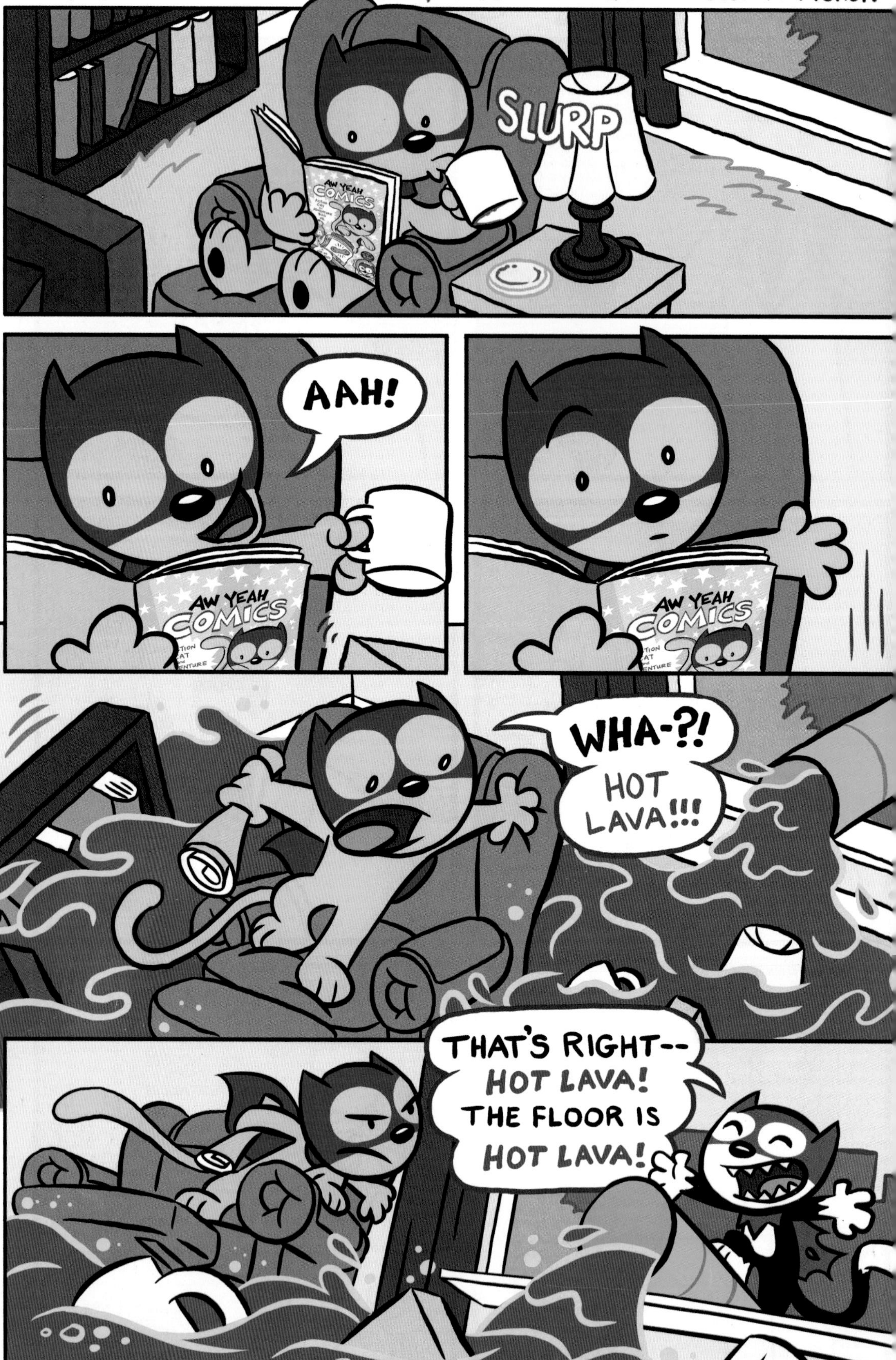
SLURP
AW YEAH COMICS
AAH!
AW YEAH COMICS
WHA-?!
HOT LAVA!!!
THAT'S RIGHT--
HOT LAVA!
THE FLOOR IS
HOT LAVA!

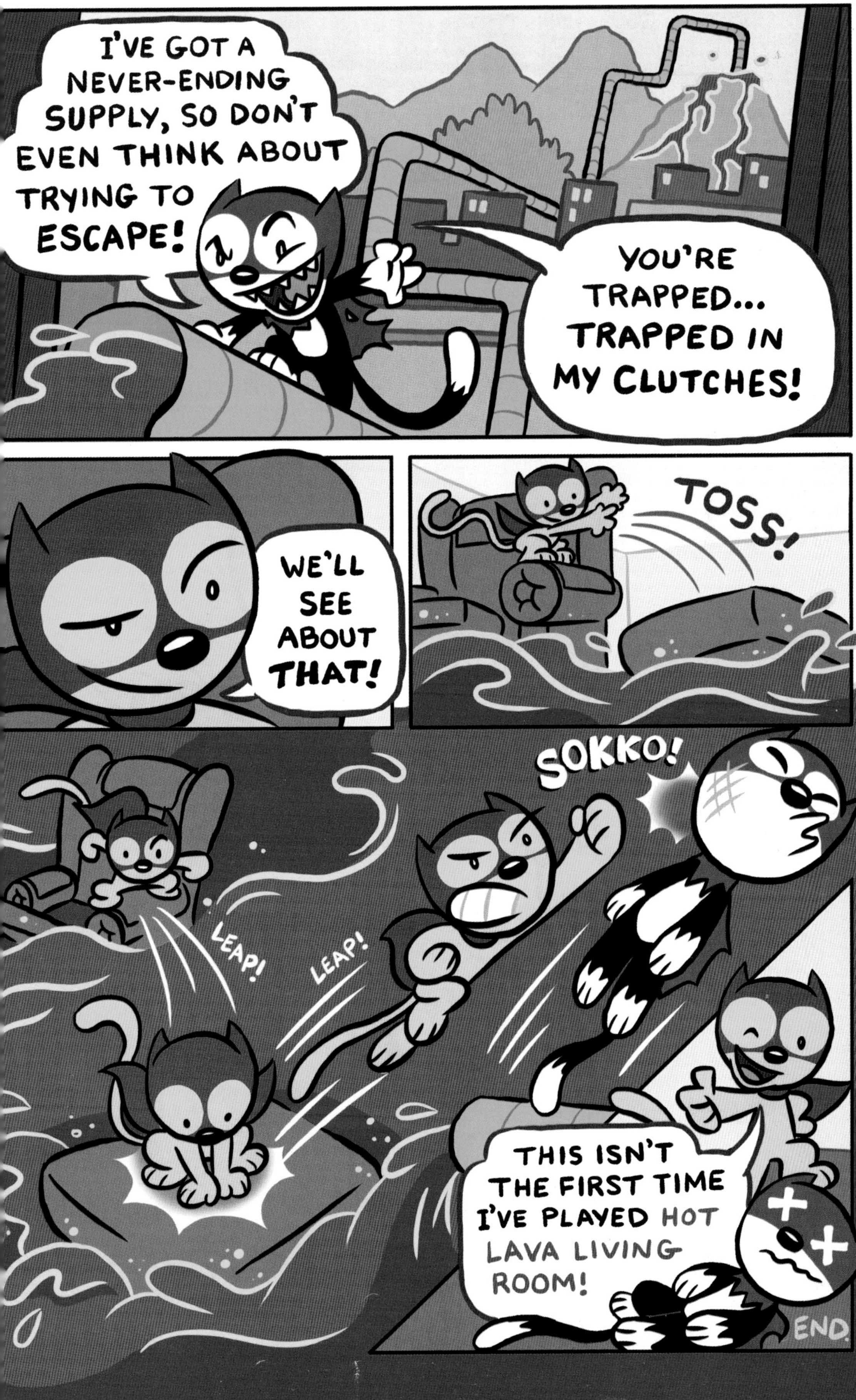

I'VE GOT A NEVER-ENDING SUPPLY, SO DON'T EVEN THINK ABOUT TRYING TO ESCAPE!
YOU'RE TRAPPED... TRAPPED IN MY CLUTCHES!
WE'LL SEE ABOUT THAT!
TOSS!
LEAP!
LEAP!
SOKKO!
THIS ISN'T THE FIRST TIME I'VE PLAYED HOT LAVA LIVING ROOM!
END.

AW YEAH COMICS! PRESENTS...

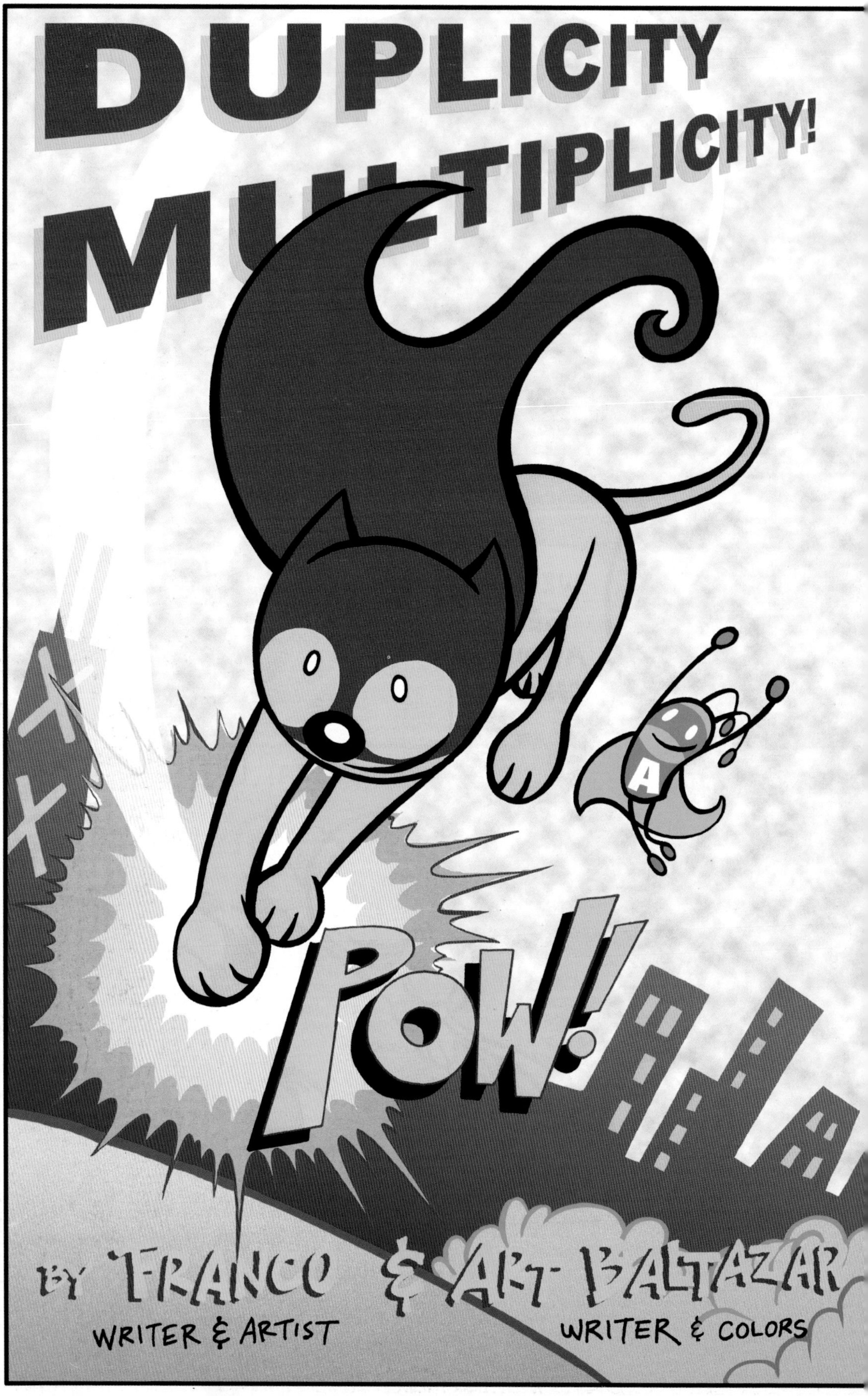

DUPLICITY
MULTIPLICITY!
A
POW!
BY FRANCO & ART BALTAZAR
WRITER & ARTIST
WRITER & COLORS

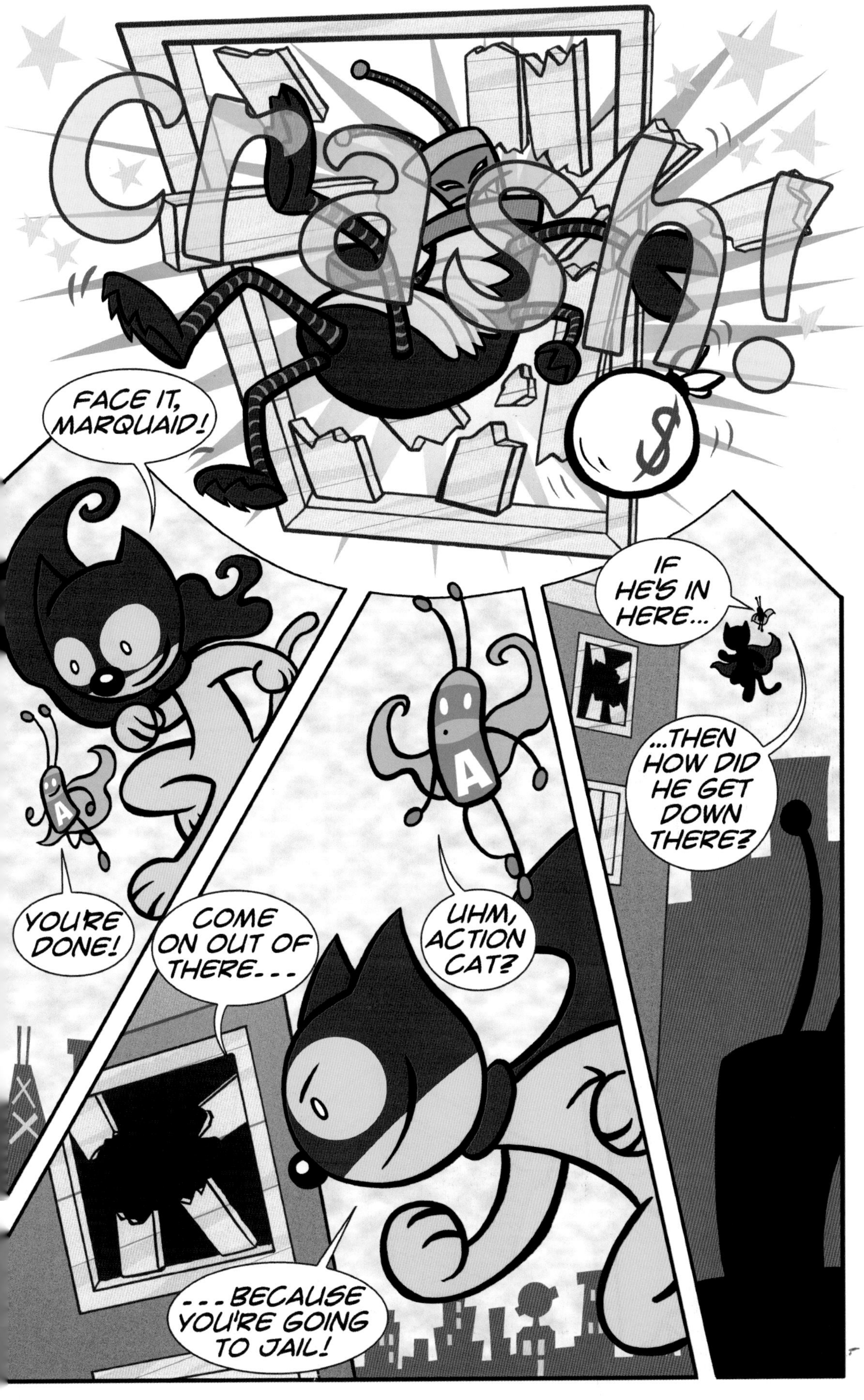
Crash!
FACE IT, MARQUAID!
YOU'RE DONE!
COME ON OUT OF THERE...
...BECAUSE YOU'RE GOING TO JAIL!
UHM, ACTION CAT?
IF HE'S IN HERE...
...THEN HOW DID HE GET DOWN THERE?

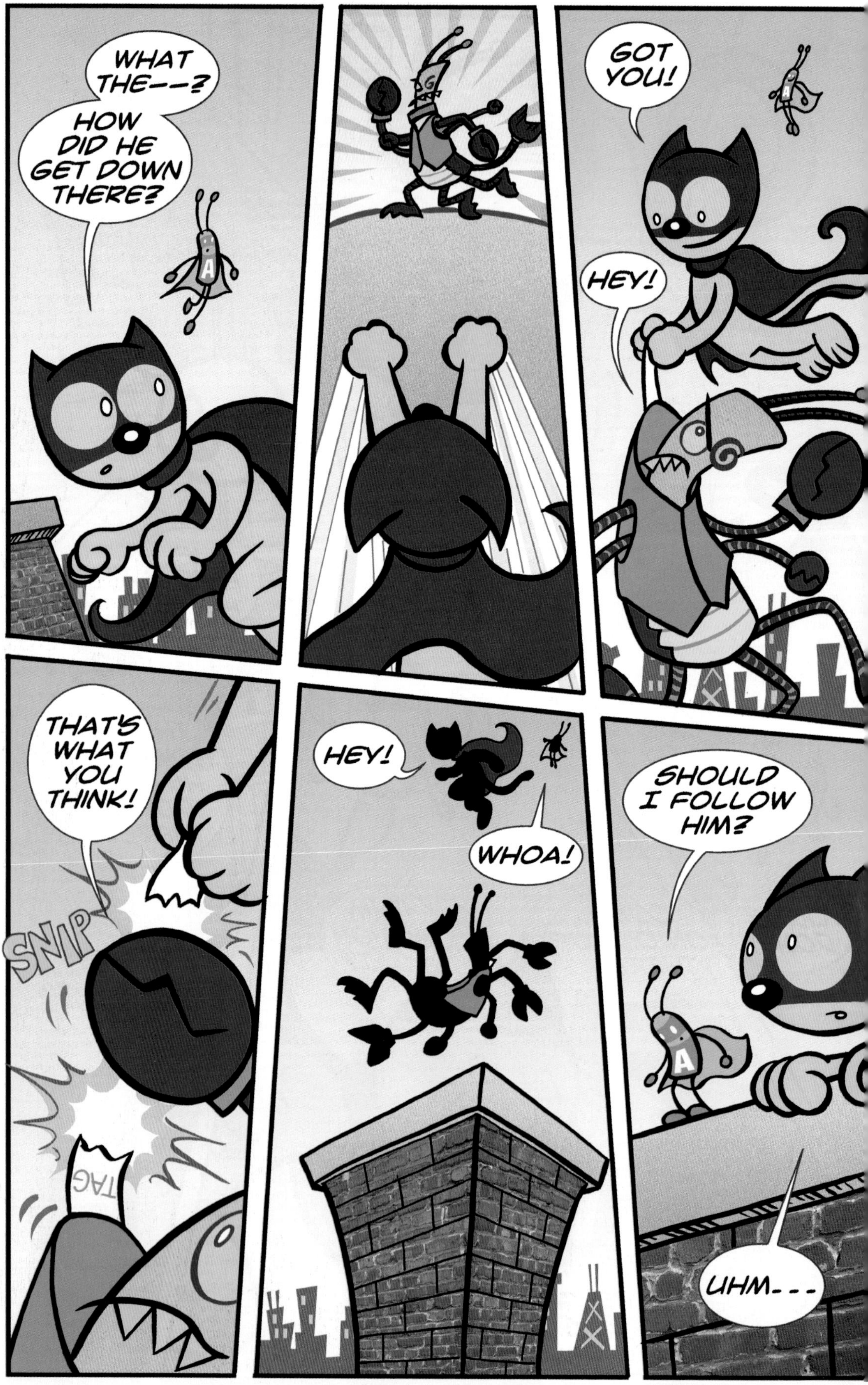

WHAT THE--?
HOW DID HE GET DOWN THERE?
GOT YOU!
HEY!
THAT'S WHAT YOU THINK!
SNIP
TAG
HEY!
WHOA!
SHOULD I FOLLOW HIM?
UHM---

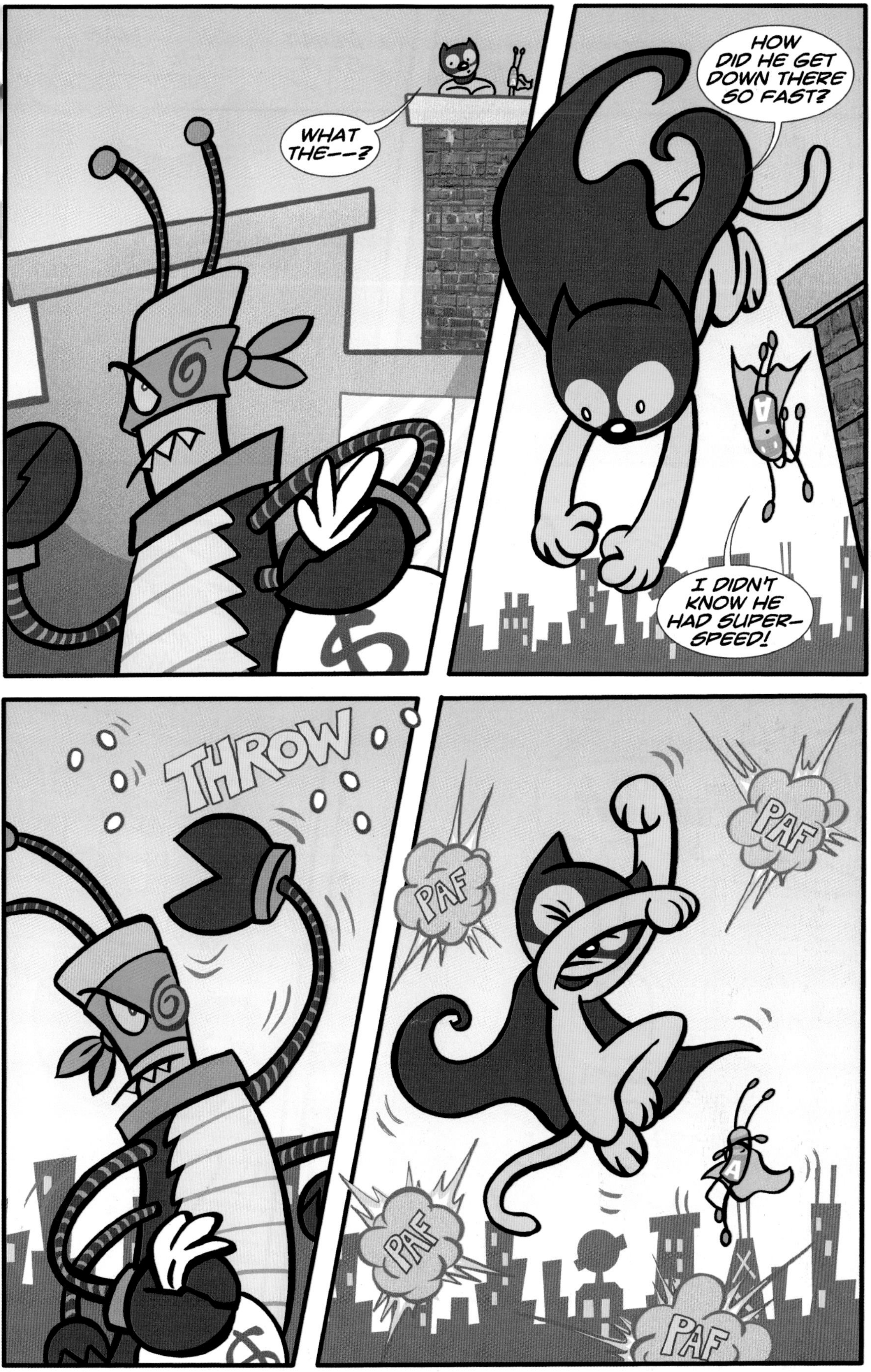
WHAT THE--?
HOW DID HE GET DOWN THERE SO FAST?
I DIDN'T KNOW HE HAD SUPER-SPEED!
THROW
PAF
PAF
PAF
PAF

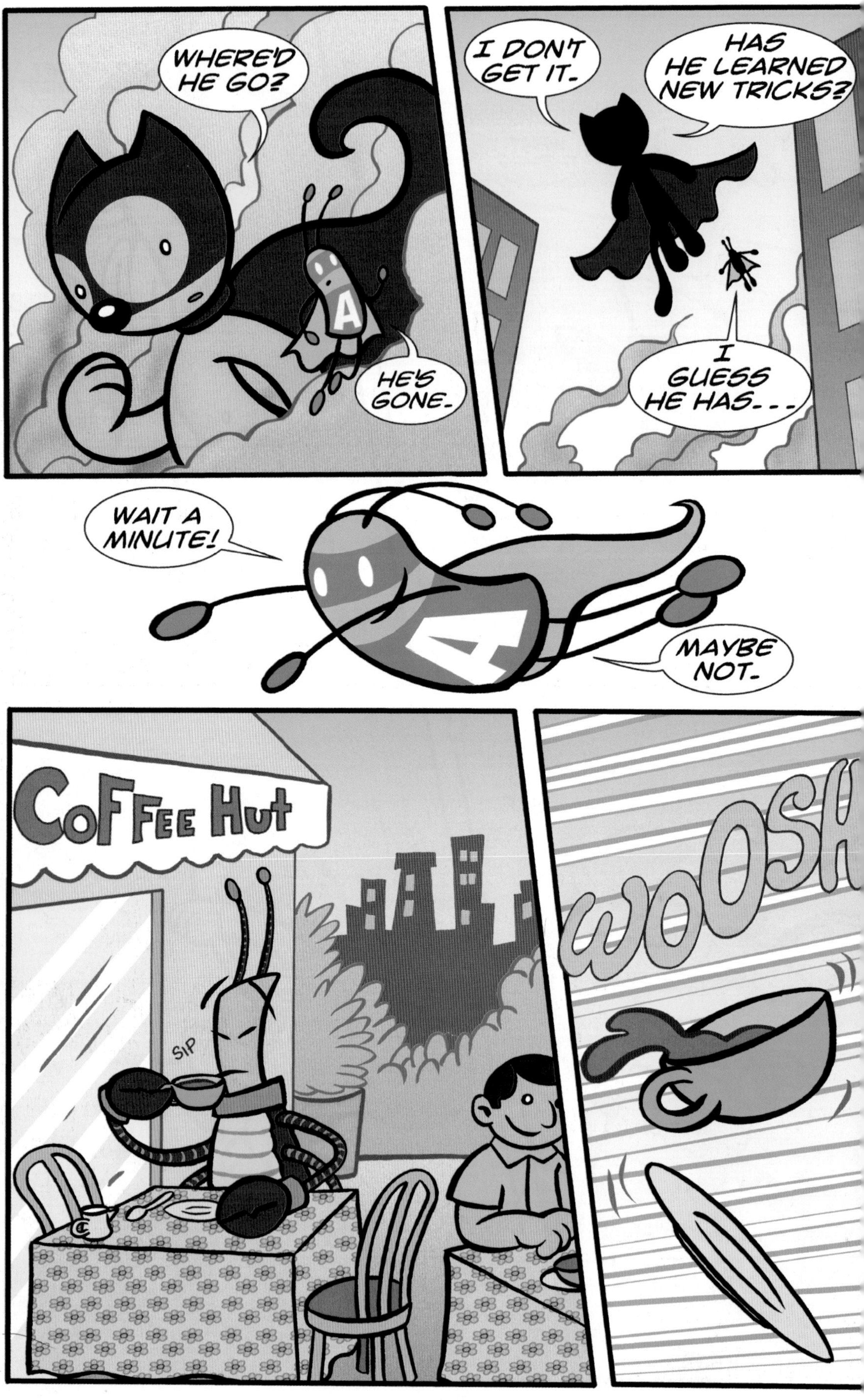
WHERE'D HE GO?
HE'S GONE.
I DON'T GET IT.
HAS HE LEARNED NEW TRICKS?
I GUESS HE HAS...
WAIT A MINUTE!
MAYBE NOT.
COFFEE HUT
SIP
WOOSH

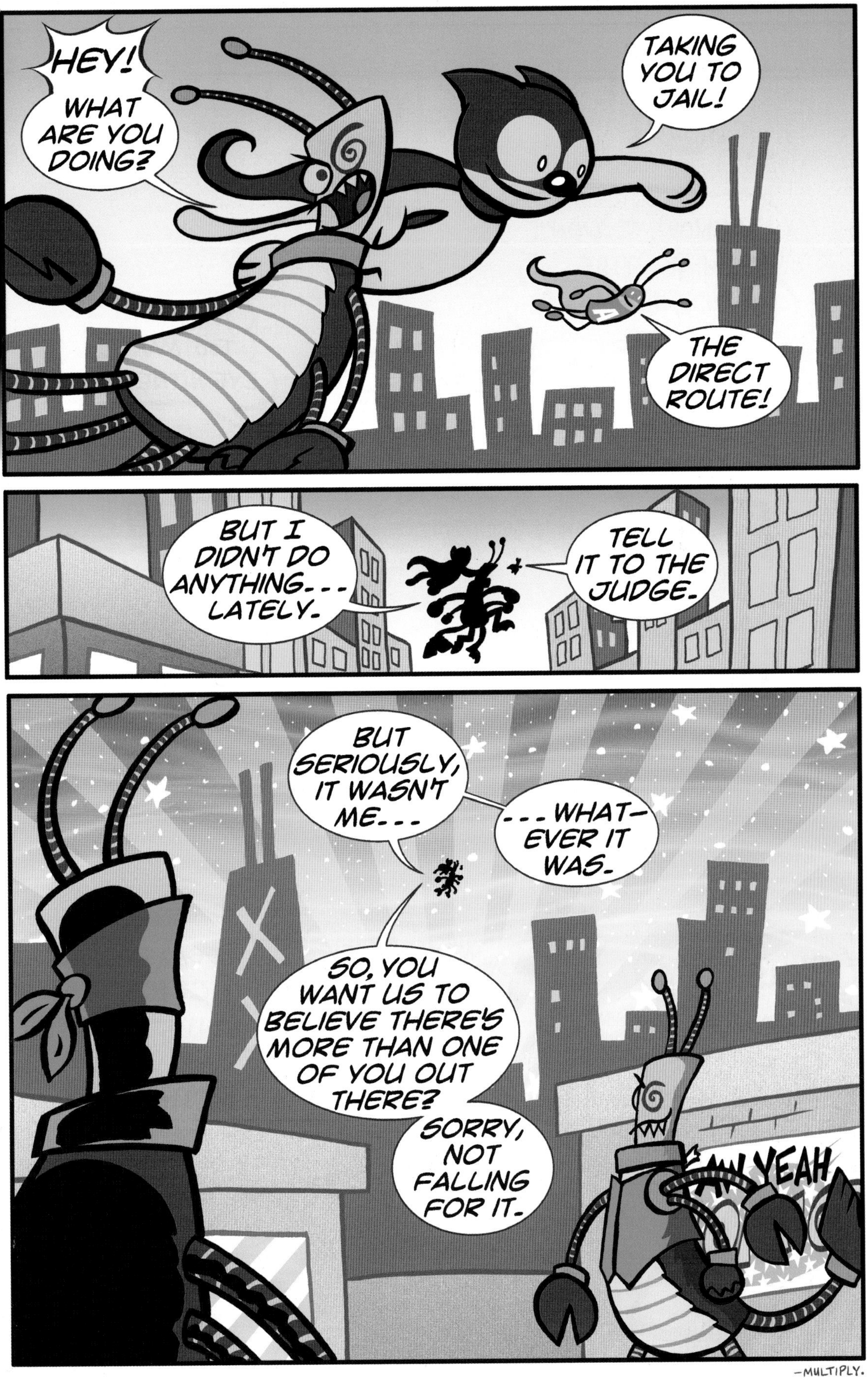
HEY!
WHAT ARE YOU DOING?
TAKING YOU TO JAIL!
THE DIRECT ROUTE!
BUT I DIDN'T DO ANYTHING... LATELY.
TELL IT TO THE JUDGE.
BUT SERIOUSLY, IT WASN'T ME...
...WHATEVER IT WAS.
SO, YOU WANT US TO BELIEVE THERE'S MORE THAN ONE OF YOU OUT THERE?
SORRY, NOT FALLING FOR IT.
AW YEAH

—MULTIPLY.

AW YEAH COMICS PRESENTS...

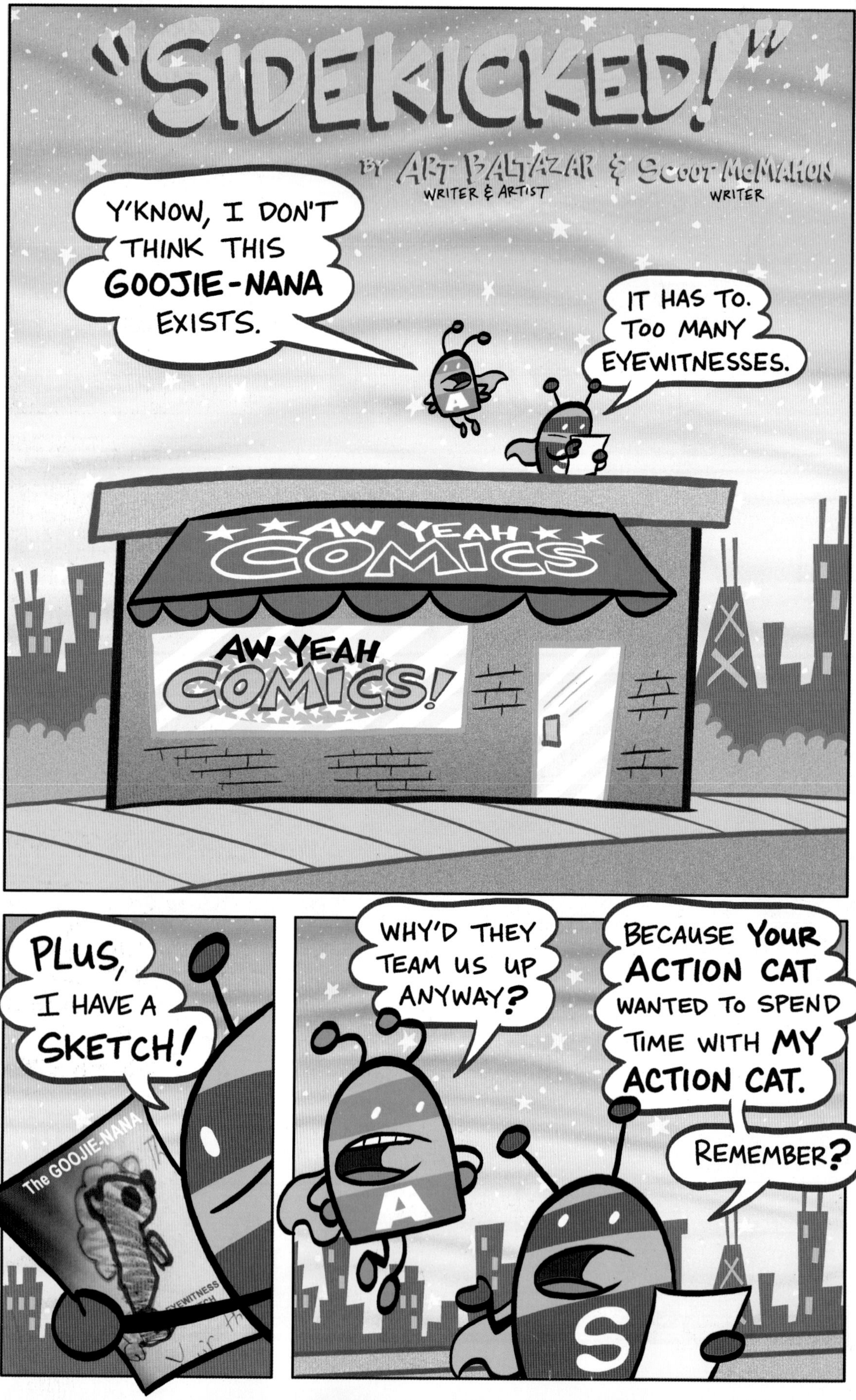

"SIDEKICKED!"
BY ART BALTAZAR & SCOOT McMAHON
WRITER & ARTIST
WRITER
Y'KNOW, I DON'T THINK THIS GOOJIE-NANA EXISTS.
IT HAS TO. TOO MANY EYEWITNESSES.
AW YEAH COMICS
AW YEAH COMICS!
PLUS, I HAVE A SKETCH!
The GOOJIE-NANA
WHY'D THEY TEAM US UP ANYWAY?
BECAUSE YOUR ACTION CAT WANTED TO SPEND TIME WITH MY ACTION CAT.
REMEMBER?

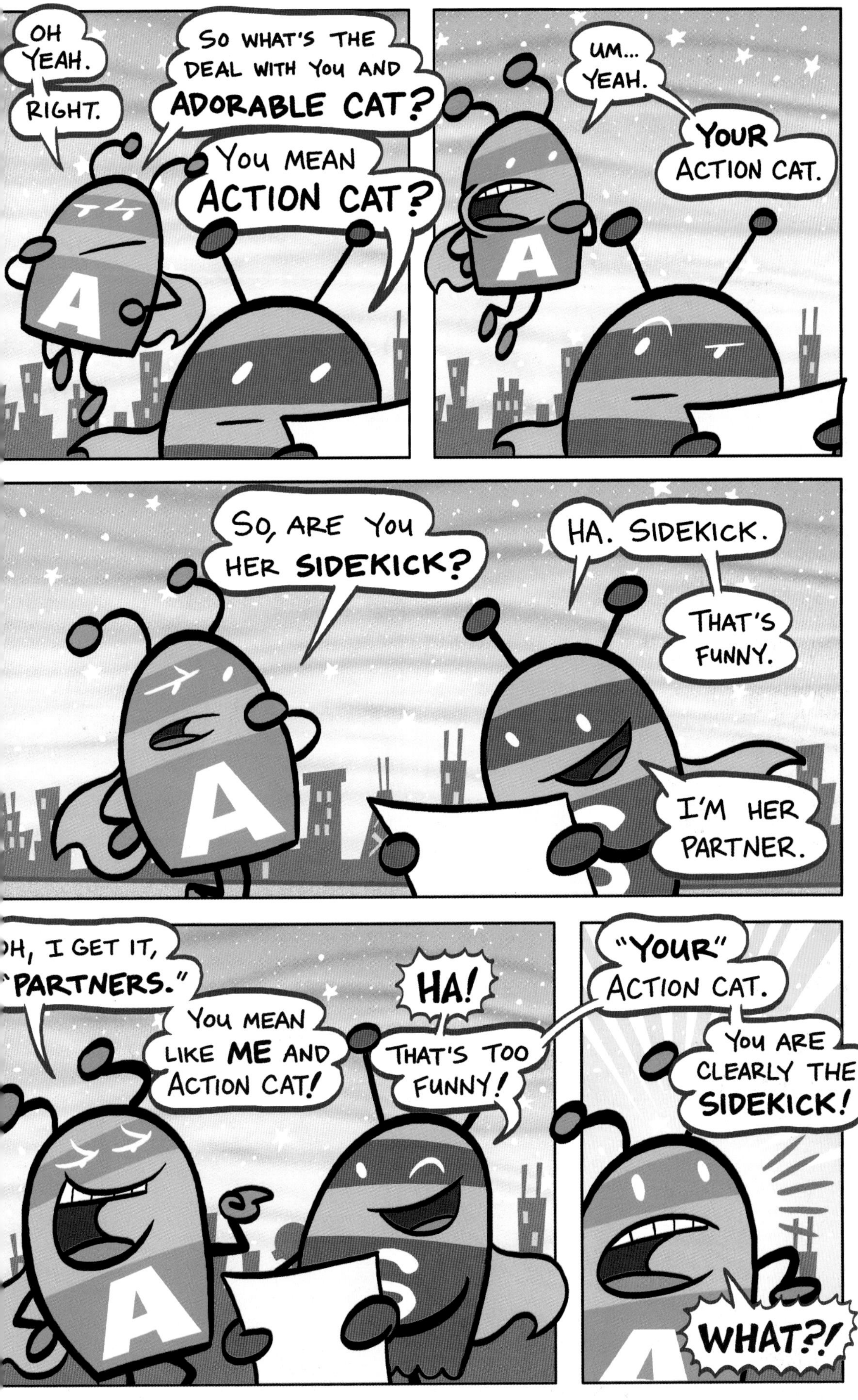
OH YEAH.
RIGHT.
SO WHAT'S THE DEAL WITH YOU AND ADORABLE CAT?
YOU MEAN ACTION CAT?
UM... YEAH.
YOUR ACTION CAT.
SO, ARE YOU HER SIDEKICK?
HA. SIDEKICK.
THAT'S FUNNY.
I'M HER PARTNER.
H, I GET IT, "PARTNERS."
YOU MEAN LIKE ME AND ACTION CAT!
HA!
THAT'S TOO FUNNY!
"YOUR" ACTION CAT.
YOU ARE CLEARLY THE SIDEKICK!
WHAT?!

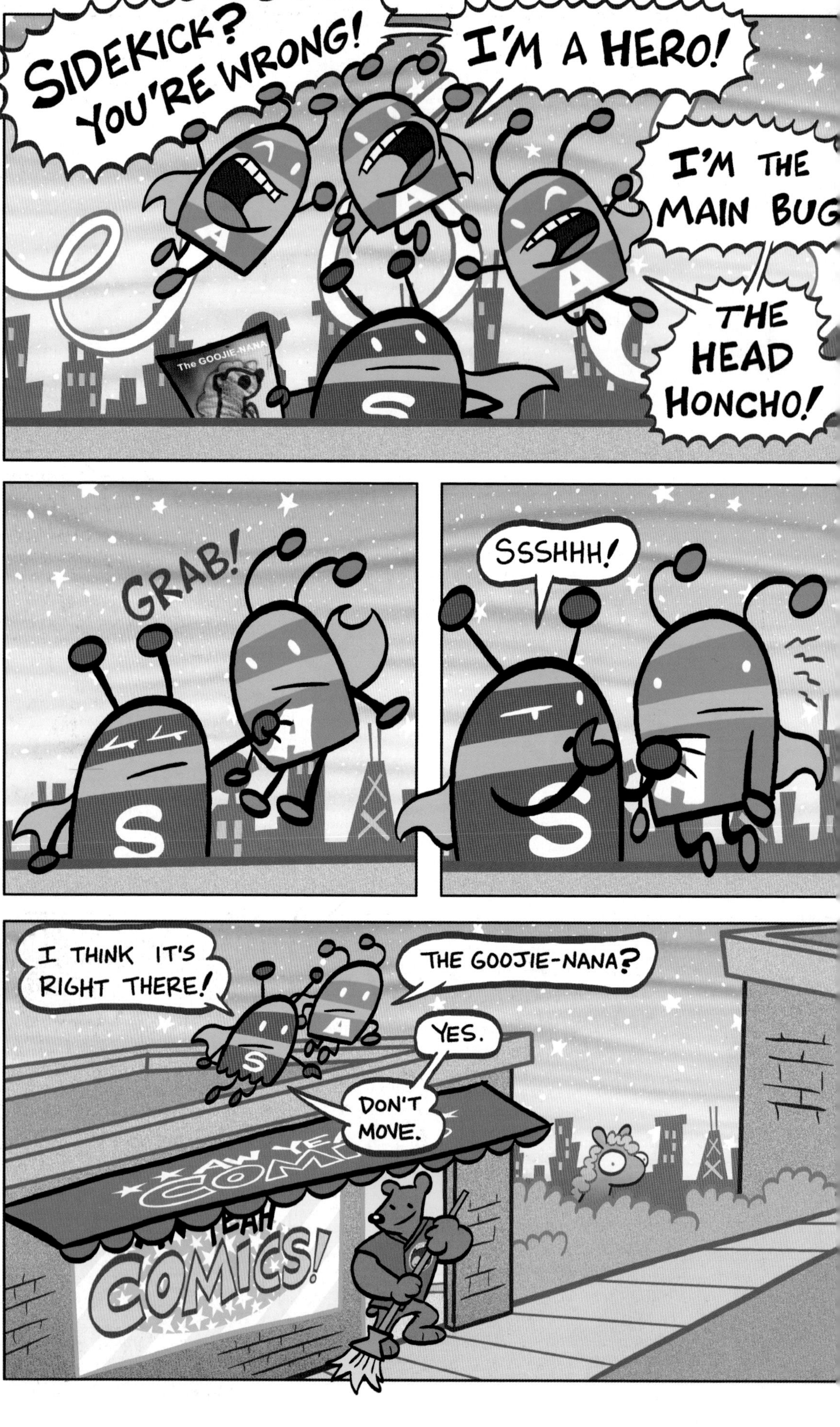

SIDEKICK? YOU'RE WRONG!
I'M A HERO!
I'M THE MAIN BUG
THE HEAD HONCHO!
The GOOJIE-NANA
GRAB!
SSSHHH!
I THINK IT'S RIGHT THERE!
THE GOOJIE-NANA?
YES.
DON'T MOVE.
COMICS!

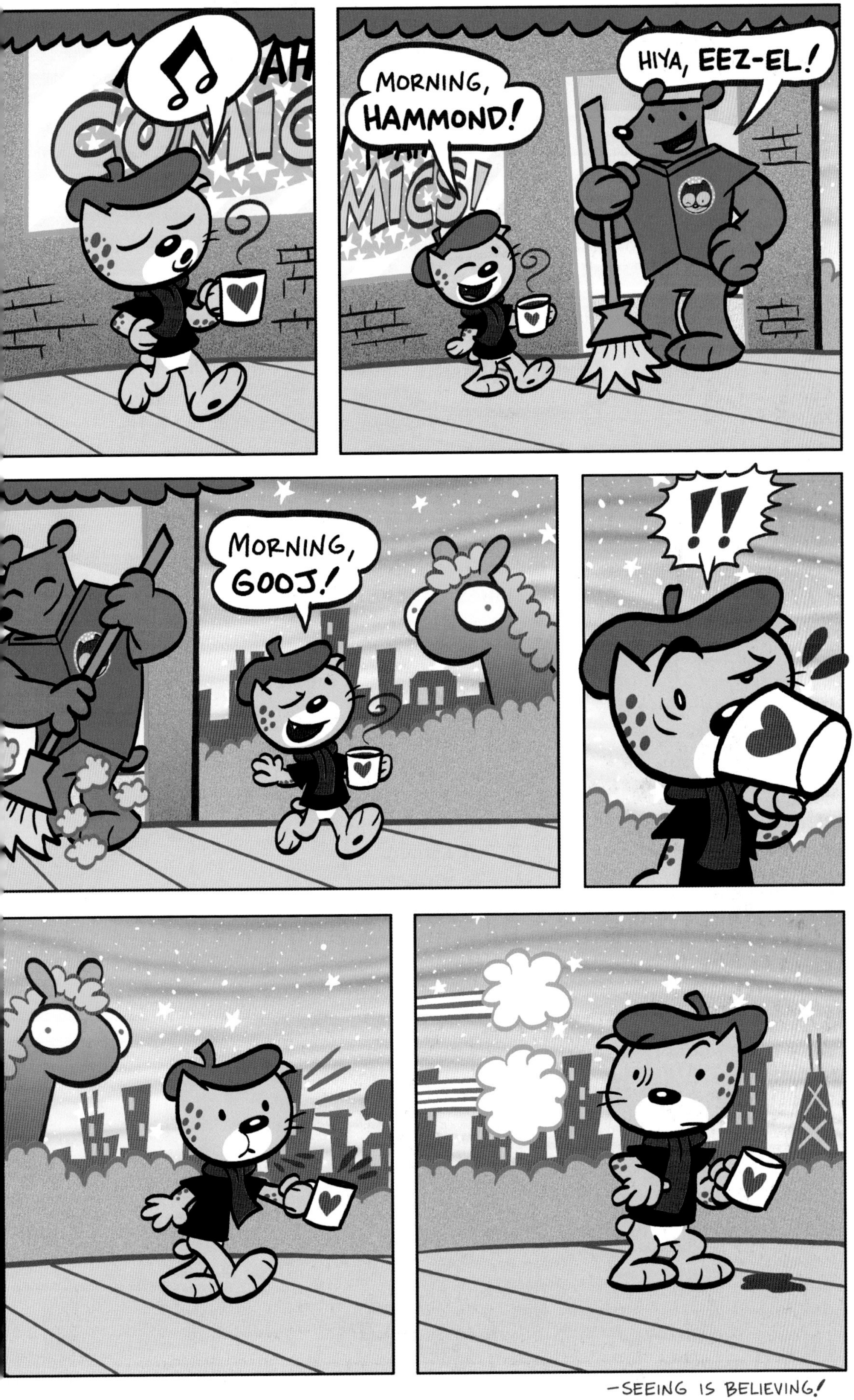
MORNING, HAMMOND!
HIYA, EEZ-EL!
MORNING, GOOJ!
!!

—SEEING IS BELIEVING!

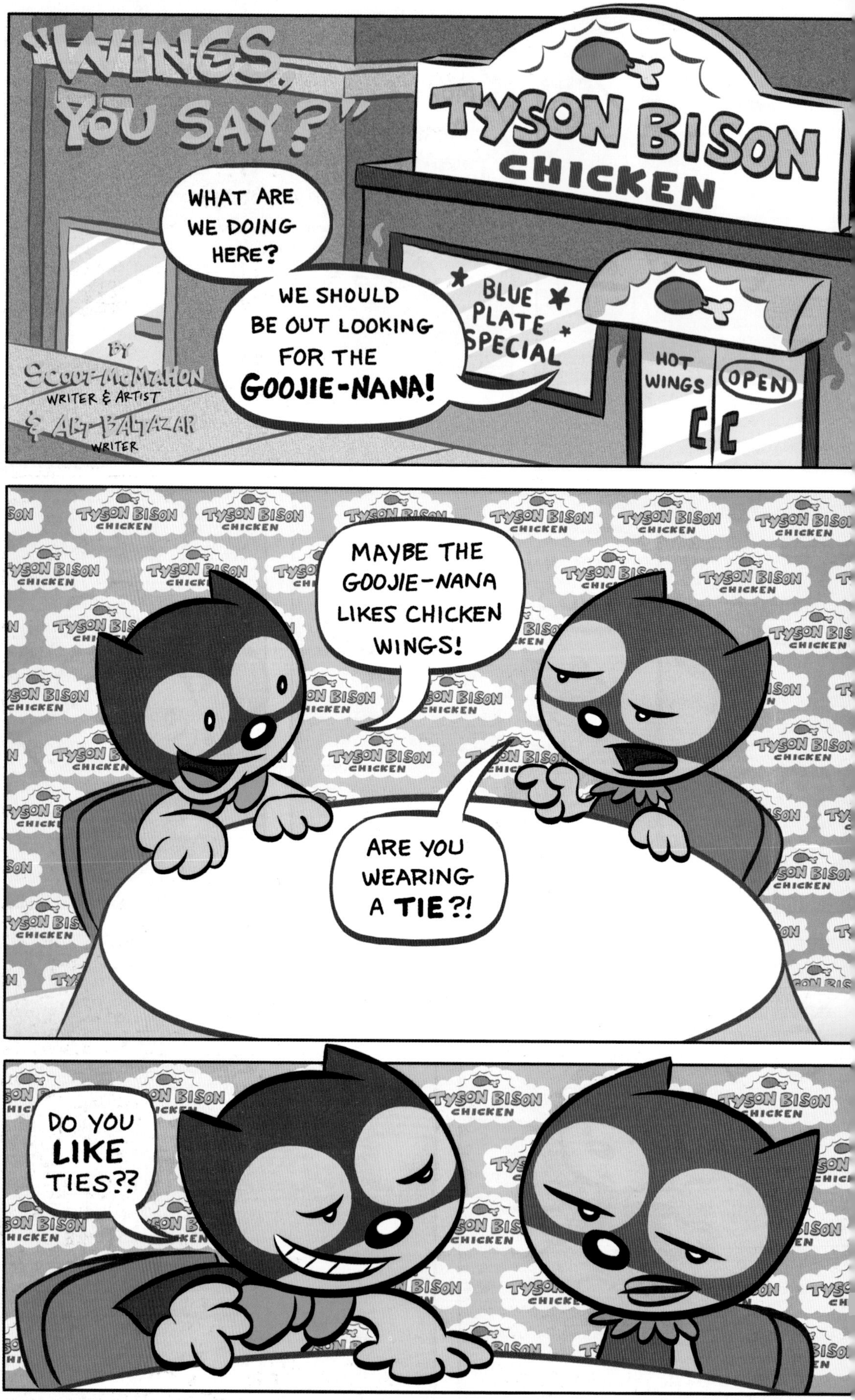
"WINGS, YOU SAY?"
BY SCOOP McMAHON WRITER & ARTIST
& ART BALTAZAR WRITER
TYSON BISON CHICKEN
BLUE PLATE SPECIAL
HOT WINGS
OPEN
WHAT ARE WE DOING HERE?
WE SHOULD BE OUT LOOKING FOR THE GOOJIE-NANA!
MAYBE THE GOOJIE-NANA LIKES CHICKEN WINGS!
ARE YOU WEARING A TIE?!
DO YOU LIKE TIES??

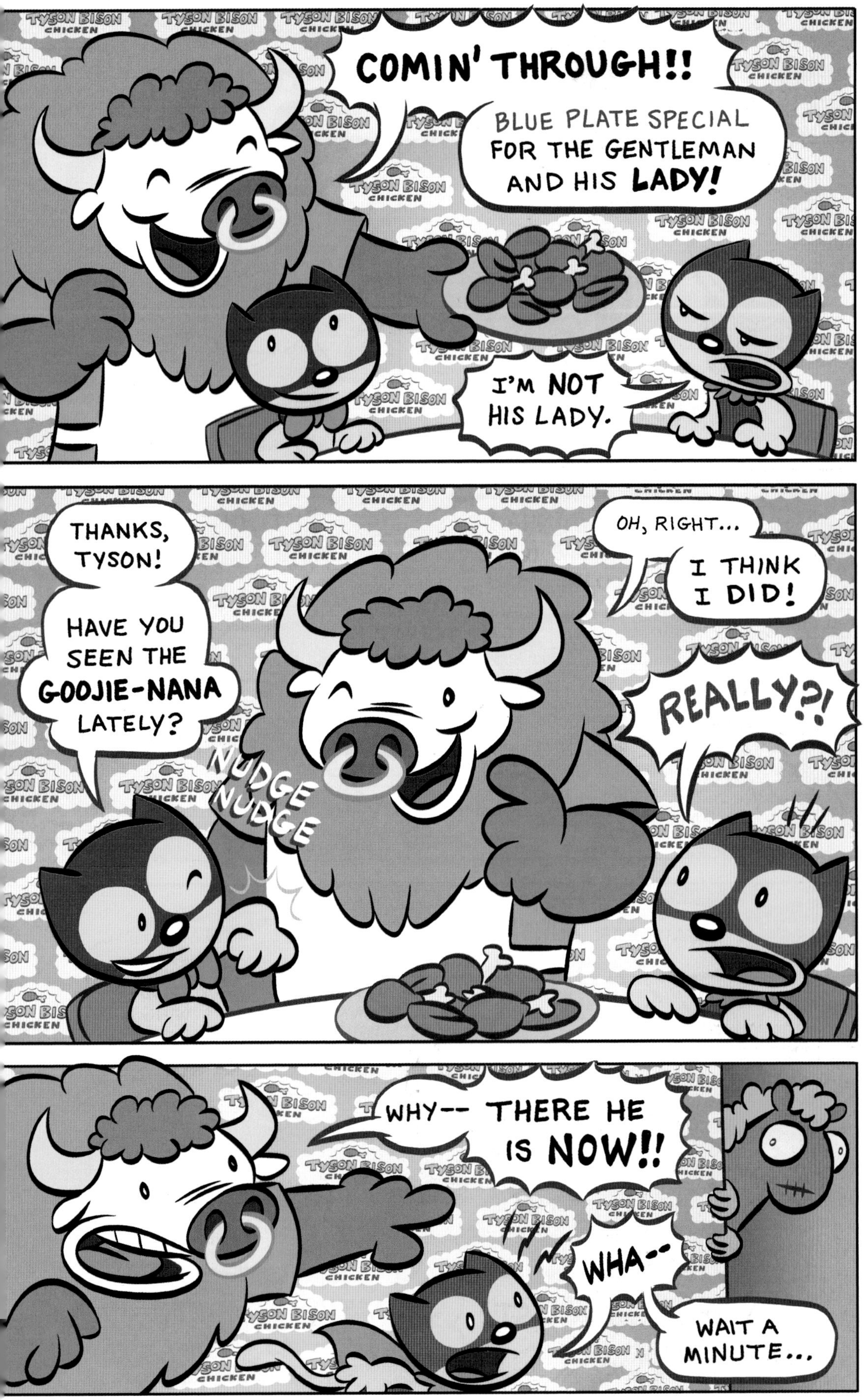
COMIN' THROUGH!!
BLUE PLATE SPECIAL FOR THE GENTLEMAN AND HIS LADY!
I'M NOT HIS LADY.
THANKS, TYSON!
HAVE YOU SEEN THE GOOJIE-NANA LATELY?
NUDGE NUDGE
OH, RIGHT...
I THINK I DID!
REALLY?!
WHY-- THERE HE IS NOW!!
WHA--
WAIT A MINUTE...

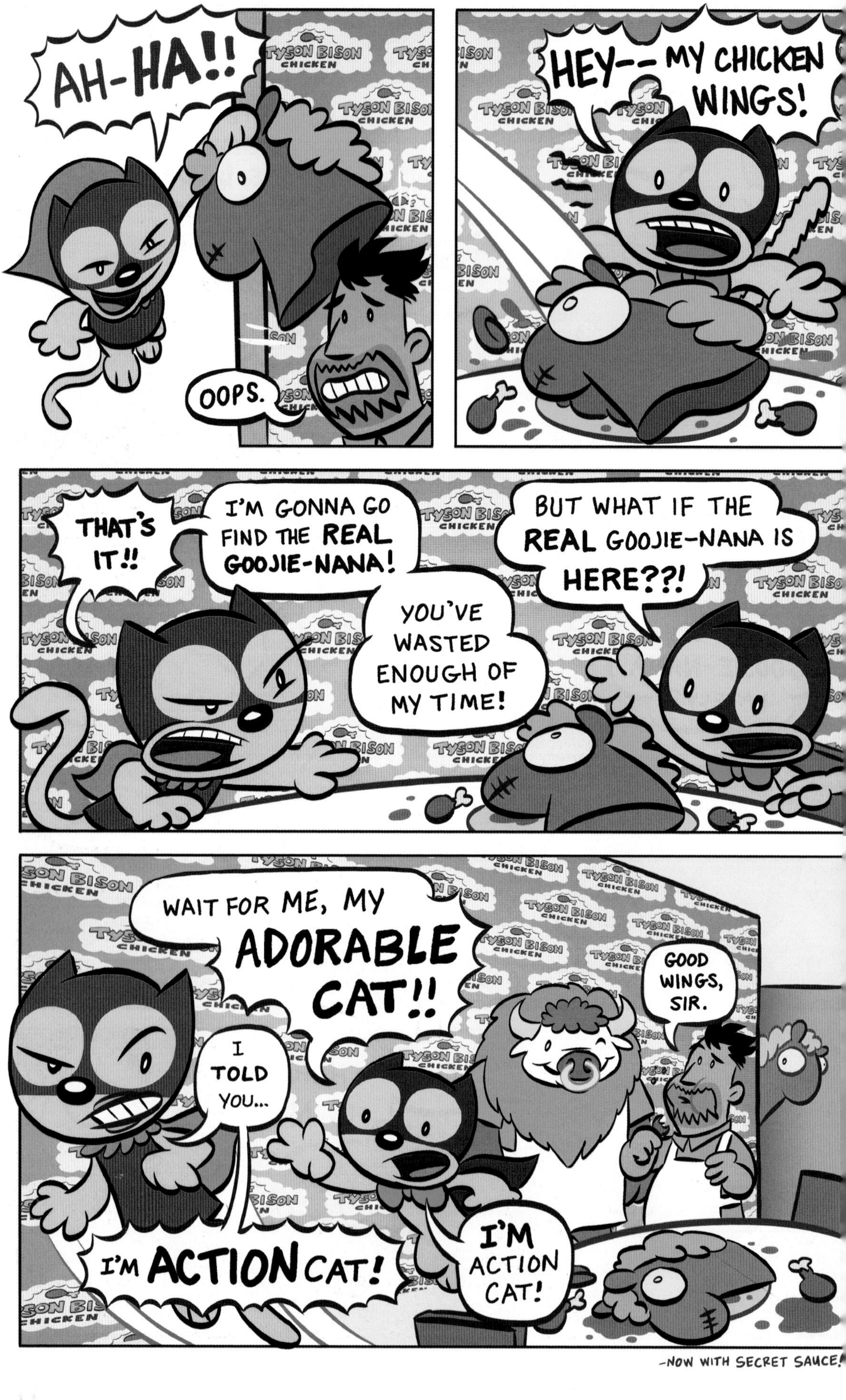
AH-HA!!
OOPS.
HEY-- MY CHICKEN WINGS!
THAT'S IT!!
I'M GONNA GO FIND THE REAL GOOJIE-NANA!
YOU'VE WASTED ENOUGH OF MY TIME!
BUT WHAT IF THE REAL GOOJIE-NANA IS HERE??!
WAIT FOR ME, MY ADORABLE CAT!!
I TOLD YOU...
GOOD WINGS, SIR.
I'M ACTION CAT!
I'M ACTION CAT!
TYSON BISON CHICKEN
-NOW WITH SECRET SAUCE!

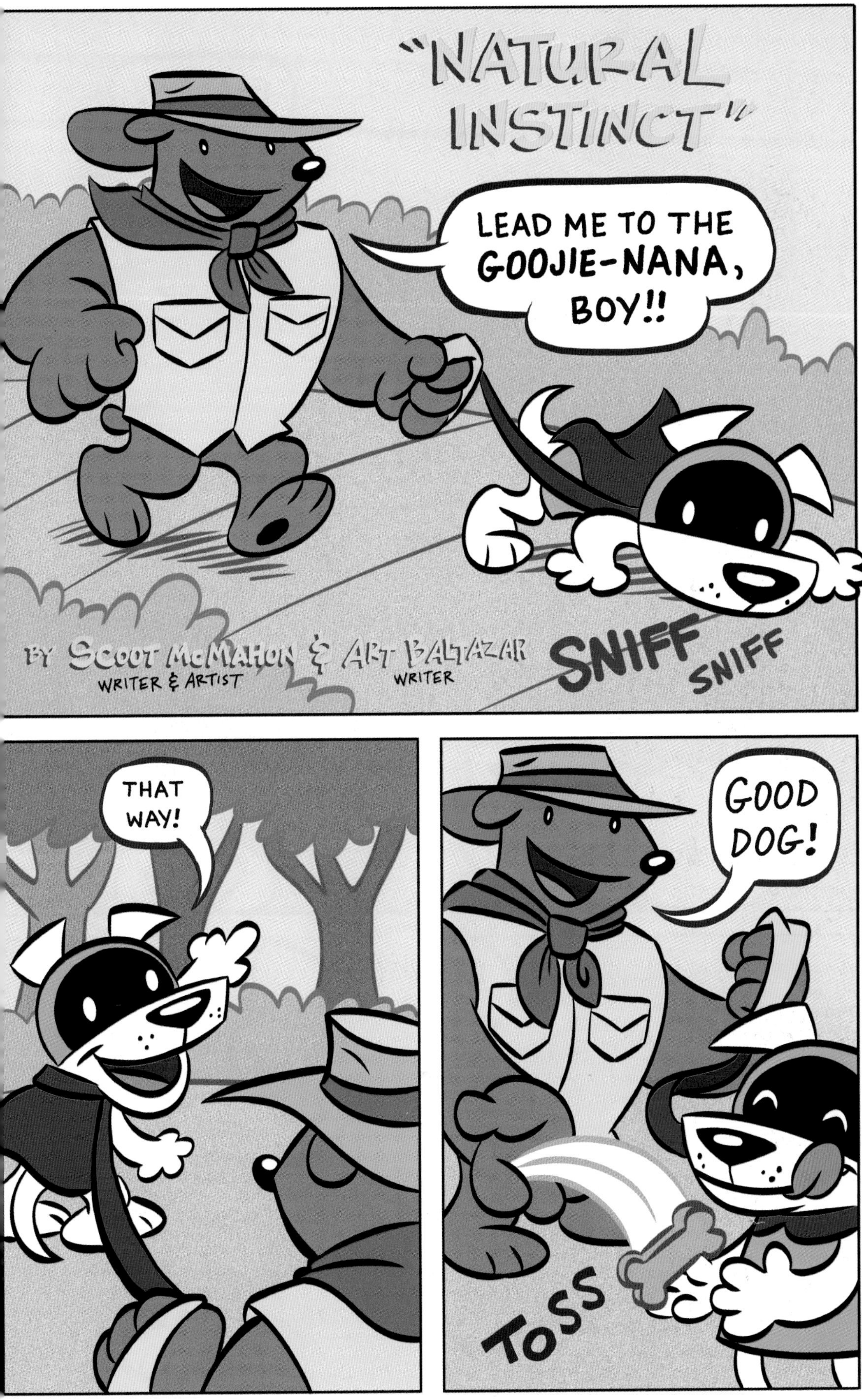
"NATURAL INSTINCT"
LEAD ME TO THE GOOJIE-NANA, BOY!!
BY SCOOT MCMAHON & ART BALTAZAR
WRITER & ARTIST
WRITER
SNIFF
SNIFF
THAT WAY!
GOOD DOG!
TOSS

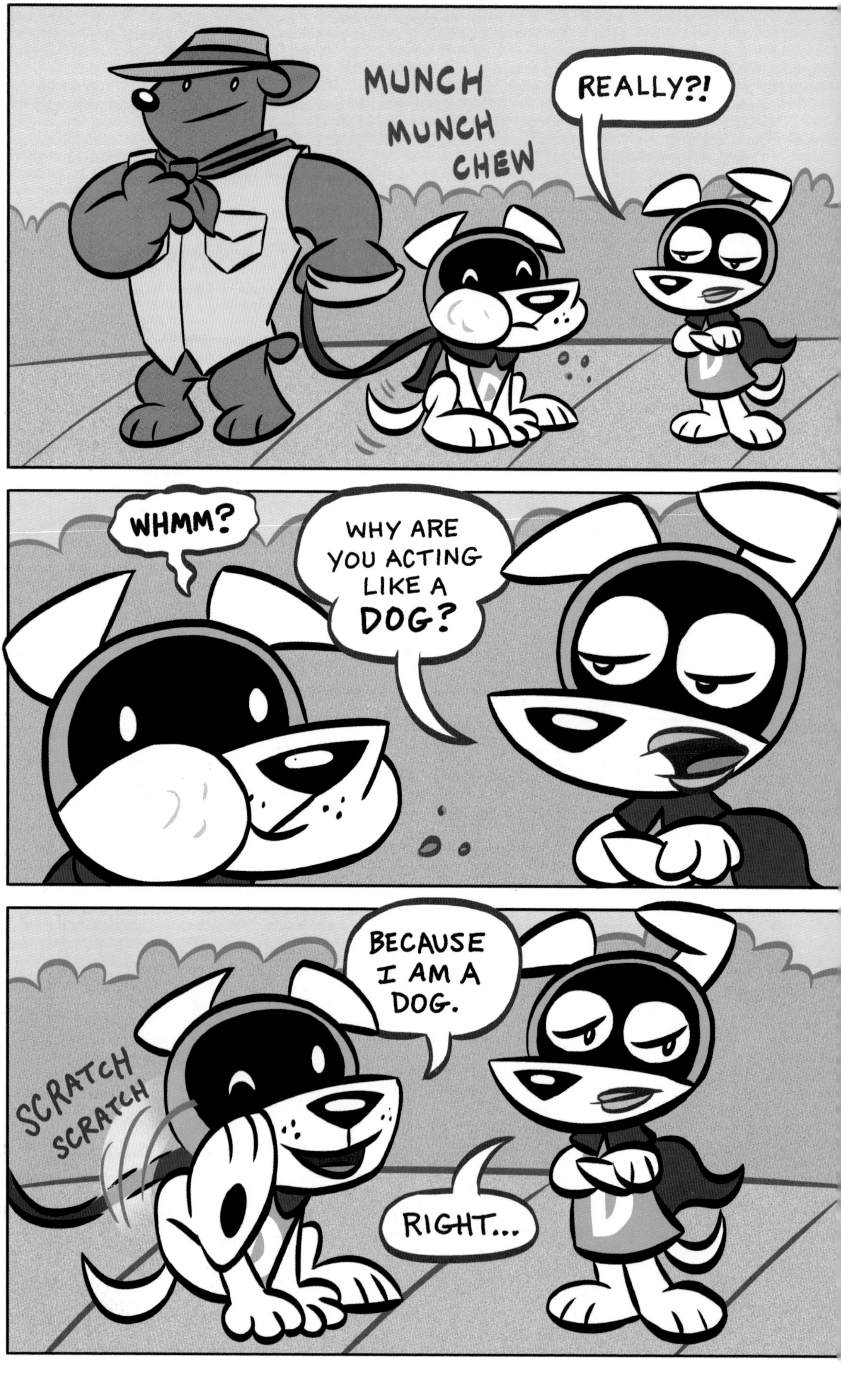
MUNCH
MUNCH
CHEW
REALLY?!
WHMM?
WHY ARE YOU ACTING LIKE A DOG?
BECAUSE I AM A DOG.
SCRATCH
SCRATCH
RIGHT...

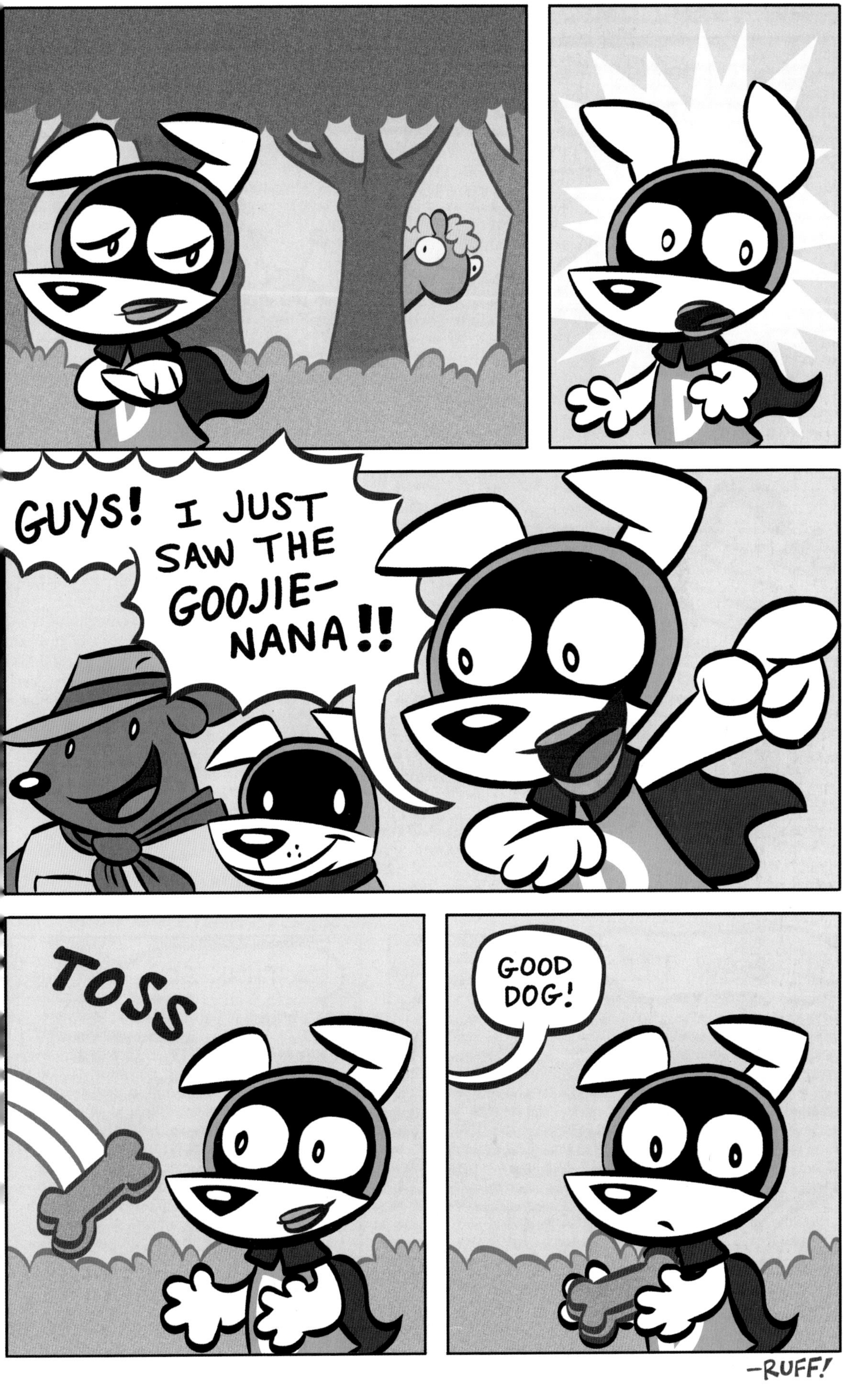
GUYS! I JUST SAW THE GOOJIE-NANA!!
TOSS
GOOD DOG!
-RUFF!

AW YEAH COMICS! PRESENTS...

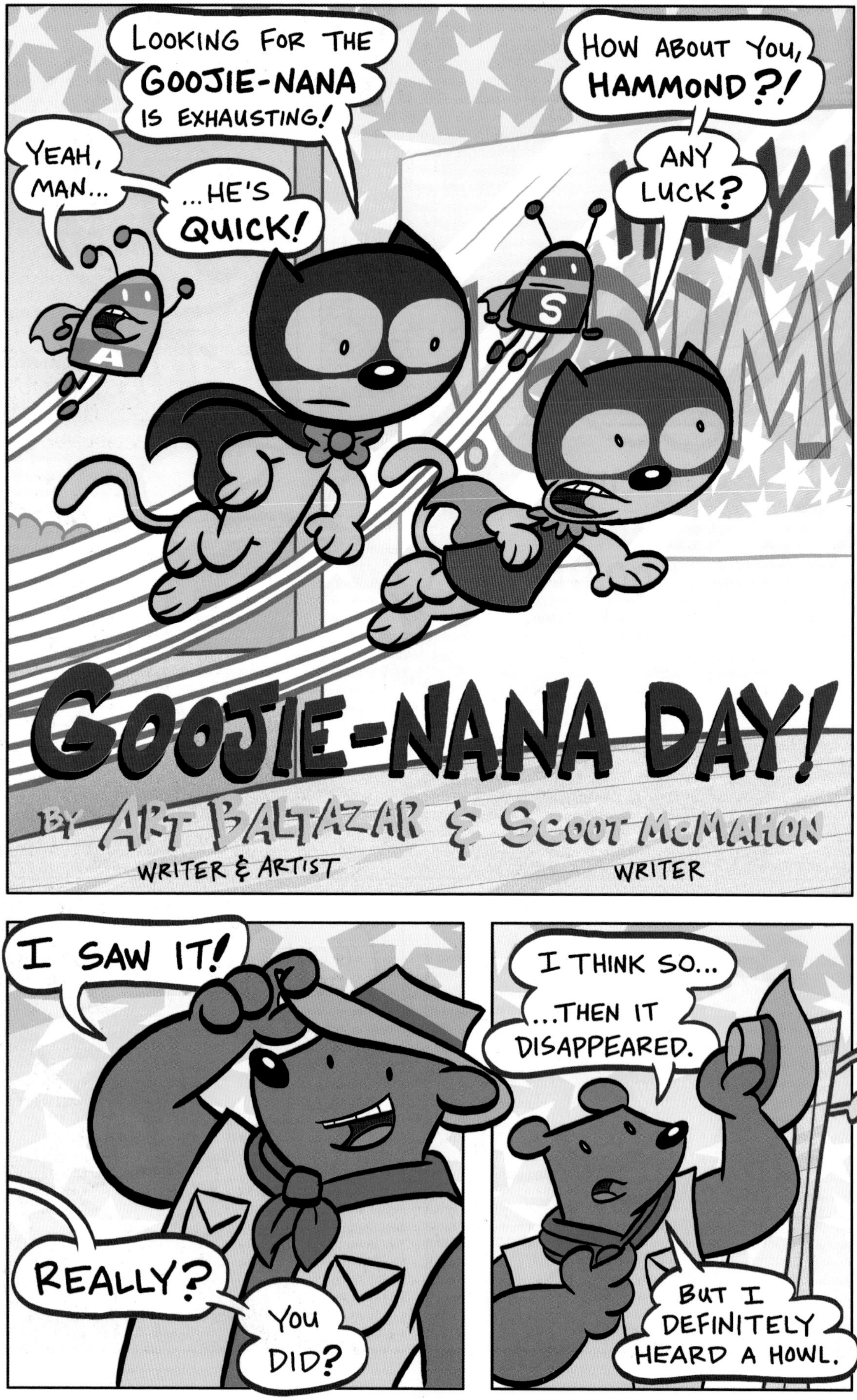
LOOKING FOR THE GOOJIE-NANA IS EXHAUSTING!
YEAH, MAN...
...HE'S QUICK!
HOW ABOUT YOU, HAMMOND?!
ANY LUCK?
GOOJIE-NANA DAY!
BY ART BALTAZAR & SCOOT McMAHON
WRITER & ARTIST
WRITER
I SAW IT!
REALLY?
YOU DID?
I THINK SO...
...THEN IT DISAPPEARED.
BUT I DEFINITELY HEARD A HOWL.

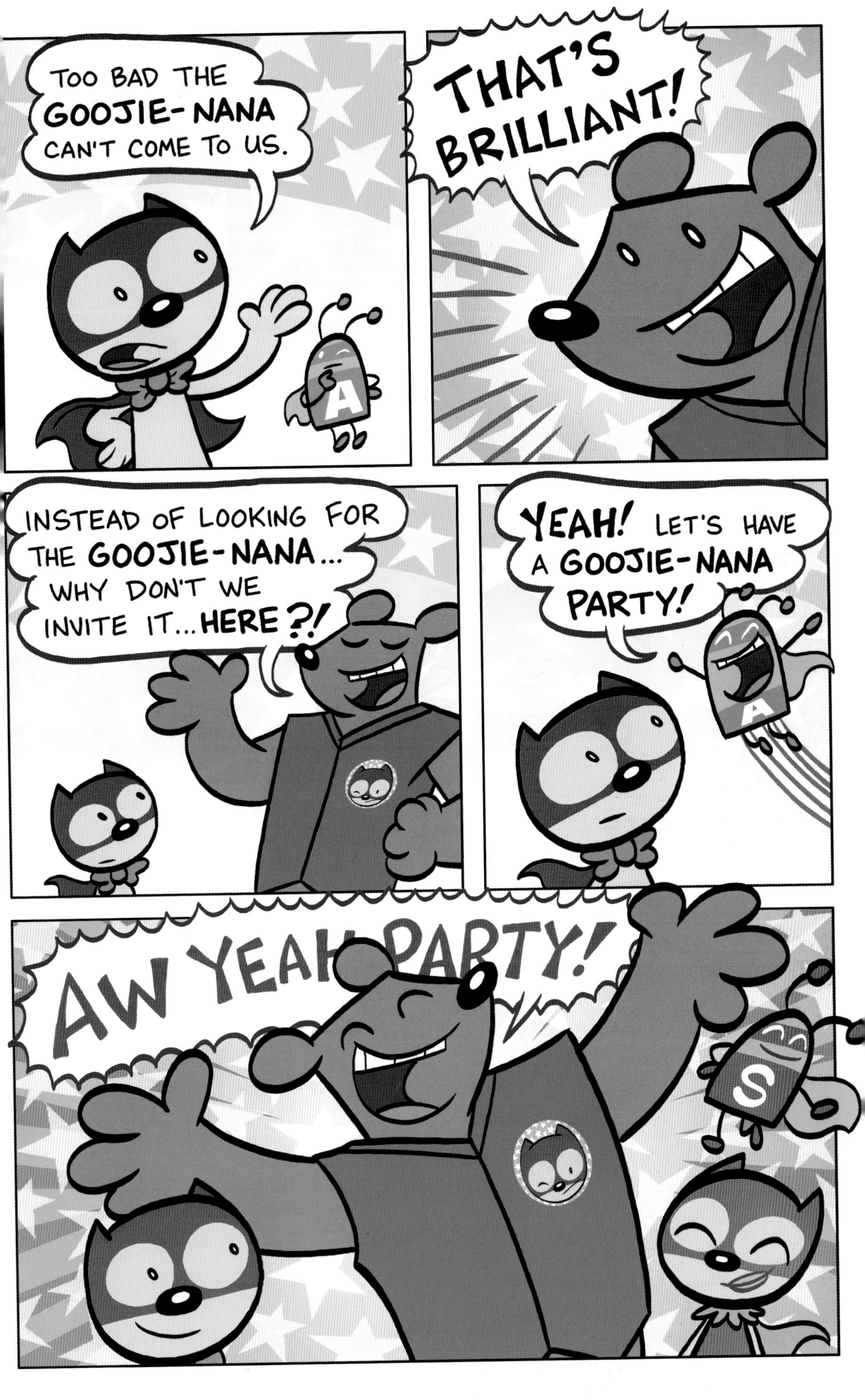
TOO BAD THE GOOJIE-NANA CAN'T COME TO US.
THAT'S BRILLIANT!
INSTEAD OF LOOKING FOR THE GOOJIE-NANA... WHY DON'T WE INVITE IT... HERE?!
YEAH! LET'S HAVE A GOOJIE-NANA PARTY!
AW YEAH PARTY!

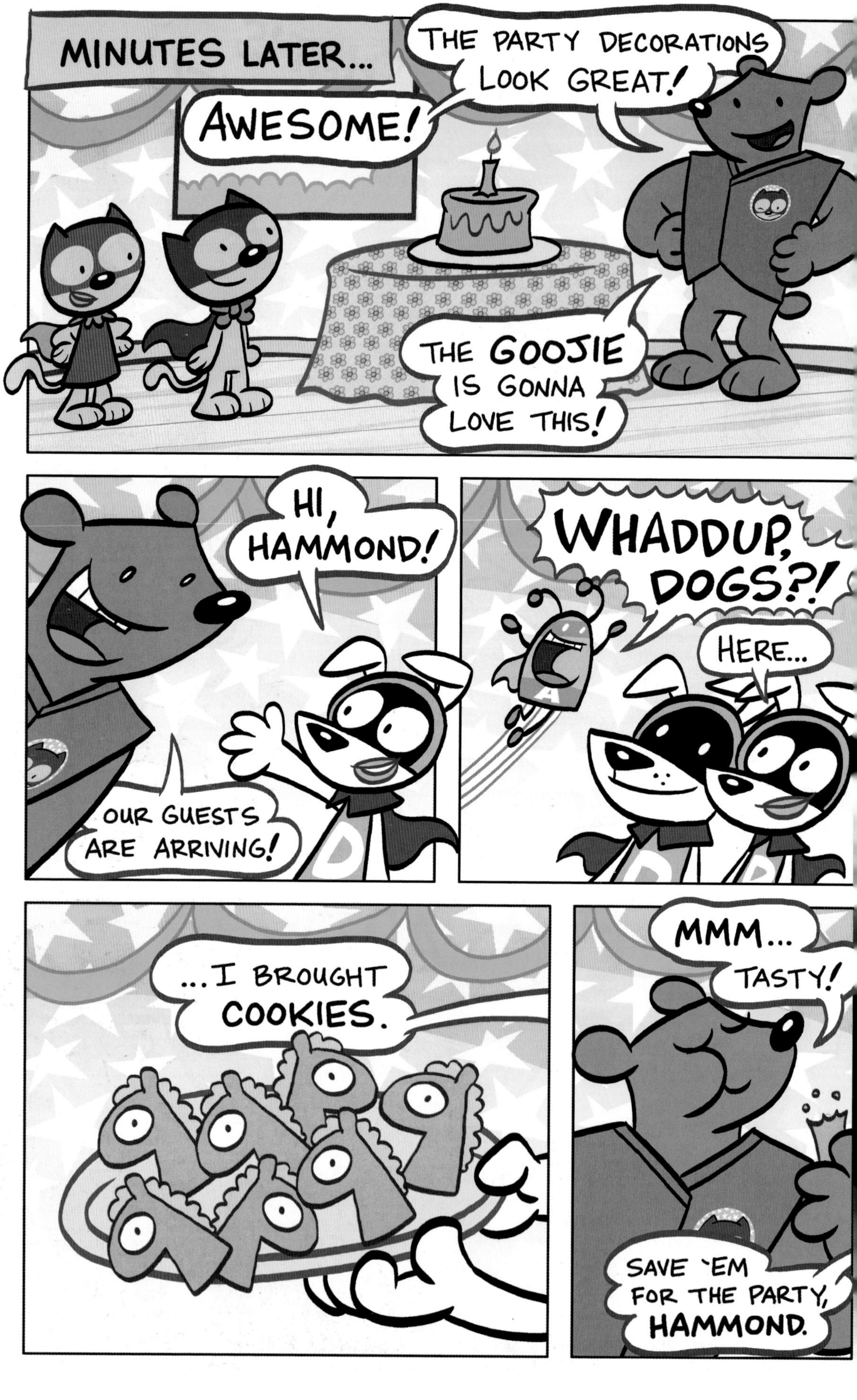
MINUTES LATER...
THE PARTY DECORATIONS LOOK GREAT!
AWESOME!
THE GOOJIE IS GONNA LOVE THIS!
HI, HAMMOND!
OUR GUESTS ARE ARRIVING!
WHADDUP, DOGS?!
HERE...
...I BROUGHT COOKIES.
MMM...
TASTY!
SAVE 'EM FOR THE PARTY, HAMMOND.

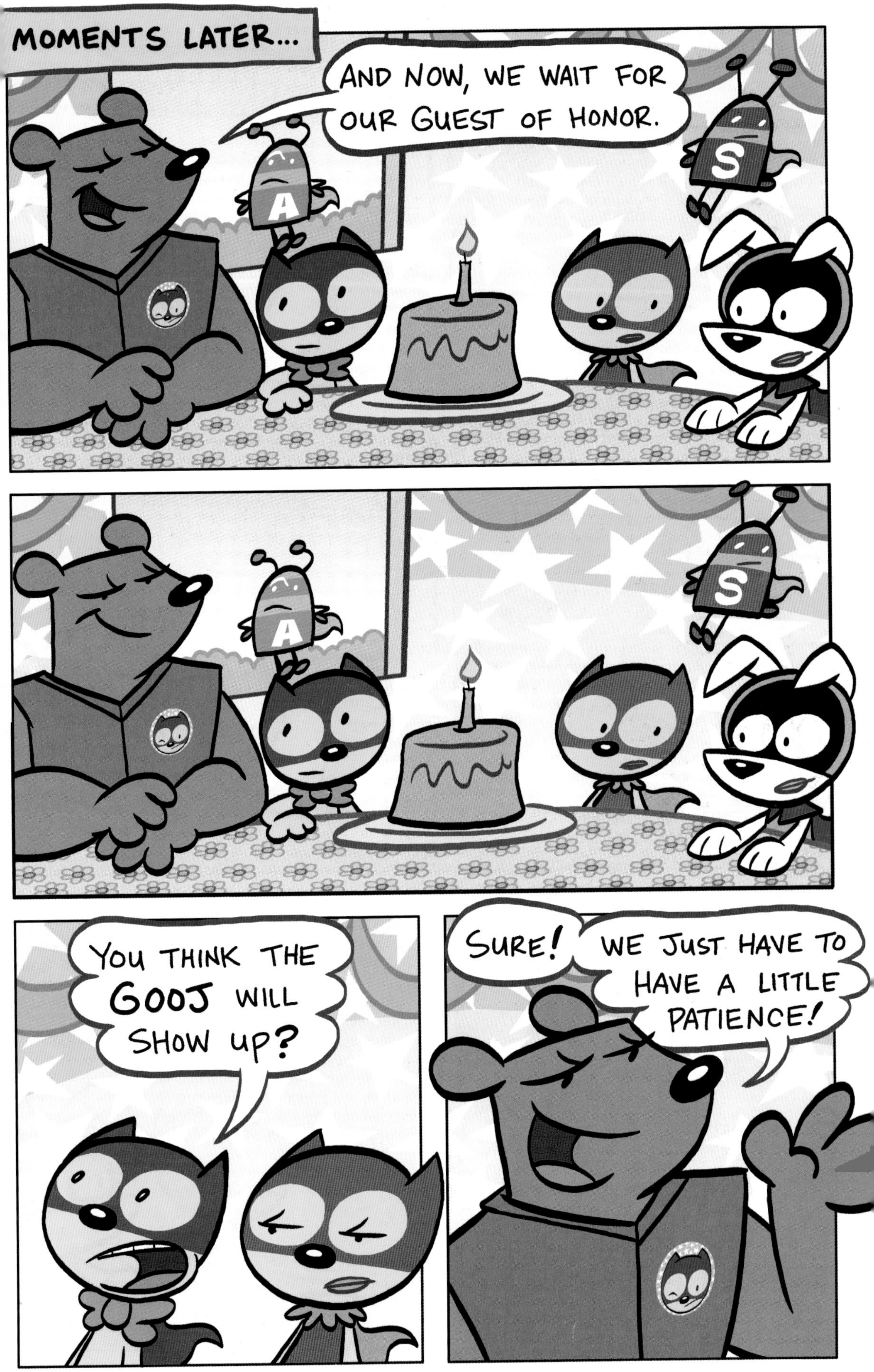
MOMENTS LATER...
AND NOW, WE WAIT FOR OUR GUEST OF HONOR.
A
S
YOU THINK THE GOOJ WILL SHOW UP?
SURE!
WE JUST HAVE TO HAVE A LITTLE PATIENCE!

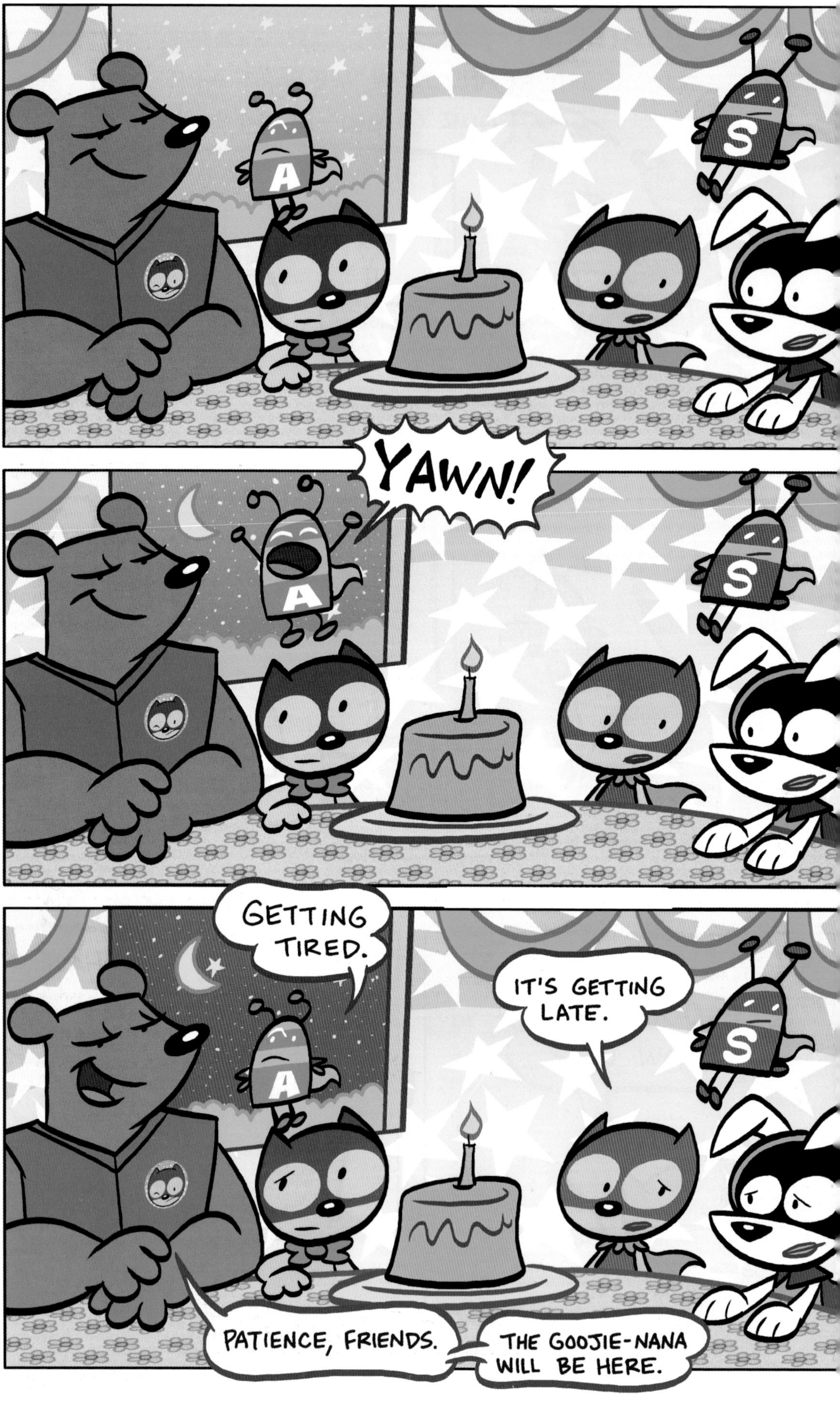
YAWN!
GETTING TIRED.
IT'S GETTING LATE.
PATIENCE, FRIENDS.
THE GOOJIE-NANA WILL BE HERE.

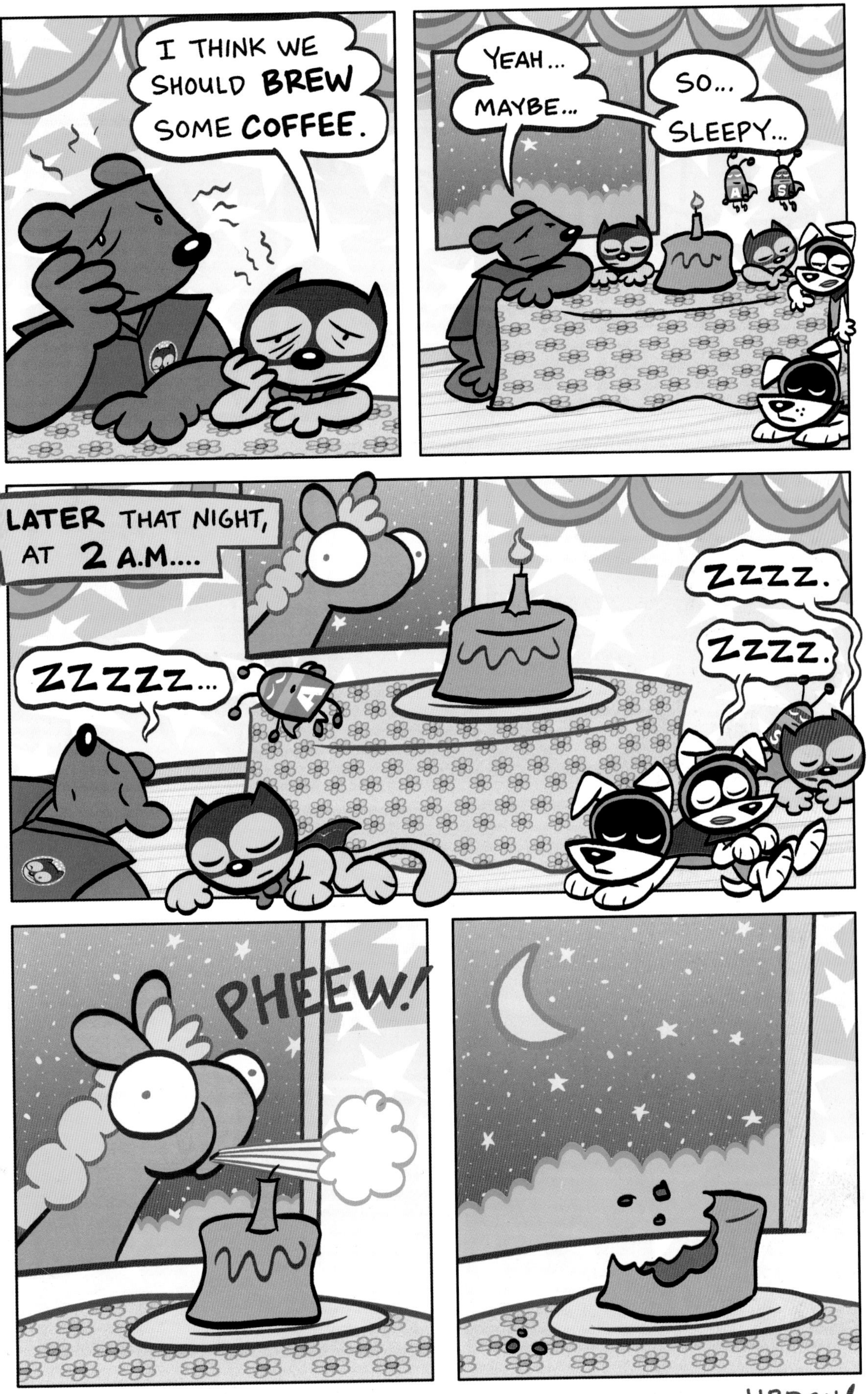
I THINK WE SHOULD BREW SOME COFFEE.
YEAH... MAYBE...
SO... SLEEPY...
LATER THAT NIGHT, AT 2 A.M....
ZZZZZ...
ZZZZ.
ZZZZ.
PHEEW!

—HBDGN!

FUTURE CAT

WORDS BY AARON PITTMAN ART BY ALEJANDRO ROSADO

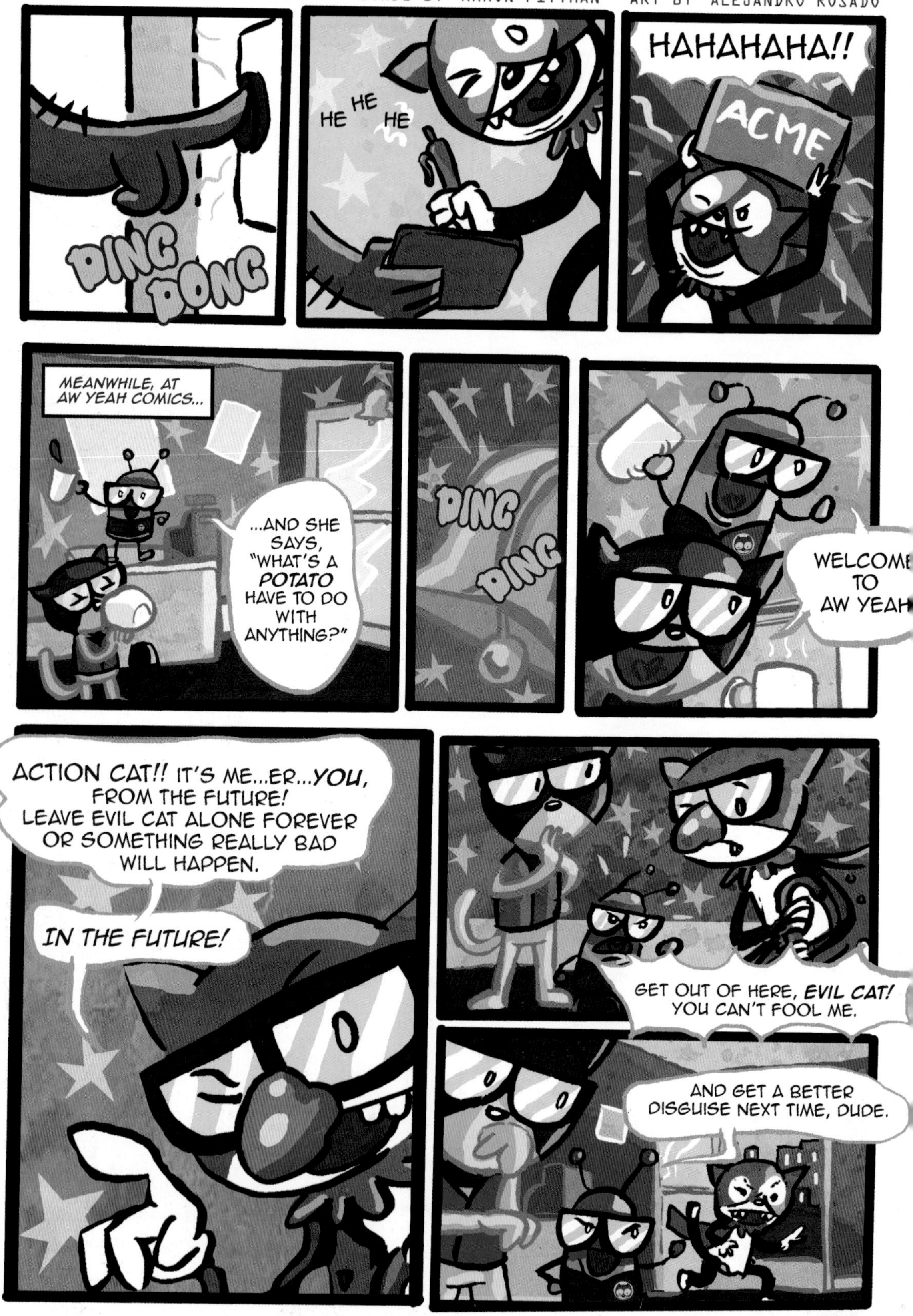
DING DONG
HE HE HE HE
HAHAHAHA!!
ACME
MEANWHILE, AT AW YEAH COMICS...
...AND SHE SAYS, "WHAT'S A *POTATO* HAVE TO DO WITH ANYTHING?"
DING DING
WELCOME TO AW YEAH
ACTION CAT!! IT'S ME...ER...*YOU*, FROM THE FUTURE! LEAVE EVIL CAT ALONE FOREVER OR SOMETHING REALLY BAD WILL HAPPEN.
IN THE FUTURE!
GET OUT OF HERE, *EVIL CAT!* YOU CAN'T FOOL ME.
AND GET A BETTER DISGUISE NEXT TIME, DUDE.

END

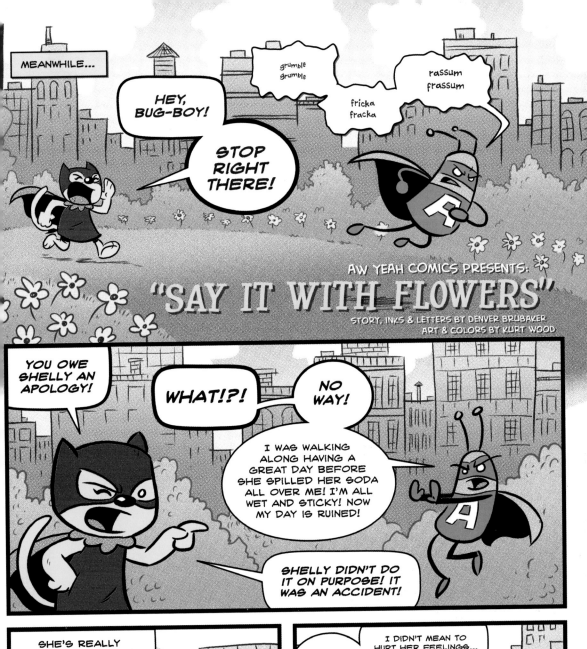

MEANWHILE...

HEY, BUG-BOY!

STOP RIGHT THERE!

grumble grumble

rassum frassum

fricka fracka

AW YEAH COMICS PRESENTS:

"SAY IT WITH FLOWERS"

STORY, INKS & LETTERS BY DENVER BRUBAKER
ART & COLORS BY KURT WOOD

YOU OWE SHELLY AN APOLOGY!

WHAT!?!

NO WAY!

I WAS WALKING ALONG HAVING A GREAT DAY BEFORE SHE SPILLED HER SODA ALL OVER ME! I'M ALL WET AND STICKY! NOW MY DAY IS RUINED!

SHELLY DIDN'T DO IT ON PURPOSE! IT WAS AN ACCIDENT!

SHE'S REALLY EMBARRASSED AND YOU YELLING AT HER DIDN'T MAKE THINGS ANY BETTER!

WELL...I...

WELL NOTHIN'!

YOU HURT HER FEELINGS!

I DIDN'T MEAN TO HURT HER FEELINGS...

≥SIGH≤ FINE!

TELL YOU WHAT...SEE THOSE FLOWERS OVER THERE?

PICK ONE, GO GIVE IT TO HER, AND SAY YOU'RE SORRY.

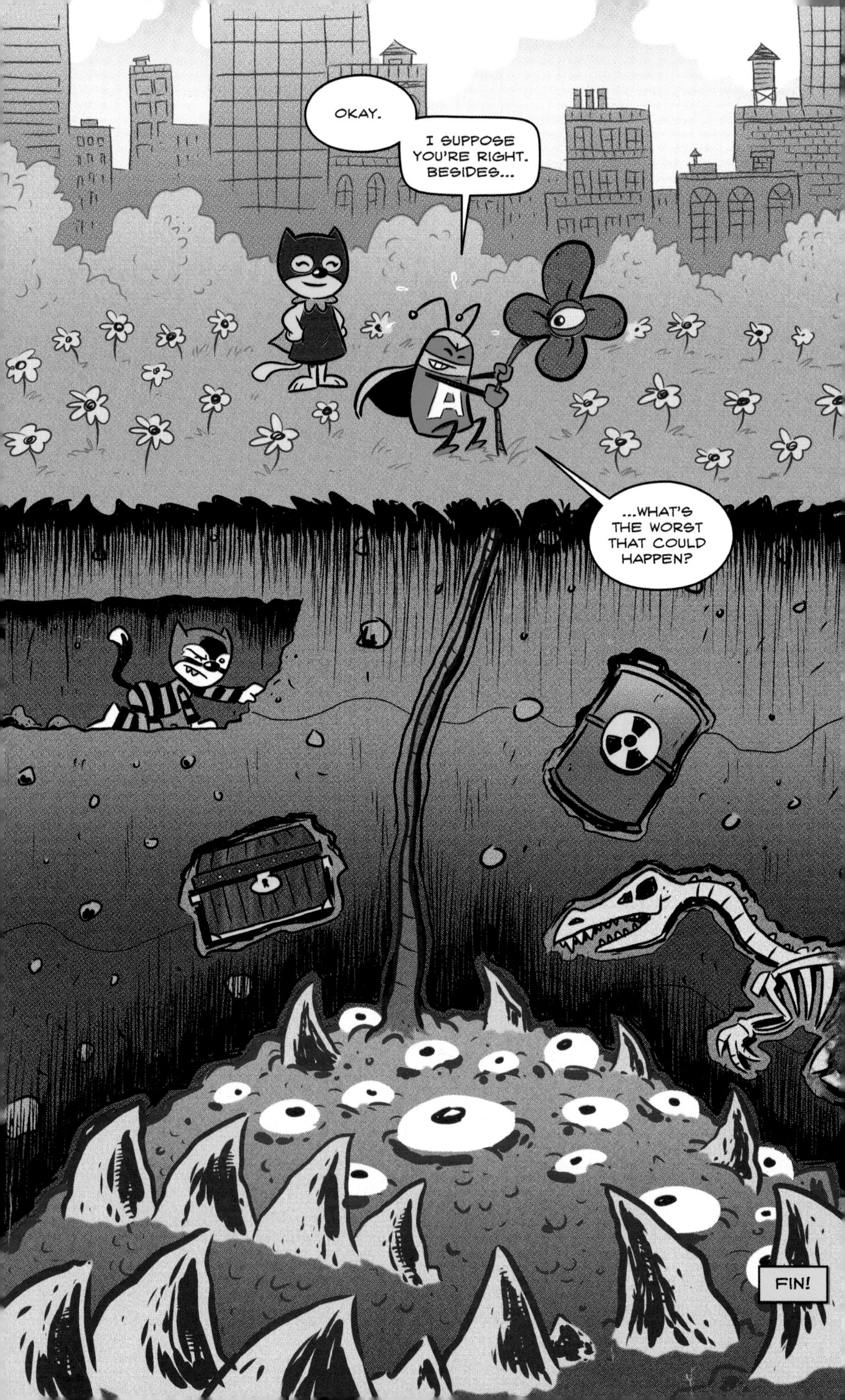
OKAY.
I SUPPOSE YOU'RE RIGHT. BESIDES...
...WHAT'S THE WORST THAT COULD HAPPEN?
FIN!

SCAREDY CATS!

- SCOOT!

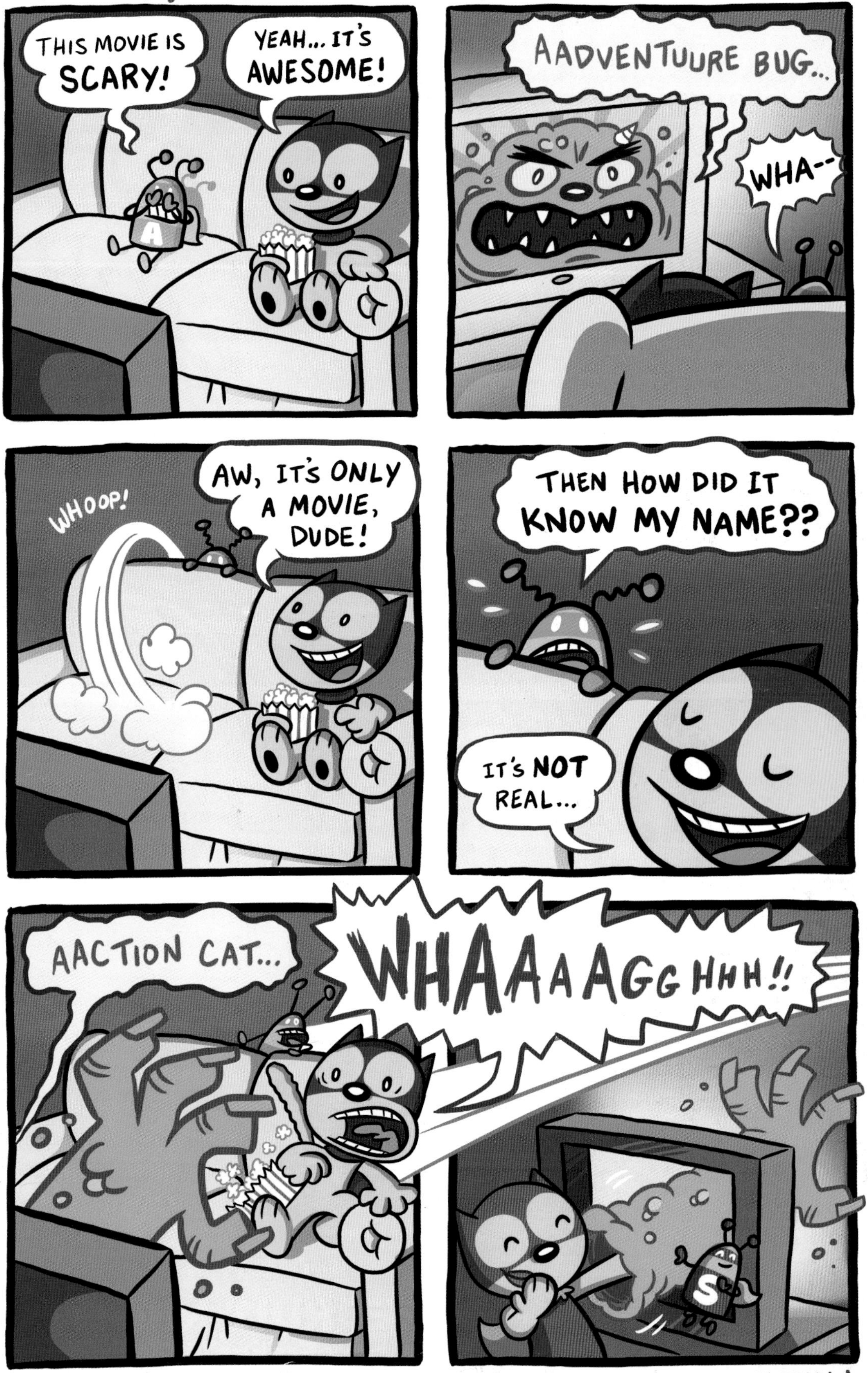
THIS MOVIE IS SCARY!
YEAH... IT'S AWESOME!
AADVENTUURE BUG...
WHA--
WHOOP!
AW, IT'S ONLY A MOVIE, DUDE!
THEN HOW DID IT KNOW MY NAME??
IT'S NOT REAL...
AACTION CAT...
WHAAAAAGGHHH!!
S

- GOTCHA!

AW YEAH COMICS! presents...

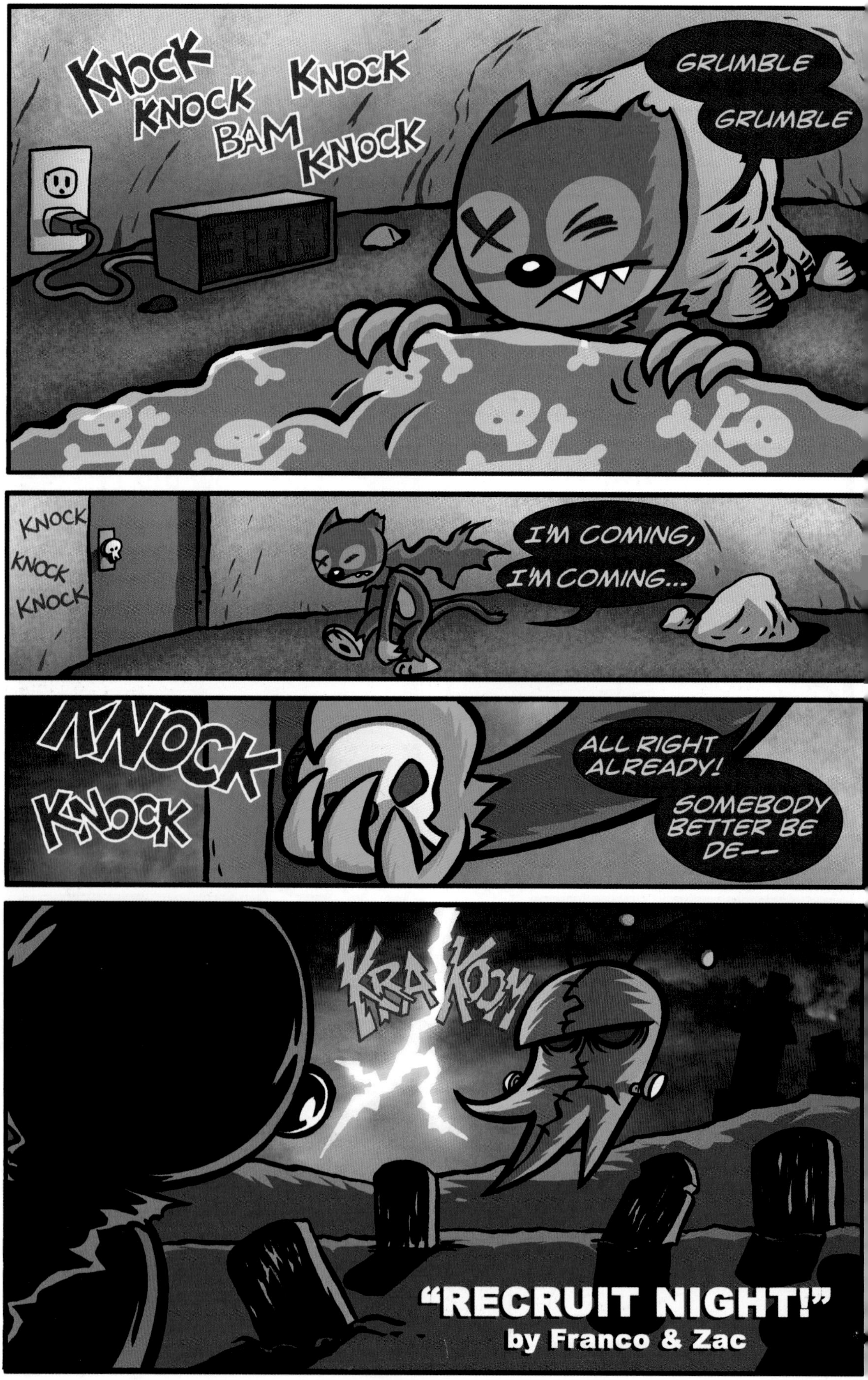
KNOCK KNOCK KNOCK BAM KNOCK KNOCK
GRUMBLE
GRUMBLE
KNOCK KNOCK KNOCK
I'M COMING,
I'M COMING...
KNOCK KNOCK
ALL RIGHT ALREADY!
SOMEBODY BETTER BE DE--
KRA-KOOM
"RECRUIT NIGHT!"
by Franco & Zac

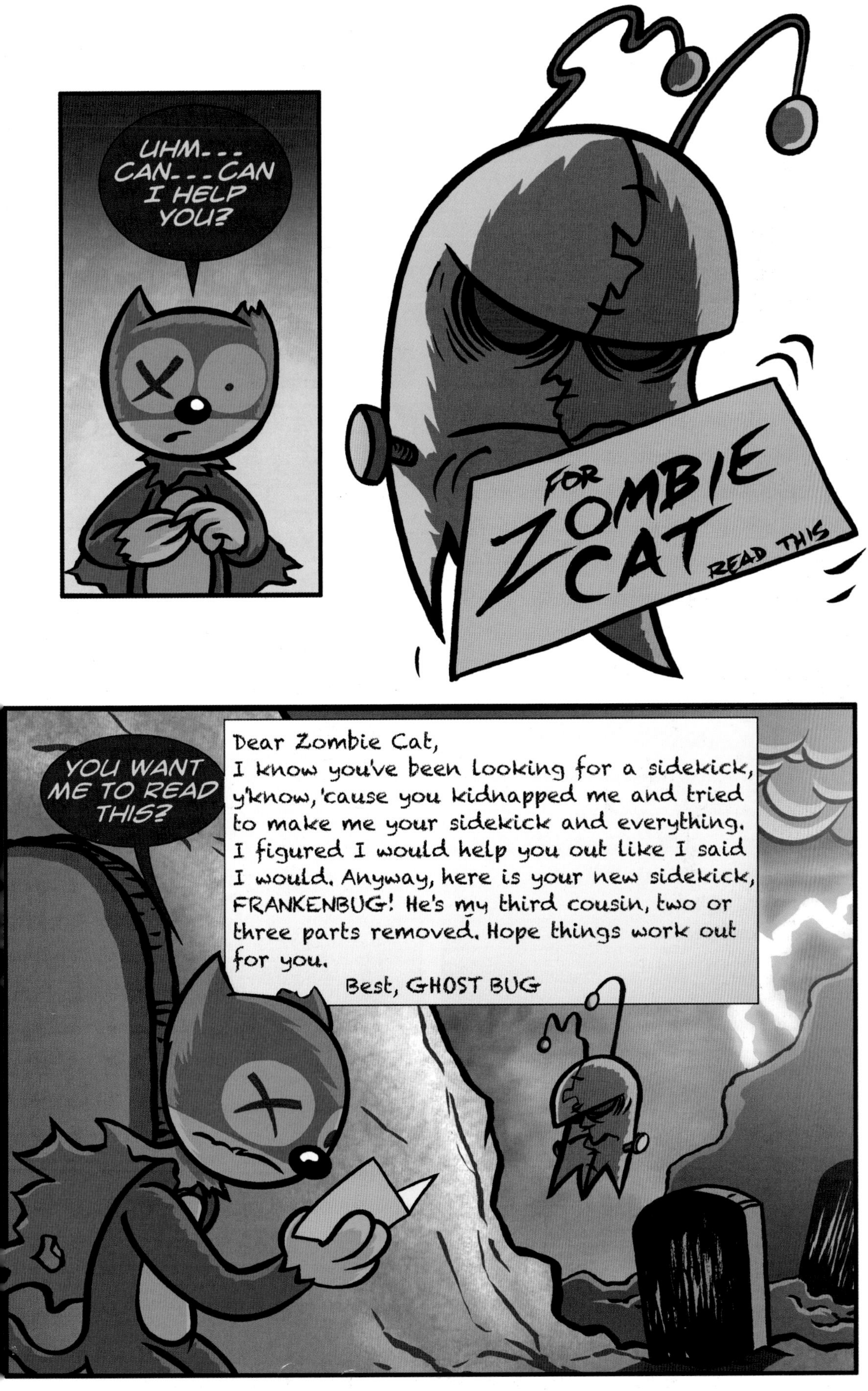
UHM... CAN...CAN I HELP YOU?
FOR ZOMBIE CAT
READ THIS
YOU WANT ME TO READ THIS?
Dear Zombie Cat,
I know you've been looking for a sidekick, y'know, 'cause you kidnapped me and tried to make me your sidekick and everything. I figured I would help you out like I said I would. Anyway, here is your new sidekick, FRANKENBUG! He's my third cousin, two or three parts removed. Hope things work out for you.
Best, GHOST BUG

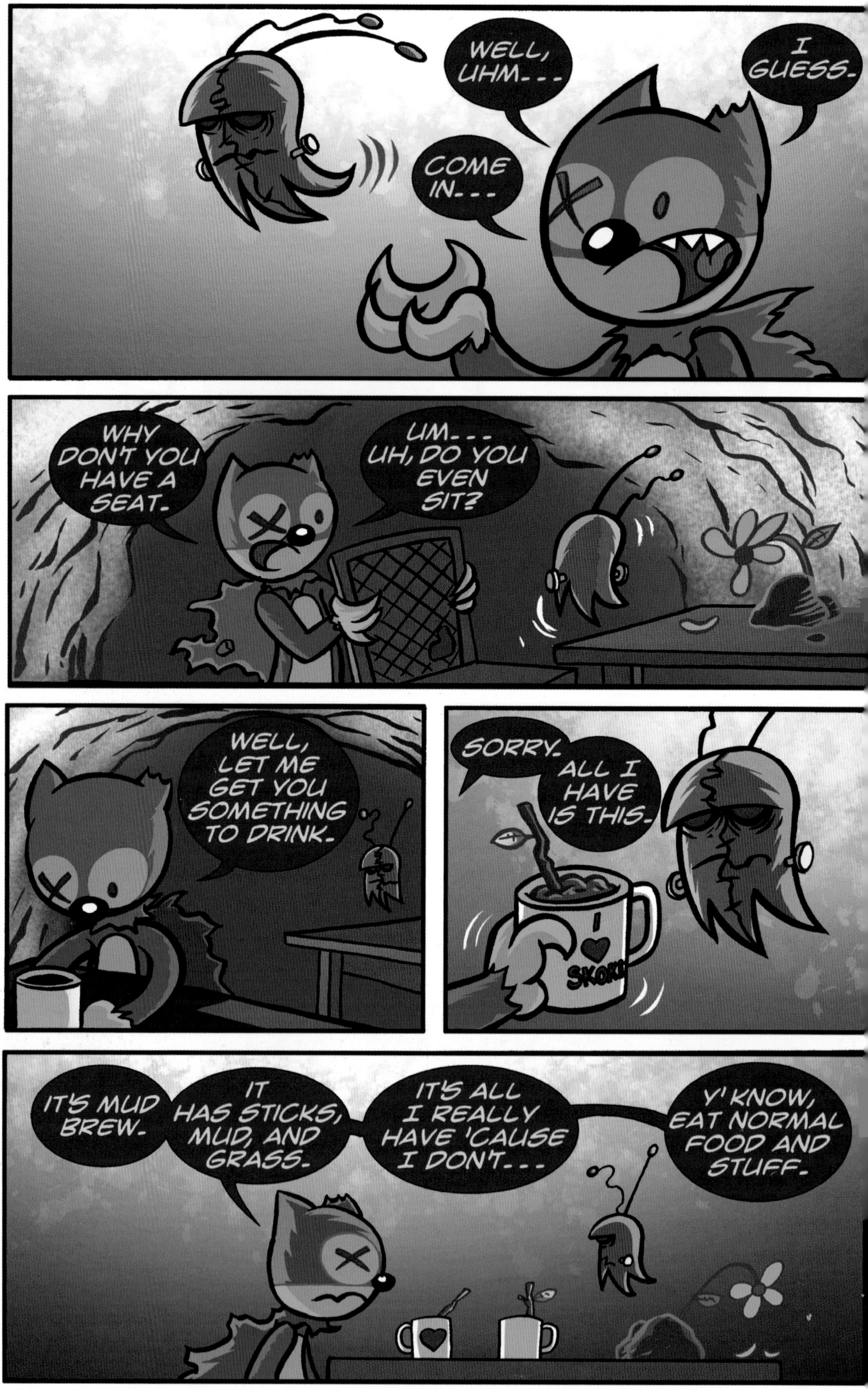
WELL, UHM...
I GUESS.
COME IN...
WHY DON'T YOU HAVE A SEAT.
UM... UH, DO YOU EVEN SIT?
WELL, LET ME GET YOU SOMETHING TO DRINK.
SORRY.
ALL I HAVE IS THIS.
I ♥ SKOKI
IT'S MUD BREW.
IT HAS STICKS, MUD, AND GRASS.
IT'S ALL I REALLY HAVE 'CAUSE I DON'T...
Y' KNOW, EAT NORMAL FOOD AND STUFF.

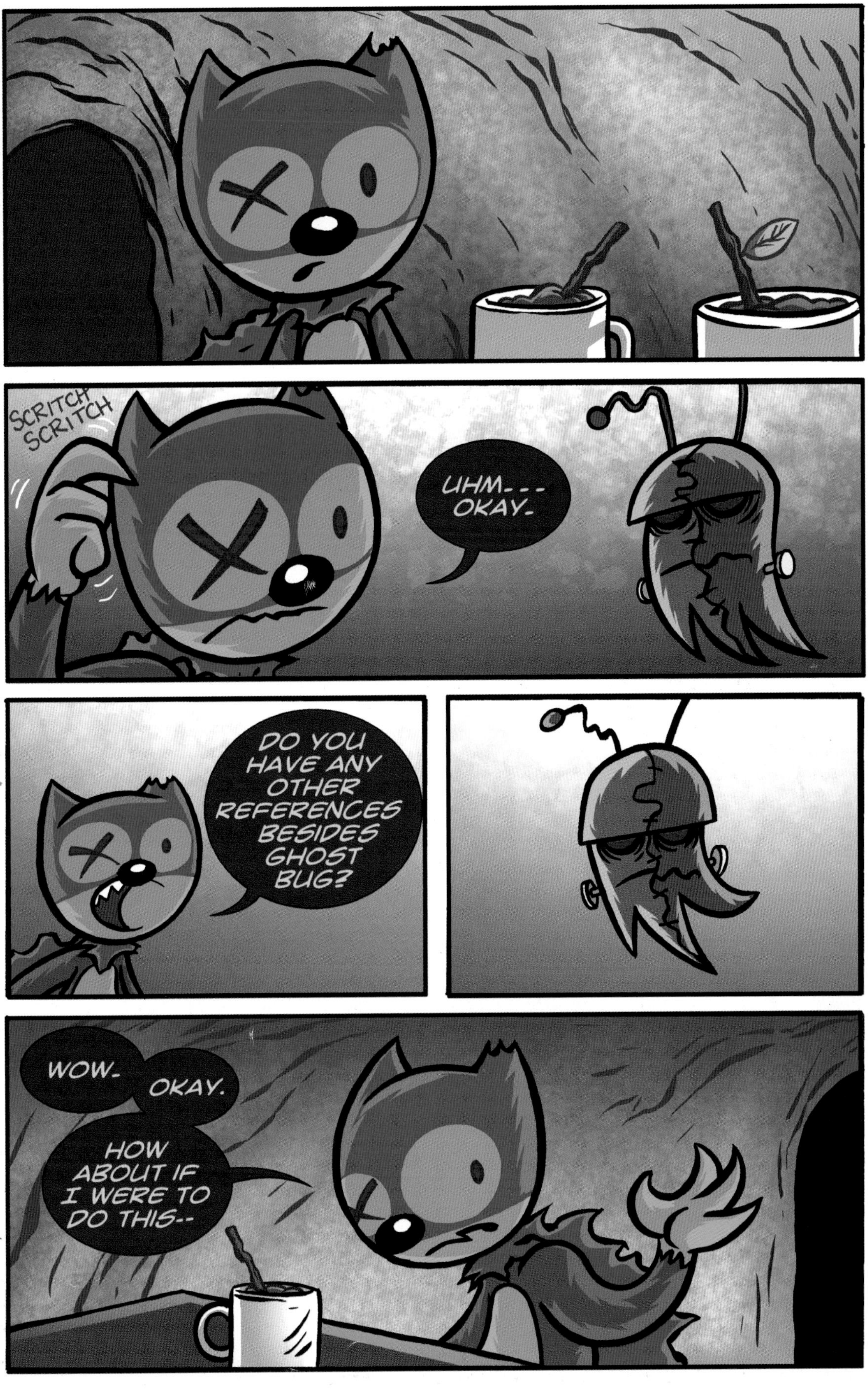
SCRITCH SCRITCH
UHM... OKAY.
DO YOU HAVE ANY OTHER REFERENCES BESIDES GHOST BUG?
WOW.
OKAY.
HOW ABOUT IF I WERE TO DO THIS--

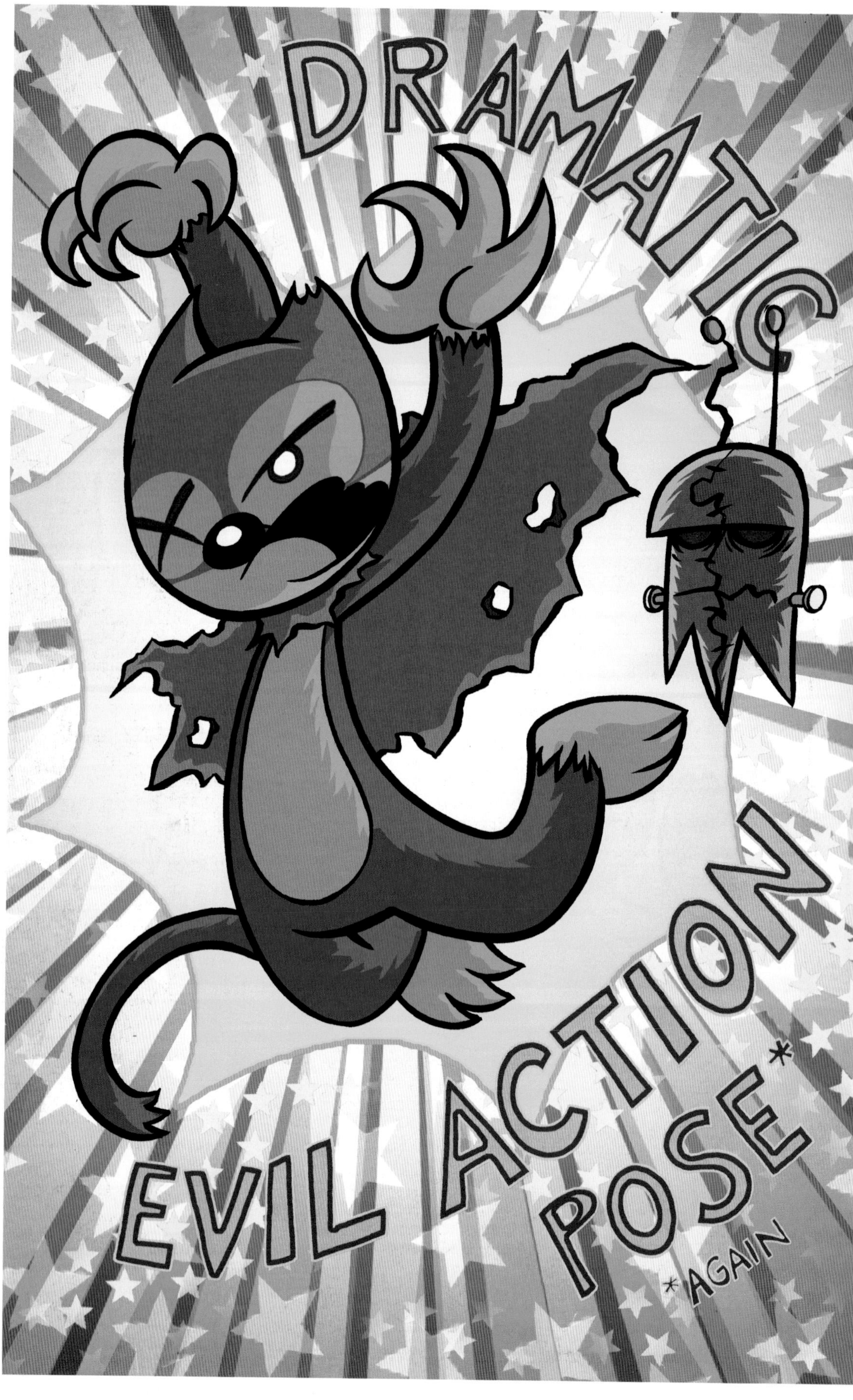
DRAMATIC
EVIL ACTION POSE*
*AGAIN

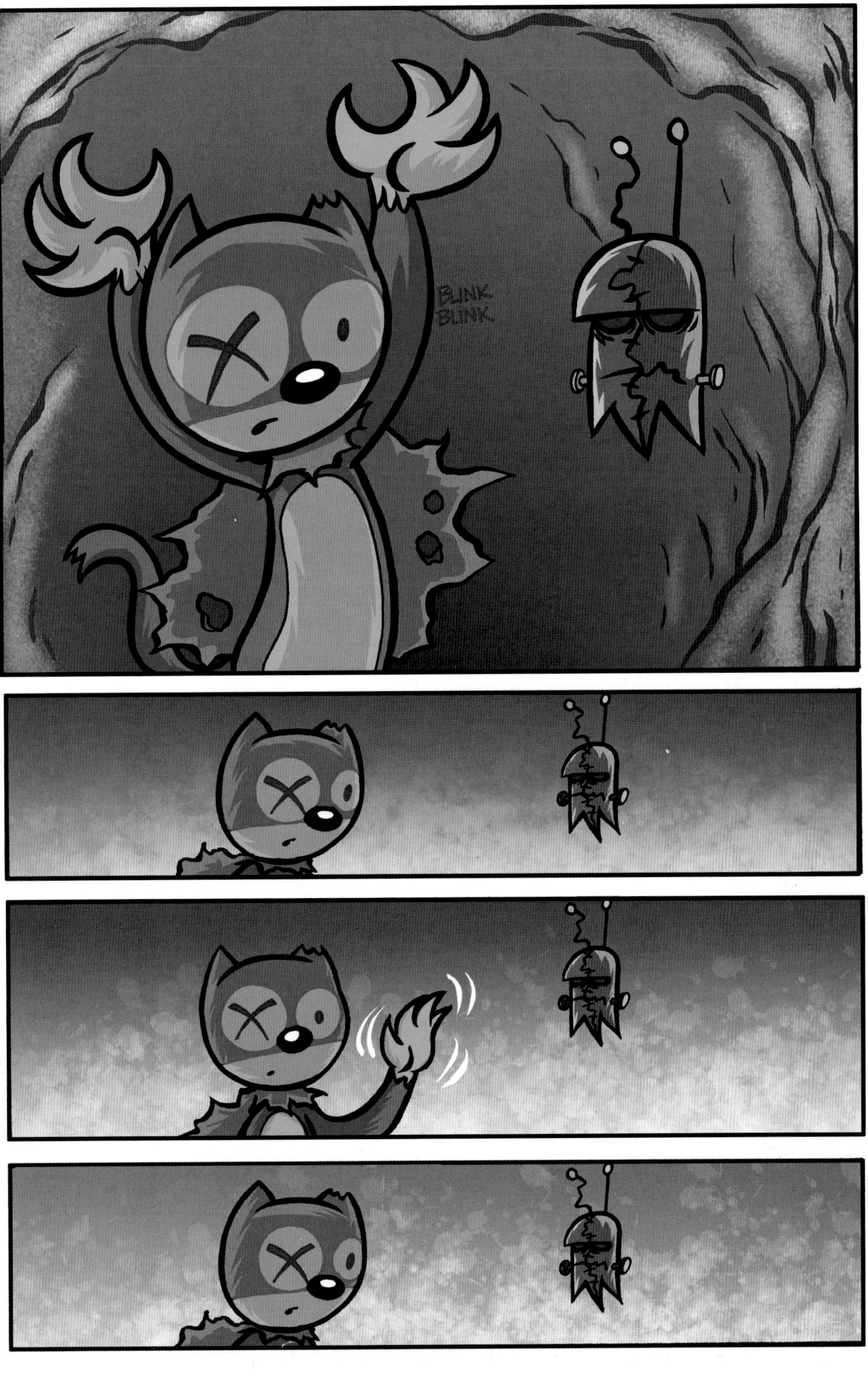
BLINK
BLINK

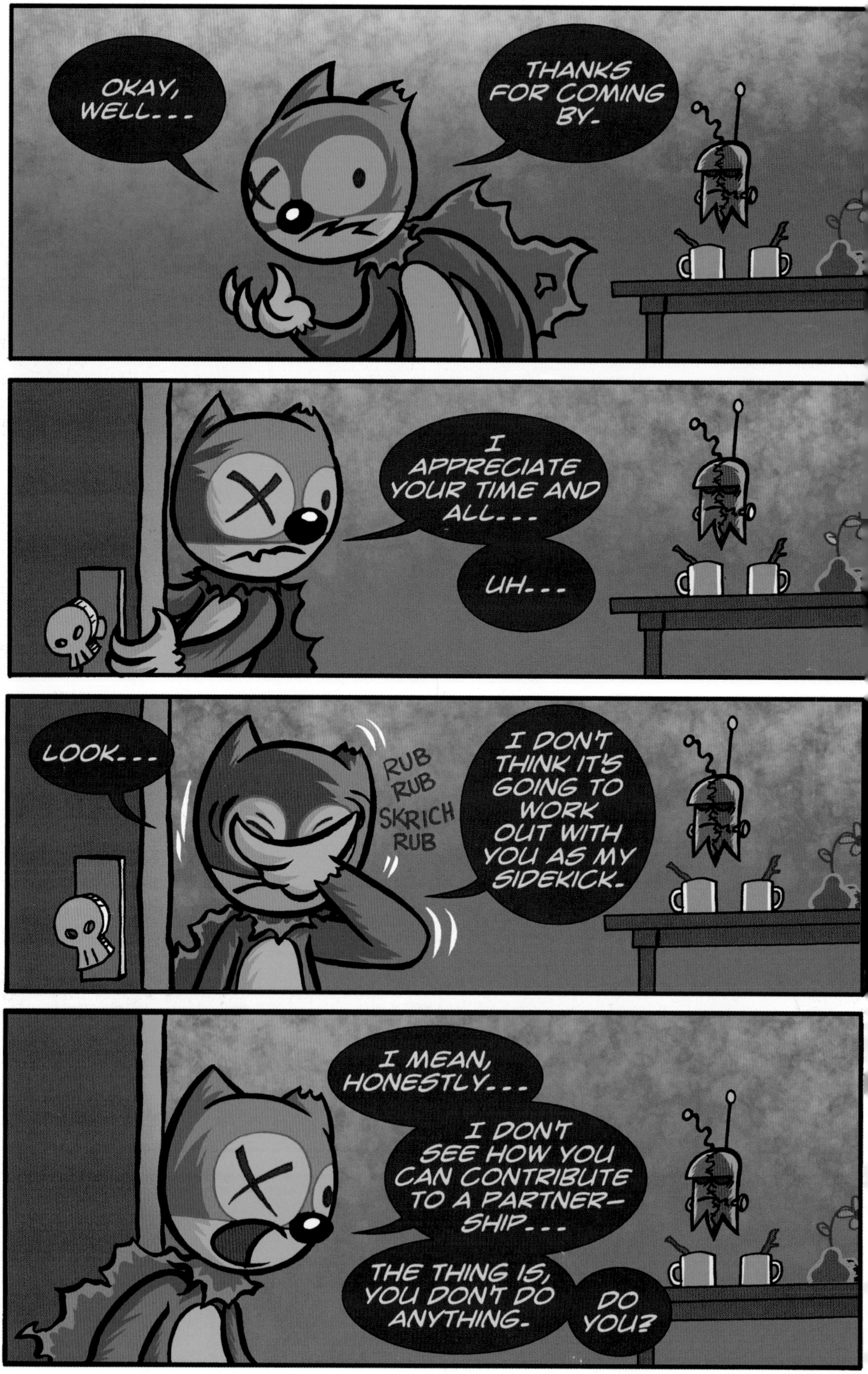
OKAY, WELL...
THANKS FOR COMING BY.
I APPRECIATE YOUR TIME AND ALL...
UH...
LOOK...
RUB RUB SKRICH RUB
I DON'T THINK IT'S GOING TO WORK OUT WITH YOU AS MY SIDEKICK.
I MEAN, HONESTLY...
I DON'T SEE HOW YOU CAN CONTRIBUTE TO A PARTNER-SHIP...
THE THING IS, YOU DON'T DO ANYTHING.
DO YOU?

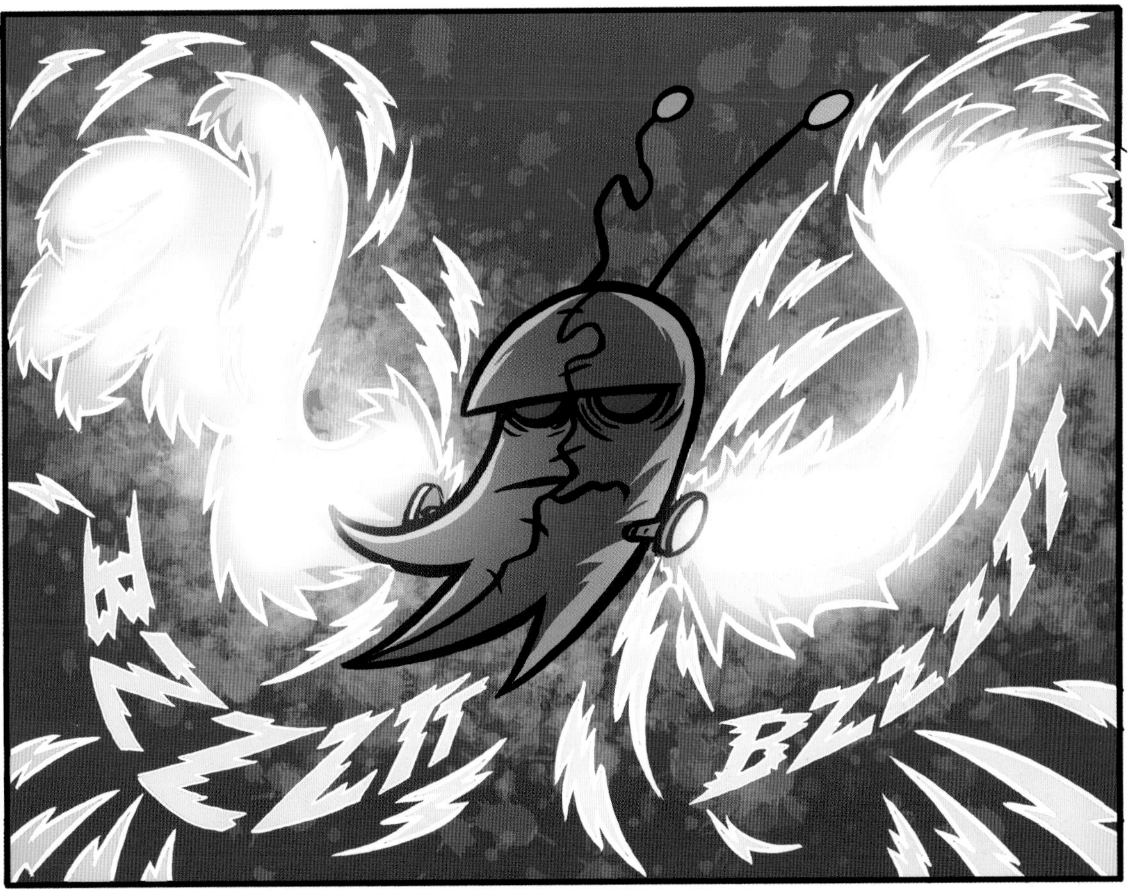
BZZZTT
BZZZTT

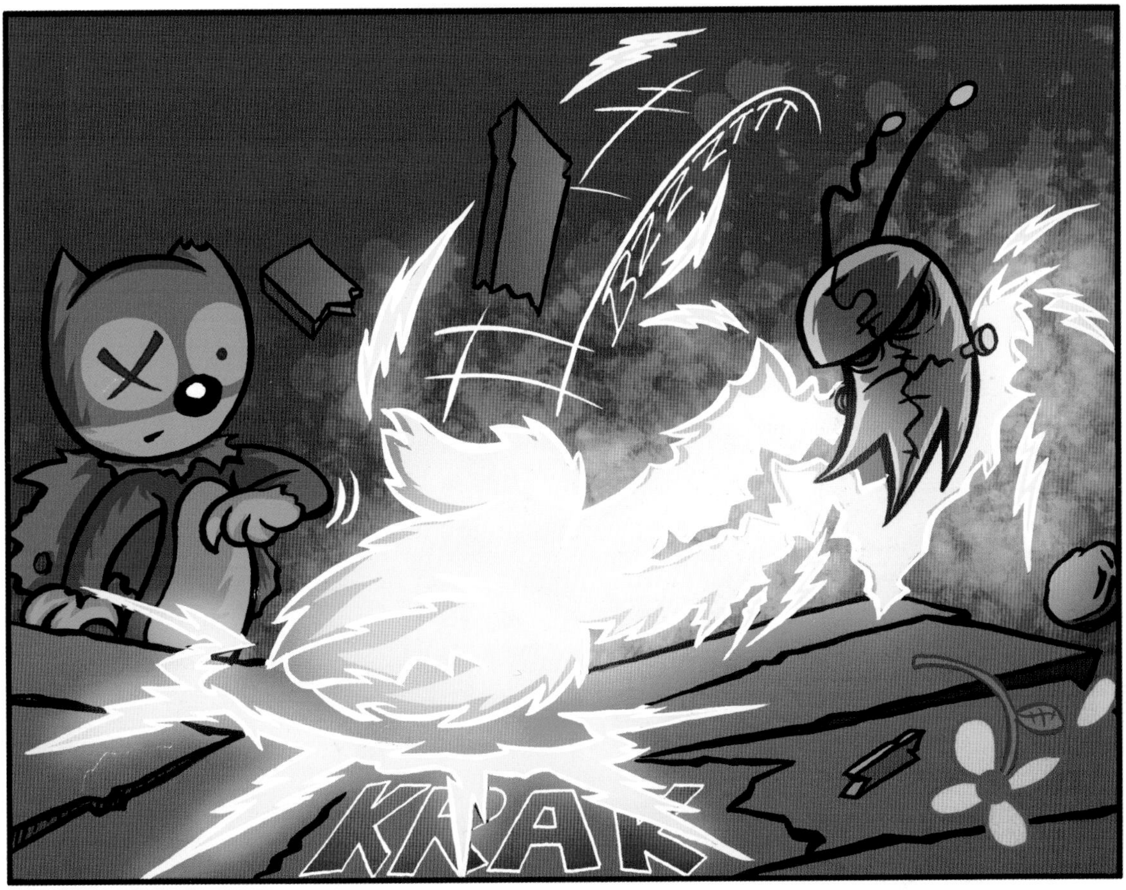
BZZZZTTT
KRAK

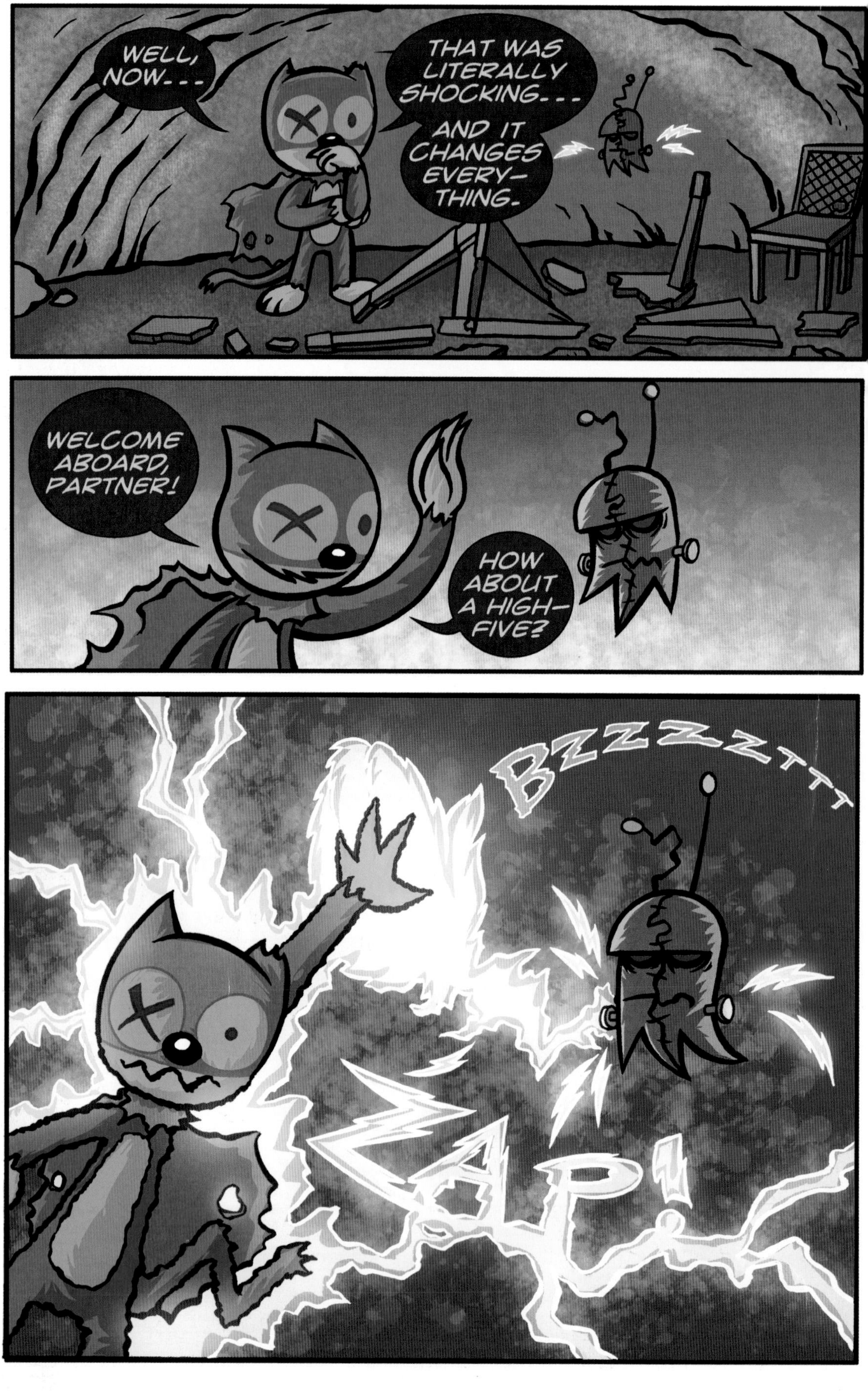
WELL, NOW...
THAT WAS LITERALLY SHOCKING...
AND IT CHANGES EVERY-THING.
WELCOME ABOARD, PARTNER!
HOW ABOUT A HIGH-FIVE?
BZZZZZTTTT
ZAP!

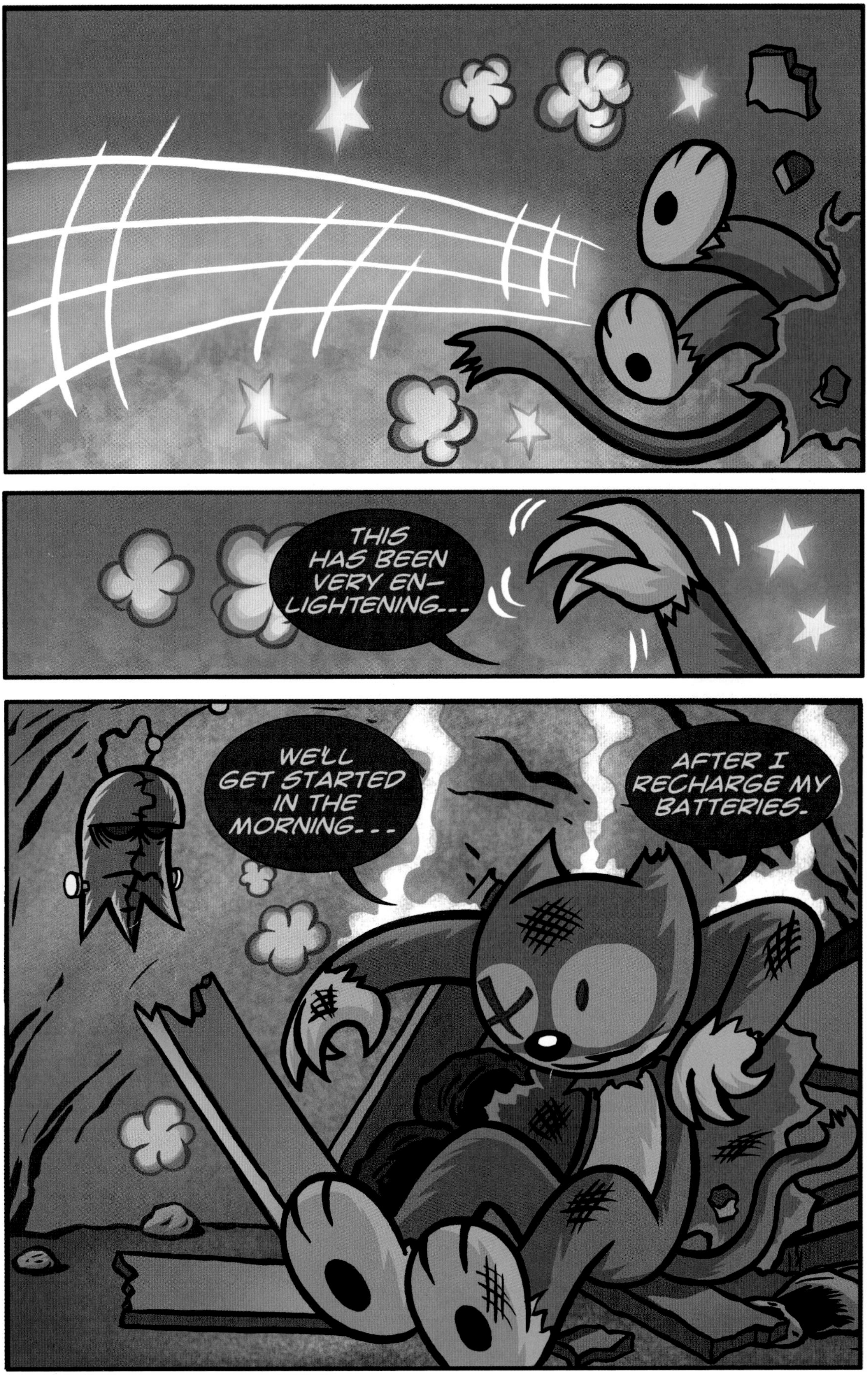
THIS HAS BEEN VERY EN-LIGHTENING...
WE'LL GET STARTED IN THE MORNING...
AFTER I RECHARGE MY BATTERIES.

PARTNERS.

"ANTI-GRAVITY BEAR" BY ART BALTAZAR

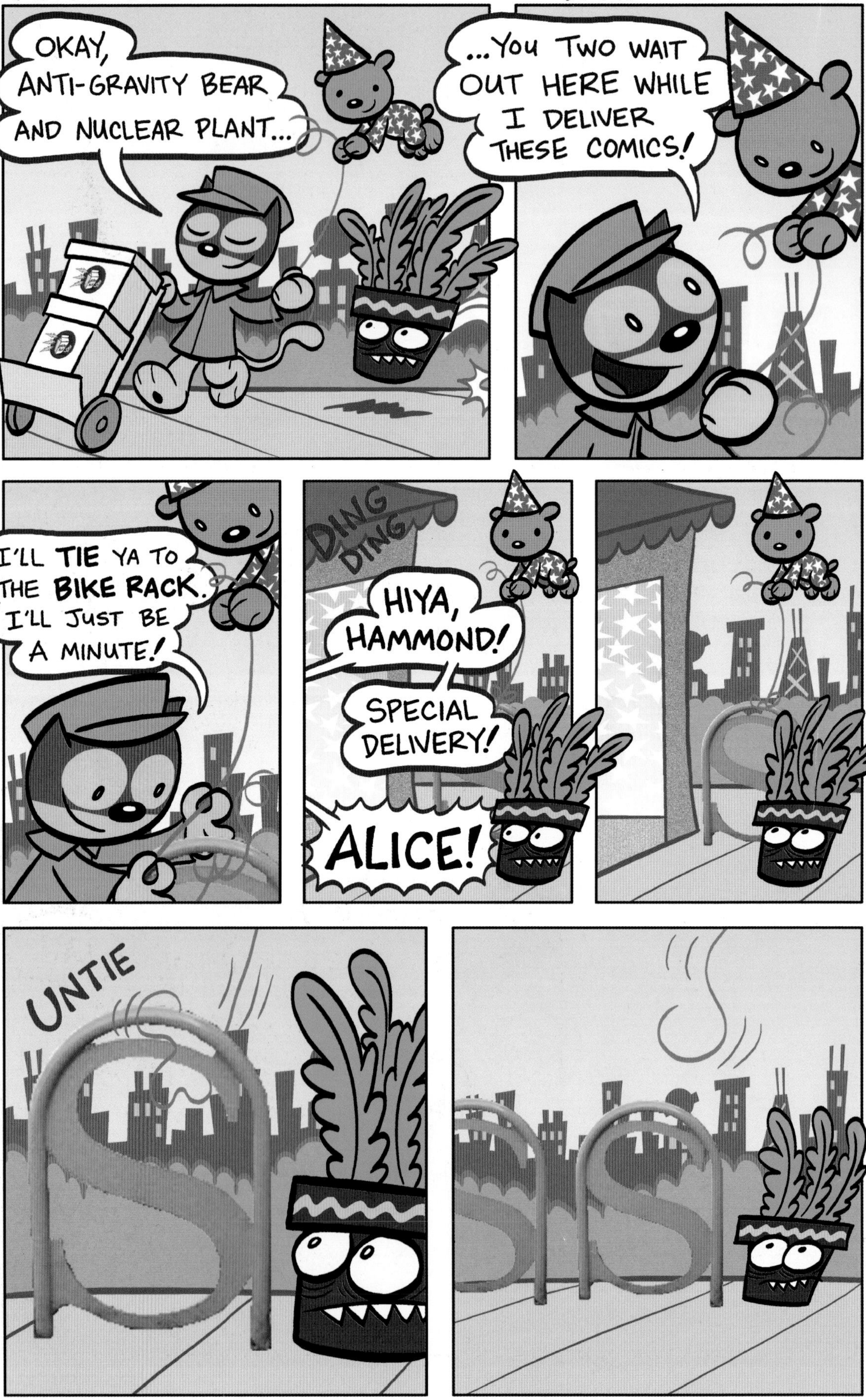
OKAY, ANTI-GRAVITY BEAR AND NUCLEAR PLANT...
...YOU TWO WAIT OUT HERE WHILE I DELIVER THESE COMICS!
I'LL **TIE** YA TO THE **BIKE RACK**. I'LL JUST BE A MINUTE!
DING DING
HIYA, HAMMOND!
SPECIAL DELIVERY!
ALICE!
UNTIE

YAWN!

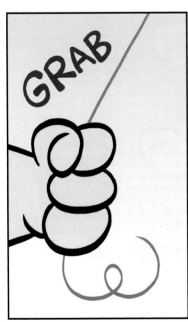

GRAB

HEY, FRIEND! WHERE ARE YOU GOING?

UP.

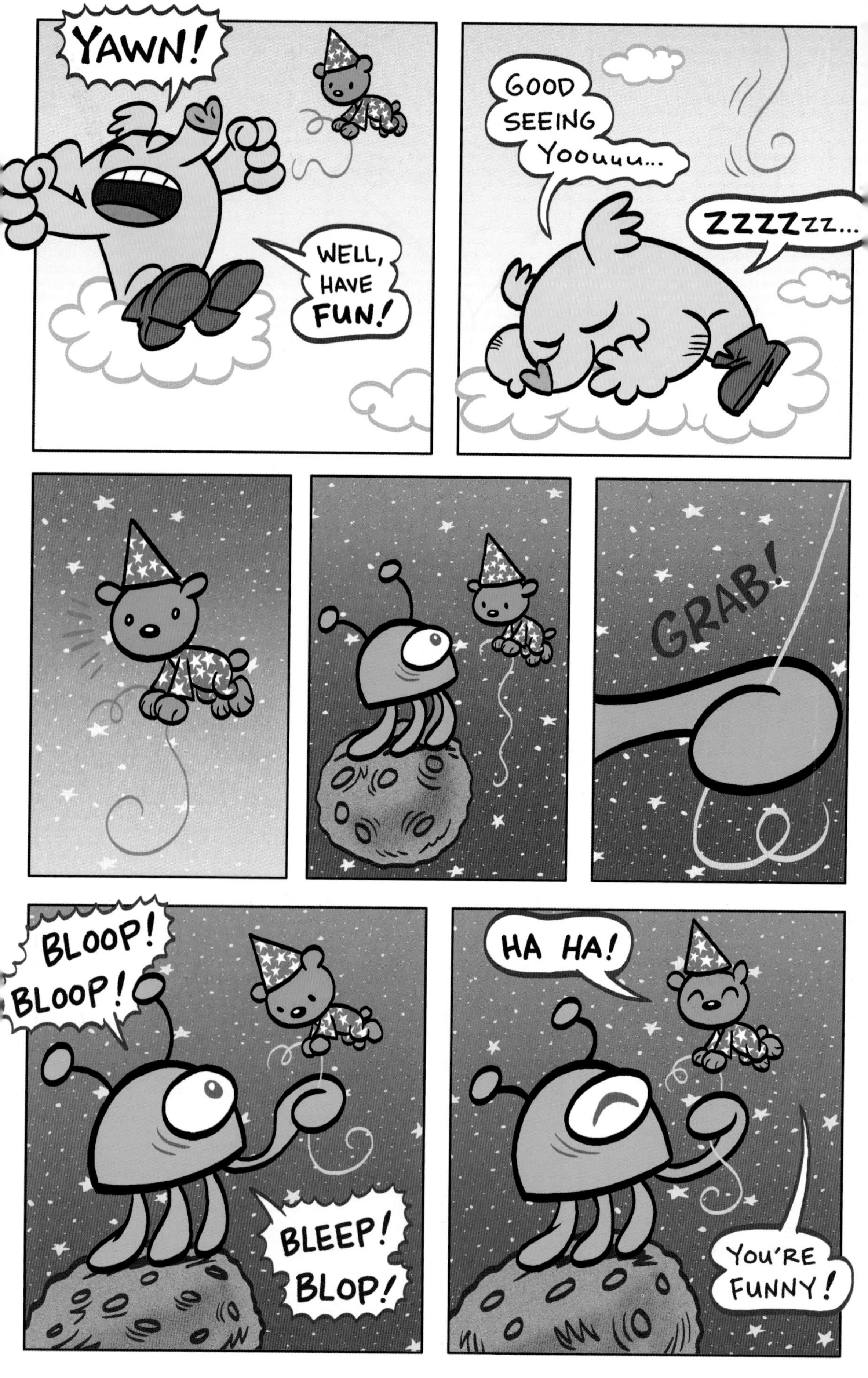
YAWN!
WELL, HAVE FUN!
GOOD SEEING Yoouuu...
ZZZZzz...
GRAB!
BLOOP! BLOOP!
BLEEP! BLOP!
HA HA!
YOU'RE FUNNY!

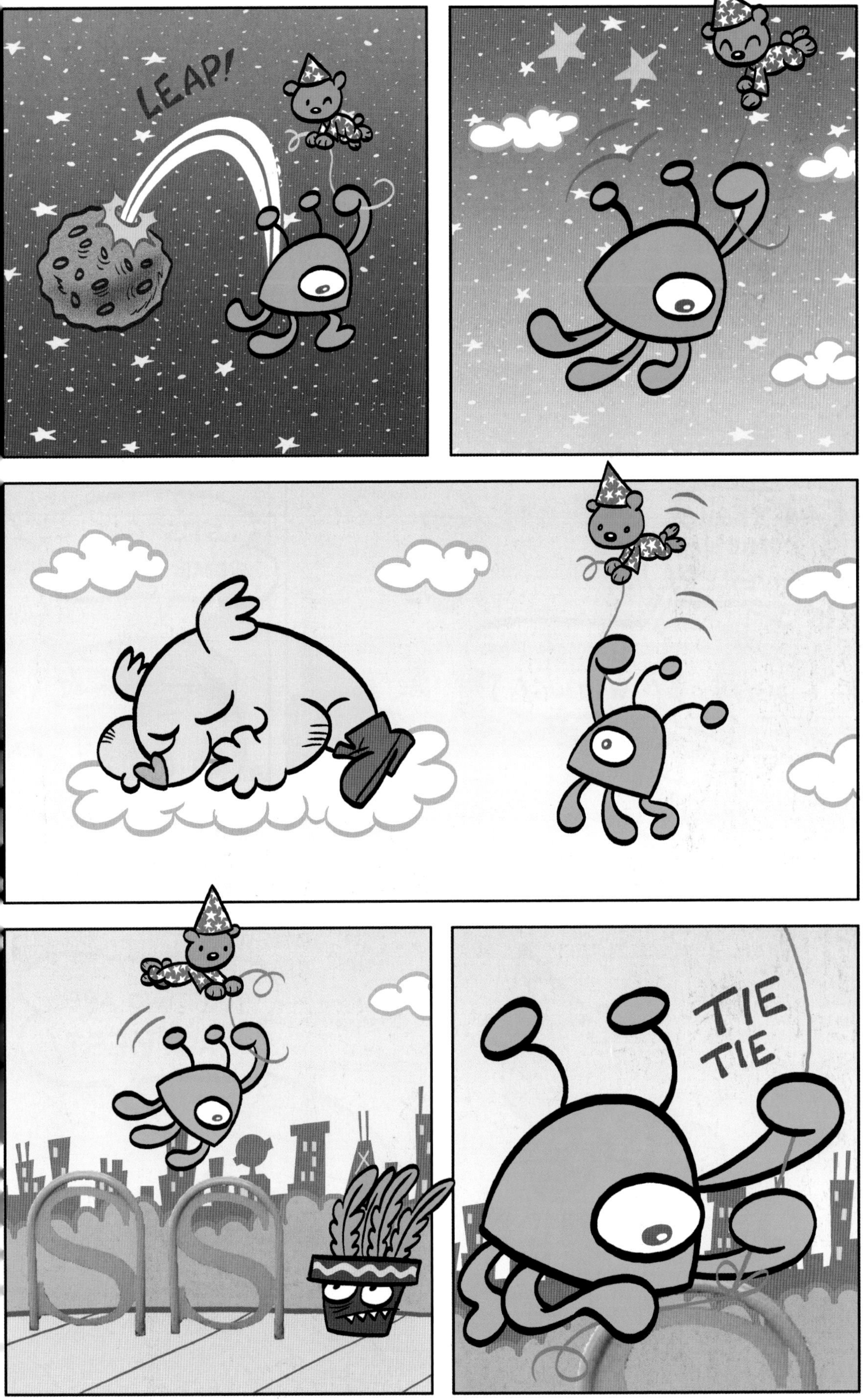
LEAP!
TIE
TIE

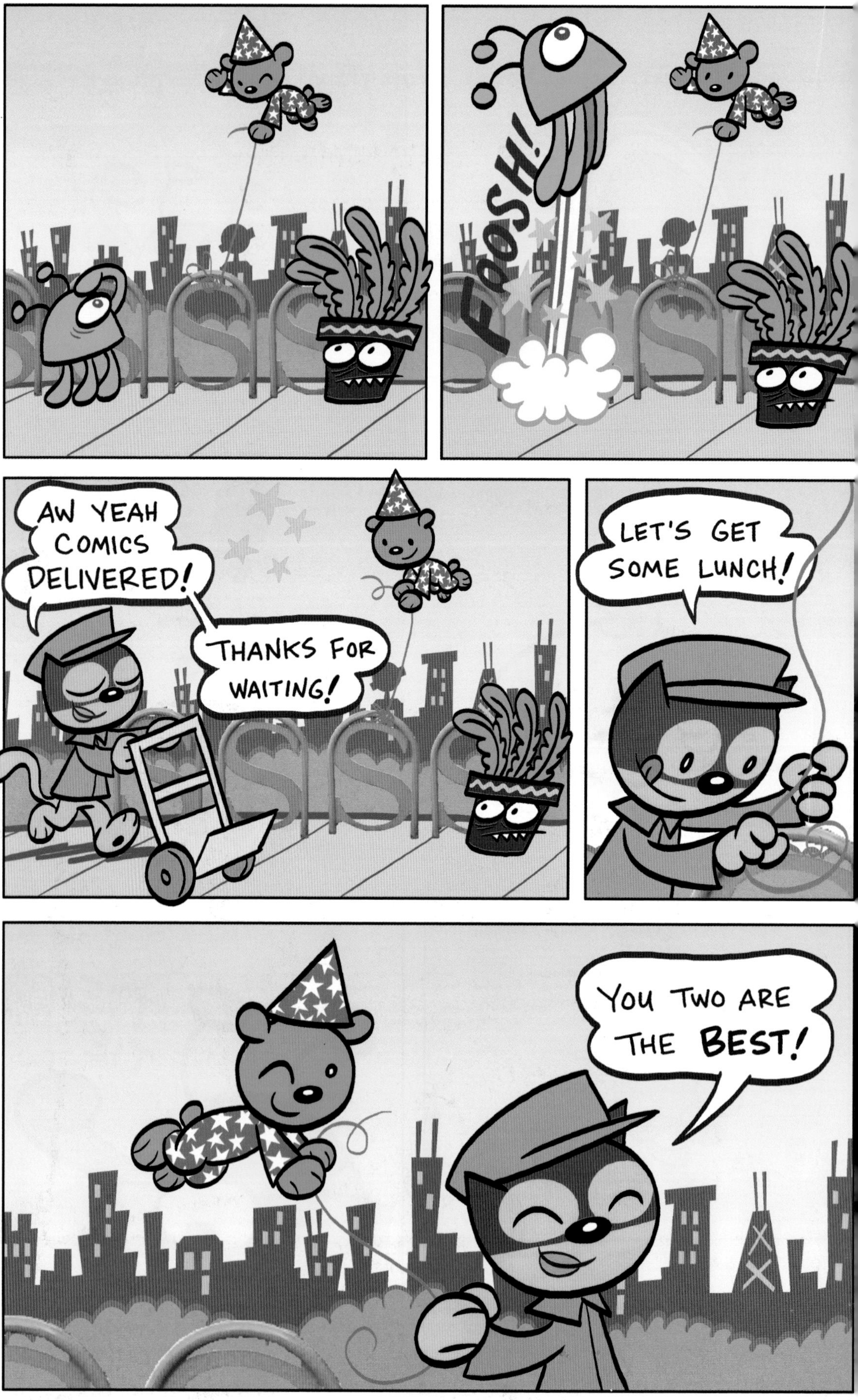
FOOSH!
AW YEAH COMICS DELIVERED!
THANKS FOR WAITING!
LET'S GET SOME LUNCH!
YOU TWO ARE THE BEST!

—ANTI-GRAVITY BEAR!

ART BALTAZAR

★ SKETCHBOOK ★

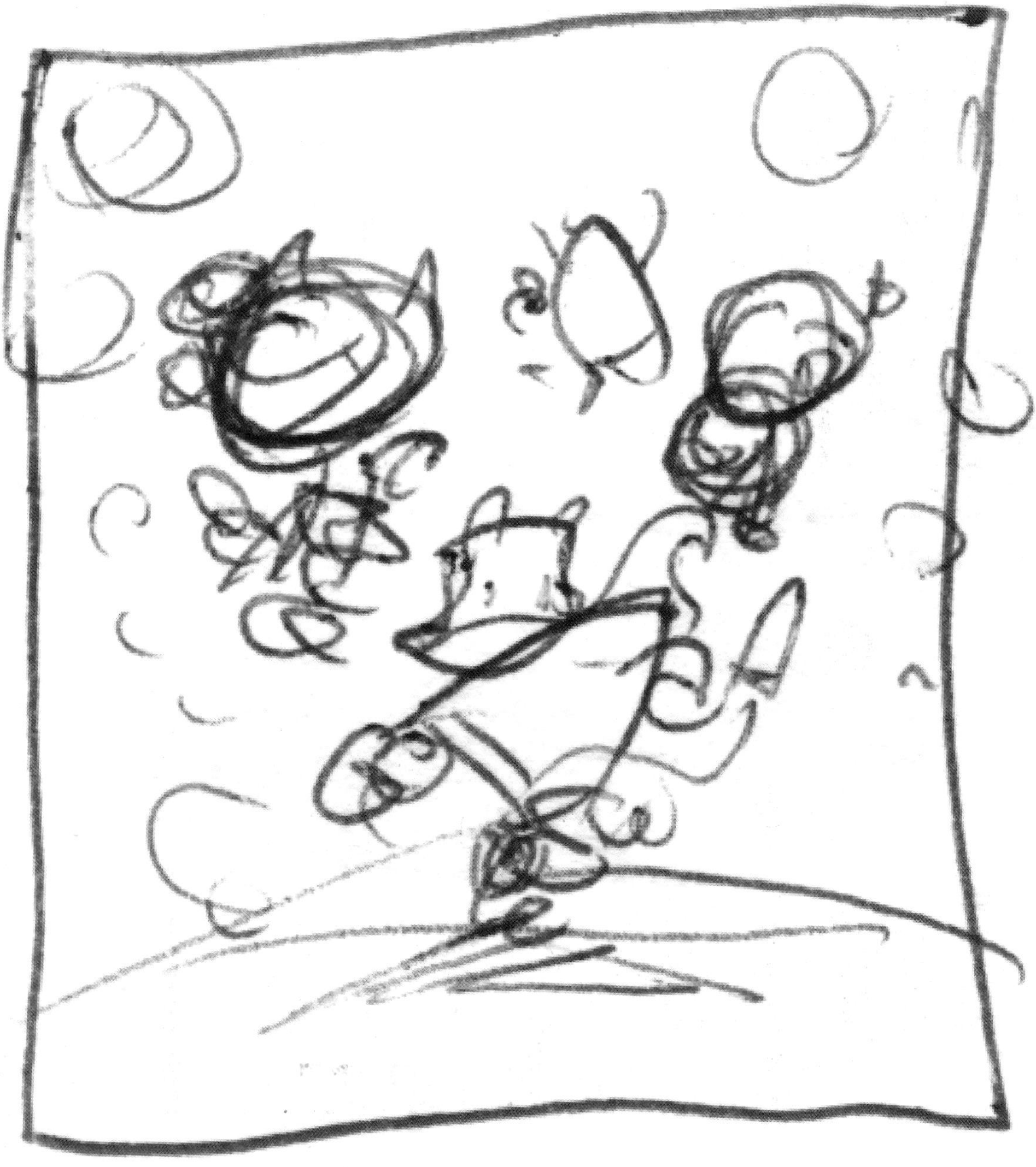

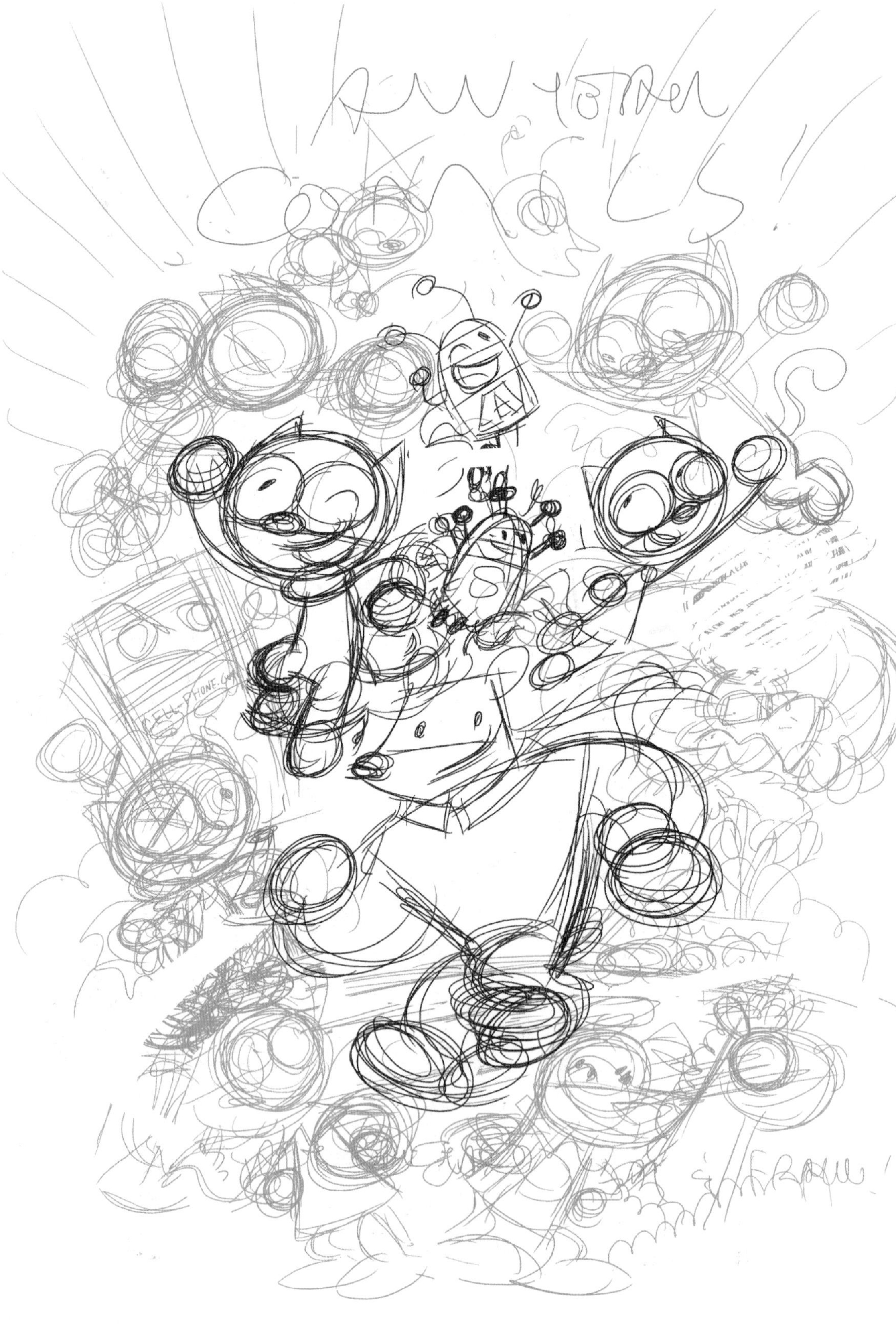

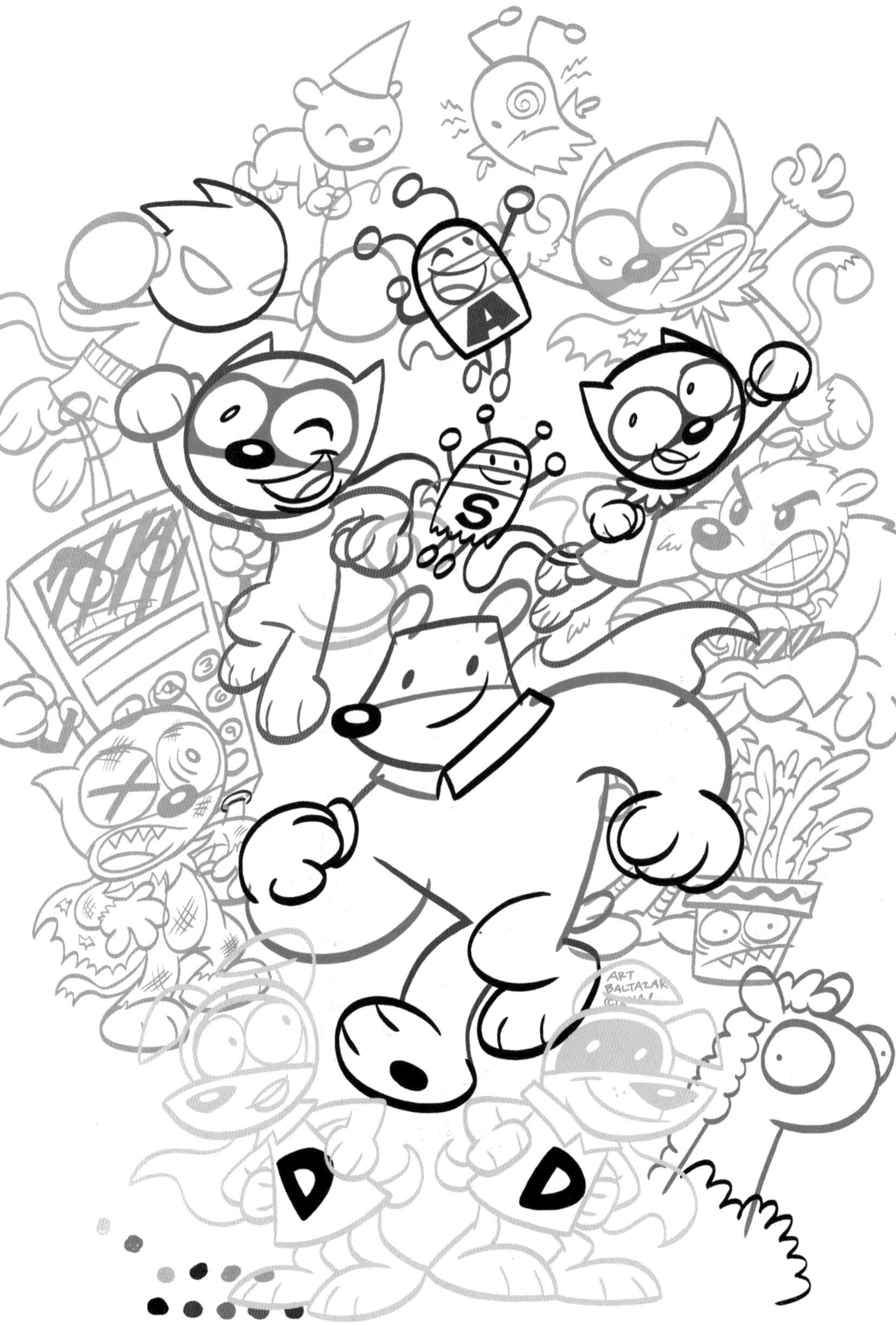
A
S
D
D
ART BALTAZAR

OTHER BOOKS FROM DARK HORSE

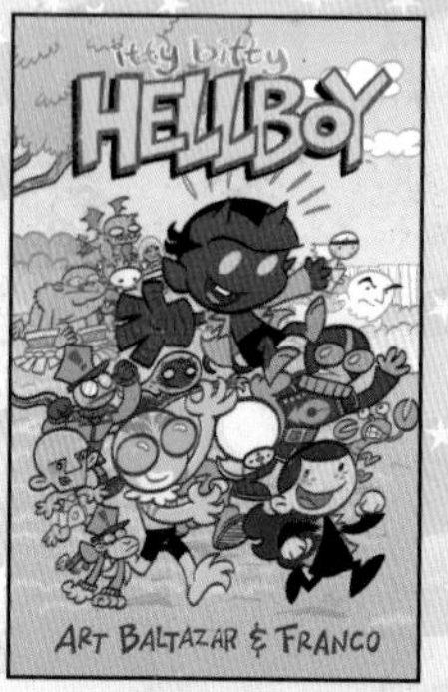
Itty Bitty
HELLBOY
ART BALTAZAR & FRANCO

ITTY BITTY HELLBOY TPB

Art Baltazar, Franco Aureliani

Witness the awesomeness that is *Hellboy*! The characters that sprung from Mike Mignola's imagination, with an AW YEAH Art Baltazar and Franco twist! This book has ALL the FUN, adventure, and AW YEAHNESS in one itty bitty package! That's a true story right there. Collects *Itty Bitty Hellboy* #1–#5.

978-1-61655-414-9 | $9.99

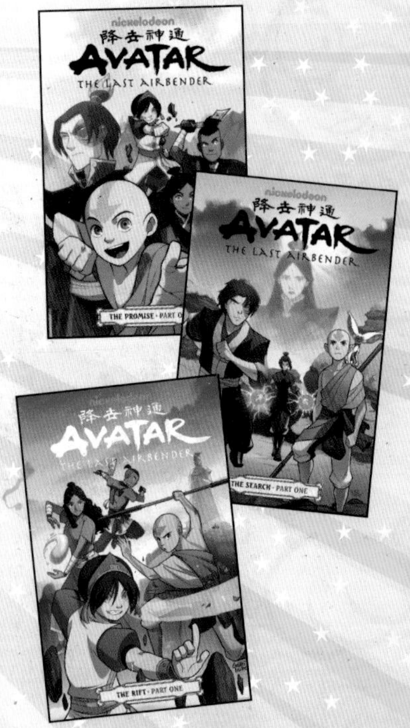
nickelodeon
降世神通
AVATAR
THE LAST AIRBENDER
THE SEARCH · PART ONE
THE RIFT · PART ONE

AVATAR: THE LAST AIRBENDER

Gene Luen Yang, Gurihiru

The wait is over! Ever since the conclusion of *Avatar: The Last Airbender*, its millions of fans have been hungry for more—and it's finally here! This series of digests rejoins Aang and friends for exciting new adventures, beginning with a face-off against the Fire Nation that threatens to throw the world into another war, testing all of Aang's powers and ingenuity!

THE PROMISE TPB | $10.99 each
Book 1: 978-1-59582-811-8
Book 2: 978-1-59582-875-0
Book 3: 978-1-59582-941-2

THE SEARCH TPB | $10.99 each
Book 1: 978-1-61655-054-7
Book 2: 978-1-61655-190-2
Book 3: 978-1-61655-184-1

THE RIFT TPB | $10.99 each
Book 1: 978-1-61655-295-4
Book 2: 978-1-61655-296-1

THE PROMISE LIBRARY EDITION HC
978-1-61655-074-5 | $39.99

THE SEARCH LIBRARY EDITION HC
978-1-61655-226-8 | $39.99

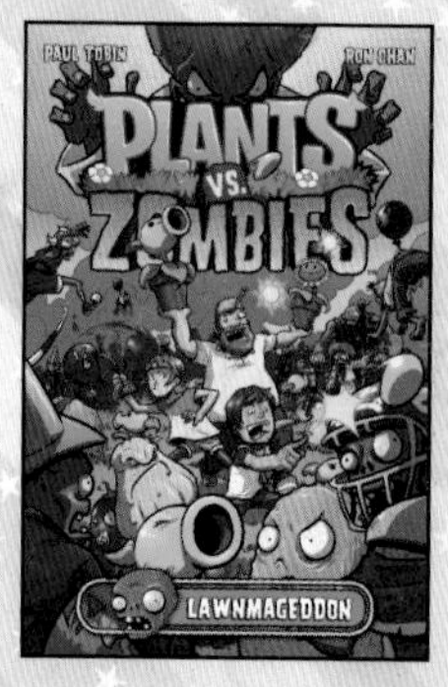
PAUL TOBIN
RON CHAN
PLANTS VS. ZOMBIES
LAWNMAGEDDON

PLANTS VS. ZOMBIES: LAWNMAGEDDON HC

Paul Tobin, Ron Chan

The confusing-yet-brilliant inventor known only as Crazy Dave helps his niece Patrice and young adventurer Nate Timely fend off a "fun-dead" neighborhood invasion in *Plants vs. Zombies: Lawnmageddon*! Winner of over thirty Game of the Year awards, *Plants vs. Zombies* is now determined to shuffle onto all-ages bookshelves to tickle funny bones and thrill . . . *brains*.

978-1-61655-192-6 | $9.99